Mrs. Henry Wood

The Castle's Heir

A Novel in Real Life

Mrs. Henry Wood

The Castle's Heir
A Novel in Real Life

ISBN/EAN: 9783744791731

Printed in Europe, USA, Canada, Australia, Japan

Cover: Foto ©Andreas Hilbeck / pixelio.de

More available books at **www.hansebooks.com**

THE

CASTLE'S HEIR.

A

NOVEL IN REAL LIFE.

BY

MRS. HENRY WOOD.

AUTHOR OF "VERNER'S PRIDE," "THE CHANNINGS," "EARL'S HEIRS,"
"A LIFE'S SECRET," "EAST LYNNE," "THE MYSTERY," "THE
SHADOW OF ASHLYDYAT," "SQUIRE TREVLYN'S HEIR,"
"FOGGY NIGHT AT OFFORD," "RUNAWAY MATCH," ETC.

Printed from the authors' Manuscript, purchased from Mrs. Henry Wood, and
issued here in advance of the publication of the work in Europe, with Illus-
trations from original designs, by the first artists in this country.

Philadelphia:
T. B. PETERSON & BROTHERS;
306 CHESTNUT STREET.

CONTENTS.

ILLUSTRATIONS.

(21)

THE CASTLE'S HEIR.

CHAPTER I.

THE FAMILY—THE CHAPEL RUINS

In a somewhat wild part of the coast of England, at least a hundred and fifty miles distant from the metropolis, is situated a small town or village, called Danesheld. The land on either side it rises above and overlooks the sea, higher in some spots than in others, and the descent of the rocks is in places perpendicular. There are parts, however, where they slope so gradually that a sure foot may descend easily, and in these the hard nature of the rock appears to have softened with time, for grass grows upon the sides, and even wild flowers. In ancient times it was a settlement of the Danes, and there is no doubt that the name, now cor-.rupted into Danesheld, was formerly written Danes' Hold. Outside the village, towards the east, a colony of straggling huts and cottages is built, not close to the edge of the heights, but some little distance from them; beyond, may be seen some scattered mansions; and again, beyond these, rise the stately walls of Dane Castle, the castle and the village being about a mile apart. The castle is a long, but not high building, its red bricks dark with age; a turret rises at either end, and a high, square turret ascends over the gateway in the middle, from which latter turret a flag may be seen waving, whenever the castle's chief, Lord Dane, is sojourning at it.

The castle faces the sea, being about a quarter of a mile distant from it, and the grass-land stretches out smooth and broad and flat between it and the edge of the heights. The high-road from the village winds up past the castle gates, and behind it is an inclosed garden. A little farther on, and almost close to the brow of the heights are the ruins of what was the chapel in the days of the monks; its walls stand yet, and its casements, from which the glass has long since gone, are sheltered round with the clustering ivy; traces of its altar, and of its once-inscribed gravestones may still be seen inside, but no roof is there, and it is open alike to the calm sky and the stormy one. A picturesque sight does that old ruin present to the eye in the slanting beams of the setting sun, or in the pale, weird beauty of a moonlight night.

On the other side of the winding road, opposite the castle, might be seen all the signs of husbandry, ploughed fields, grass-lands; with here and there a farm-house, surrounded by its substantial ricks and barns. And one sunshiny day in spring, perched upon a gate leading into a clover-field, and doing something to a fishing-rod, was a young man in the careless attire favored by country gentlemen. He looked about eight-and-twenty, was tall and slender; his features were thin and sharp,

(23)

and his eyes dark, but they had not a very open expression. His velveteen sporting-coat was thrown back from his shoulders, for the day was really warm. Hearing footsteps, he lifted his eyes, and saw approaching, from the direction of the village, a middle-aged man, who wore the dress of a gentleman sailor. The latter lifted his glazed hat from his head as he neared the gate, but whether in courtesy, or whether merely to wipe his brow, which he proceeded to do, was uncertain.

"Is that Dane Castle?" asked the stranger.

"Yes."

"I thought it must be," was the comment of the sailor, spoken in an undertone. "Perhaps you have no objection to tell me a little of the present history of its inmates," he continued: "I made acquaintance with one of the sons abroad."

"With all the pleasure in life," carelessly replied the young gentleman, still intent upon his fishing-rod. "The family are at the castle now, Lord and Lady Dane, and one of the sons. Lord Dane more helpless than ever."

"Lord Dane helpless!"

"He fell from his horse last autumn, hunting, and the spine was injured, paralysis of the spine, I believe they call it. The effect is, that the entire use of his lower limbs has left him, and he is nearly as helpless as a baby."

The sailor looked at him.

"No power in his legs, I suppose?"

"None. Lady Dane retains power in hers, though, and in her tongue, too," said the young gentleman, breaking into a whistle. "She rules the roast, now the Baron's laid by."

"Which of the sons is at home?"

"The younger one, the captain. The heir is in Paris. He is a fast man, and a Parisian life suits him."

"There was a young lady at the castle. I forget her name—"

"Adelaide Errol. A wild, Scotch girl. I dare say you may have heard, for that is what she is styled here by the gossips."

"I have heard her called an an-

gel," returned the sailor, with an imperturbable countenance; "nothing less laudatory."

The other lifted his eyes from his fishing rod, and fixed them on his face.

"Then, if you have heard that, I'll wager it was from no other than Harry Dane."

"From William Dane."

"William Henry; it's all one; we dub him Harry here. The old peer is fond of the name of Harry, and rarely called his son any thing else. Geoffry is the name of the eldest."

"I know. Is William to marry Adelaide Errol?"

The young gentleman raised his eyebrows.

"People profess to say so. The captain, gallant son of Mars though he is, has singed his wings in the brightness of her fascinations. He—"

"I wish you'd talk plain English, sir," testily interrupted the stranger.

The other accorded him a prolonged stare.

"Why, what else am I talking? Dutch?"

"Rhapsody—and I don't understand it. Is Captain Dane to marry the young lady, or is he not?"

"What a very unreasonable person you seem to be!" was the equable rejoinder. "Don't I tell you that it is said he will? He is *fou* after her—if you understand the French term in all its force; worships the very ground she treads on. If that's not English, I don't know what is."

"And she?"

The young man shrugged his shoulders.

"There's no answering for women. Perhaps she returns his love; perhaps she does not. My lady impresses upon her the fact that the Honorable William Henry Dane is no bad match for a portionless damsel."

"Captain Dane is rich."

"I wish I were a tithe as rich. Some arrangement exists in the Dane family by which the younger sons step into their fortune when they become of age, and the captain took possession of his; fifty thousand pounds.

"A large portion," remarked the sailor.

"It's not to be sneezed at. But he comprised all the younger children in himself, remember; sons and daughters too. Had there been ten, the fifty thousand would have been divided among them. His uncle, William Henry, whom he was named after, left him his fortune also, for he had never married; and that was at least fifty thousand more. It is thought, too, that the gallant captain saves, does not live half up to his income. Of course, now that he is in England, visiting at home, he does not want to spend—"

"How long has he been at home? It is two years since he quitted the States."

"Ay, but he went traveling, we hear; he is a close man upon his own movements. He appeared at home about six months ago, saying he was come for a few days; but the few days have lengthened into months."

"Why did he remain?"

The younger man laughed.

"Ask Adelaide Errol."

"He and his elder brother are at variance."

"And always will be. There's bitter blood between them. But for this mad passion for Adelaide, he was about to repurchase into the army; I can't think, for my part, why he ever sold out."

"Why do you term it a mad passion?"

The young man took out his penknife, and scraped a spot off the fishing-rod before he answered.

"Random figures of speech slip from us at times; they convey no meaning. And now, Mr. Sailor, I must wish you good-morning."

"I thank you for your courtesy in answering my questions," said the sailor.

"I have answered nothing that you might not hear from any man, woman or child in the dominions of Lord Dane," was the reply. "The politics of the family are patent to all."

He moved away as he spoke, with that indolent, gentlemanly languor, somewhat common to Englishmen of the upper classes; sauntering towards a group who had appeared in sight, and were approaching the castle.

An invalid-chair, in which reclined a fine-looking old man, whose gray hairs were fast turning to white. It was pushed behind by a man servant in livery, white and purple, and a tall and stout old lady walked by the side. Behind, came a man of noble features, who might be approaching his fortieth year, upright and stately, and far above the middle height; and a fair girl of nineteen, with large, blue eyes, and, auburn hair, smiling and lovely, was chatting to the latter. The sailor recognized the livery as that of the Dane family, and at once divined that he saw Lord and Lady Dane; Captain Dane he recognized; and the young lady talking to him, must be Adelaide Errol.

The party were not on the highway: they were on the greensward, and passed him at some little distance. Lord and Lady Dane both seemed to look at him, but Captain Dane never turned his head from the fair vision at his side. The young man with the fishing-rod joined the group, and fell into line on the other side of the baron's chair. And just at that moment, another person came in view, a short, thickset man, dressed in black; he looked like what he was, an upper servant in plain clothes. He was walking in the road, and appeared to hang back, as if he did not care to overtake his superiors. The sailor, —as we have been calling him all along, although he was not one, in spite of his dress—accosted him.

"Can you tell me who that gentleman is?" he asked, indicating the young man with the fishing-rod, who had just quitted him.

"It is Mr. Herbert Dane."

"Not a son of Lord Dane?" cried the other quickly.

The man threw back his head, as if the question rather hurt his consequence.

"Oh, dear no; he is nothing but a

relation. *That* is Lord Dane's son, the Honorable Captain Dane."

He was moving on after speaking, but the sailor once more arrested him.

"Ravensbird, I think you have forgotten me."

The man turned and stared, and then respectfully touched his hat.

"Indeed, sir, I beg your pardon, but I don't think I looked at you: I took you for a sailor: we often see strange sailors about here. Colonel Moncton, I believe, sir."

"The same. Will you inform your master that I am here? Stay—Ravensbird—don't tell him who: say a gentleman craves speech of him."

The servant touched his hat once more and hastened forward, overtaking the family just before they reached the castle gates.

"If you please, sir," he said, addressing Captain Dane, whose personal attendant he was, "a gentleman wishes to speak to you."

Captain Dane looked casually round, and saw no one.

"Who does? Some one in the castle?"

"No, sir," slightly pointing to the gate where Colonel Moncton stood. "That gentleman: he bade me follow you and say so."

"Excuse me an instant, Adelaide," said the captain, as he turned in the direction.

She threw her bright, laughing gaze after him, and then bent it on the servant.

"Who is it, Ravensbird?"

"A stranger, my lady."

The two friends met, Colonel Moncton and Captain Dane, and their hands were clasped instantly. Colonel Moncton was an American, and it was in the States that they had first made each other's acquaintance, which had gone on to intimacy. They had been a great deal together, and corresponded yet: it was in this correspondence Colonel Moncton had heard of Adelaide Errol. Both had served in the army, but were free men now, and wealthy.

"Where in the world did you spring from?" uttered Captain Dane. "Have you taken a tour through the bowels of the earth, and turned up on this side?"

Colonel Moncton laughed.

"I invested some funds in a yacht, and must needs try her. We came over to England, have been cruising about the coast, and put in here this morning for a day's sojourn."

"A day! nonsense! The castle won't let you off under a week."

"The castle is not going to be pestered with me," was the interruption of Colonel Moncton, in a graver tone. "I have received news from home that compels me to go back without loss of time. Pardon the seeming discourtesy, Dane; I cannot spare time for the castle; but, as I was here, I would not leave without trying to see you."

"You did not put in on purpose, then?"

"The yacht's master put in for some purpose of his own. You will come down on board with me."

"I heard an hour ago there was a smart, clipper-built yacht in the bay, sporting the stars and the stripes; but I never thought of you. I'll come down with you now, and have a look at her. I had a passion for yachting once."

"Talking about the stars and the stripes, what is that great flag for, may I ask, surging over the castle?" demanded Colonel Moncton.

"Oh, that is nothing but one of the old Dane customs," laughed Captain Dane. "When my father is at home, that flag waves there: in his absence, it does not show."

"One more question, Dane. Who was that bright looking girl you were walking with but now?"

The color actually flushed into the face of Captain Dane, as brightly as to any school girl's. His love was powerful within him.

"The Lady Adelaide."

"I thought so. And when are you to take possession of her?—as we say of other things."

Captain Dane shook his head with a smile.

"It is impossible to say. She is a capricious little beauty, and plays fast and loose. Sometime before the year is out, I suppose."

"And when are we to see you over in the new country again? Never?"

Captain Dane turned his face in surprise on the questioner.

"Can you doubt it? I shall come, and bring my wife with me; she says she should like the trip. But I shall not take up my residence there again; I must make arrangements for having—"

At that moment Mr. Herbert Dane overtook them, his fishing-rod still in his hand. He joined them, speaking a few idle sentences; but Captain Dane did not appear to encourage him, and made no advance to introduce him to his friend. So Herbert Dane walked on.

"That is a relative of yours," observed Colonel Moncton, when he was out of hearing.

"A cousin. His father was the Honorable Herbert Dane, Lord Dane's brother. But the Honorable Herbert got out of his money, and has left his son nearly penniless. I don't think it is of much consequence in the long run, for Mr. Herbert has a talent for spending, and would have run through it, if his father had not. A mine of gold, more or less, would be nothing to him, could he have his fling at it."

"Does he live at the castle?"

"Certainly not. A small house came to him with what patrimony was left, and he occupies it. You may see it to the right, as we walk on,—a low house covered with ivy. There he vegetates, leading an idle life—save for out-door sports. The worst thing his father ever did for him, was to bring him up without a profession. There was the army, and there was the church; either of them legitimate occupation for a man of family."

They walked on towards the town, beyond which was situated the small bay,—so small that no craft larger than a yacht or a fishing-boat could find

shelter in it. She was a beautiful little thing, this American yacht, named the "Pearl," and was at the present moment the pride of Colonel Moncton's life. He was somewhat fond of fresh pastimes and fresh favorites, which reigned pre-eminent while his fancy for them lasted.

Meanwhile Mr. Ravensbird had entered the castle, and sought a companionship he was rather fond of seeking,—that of Lady Adelaide Errol's French maid, Sophie. He was a dark, stern-looking man, with a sallow complexion, but nevertheless he had an honest face, and there was a kindly expression in his black eyes. Nobody could deny that he was very ugly; but ugly men sometimes find great favor with women. The castle wondered what pretty Sophie could find to like in Mr. Ravensbird.

"There's your commission executed," said he putting on the table a paper which contained a few yards of ribbon. "Will it do? Is it right?"

Sophie unfolded it, and held it up. She was a neat, trim damsel, with rather saucy features, quick gray eyes, and an exceedingly smart cap. Sophie stamped her foot petulantly.

"If ever I saw the like!" cried she, for she spoke English pretty fluently. "I ask you to go and buy for me four yards of blue ribbon, and you bring me purple! I have told you fifty times and fifty, that you have not the eye for colors."

Ravensbird laughed.

"I did my best. Won't it do?"

"It must do. I wait for it; I am in the hurry for it. But don't you go and be so stupid again. Who was that sailor gentleman you were talking to by the swing-gate?"

"How did you see me?"

"I stand at the turret-window in my lady's room; I was looking out for you and the ribbon. 'He is taking his time,' I said to myself. Who was it?"

"A friend of the captain's; a gentleman we used to know in America. What do you think he asked me? if that Herbert Dane were my lord's son."

"He did not know better," responded Sophie. "I wish he was my lord's son; things might go smoother."

"What things?" inquired Ravensbird, opening his eyes.

"Well, I should think that you and your master are the only two in this castle who can't see, who have got no sight for what's going on!" uttered Sophie, somewhat contemptuously. "You think my Lady Adelaide will marry your master; he thinks so. Bah!"

"What is now up?" inquired Ravensbird. "What do you mean?"

"There is nothing up that there has not been all along," imperturbably rejoined Sophie, "but you have not got any eyes, and he has not got any wits. My lady's a flirt, she's vain, and she just lives in admiration; but she has got one in the corner of her heart that is more to her than your master and all his gold,—more to her than the whole world. And she had him there long before your master came home, and upset things by wanting her for himself!"

Exceedingly astonished looked Richard Ravensbird.

"I don't know what you are driving at, Sophie," he said. "If she has got her heart fixed on somebody else, and is palming off false smiles upon my master, she's a worthless jilt."

"We can't control our likings," returned Sophie; "and her heart was given, I say, before the captain ever came here. But Lady Dane began to suspect that there was more between them than there ought to be, considering he was poor; and my young lady got frightened lest they should be separated, and he, or she, sent away. So, when the captain came forward with his love and his grand offers, she made a show of accepting him, just to gain time; but, bless you, it was nothing but to blind my Lady Dane, and throw her off the scent. She'll never marry him; she loves the other too well."

"Sophie, tell me who you are speaking of? Squire Lester?"

"Bah! Squire Lester! She likes his gallant speeches and his flattery of her beauty, but what else cares she for Squire Lester? I speak of Herbert Dane. They are engaged in secret, and they love each other to folly."

Richard Ravensbird paused, and then, as past events crowded on his memory, bringing conviction of the truth of Sophie's words, he broke into a low, prolonged whistle.

"If this does not explain much that was dark to me! Sophie, I have wondered to see them so often together in secret. I have seen them walking together on a moonlight night. But I never gave a thought to the true cause. I deemed her childish, wild, fond of laughter and of liberty."

"That is their hour of meeting. When my Lady Dane and Lady Adelaide leave the dinner-table, my lord and the captain remain. Then my Lady Dane falls asleep in her chair, and she steals out in her gray cloak, and meets him; and they walk about for ten or twenty minutes, as long as she thinks she dares stay. Bah! my young lady need not flatter herself I have had my eyes shut."

"I have seen them go to the ruins."

Sophie nodded.

"It's their favorite walk. Once at the old chapel they can shield themselves from the curious, and pace about at leisure under cover of its walls."

"They are a couple of treacherous serpents!" exclaimed Mr. Ravensbird, in a heat.

Sophie laughed.

"You English say that all things are fair in love and war. One wise noodle will exclaim, 'Why does not that Mr. Herbert be off to the wars, or to travel, or to amuse himself, as other young men of quality do?' And another says, 'What does he stop, moping at Danesheld for? why not he go elsewhere and try for a place under government, or do something to amend his fortunes?' And I have smiled to myself to hear them, and wondered they did not look at Lady Adelaide, and see the cause."

"Sophie it is treacherous, *treacherous* towards Captain Dane!" exclaimed Ravensbird, in excitement. "He is honorable and unsuspicious; and those are the natures that get played upon! He ought to be told: he ought to be enlightened: if nobody else does it, I will."

"My friend," said she, gently, "you just take my advice, for it's good: *don't you interfere.* Folks that tell unpalatable truths never get thanked. Let them battle it out for themselves; let things take their course. Captain Dane cannot remain blind long; something or other, rely upon it, will turn up to open his eyes, and then Lady Adelaide must answer for herself, and choose between them. But don't you go and break your head against a wall."

The man-servant was silent. He sat stroking his chin,—a habit of his when in deep thought.

"Sophie," he presently said, "are you sure you are not mistaken? It does seem incredible that a high-born lady should behave so."

Sophie tossed her head and laughed at his simplicity.

"As if there were any difference between high-born and low-born in such matters as these! My Lady Adelaide's a deal less prudent than many a poor girl who has to work for her bread. She means no harm," added Sophie, emphatically; "she's not the one to run into real harm, but she is as flighty a young Scotch girl as ever ran wild on the heather: her spirits are high, and she's thoughtless and young."

"How came she to be living here?" resumed Mr. Ravensbird.

"How came she? why, don't you know?" returned Sophie, in her quick, impetuous way. "Her mother, the Countess of Kirkdale, was Lady Dane's sister. She was a widow, and when she died, Lady Adelaide came here for a home. She has no other: her brother, the young earl, a wild harum-scarum chap, stops on the Continent; he is here, he is there, he is everywhere. Ah! it was a sad position: there she was left motherless and homeless, with barely enough in-come to supply herself with decent clothes. But for Lady Dane, I don't know what she would have done. She was seventeen then, and I came here with her: I had been maid to the countess."

"I thought those well-born young ladies always had some fortune."

"She hadn't. When her father and mother married he was a younger son—as you call it in England, and there were no settlements made: for a very good reason; because there was nothing to settle. He became the earl afterwards, but he was the poorest man in the Scottish peerage."

"So they are all three cousins!" exclaimed Mr. Ravensbird.

"Who? what three?" returned Sophie.

"Lady Adelaide and my master and Herbert Dane."

"Lady Adelaide and your master are; but you can't call her cousin to Mr. Herbert. They are—what's your word for it?—connections; nothing more."

Richard Ravensbird made no reply. He was boiling over with indignation at the duplicity practised on his master, to whom he was much attached. He was a man cool and phlegmatic in general manner, but capable of being aroused to gusts of fierce passion—and in that respect he and Captain Dane were alike.

"If you don't believe me," cried Sophie, fancying he was still incredulous, "go and hide yourself in the ruins to-night, and watch them."

CHAPTER II.

THE QUARREL—THE LADY'S SHRIEKS.

WHETHER in compliance with the suggestion of the French maid, or whether in the gratification of his own curiosity, certain it is that Richard Ravensbird did determine that night to watch the ruins.

His master was dining on board the

yacht, and Squire Lester made the fourth at the dinner-table. Lord Dane could sit at table and enjoy his dinner as much as any one. To see him seated there, with the full use of his hands and arms and mouth and speech, no stranger would have suspected that he was held upright through mechanical support, or that his legs, covered-up under the table, were powerless. He retained all his mental faculties; and he had ever been a man of brilliant intellect.

Richard Ravensbird had no service to render in the dining-room, and when once he had assisted his master to dress for dinner, his evenings were mostly at his own command, to spend as he liked; this evening his movements were entirely unfettered.

The time seemed to drag on with weary wings; he was impatient, and just before the hour, when he expected the ladies would be quitting the dinner-table, he put on his hat and went out. He stood for some moments outside the gates and waited, gazing at the scene. Before him stretched the green table-land, the sea beyond it; standing, however, where he did, he could not see much of the sea. He was too low; on the right were the scattered villas, and the lights of Danesheld beyond them, and on the left the most conspicuous point visible was the old ruin. It was a fine, calm, moonlight night, and there was something ghostly and weird-looking in the ivied walls and glassless windows, as the moon shone on them. He stepped softly over the grass to the left in a slanting direction, and soon came to the ruins.

He went inside the door and looked about him—or rather in at the aperture where a door once had been. Grass was growing in places; an ancient gravestone or two, cold and gray, covered the remains of those who had for centuries been dust of the dust; and, at one end, part of the marble flooring was left still. Traces of niches and nooks, and of little chapels or altars, after the manner peculiar to the Roman-Catholic places of worship,

might be seen: altogether, these old chapel-ruins would afford pleasure to the antiquary, and to those minds given to speculative romance.

Richard Ravensbird, however, had nothing of the antiquary about him, or of romance either; few men less; he was constituted of hard, practical reality. He looked keenly around in the nooks and corners, satisfied himself with pretty good certainty that no interlopers were lurking there, and then he crossed the open building and emerged by the opposite door, which brought him out on the heights within a few yards of their brow. He walked over those few yards, and stood looking down at the sea underneath; he was not so much above it there as he would have been in some other parts, for the chapel lay rather in a dell. Close under the rocks was a narrow strip of beach, extending for some miles on either side; when the tide was at its height, for about two hours this beach would be covered with the water, but at other times the preventive-men paced it,—for tales were told, and believed, of smugglers' work being done there.

These preventive-men had each his marked beat, extending about a mile in length; and their pacings were so timed (or ought to be) that they met at the given boundary at a certain moment, exchanged the signal "All right," and then turned away again. Scandalmongers said that they sometimes lingered in each other's company at these meeting-points longer than they ought to have done, took their seats under the friendly shelter of the rocks, produced pipes and a substantial black bottle from their pockets, and made themselves comfortable. The supervisor heard the rumor, and said they had better let *him* catch them at it.

A sad event had occurred the week before. The man on this particular beat, underneath the chapel, fell asleep, as was supposed, on his post, and the tide overwhelmed him, and carried him out to sea. The body was washed ashore the next day, and a subscription was now being raised for the widow and children, Lord Dane having headed it with five pounds.

As Ravensbird stood looking down, the preventive-man on duty that night came slowly round the point where the rocks projected, shutting out the view beyond. Ravensbird called to him.

"Is it you, Mitchel?"

The man looked up. He could not distinguish who was speaking.

"Don't you know my voice, Mitchel? Take care you don't go to sleep, as poor Biggs did."

"Oh, it's you, Mr. Ravensbird. No, sir, I'll take care of that. We think it's just about in this very spot as he must have sat down and yielded to drowsiness—if he did yield to it. We have been talking pretty freely among ourselves since he died, a saying the nonsense it is to make us pace this strip of beach; why, in some places it's not a foot broad that we have to wind round; and some of us think he's just as likely to have slipped off, and got drowned that way, as to have dropped asleep."

"If you can make the supervisors think it's nonsense, and take you off the duty, the smugglers will be obliged to you."

"Not at all, sir. We could be moved on to the heights up there, and keep quite as good a look-out. Better, I think; and there we should be out of danger."

"You must be very timorous men to fancy there's danger down there. A child might keep himself from it."

"Being on the watch constant, perhaps he might; but one gets off the watch sometimes."

"Thanks to what you take to warm you on a chilly night," laughed Ravensbird.

"No, indeed, sir, you are out there; we take nothing, and daren't: it would be as much as our places were worth. But when a comrade gets drowned, all in a half hour, one can't tell for certain how or why, it puts us up to think that what has happened to him

might happen to us. I say, sir, don't you lean over so far: it makes me twitter to see you. You might be took with giddiness."

"I am all right; my brain is strong, and my nerves are steady. I like looking down from heights."

"It's more than I do," returned the man. "And that would be a nasty fall. It might take life; and it would be sure to break limbs."

"I don't covet the fall. Good-night, if you are progressing onwards."

The preventive-man passed on, and Richard Ravensbird turned round and walked to the chapel again. During his colloquy with the officer, he had kept a continual look-out in the direction of the castle, but had seen no signs of any approach. He took his station in the chapel, in one of its gray, dark corners, near to a window-aperture; and scarcely had he looked again when he saw some one sauntering slowly towards it, whom he soon recognized to be Herbert Dane.

"Then Sophie is right!" he muttered.

Mr. Dane came up, whistling, leaned against the ivy that trailed round the doorway, and looked back the road he had come, whistling still. Ravensbird likewise continued to look, for he was sheltered from observation.

Presently, a light figure, swift of foot, and enveloped in a gray cloak, came running along. The hood was drawn over her head, and but for her voice the servant would not have known her for Lady Adelaide. Mr. Dane threw back the hood, clasped her in his arms, and laid her pretty face upon his shoulder. The indignant servant nearly groaned.

"My darling Adelaide!"

"I was quite determined to come to-night; and, see what a lovely night it is! But we were later than usual at the dinner-table."

"Is the gallant captain at home?"

"Not he. He is dining on board some yacht that is in the bay. Squire Lester is dining with us. Herbert, between all my admirers, I think I shall go deranged. I have pretty trouble to stave off attacks ; the squire is growing demonstrative now."

She laughed merrily as she spoke, and Herbert Dane held her closer.

"The squire's nobody, Adelaide : he may be kept at arm's length, or summarily dismissed. The one I fear is nearer home."

"You need not fear," she impulsively answered. "I hate and despise him ; he may be a man that men esteem and women admire ; but because he has set his love on me, I hate him."

"He is the Honorable William Dane, and his purse is full," was the bitter answer. "No mean rival."

"Oh, Herbert, my dearest, why will you torment yourself ? Don't I tell you—have I not repeatedly told you—that I only care for you, and that nothing, in the earth or above it, shall tear me from you ? I will never marry but you. I am obliged to appear to tolerate him : I even give him gracious marks of favor to keep him in good humor, but you know why I do this. I dare not let my aunt suspect that I care for you : I am obliged to let her think I shall marry him. We should be separated forever : forever, Herbert."

"Things cannot go on long as they are going on now. He will insist upon an explanation with you. Stave it off as you will, it must come."

"Yes, I know it must come."

"And what then—when it does ?"

"Oh, I don't know," she carelessly replied. "Let us throw worry to the winds, and leave the future to the future. Some one may have left you a fortune by that time, Herbert," she merrily added.

"Ah, that they would! that I might claim my darling Adelaide !"

"Why do you come so seldom now to the castle ? I don't know when you have been there before to-day."

"Because I cannot contain myself," he answered with emotion ; "or I fear I cannot. When I see him paying you attentions as a matter of course, as though he made sure of you, my hands tingle to knock him down."

"I wish he was in that sea !" uttered Lady Adelaide.

Heedless words. Spoken not in wickedness, but in her careless impetuosity. Herbert Dane laughed, as if he would welcome the fact with all the pleasure in life. And Richard Ravensbird, from his hiding-nook, threw up his hands menacingly towards Herbert Dane, as though they tingled to put him in it instead.

Mr. Dane and Lady Adelaide moved from the entrance, and began to pace slowly round and round the chapel, outside, conversing confidentially, she drawn close to his side. It was their general walk when they met there ; keeping close to the dark ivied walls, their presence and movements could not be detected from a distance, should there be any night stragglers about. Richard Ravensbird caught a sentence now and then, sufficient to hear that their themes of conversation were their own mutual affection, their plans for the future, and mocking ridicule of the credulity of the Honorable Captain Dane. His blood bubbled up to boiling heat, as it had done in the interview with Sophie ; but he had no resource but to force it down to calmness.

They lingered together for about a quarter of an hour, pacing round continually, and then Lady Adelaide, enveloping her head once more in the hood, flew back, alone, to the castle. Mr. Dane leaned against the ivy, and watched her to it, as he had watched her come. Prudence suggested that she should go alone. That the Lady Adelaide, giddy girl, should trip out in the moonlight within the precincts of the castle, might be thought nothing of, did any prying eye observe her ; but for her to trip out with Mr. Herbert Dane would have set eyes speculating and tongues talking. Next, when she was fairly in, Mr. Herbert Dane sauntered away, and he was followed, after awhile, by Richard Ravensbird. The latter had decided on his line of conduct ; for he was a man given to form plans with prompt decision, and to execute them firmly.

THE SECRET MEETING.—*See page 31.*

The following morning, Lady Dane, her son, and Adelaide, met at breakfast; Lord Dane never rose so early. Adelaide was dressed in a flowing muslin robe, whose prevailing tint was peach color, while lace open sleeves shaded her wrists, matching her lace collar; her cheeks were flushed, her blue eyes were bright, and her auburn hair gleamed in the morning sun.

"You were home late last night, Harry, were you not?" Lady Dane observed to her son.

"Rather so," he replied. "It was past twelve, I think. Moncton and I got talking over old days, and the time slipped away."

"I suppose the yacht leaves this morning: or has left."

"Not until to-night. Her captain found out something wrong in her, some trifling damage to be repaired, which was the reason he put into the bay; and they could not get it completed yesterday, so they don't leave till evening."

Lady Adelaide looked up.

"Colonel Moncton will be here, then, to-day?"

"Very probably. He gave me a half promise last night that he would come for his introduction. I know you will like him, Adelaide. And he is looking forward to the future pleasure of welcoming you to his own home."

She tossed back her pretty head somewhat defiantly.

"I don't know about liking him. Many of your friends, whom you praise up to the skies, I don't like at all, Captain Dane."

"Captain Dane!" he echoed; and there was a pained irritation in his voice, reproachful tenderness in his glance.

"'Harry,' then," she good-humoredly rejoined, for Lady Dane had turned her disapproving eye upon her, "if you are ashamed of the other name."

"Not ashamed of it, Adelaide: but I like a different one from you."

"Oh, dear!" sighed Adelaide, half laughing, half in petulance, as she threw herself back in her chair. "How crooked and contrary things do go in this world!"

"What goes crooked with you, Adelaide?" asked Lady Dane.

"Oh, I don't know, aunt. Plenty of things. Sophie was as cross as two sticks this morning; and my little canary is ill."

"Grave sources of discomfort," said Captain Dane, with a smile; "but scarcely sufficient to make you unhappy, Adelaide."

"Do you dine on board the yacht again to-night?" was all her rejoinder.

"I shall get Moncton to dine here, if I can," was his reply, "should it not interfere with his sailing. But I expect they will be putting to sea about that time."

"At what hour does the tide serve?" asked Lady Dane.

"High tide at ten to-night. They'll be off by nine, I dare say. Adelaide, would you like to go on board and inspect her? she is a beautiful little thing, and Moncton would be so pleased to welcome you."

She gently shook her head.

"No, thank you, Harry; I don't care for yachts. But I shall be glad to make the acquaintance of Colonel Moncton, should you bring him here."

As Captain Dane was quitting the room after breakfast, his servant accosted him:

"Could you allow me to speak to you for a few minutes, sir?"

"What about?" asked Captain Dane, feeling a sort of surprise.

"I wanted to say a few words upon a matter personal to yourself, sir."

"Very well. I am going to my room to write letters: you can come now."

They proceeded to the captain's apartment. Ravensbird held the door open for his master to enter, and then followed him in; and the door was closed upon them.

Lady Dane rang the bell for the servants to clear away the breakfast things; and it was done. She then reached her prayer-book, and began reading to herself the morning psalms, as was her custom upon the conclusion of breakfast. Adelaide did not care to join in the exercise, and Lady Dane would not press it: she was wise enough to know that none can be forced into religion. It must come spontaneously, of their own conviction, their right feeling; and she hoped it would in time come to Adelaide. She sat in her easy-chair, near the fire: Adelaide stood behind her, looking from the window.

It was one of those warm, balmy, brilliant mornings that we sometimes get in early spring. The sky was blue, the sun was shining, the hedges were putting forth their green, and the spring flowers were opening. But not at any of these, pleasant objects though they were, gazed Lady Adelaide: genial sun, the calm sky, the shooting hedges, and the smiling flowers were as nothing to her: she did not cast a thought to the blue expanse of sea, stretched out in the distance, or to its stately vessels sailing along; she did not heed the cheerful villas near, or the busy laborers at work on the farm-lands: no; her attention was fixed on something else.

Astride upon the very gate where you saw him yesterday, was Herbert Dane. He might often be seen there: was it so favored by him because it was in full view of the castle windows, and of a beautiful face which was wont to appear at them? He had discarded the fishing-rod of yesterday, but he held in his hand a silver-mounted riding whip, with which he kept switching, first his own boots, then the bars of the gate. Think you Adelaide Errol could see any other object, with *him* in view? As she appeared at the window, he raised his hat, though so far away: a stranger would have seen nothing in the act but the ordinary courtesy of a gentleman; Adelaide probably saw much, and imagined more.

How long she stood there, looking, she could not have told, for she was taking no heed of the time; ten minutes it may have been. And then she was abruptly startled, as in fact

was the whole castle, by unusual sounds of anger and contention on the corridor above. Lady Dane started from her chair in alarm, and Adelaide sprang to the door and pulled it open. Captain Dane and his servant, Ravensbird, were quarrelling,—quarrelling as it appeared, for the voices of both were raised in a fierce passion. Both seemed in violent anger, in uncontrollable excitement; the captain was red with fury, the servant was livid; and just as Lady Dane and Adelaide appeared, the captain pushed the man to the top of the stairs, and kicked him down them.

Ravensbird stumbled as he got to the foot, where stood the ladies. He took no notice of them, but he turned round, looked up defiantly at his master, and raised his clenched fist.

"Take care of yourself, Captain Dane," he hissed. "I shall never lose sight of this insult, until I have repaid it."

"Good heavens, Henry!" uttered Lady Dane in agitation, as the man disappeared down the lower stairs, "what is this about? what has he done?"

"Never mind, mother; he won't trouble the peace of the castle a second time. I have dismissed him."

"But what had he done?"

"The wicked hound!" burst forth Captain Dane. "He would have traduced one who is dear to me."

Richard Ravensbird was already outside the gates of the castle, first ordering one of the wondering footmen to send his clothes and other property after him. As he passed Herbert Dane, who was still astride on the gate, the latter was struck with the ghastly, enraged look of his face.

"What's up, Ravensbird?" he hastily asked.

The man stopped, and answered, giving each word its full force.

"I have been kicked out of the castle, sir."

"Kicked out of the castle!" repeated Herbert, in astonishment. "By whom? Not by its lord?" he added, with an attempt at a joke.

"I have been ignominously kicked down-stairs, in the sight of Lady Dane, and ordered out of the castle. He who did it was my master. But let him look to himself. There are some insults, sir, that can only be wiped out by revenge. This is one."

"And what on earth was it for? How had you offended him?" reiterated Herbert.

"I was endeavoring to do him good, to serve him; and my friendly words—friendly I meant them to be —were taken up in a wrong light. Let him take heed to himself, I say."

Ravensbird strode on, and Herbert Dane watched him, beginning again gently to switch the little whip, which, since Ravensbird's approach, had been still.

"A queer customer to offend, he looks just now," quoth he. "What a livid face of anger it was! I think Mr. Harry *had* better take heed to himself."

Nothing more came out, as to the cause of the squabble in the castle. Lord Dane, to whose ears the noise had penetrated, summoned his son, but the latter would enter into no details. Ravensbird had behaved infamously, and he had given him his merits, was all that could be got from Captain Dane.

Colonel Moncton came up in the course of the morning, and paid a short visit. He was introduced to Lord and Lady Dane and Adelaide, and then he and Captain Dane went out together. Adelaide watched them from the windows; they were strolling about arm-in-arm. She saw them go inside the ruins of the chapel; she saw them standing on the heights and looking down at the strip of beach and the sea underneath : it appeared that Captain Dane was pointing out the features of the locality to his friend. The colonel had declined the invitation to dinner : they should be getting away, he said : but he asked Captain Dane to dine with him on board the Pearl instead, and the promise was given.

Somewhat, then, to the surprise of Lord and Lady Dane, when they assembled in the dining-room at seven o'clock, Captain Dane entered, and sat down with them.

"How is this, Harry?" inquired his father. "I thought we were not to have your company this evening. Is the Pearl gone?"

"I changed my mind about going, and have despatched an apology to Moncton."

The answer was delivered in a short, cold tone, as if the speaker did not care to be questioned.

Lord Dane looked at his son keenly : he thought something had occurred to annoy him.

"You are letting that affair with Ravensbird vex you, Harry," said he.

"It has vexed me, very much indeed."

"Harry, you must take care of that man," observed Lady Adelaide. "I hear he vows vengeance against you."

Captain Dane smiled contemptuously.

"How do you know that, Adelaide?" asked Lord Dane. And the question—or the having to answer it —brought a pretty blush to her face.

"I met Herbert Dane when I was out this afternoon, and he said Ravensbird had passed him on his way from the castle, uttering threats of revenge," she replied. "Herbert said he would not care to have Ravensbird for an enemy; he thought he could be a powerful one."

A peculiar smile of anger, mixed with irony, flitted over Captain Dane's face.

"If I have no more formidable enemy than Ravensbird, I shall not hurt," he sarcastically uttered.

After that, he relapsed into silence, and, when addressed, answered only in monysyllables. Nearly everything put before him he sent away untasted; there could be no doubt that he was smarting from some inward annoyance or vexation.

Lady Dane and Adelaide quitted the dining-room, leaving the two gentlemen together. The former hoped that Lord Dane would succeed in drawing from Harry what was amiss. Harry was her favorite son, and it pained her to see him like this. She took her easy-chair, sat down in it before the fire; and, in thinking over matters, dropped into her usual after-dinner sleep.

Then came the turn of Lady Adelaide—the moment for her stealing out of the ruins: yet she was not sure that night of meeting Herbert, for he had told her in the day he did not think he should be able to visit them. She loved him far too much, however, not to run the chance, and with quiet movements and stealthy treads, she glides down the staircase, seized the old gray cloak from its hanging nook, threw it on, stole out at a side door, and across the grass. Very quickly went she, for she was late: if Lady Dane had been one minute dropping off to sleep that night, she had been five-and-twenty.

Into a very comfortable sleep, however, had Lady Dane dropped. And longer would she have continued to enjoy it, but that she was abruptly aroused. A sound of shrieks from the direction of the ruins, broke suddenly forth on the still night air, so loud, so terrific that they disturbed even the sleeping Lady Dane. She rubbed her eyes, she listened, she raised her ear: and then she darted to the window, and threw it open.

In the clear bright moonlight might be discerned a form speeding towards the castle from the ruins,—a gray form, enveloped in a cloak, or other shrouding garment, and uttering shriek upon shriek.

Lady Dane heard the servants, whose ears had likewise caught the ominous sounds, rushing to the great gates, and in her consternation she sped thither also. The warm flood of gas from the gateway-lamp threw its light upon the entrance, and into that light, shrieking still, darted the gray form—that of Lady Adelaide Errol. She fell into violent hysterics as they caught her in their arms.

CHAPTER III.

THE FALL FROM THE CLIFF.

THEY bore Lady Adelaide into the hall,—a spacious room, hung round with pictures, which opened from the left-hand side of the great gateway. On that side, on the ground-floor, there were but two apartments, the hall and the dining-room. At the back of the hall a handsome staircase wound up to the floor above, and near the foot of the staircase a door opened to some back passages, which led round to the kitchens and the apartments of the servants, on the other side the gateway.

Adelaide was shrieking still, sobbing and crying in strong hysterics; she was evidently under the influence of some powerful terror. The servants put her into a large arm-chair, took off her cloak, and ran for water and for smelling salts; Lady Dane chafed her hands, and somewhat angrily demanded of her what had happened, and where she had been.

Lord Dane was in the dining-room, alone. He pulled sharply the silken string, tied to his chair and attached to the bell-rope, and when Bruff, the butler, answered it, inquired haughtily what all that unseemly noise meant.

"My lord, it is Lady Adelaide. She seems to be taken ill."

"Lady Adelaide shrieking like that! What brings her down in the hall?"

"She was outside, my lord, as it appears. We heard the screams, and went to the gate, and Lady Adelaide came flying in from across the grass. I should think she must have been frightened in some way, my lord."

"I never heard of such an improbable thing!" ejaculated Lord Dane. "Lady Adelaide out at this hour! it is not likely."

The butler was too wise to maintain his assertion.

"My lady is with her," he said. "She heard the cries too, and came down."

" Undo this," cried Lord Dane.

He meant the silk ribbon attached to his chair. The butler obeyed him, and Lord Dane touching the spring, the chair propelled itself into the hall, for it was one of those invalid-chairs running upon wheels, so useful to helpless persons.

Lord Dane took himself and his chair immediately opposite to Adelaide. There he stopped. He saw that her breath was labored, that her whole frame trembled, and that she was as white as death; but she was not screaming now.

" What is all this ?" he inquired, looking first at her, and then at his wife. " Have you been frightened, Adelaide ?"

The question threw her into hysterics again ; and Lord Dane turned for an answer to his wife.

" I know nothing about it," said Lady Dane. " I was dozing in the drawing-room, and was awakened by screams, outside. I put up the window, and saw some one running from the direction of the ruins, shrieking awfully. It proved to be Adelaide."

" But what brought Adelaide out there ?"

" That is what I want to learn. When I dozed off, she was sitting quietly in the drawing-room, reading."

" My dear, what took you out ?" inquired Lord Dane, when she grew quiet.

She shook terribly as she answered him :

" I—I don't know."

" But you must know," reiterated Lady Dane, " you could not have walked out in your sleep. What took you out ?"

Adelaide's very teeth shook as she answered the question, and she turned if possible, more deadly white. But she pressed her two hands for full a minute upon her forehead before she spoke.

" I don't know what made me go out," she faltered ; " it was very foolish. In looking from the drawing-room window, I observed what a lovely night it was, nearly as light as

day, and the thought came over me that I would put on my cloak and run as far as the ruins and back. I meant no harm."

" The most senseless thing I ever heard of ! such a wild-goose trick, sure, was never performed," exclaimed Lady Dane. " Had any one told me, but yourself, I could not have believed it."

Adelaide did not care for that ; her aunt might call her senseless, and a " wild-goose" for an hour, if she pleased ; but what she did care for, and dread, were the keen eyes of Lord Dane, fixed penetratingly upon her. She saw he did not believe her fully.

" Let that pass," he said, as if answering his own thoughts. " What caused you to scream ?"

" Oh—I cannot tell," she answered, clasping her hands in agony.

" Did any one accost you ?" proceeded Lord Dane.

" No, no," she answered eagerly. " I—I—I think I got frightened at finding myself all alone by moonlight in ↗those chapel-ruins, where the graves are."

" And so you ran home, shrieking, thinking a ghost was after you ?" cried Lord Dane, who readily accepted the version.

" Y—es, I suppose so."

As Adelaide spoke the hesitating answer, she happened to catch the look of her maid, Sophie. Most strangely and earnestly was the woman's gaze fixed upon her, almost, as it seemed, in terror. Adelaide shuddered, and once more hid her face in her hands.

" I hope it will be a warning to you, my dear," said Lord Dane, " not to attempt a moonlight escapade again. You might meet a real ghost another time—or something worse."

" And you cannot say but you would deserve it," added Lady Dane, crossly. " You are as flighty as your brother. The best thing you can do now, is to go to bed."

" Oh, no, no, pray no !" eagerly returned Adelaide. " I am not ill ; I am not frightened now. I would rather sit up."

She looked both frightened and ill, but it was not urged. Lady Dane put her head in at the dining-room door.

"I wonder you can remain contented there, through all this noise, Harry," she cried. "Is he asleep?"

"Harry's not there," said Lord Dane. "He went out."

"Oh. Down to the yacht, probably, to see his friend off."

"I fancy so."

Lord Dane retired to the dining-room; he never appeared in the drawing-room at night. The two ladies went up-stairs, and the servants dispersed. But a sudden freak — or whatever you may please to term it— took Lady Dane.

"You have made me quite nervous, Adelaide, with your shrieks and your absurdity," she exclaimed. "I should feel more comfortable with Lord Dane than up here." And, ringing the bell, she ordered the tea taken into the dining-room. So they both went down again.

Now, somewhere about the time that Lady Adelaide's cries were first heard, Mitchel, the preventive-man, to whom Ravensbird had spoken the previous evening, was again nearing the same spot, in pursuance of his duty. As he turned round the ledge of rock, which there projected so far as to leave scarcely a foot of ground to walk upon, he heard angry voices on the heights, close to the ruins of the chapel. The man naturally looked up to whence they proceeded, and there, in the bright moonlight, he perceived, or thought he perceived, two men scuffling together at the edge of the cliff, as in a deadly struggle. The next moment one fell, or was propelled over the cliff, and awful shrieks from the chapel, or near it, broke out upon the night air.

For an instant Mitchel stood in dismay, in fear, his heart leaping into his mouth. As may have been gathered from his conversation with Ravensbird, he was not a particularly

brave man: few men, permanently weak in health, are so. Mitchel, though he managed to keep up and go about his duties, was always ailing, and earlier in life he had been subject to epileptic fits. He drew near to the fallen, prostrate man, in tremor and dread, expecting to see him lifeless.

Lifeless he appeared to be. The face was upturned to the moonlight, the eyes were closed, the skin looked blue and ghastly, and the mouth was open. Mitchel's terror and dismay were not lessened when he recognized the features; for they were those of the Honorable William Henry Dane.

The man was perfectly ignorant of what it would be best to do. He shouted out at the top of the heights for help, but there was no answer: little fear that the murderer—whether one in intention or by accident—would answer him. He then took off his coat, laid it under Captain Dane's head, rubbed his hands, and rubbed his heart.

But Captain Dane, poor fellow, never moved, or gave the faintest signs of life. Mitchel felt that he was dead: and—what was *he* to do? The body must be got away, for in an hour's time the tide would be up: and indeed this had been Mitchel's last turn before going off duty, until the tide was gone again.

He pushed the hair from the clammy brow. The face was not injured in falling: he lifted one of the hands, but it fell dead again. And then Mitchel turned, and tore away at a break-neck speed, expecting to meet his comrade on the next boundary.

But he did not: whether the man had stolen a march upon time, and gone off too early, or whether he might have been seated under the rocks, and had suffered Mitchel to pass him, the latter could not tell. All he had to do was to tear on again at the same speed, and gain what they called the coast-guard station.

The coast-guard station was a low building; in outward appearance for all the world like a barn. Inside, it consisted of two rooms and a sleeping closet. And on this night, sitting round a blazing fire in the first room, to which the door opened, were a supervisor and three of his men. They were talking over the chief occurrence of the day—which had been known from one end of Danesheld to the other in an hour's time after it happened; namely, the quarrel at the castle between Captain Dane and his servant, and the kicking of the man out. Never was there a more scandal-loving place than Danesheld. Exceedingly astonished were they to be interrupted by Mitchel. He burst in upon them, his hair standing on end, and his face in a white heat.

"What's the matter with you?" exclaimed the supervisor, whose name was Cotton.

Mitchel could not answer. His heart was beating wildly, as he never remembered it to have beaten before, and he laid his two hands upon it, and staggered against the wall.

"Why have you left your beat? What brings you here?" continued Mr. Cotton in wonderment. "Can't you speak?"

"He's dead, he's dead," Mitchel at length panted. "I want assistance."

The supervisor stared, and the men turned round.

"Who is dead?"

Mitchel opened his lips to answer, but no sound came. They sprang forward and caught him just in time to prevent his sinking to the ground. The fright of seeing Captain Dane fall, the excitement, or the running, or perhaps all combined, had brought on what he had not been troubled with for years—a fit.

Of course they could make nothing of what he had said, about somebody's being dead and wanting assistance. The supervisor gave it as his opinion that he was only wandering in mind, the precursor of the illness. He sent one of the men out for a doctor.

The latter, Mr. Wild, was not at home; he was gone to spend an hour with Mr. Apperly, so the man went there after him. Mr. Wild hastened to obey the summons, and Mr. Apperly, who was a solicitor, accompanied him.

"What has brought this on?" demanded Mr. Wild of the supervisor, as he busied himself with Mitchel. "I suspect he must have been excited or agitated, and in no measured degree."

"He rushed in here like one possessed," was the supervisor's answer. "I never saw a man so agitated. His breath all panting, and his speech gone."

"Did he give no explanation?"

"Nothing that one could make top or tail of. He spluttered out some confused words about wanting assistance for somebody who was dead. I think his brains must have been moonstruck."

"I don't then, sir," spoke up one of the men. "I think his agitation was caused by something real. Mitchel's a quiet man, not given to drink, or to any thing of that sort. Something extraordinary must have happened."

Whatever might have happened their only chance of coming to the solution of the mystery was, by endeavoring to restore consciousness and speech to Mitchel: and this was effected in about an hour's time. The man was raised from his recumbent position, placed in a chair in front of the fire, and some refreshment given him to drink.

"Now, Mitchel," began the doctor, "let us have it out. What upset you like this?"

Mitchel did not answer for a minute or two; he was probably recalling his recollection.

"What's the hour?" he suddenly asked. And the supervisor cast his eyes up to the clock.

"Getting on for ten."

Mitchel staggered up from his chair, but sank down again. He was weak yet.

"Then its too late!" he uttered in excitement, "and his body will have been washed away."

"What is this mystery, Mitchel?" inquired Mr. Wild.

"I'll tell you, sir, as well as I'm able, but I don't understand it myself," was Mitchel's answer. "I had just got around Rock Point, as we call it, when I saw a man thrown over the cliff. I ran up to succor him, but he was dead."

"Thrown over the cliff!" was echoed by the bystanders. "From the top down to the beach?"

"Pitched right over, he was. They were having words and scuffling together, whoever the other was—and nobody need go far to guess at him, knowing what's known."

"Why, who were they? who was pitched over?" cried the doctor, impatiently.

"Captain Dane, sir."

The name startled them all. Their thoughts had been cast to nothing more than some poor fisherman or smuggler; certainly not to Lord Dane's son. Mr. Apperly broke the silence.

"Do you say there was a scuffle between two people on the heights, and that Captain Dane was pushed over?" he asked of Mitchel.

"As it seemed to me, sir. They were quarreling and struggling; and it is not likely Captain Dane would throw himself down."

"I fear, then, his assaulter must have been the servant, Ravensbird," gravely observed Mr. Apperly. "He has been heard uttering threats of revenge against Captain Dane to-day."

"Not the least doubt of that, sir," returned Mitchel: "who else would attack Captain Dane? But I never thought the man would have done such a thing. I didn't dislike Ravensbird. But what's to be done?" he added in a more energetic tone. "The tide will be safe to have carried away the body."

"Was he dead?" asked the surgeon, in a low tone.

"Stone dead, sir. It was that frighted me."

What was to be done, indeed? They might well ask it. A moment's consultation and then they all, Mitchel and one of the men excepted, started off towards the spot, by way of the land: the beach they knew would be impassable from the tide.

They laid their plans as they went along. Mr. Apperly and Mr. Wild would proceed to the castle, and break the news to Lord Dane, and the rest would go on to the chapel and look down from the heights: they knew there was not the slightest possible chance that the body had not been carried out to sea, but it would be some consolation—to their curiosity, at any rate—to gaze down at the spot.

"I don't like the task," abruptly exclaimed the doctor as they went along. "The captain was the favorite son."

"I'm sure I don't," returned Mr. Apperly. "It has been occurring to me for the last few minutes that the better plan might be to call on Herbert Dane, and get him to break it to them."

The surgeon eagerly caught at it, and they turned off to the right to the house of Mr. Herbert Dane, and found him at home. He appeared to be making himself comfortable, had a sofa drawn before the fire, a cigar in his mouth, and some bottles and glasses on a table at his elbow.

"This is your promised nine o'clock!" he called out, as they were entering. "A pretty long while to keep a fellow waiting: it's too bad, Harry. Oh! I beg your pardon," he added, as his visitors advanced. "I thought it was Captain Dane, whom I am expecting."

They did not take the offered chairs, but looked gravely at Herbert—as if hoping their grave looks might prepare him for what was to come.

"We have an unpleasant task to perform, Mr. Herbert Dane, and we have called on you, to request that you will help us out with it. We are on our way to the castle, bearing evil tidings to Lord Dane. An accident has happened to his son."

Mr. Herbert Dane did not appear to take in the ominous sound of the words: he was more intent on hospitality. He pushed aside the sofa, rang the bell for more glasses, and extending his hand to turn the gas on brighter. Instead, however, of turning it on, he—turned it out.

"A plague on my clumsiness! I am not used to the thing, and must have turned it the wrong way. The servant will be in in a minute, gentlemen: a cheery welcome, this, for you!"

"Mr. Herbert," cried the surgeon, "you did not understand us. Never mind the gas. We came to inform you of a shocking event that has occurred to Captain Dane."

"To Captain Dane! What is it?"

"He has fallen—or been thrown—over the cliff, by the chapel. There is little doubt that it has killed him."

Herbert Dane put down his cigar, and turned his dismayed face upon them. They noticed how pale it looked as the fire-light shown upon him.

"Fallen over the cliff!" he uttered. "When? How? When did it happen? I have been expecting him here since nine o'clock."

They told him all they knew, and asked him to break it to Lord Dane. He had rather not, himself, break it to him, he answered: Lord and Lady Dane had not been very cordial with him lately, and he should dread the effect of the communication on Lord Dane, coming from *him.* He would, however, go with them to the castle, and join in consulting as to what was best to be done. "What will you take!" he asked.

They would prefer not to take any thing.

"Had you not better?" he urged. "Tidings such as these require support of some sort. Which of the preventive-men, do you say, saw the affray?"

"Mitchel. A thousand pities that it should have been he. Any other of the men would not have lost his senses over it, and help might have reached Captain Dane in time, in case he was alive. There is sure to be some untoward fatality attending these cases!"

Herbert Dane tossed his hair from his brow, and then leaned his forehead on his hand, his elbow on the mantelpiece. "Did Mitchel not distinguish the other on the cliff with Harry—with Captain Dane?—who it might be?"

"Fast enough," cried the lawyer, who was a quick, fiery little man. "Who should it be, but the discharged man, Ravensbird?"

"Ah!" uttered Herbert Dane, a glow flashing into his pale countenance. "I told Harry, when I met him this afternoon, to take care of him."

"We are wasting time, Mr. Herbert," said the surgeon. "Lord Dane must be informed of this."

Herbert rang the bell for his hat, and went out with them. The man-servant addressed his master as he was showing them to the door.

"If Captain Dane comes, sir, am I to ask him to wait?"

"No," mechanically replied Herbert.

Arrived at the castle, they asked for an interview with Lord Dane. The butler resolutely refused them. "You know, Mr. Herbert," he said, in a tone of remonstrance, turning to the latter, "that my lord will now never be disturbed in an evening. Could not these gentlemen come to-morrow? Or perhaps they will walk in and wait till the captain enters. I don't suppose he'll be late: he dined at home."

"Bruff," cried the surgeon, who knew the servant, "we *must* see Lord Dane. An accident has happened to the captain, and—I do fear—you will never see him home again. Go in to his lordship: say that we have heard bad news, and have come to tell it him: he will be sure to admit us."

The butler turned from them in doubt and dread, and entered the dining-room.

"My lord will see you, gentlemen," he said, when he came out. "My lady and Lady Adélaide are there," he added, in a low voice.

They entered. Not Herbert: he lingered outside. The butler held the door open for him, but he shook his head, and the man stepped back and closed the door.

"I declare I don't like to face them, Bruff. It will be awful tidings, especially for Lady Dane. I'll go in presently, when the brunt of the shock is over."

"What has happened, Mr. Herbert? They spoke of the captain, but he was quite well when he went out from dinner."

"I really cannot tell you what has happened: I don't understand," was the reply of Herbert. "They called upon me with a tale that he had fallen over the cliff, and asked me to come up here. It is incredible."

How the two gentlemen contrived to break the news to Lord and Lady Dane they scarcely knew themselves. Soon the house was in commotion. His lordship had not the use of his own legs, but he speedily set in motion those who had. Some of the servants were sent flying for the man, Mitchel, some for the police-inspector, some across to the brow of the heights, some down to the bay to see if the American yacht was gone. Lord Dane was in great excitement, though he did not wholly believe the tale: as Herbert had said, it was incredible.

"What do you know of this, Herbert?" Lord Dane asked of the latter, when he at length went in. "When did you last see Harry?"

"In the afternoon: about two, I think it was. He was with that Colonel Moncton—or whatever the man's name is—they were coming out of the castle. Harry stopped me and said he would come in and smoke a manilla at my house this evening, and it was agreed upon. Nine o'clock he named. He was going to dine on board the yacht, but would be back by nine, for she would be setting sail."

"Did he come?"

"No. I was waiting for him still, when Mr. Apperly and Mr. Wild called."

"What do you think of this tale?"

"I can only hope that the man, Mitchel, was wandering in his brain before falling into the fit, and that Harry will be found safe on board the yacht," was the reply of Herbert Dane.

Lady Dane was pacing the room restlessly: she occasionally put a question to Herbert. Lady Adelaide sat on a sofa, her head bent down and buried in the cushions.

"Any one, but you, would be over on the brow of the heights," cried Lord Dane, sharply, to his nephew, "looking out for—"

"I have been," interrupted Herbert. "I went over with Bruff while the news was being broken to you. Supervisor Cotton and some of his men were there."

"And what did you see?" interrupted Lady Dane.

"Nothing at all. The tide was up and the beach underneath was covered with it. Every thing seemed calm and quiet."

"Were there any traces of the scuffle on the heights?" rejoined Lord Dane.

"None whatever, so far as we could see by this light. I don't know what may be visible by day. Cotton declares he does not believe a word of the story."

"Neither do I?" cried out Lord Dane, very much in the manner of a man who would like to brave out something that he does believe.

Of the messengers sent out, the first to return was the servant who had been despatched to the yacht. The yacht had gone when he reached the bay, had sailed out nearly two hours before, and must be then far away, for the wind was fair.

"Then there's no knowing whether Harry went on board or not," groaned Lord Dane. He had unconsciously clung to the hope that the Pearl might still be in port and his son on board of her, and to find that it was not so, came upon him like a keen blow.

"The captain had not been on board, my lord," rejoined the servant. I saw Mills, the sail-maker, who was on the Pearl at work all day, only quitting her at the last moment. He said Colonel Moncton was disappointed that the captain did not come to dinner, and that he had to sail without seeing him. I asked Mills if he had seen Captain Dane about, down there, this evening, but he said, No; he had come on board with the colonel in the afternoon, for an hour, but he had not seen him since."

The inspector of police was the next to arrive; but Mitchel did not come at all. He was not sufficiently well to venture out again that night. The inspector heard the various stories, and received Lord Dane's orders to apprehend Ravensbird, and to bring him before him the following morning. At length the castle was cleared. But the old Lord and Lady Dane sat up the livelong night hoping that Harry might return, hoping against hope. Had they heard Mitchel's testimony by word of mouth, they might have been less sanguine; but they sat on in sick expectancy. The tide receded from the strip of beach, leaving nothing on it, leaving no signs that any thing dead or alive, had been on it. And the morning light dawned upon the earth, and the morning sun shone out to gladden it; but Harry Dane had not come.

CHAPTER IV.

LADY ADELAIDE'S OATH.

JUST before entering Danesheld, standing in a somewhat obscure spot, though near to the fishermen's huts, was a small inn, or public house, called the "Sailor's Rest." It was kept by a man of the name of Hawthorne, who had once been gamekeeper to the Dane family. It was a well conducted inn, of rather a better class than a common public-house, professed to afford good bed and board, and had its share of custom. Among those fond of frequenting its bar and parlor were the men-servants from the castle; and it was to this place that Ravensbird proceeded when turned out by his master, intending to take up at it his temporary sojourn.

On the morning afterwards, the landlord was in the bar alone—or, at any rate, he thought he was alone. He was busy polishing his taps, and setting things straight, according to his custom before breakfast, when one of the preventive-men, on his way down to the beach, came up the passage and entered.

"Half a gill of rum, landlord; the morning air's chilly."

"'Twas a bit of a frost I fancy last night," responded the landlord, as he handed him what was called for, "but it'll be a fine day."

"I hope it will, for the work that's got to be done. They'll be dragging for the body in shore, and all Danesheld, I suppose, will turn out to see."

"Dragging for what body?" returned the landlord. "Has anybody been lost?"

The man was in the act of putting the glass of rum to his lips; he drew it back in astonishment, and gazed at the landlord.

"Why! you don't mean to say you have never heard?"

"What is there to hear?"

"Of the calamity that has overtook the castle. Captain Dane's murdered."

"Captain Dane murdered!" echoed the landlord, doubting whether his ears were not playing him false.

"He was murdered last night. It's a odd thing you didn't hear of it—though perhaps you were shut up when the folks came back from the castle. Mitchel was on his beat, and saw a scuffle on the heights between two men, not knowing then who they were, and one pitched the other over, and killed him. When Mitchel got up to the fallen man he found it was Captain Dane—stone dead."

"Good mercy preserve us!" uttered Hawthorne.

"And that fool of a Mitchel comes rushing up to the guard-station at the pace of a steam-engine, which we conclude upset his heart, or some other vital part of him, and must needs fall into a fit. The consequence was, that nobody knew any thing about it till he came-to, which was more than an hour after, and then the tide had covered the beach, and washed the body away. Sickly fellows like Mitchel are never good for much."

"Poor gentleman!" exclaimed the landlord. "It was only the day before yesterday he stopped at the door here and spoke to me as he went by. What an affliction for my lord and my lady. Who was the quarrel with? Who threw him over?"

"His late servant, Ravensbird."

The landlord backed against the shelves as if thunderstruck, and an iron ladle which he held in his hand clattered on to the ground.

"Ravensbird!" he uttered, in a low, awe-struck stone, "Ravensbird!"

"Ravensbird, and nobody else. He was not long carrying out his threats of vengeance."

"Why, he has been lodging here ever since yesterday morning. He is up-stairs in bed at this moment. I couldn't have slept in the same house with him, if I had known this last night."

"He must have dodged Captain Dane, and waylaid him on the heights. The curious part of the affair is, what took Captain Dane over to the brow at all; some think that Ravensbird, in some cunning way, entrapped him into going, and then—"

At this moment an interruption occurred which nearly made the landlord and the speaker start out of their skins. A high-backed, wooden screen went partially across the bar, its seat in front facing the fire. At the back of the screen stood the landlord and his customer; and at this critical juncture the head of Mr. Ravensbird was propelled round it, glaring at the two in indignation. He had been quietly seated there all the time.

"Your name's Dubber, I believe," he said, looking at the preventive-man. "How dare you stand there to traduce me?"

Dubber was, as the saying runs, taken-to. He was too confused to make any reply. And Ravensbird walked round and confronted him.

"By what authority do you accuse me of the crime of murder?"

"Well, now, Mr. Ravensbird, if what I've said is not true; if you are innocent, I'm sure I beg your pardon," he answered, gathering courage and his wits together. "But you must not blame me. If I had not told Hawthorne, the next comer-in would. When events like this happen, people will talk; and if you were not mixed up in this, you'd be the first to talk of it, yourself. Mitchell saw the affair, and saw the captain pitched down; and he says the other was Mr. Ravensbird."

"Mitchel says that it was I? That he saw me?"

"As I hear; the men were saying so last night. I didn't hear Mitchel speak myself, for I wasn't in the guard-house till he had gone."

"Is what you have been asserting true?—that Captain Dane is murdered?" pursued Ravensbird.

"Oh, that's true, safe enough. They are getting ready the drags to search for the body."

"On what part of the heights did it happen?" proceeded Ravensbird.

"Off the chapel-ruins. He fell down just beyond Rock Point. But I must be off, for my time's up," added the man; "unless I'd like to get reported."

He turned round as he spoke, and departed, glad to be away from the stern eye, the sallow face of Ravensbird. "Putting them questions as if he'd like to make believe he was an innocent know-nothing," thought Dubber. "But they won't avail him much, when he's carpeted before my Lord Dane."

Ravensbird turned his eyes on the landlord, when they were left alone. "What do you know of this business, Hawthorne?"

"If you were sitting in the screen, Mr. Ravensbird, you must know as much as I. I have only heard what Dubber said."

"What do you think of it?"

"I can't think. Who would do harm to Captain Dane? He had no enemies, that I know of. I'm sure the quarrel with you was quite unlike him."

"Unlike his general nature. He was put up—and so was I. Where's my hat? Up-stairs, I think. I shall go out and ascertain the truth of this business."

He quitted the bar to go to his chamber, and almost at the same moment the inspector of police entered it. He ranged his eyes round and round, as if in search of some object, and then nodded to the landlord.

"Good-morning, Hawthorne. You have got Master Ravensbird lodging with you, I hear. Is he up yet?"

"He was here not an instant ago, sir. He's gone to his room to fetch his hat. He wants to go out and learn the particulars of this sad business about the captain. Dubber has just been in to tell of it. I'm sure you might have knocked me down with a puff."

The inspector withdrew from the bar to the passage, and there he propped himself against the wall. The position he had chosen commanded a view of the back-door of the house, as well as of the front. Almost immediately Ravensbird appeared, and the inspector accosted him.

"A fine morning, Mr. Ravensbird."

"Very. I am going out to enjoy it."

"An instant yet. I want to say a few words to you."

"Not now," impatiently returned Mr. Ravensbird.

"No time like the present," was the reply of the inspector, as he laid his hand upon the man's shoulder. "Don't be restive: I *must* detain you."

Ravensbird turned his sallow face on the officer, his eyes flashing with anger. "By what right? What do you mean?"

"Now, Ravensbird, don't be unreasonable: take things quietly. You are my prisoner, and all the resistance in the world will not avail you."

Ravensbird's answer to this *was* resistance. He strove to wrench himself from the inspector's grasp, and,

though short of stature, he was a powerful man. Had it come to a tussle of strength between the two, he might have gained the victory; but before he well knew where he was, or what had happened, he found a pair of handcuffs on his wrists.

"The most senseless thing a man can be guilty of is to try and resist an officer in the execution of his duty." observed the inspector, in a tone of pleasant argument, as though he were discussing the point with a knot of friends. "You need not suppose we do our work by halves, Ravensbird: had you escaped me, you would only have jumped into the sheltering arms of my men, who are planted outside of the house, front and back."

"Planted for what?" fumed Ravensbird.

"For you. And there they have been all night, since Lord Dane gave me the orders to arrest you. I thought I'd do the thing politely, and wait till morning: or I might have knocked up the house and taken you then."

"How dare Lord Dane order me into custody!"

"That's his affair."

"He is no magistrate: by what right does he grant warrants? He—"

The inspector burst into a laugh. "A stipendiary magistrate, no. But he *is* lord of the manor, and lord-lieutenant of the county. Don't question Lord Dane's *rights*, my man."

Ravensbird appeared to be cooling down. "Understand me," he said. "I do not want to resist the authority of the law, and if I were free as air this moment, I should stay and face this matter out. But, what I am vexed and annoyed at, is this: I was on the point of going out to inquire; to ferret out particulars; I have a motive for doing so that you know nothing of: and I'd rather have given a ten-pound note out of my pocket, than have been stopped in it."

The inspector coughed,—as incredulous a cough as ever man gave vent to. In his opinion, there was not a shadow of doubt that the attacker of Captain Dane was the man before him: and he looked upon the words as being put forth in cunning deceit.

"I'm sorry I can't spare you. If you can convince Lord Dane of your innocence, why you'll be at liberty perhaps before the day's over. But there are no particulars to learn beyond what are universally known. The struggle took place, Captain Dane was thrown down, and the tide washed the body away."

"Dubber says the struggle took place by the ruins."

"Not ten yards from them," replied the inspector, who was a good-tempered man, and liked to humor his prisoners. "But what's the use of your keeping up this show of ignorance, Ravensbird?" he added. "You have got an old card to deal with, in me. As if there was any living man could tell the time, the place, the facts altogether, so certainly as you."

Ravensbird looked the inspector steadily in the face, never quailing. "You may be an old card—experience has made you one—but you have taken the wrong man in taking me. I did not know that any accident, any ill had happened to Captain Dane, until Dubber just now told it; I did not know but he was alive and well; and that I swear."

"Now, don't you take and swear to any nonsense, or it may be used against you," was the retort of the inspector. "I never care to make bad worse, for those who come into my custody; it's not my way; but when prisoners get chattering, and letting out all sorts of slip words in their folly, why I'm obliged to repeat it again. The best thing you can do is to sew your mouth up, until you are before Lord Dane. And that's friendly advice, mind."

Possibly Ravensbird felt it to be so: for, if he did not observe it literally and sew up his mouth with thread, he at any rate relapsed into silence.

Between nine and ten he was conveyed to the castle. Lord Dane was seated in his audience-chair in the great hall: though so physically powerless, his mind was as vigorous to conduct the investigation as it had ever been. Mr. Apperly, in his legal capacity, sat near him, a small table and pen and ink before him; Squire Lester, Supervisor Cotton, and a few others were present—but not Mitchel. He was expected, but had not come. A sensation was created when Ravensbird, in his handcuffs, was introduced by the inspector.

"You bad, wicked man!" broke forth Lord Dane, in anguish, forgetting the dignity of a magistrate in the feelings of a father. "Could nothing serve your turn but you must murder my poor son?"

"I did not murder him, my lord," respectfully answered Ravensbird.

"We don't want quibbling here," interrupted the lawyer, who was of an excitable temperament, apt to put himself into heats. "If you did not deliberately murder him with a knife, or a club, or a pistol, or any thing of that sort, you attacked him and threw him over the cliff. I don't know what else you can call it, but murder."

"I never was on the heights last night. I never saw Captain Dane after he turned me from the castle in the morning," responded Ravensbird. "Who accuses me of this?"

"Now, my good man," impetuously broke forth the lawyer, "this absurd equivocation will not avail you, and you only waste breath and my lord's time in using it. You have brought enough sorrow upon his lordship, without seeking to prolong this trying scene."

"I asked who was my accuser, Mr. Apperly," doggedly repeated the prisoner: "and I have a right to be answered."

"Circumstances and your own actions are your accusers, and Mitchel is evidence," returned Mr. Apperly. "He witnessed the struggle on the heights, and he saw you push down Captain Dane."

"Could not Mitchel have been here by this hour?" feverishly put in Lord Dane, looking at the supervisor.

"I thought he would have been up before this, my lord," was the reply

RAVENSBIRD'S INDIGNANT DENIAL.—*See page 46.*

3

of the latter. "I'll go out and see after him."

"Does Mitchel say it was I, struggling with Captain Dane?—that he saw me?" inquired the prisoner, as Mr. Cotton left the hall.

"Of course he does," answered the lawyer. "Do you imagine he would conceal it?"

"Then he tells a malicious, gratuitous lie," exclaimed Ravensbird. "And he must do so to screen the real offender."

Lord Dane bent his head forward, and spoke. "Ravensbird, as Mr. Apperly says, this line of conduct will only tell against you. Had no person whatever seen the transaction, there could not have been any misconception upon the point, for who else, but you, was in ill-blood with my son? Of the nature of the quarrel between you and him, yesterday morning, I am in ignorance, but it is certain that you must have provoked him most grievously, and you quitted my roof, uttering threats against him."

"My lord, so far, that is true," replied Ravensbird, calmly and respectfully. "I gave Captain Dane certain information, by which I thought to do him a service, but he received it in a contrary spirit. It was connected with his own affairs, not pleasant news, and it called forth anger on his part towards me. I felt that it was unmerited, that I was harshly treated, and my own anger was roused. I answered my master as I confess I had no business to answer him. We both grew excited, he beyond control, and he ordered me out of the house and kicked me down the stairs. I ask you, my lord, whether it was likely I could take it calmly, without a retort? I had been a good servant to my master, had served him faithfully for years, and that only made me feel the insult more keenly. I left the castle, and for the next two hours all I did was to give vent to my feelings in harsh words—"

"You said you would be revenged," interrupted Lord Dane.

"Ten times, at least, I said it, my

lord, and many heard me, but by the end of the two hours my anger was spent. Harsh words they were, but idle as the wind. I never seriously entertained the thought of taking vengeance on my master. I had but spoken in the heat of passion; and, before long, I actually began in my own mind to find some excuse for him."

"You forget that your struggle with him was witnessed by the preventive-man."

"It never was, my lord, for no struggle with me took place. What Mitchel's motive for accusing me can be, I cannot tell: either his eyesight deceived him, or he is screening the real offender at my cost. But I don't fear; the truth is sure to come to light."

"The truth is to the light already," sarcastically replied Mr. Apperly. "I am astonished at your ridiculous persistence, prisoner. You may just as well hold to it that the sun is not shining into the room at this present moment. But all this is most irregular, and only a waste of time. Inspector, is there nothing we can proceed with in order, while waiting for Mitchel? Are there no witnesses to be examined?"

The police-inspector stood forward and addressed Lord Dane. "Your lordship has done me the honor to put the conducting of this case into my hands," he said, "and I must ask to be allowed to question a witness—or that your lordship would question her. It has come to my knowledge that there is one of your lordship's family, who perhaps may be enabled to throw some light upon the affair: I speak of Lady Adelaide Errol."

There was a pause. Lord Dane did not reply. Mr. Apperly stared, and the inspector continued.

"I have been informed that the Lady Adelaide proceeded as far as the ruins last night, just about the time the affray must have happened, and came back screaming, in a state of extreme terror. It strikes me, my lord, that her terror may have been caused through having seen something of the affray: and I should like to question her."

"I have questioned her," replied Lord Dane. "She says not."

"Pardon me, my lord, if I hold my own opinion. Her ladyship is but young, most likely timid, and she may feel afraid to confess to it. It may be necessary—with your lordship's sanction—to administer the oath."

Lord Dane despatched a summons for Lady Adelaide. The reader must not suppose that things were conducted with the regularity that they would have been in a formal court. Nothing of the sort. Lord Dane ruled, and the rest bowed to his will.

Adelaide came in, not daring to disobey. She was in a white morning-dress, ornamented with blue ribbons. The sunlight fell upon her auburn hair, and her color went and came painfully: one minute she was crimson: the next, white as her robe. She shivered and shook as she took the oath.

"Had your ladyship any motive in going out to the ruins last evening?" asked the inspector.

"It was a fine night," she faltered, her voice scarcely audible.

"You had no suspicion that any quarrel or affray was about to take place there?"

"Oh, no!" she vehemently answered.

"It took you by surprise, then. Will your ladyship tell us what you saw?"

She burst into tears. But for her oath, she would have denied seeing any thing, as she had hitherto done.

"Speak out," said Lord Dane, sternly.

"I ran across to the ruins: it was very stupid and thoughtless of me: and I went inside," she sobbed. "I stood a few moments to take breath, and I fancied I heard voices, as if in dispute."

"And then?" eagerly questioned Lord Dane, for she had paused.

"I crossed the ruins to the other door—the one nearer the sea—and looked out. Two men seemed to be struggling on the brow of the precipice, and I saw one fall over. I was

nearly terrified out of my senses: I believe that, for the moment, my senses did leave me: all I remember is, that I tore out of the ruins, and back here, screaming."

"Why did you not state this?" sharply demanded Lord Dane.

"Oh, I was too frightened," she shivered. "I was sick with fear. I thought if the men should come after me, and kill me for watching them."

"Did you recognize one to be Harry?"

"No, no. How could I recognize them in that short moment?"

"My lady," interrupted Mr. Apperly, "did the other seem to bear any resemblance to the prisoner here?"

"Not that I saw or thought of," she answered. "It did not strike me that either of them was Ravensbird."

"If she could not recognize my son, she could not recognize Ravensbird," observed Lord Dane.

"My lady," struck in the inspector, "did no idea, ever so faint, convey to your mind who either of them might be?"

The question—from him—seemed to excite her anger, and she turned her face haughtily upon him.

"Did you not hear my replies to Lord Dane and Mr. Apperly? Had I recognized Captain Dane or his adversary, should I be likely to say I did not? To what end? What had the affair to do with me?"

It takes a great deal to stop a police-inspector. And this one proceeded as deliberately as though he had received no reproof.

"Nor the voices either, my lady? Did you not recognize them?"

"I recognized nothing," she impatiently answered. "I was too terrified. May I retire?" she added, turning to Lord Dane. "If I stop here forever, I can say no more."

"An instant yet, my lady," interrupted the inspector. "Did the other—the one who did not go over the cliff—attempt to follow you, when you ran away?"

"Not that I saw—not that I know of. I did not look round to see."

"My lady," continued the undaunted inspector, "I must ask you one more question; and you will pardon me for reminding you that you are upon your oath, before you answer it. Have you told *all?* Is there nothing that you are keeping back?"

But the question was never answered. For Lady Adelaide, overcome by emotion, caused perhaps by past remembrance, perhaps by present perplexity, turned deadly white, and fell back on a chair.

"She knows no more," said Lord Dane. "Take her up-stairs to my lady."

CHAPTER V.

RICHARD RAVENSBIRD.

LORD DANE grew impatient in his chair of state. The warrant, committing Richard Ravensbird for the wilful murder of his son, was already made out; it wanted only the signature, and that waited but for the formality of Mitchel's evidence. Mr. Apperly busied himself with his papers, the prisoner leaned against the wall, the inspector was in a brown study, his arms folded, while the servants collected outside in groups, to express their horror and aversion of their late comrade, Ravensbird.

"Here's Mitchel, here's Mitchel," briskly cried out Mr. Apperly, seeing the approach of the man. "Now, then, we shall soon have it over."

The preventive-man came in, under the wing of Supervisor Cotton. He looked pale and ill still, and Lord Dane ordered him a chair, while he gave his evidence. He testified to hearing the disputing sounds, to seeing indistinctly the struggle, and to the fall of Captain Dane.

"Thrown over by Ravensbird," said hot-tongued Lawyer Apperly.

"Yes," responded Mitchel.

"Were there no signs of life whatever in my son?" inquired Lord Dane, struggling with his inward feelings.

"None, my lord: he was as dead as ever I saw anybody. I wish I could have carried him away with me in my arms, my lord, instead of leaving him to be washed away with the tide; but it was beyond my strength. I wish I had not fell into that fit: there'd have been time to get to him."

"You could not help it, Mitchel," replied Lord Dane, in a sad, kind tone. "Did you recognize him to be my son on the heights before he fell?"

Mitchel shook his head.

"Impossible, my lord. It was only moonlight, and the scuffle did not seem to last a moment hardly before he was over. It was only when I got to him, trying to lift him up, that I saw it was Captain Dane."

An interruption came from the prisoner. He had fixed his stern, black eyes on Mitchel when the man first entered, never removing them; they seemed to devour every turn of his countenance, every word that fell from his mouth.

"My lord," said he, turning to Lord Dane, "the worst criminal brought to the bar is allowed an advocate, by the English law; but I have been hurried here without one. Having none, I should like to ask the witness a question myself."

"Ask it," assented Lord Dane.

"You have just sworn that it was impossible you could recognize Captain Dane upon the heights, that it was only moonlight, and the scuffle lasted but a moment," proceeded the prisoner to Mitchel, availing himself of the permission. "If you could not recognize him, how could you recognize me?"

"I did not recognize you," returned Mitchel.

A pause. The prisoner spoke out again eagerly, passionately.

"Then why did you say you did?"

"I didn't say it."

"You did. As I am told."

"I, I did not say it. My eyesight did not carry me so far," was Mitchel's rejoinder; but he was interrupted by the police-inspector.

"Do you mean to deny, Mitchel,

now you are on your oath, that it was Ravensbird who flung over Captain Dane?"

"I couldn't say that it wasn't, or that it was, sir. It might have been him, or it might have been anybody else in this room, for all I saw."

The inspector looked at Lord Dane.

"I understood your lordship, last night, that Mitchel had seen and recognized Ravensbird as the offender."

"I understood so," returned Lord Dane, "I was so informed. You, for one, Apperly, certainly said so."

Mr. Apperly brought his spectacles severely down upon the countenance of Mitchel and spoke in a sharp quick tone.

"You know you said last evening in the guard-house, that it was Ravensbird."

"I said it was sure to have been Ravensbird, because of the quarrel he had with his master in the morning," answered Mitchel. "As I was coming-to, after my attack, and telling what I had seen, somebody exclaimed —and I do believe it was yourself, Mr. Apperly—that it must have been Ravensbird, and I agreed, saying there was no doubt of it. But I never said it was Ravensbird from my own knowledge; from my own eyesight."

"Then are we to understand, Mitchel, that you do not positively know who it was that was engaged in the conflict with my son?—that you did not recognize the person?" asked Lord Dane.

"I did not, my lord. I surmised it to be Mr. Ravensbird, on account of the quarrel, but I could not see who the people were scuffling on the heights. Had Captain Dane not fallen, I could not have known him to be one. The other might have been a woman, for all I could see."

The party felt rather nonplussed. Every one present, including the usually keen and correct inspector, had fully understood that Mitchel would swear to Ravensbird. The misapprehension had gone abroad, carried from one to the other.

"It makes little difference," cried Lawyer Apperly, who was the first to speak. "It *could* have been nobody but Ravensbird. He owed his master a grudge, and he paid him out: he may not have intended a fatal termination—"

"But it makes every difference," interrupted the prisoner, in agitation. "If a credible witness says he saw a man commit murder, he is believed; but, if it turns out that he never saw it, it makes all the difference. My lord," he added, "I swear I was not the assailant of your son: I swear I never saw him after I left here this morning."

Lord Dane looked annoyed at the appeal. His belief that Ravensbird was the guilty man was firm as a rock. Mr. Apperly spoke up authoritatively.

"Assertions go for nothing, prisoner. Perhaps you'll account for your time yesterday, hour by hour, up to ten o'clock at night."

"Yes, I can," somewhat doggedly returned the prisoner. "After I quitted the castle I went straight to the Sailor's Rest, and the landlord can tell you so."

"But you may not have stopped at the Sailor's Rest."

"I did stop at it; and twenty people, going in and out, saw me there; and I dined and had tea with the landlord and his wife."

"Well—after tea?"

Ravensbird hesitated.

"After tea I sat in the parlor with the landlady till it was hard upon seven, and then I went out for a stroll."

The inspector pricked up his ears and exchanged glances with Mr. Apperly. The latter continued, his dry, hard tone speaking volumes.

"Where did you stroll to? Which road?"

"I don't know that that matters to anybody," was the somewhat sullen answer.

"Perhaps it was up this road?"

"Perhaps it was, perhaps it wasn't," returned the prisoner. But all present felt that it was.

"Why, bless my heart!" uttered the lawyer, nearly jumping from his chair with the suddenness that the recollection flashed upon him, "I met you myself, Ravensbird; I was on my way home from a client's, and encountered you coming up this way. It was about seven o'clock. You cannot deny it."

"I have not attempted to deny it, Mr. Apperly."

"Well, now, the question is, What time did you get back again to the Sailor's Rest?"

Ravensbird answered the question by asking another, looking at Mitchel as he did so.

"What time was it that you saw the scuffle, and the fall?"

"It had gone the half-hour past eight," was the immediate reply of Mitchel, "it was hard upon the quarter to nine."

Ravensbird coolly folded his arms and drew back.

"That settles it, then," said he, with the air of a man who has done with contention; "I was back inside the Sailor's Rest at twenty minutes past eight, and I did not stir out again."

It, however, by no means "settled" it. For not one believed him. They could not have been more fully persuaded that he was the culprit had they actually seen him with their own eyes pitch over Captain Dane.

"I gather," said Lord Dane, "that you were—according to your own account—absent from the inn somewhere about an hour and a half. Where did you pass that interval?"

"My lord, I must decline to answer," promptly replied the prisoner.

"You refuse to state, sir?"

"Yes, my lord. I was at the Sailor's Rest at the time the crime is stated to have been committed, and could have had nothing to do with it; therefore I would respectfully submit to your lordship, that my movements, preceding it, have no right to be inquired into."

"Now don't you go drifting against rocks, prisoner, or may be you'll split upon them," interposed the inspector.

"When a man's arrested on a capital charge, it is the business of the law to work up and bring to light, not only his movements and doings, but every particular respecting him. So you will do well to answer his lordship."

"I decline to answer," was the only response reiterated by the prisoner.

However convinced Lord Dane, the solicitor, and the police, might feel, that Ravensbird was guilty, it was yet necessary to show justifiable grounds for the opinion, ere the warrant was acted upon. Ravensbird was detained in custody at the castle, while the inspector went to make inquiries in the town. And he brought back news which completely baffled Lord Dane.

Hawthorne and his wife, in conjunction with two or three other respectable witnesses, declared that Ravensbird *was* back at the Sailor's Rest by twenty minutes past eight, and that he did not quit it again. He sat in the parlor, common to the guests, till eleven, when the house shut up, and then retired to his chamber. The inspector confessed himself "floored" by the news.

But what about the warrant? Why, it was of no use, and had been made out for nothing; for it could not be put in force against Ravensbird. Neither was there any plea for detaining him in custody in the face of so distinct an alibi; and he was discharged.

"Only to be retaken," observed Lord Dane, as the man quitted the hall. "I do not clearly, at present, understand how it could be; either there is an error in the stated time, or some other false plea has been set up; but that Ravensbird is the guilty man, I feel a positive conviction. And he will soon be retaken on the charge."

"Not he," angrily dissented Mr. Apperly, who was more vexed than anybody at the termination; not that he was a malicious man, but *his* mind also was fully made up. "Now that he has got his liberty, my lord, he'll be putting distance between himself and this place with the seven-leagued boots of Jack in the fairy tale; and when any thing fresh turns up to re-take him upon, he'll be *non est.*"

"I could not do otherwise," re-turned Lord Dane. "I could not commit him in the teeth of evidence. Nevertheless, I am certain the man is guilty; and the very fact of his re-fusing to state where he was, or how he passed his time during a portion of the evening, would almost condemn him. An innocent man has nothing to conceal."

Near the gate before mentioned, stood Herbert Dane, when Ravens-bird was released from the castle. Not perched upon it, as was his wont in gayer times, but leaning against it in pensive sadness. That the untime-ly fate of his cousin gave him much concern, was evident. He looked ex-ceedingly surprised to see Ravensbird approach, released from the handcuffs, and unattended by the guardians of the law.

"What! have they let you off, Ravensbird?" he uttered, as the man neared him.

"Could they do otherwise, Mr. Herbert?" was the response of Ra-vensbird, stopping short before him, as though he disdained to shun in-quiry.

"Do otherwise!" echoed Herbert. "Why, the whole place is saying that there never was a clearer case. Mitchel testifies that he saw you push him over."

"No, he does not, Mr. Herbert," steadily answered the man, bringing his piercing black eyes to bear fully on the face of Herbert Dane.

"Has he eaten his words, then, be-fore my lord?"

"No, sir. He never spoke the words; it was a misconception alto-gether. When you see Mitchel; you had better inquire for yourself, and you will find that he did not dis-tinguish who the strugglers were. He would not have known the captain, but for his falling at his feet."

"And so, on the strength of the un-certainty, they have given you your liberty! I suppose you will hasten now to put the sea or some equally

effective barrier, between you and England."

"Why should I?" returned Ravens-bird. "An innocent man does not fly like a craven."

Herbert Dane very nearly laughed. "Innocent!" he exclaimed, his tone savoring of ridicule. "You know, Ravensbird, it is of no use to be on the exalted ropes before me. The words you spoke in my presence, yesterday morning, in this very spot, the threats of vengeance you uttered against your master, would be enough to hang you. But—"

"Do you believe me guilty, Mr. Herbert?" interrupted the man, draw-ing nearer with his fixed, penetrating eyes.

"I was about to say, Ravensbird, that you are safe for me," proceeded Herbert Dane. "I make no doubt that you dropped the words in the heat of passion, almost unconscious (if I may so express it) that I was within hearing, to take cognisance of them. I felt sorry for you at the time, feeling that my cousin, in *his* passion (whatever may have called it forth), must have been unjustifiably harsh, and I will not put myself forward against you. Moreover, were you gibbeted on the nearest tree this day, it could not bring your master back to life."

"Sir," repeated Ravensbird, in the same calm, matter-of-fact voice, "I asked if *you* believed me guilty."

"What a superfluous question!" was the retort. "Do you suppose there's a soul in the place but must believe it?—although you have con-trived to escape bonds. You ask me if I believe you guilty, when I say that I could hang you!"

"Then why don't you hang me?" returned Ravensbird.

"I have told you why. I do not care to go out of my way to do you harm; and it could not benefit the dead. But guilty you certainly are."

The way in which Ravensbird stood his ground before Herbert Dane, stony, self-possessed, not a muscle of his face changing, not a tremor in his voice, and his searching eyes never moving from Herbert's face, astonished the latter not a little.

"Then let me tell you that I am *not* guilty, Mr. Herbert," spoke Ravensbird. "Let me tell you something more, shall I?"

"Well!" responded Herbert, lifting his questioning eyes.

"That I could this hour put my finger out upon the guilty person. As certain as that you and I, sir, are standing here, face to face, I know the one who did the deed."

"What absurd treason are you uttering now?" demanded Herbert, after a pause of blank astonishment.

"No treason, and nothing absurd," was the undaunted reply. "I could lay my hand upon the party who murdered my master, as readily as I now lay it upon this gate. But I don't choose to do it; I bide my time."

Herbert Dane stared at the speaker from head to foot; wondering, possibly, whether the man was not giving utterance to a most audacious falsehood.

"Will you venture to assert—allowing that you were not one of the actors in it—that you witnessed the scuffle on the heights?" he inquired.

"No, sir, I did not witness it; I was not there. I was in the public room at the Sailor's Rest at the time it took place, which proved fact has baffled my 'lord and the police, and compelled them to release me. But I know who was on the heights, though I was not."

"And what may be your reasons for holding it secret, if you know so much?"

"That, sir, you must excuse me if I keep to myself," was Ravensbird's reply. "But I hope, Mr. Herbert, you will not again accuse me of being the guilty man. Good-day, sir."

Ravensbird turned off towards Daneshold as he concluded, and Mr. Herbert Dane stood watching him, deep in puzzled thought. Not until the former was out of sight did he awake from his reverie, and then he bent his steps towards the castle.

"I'll know, at any rate, what grounds they had for letting the fellow off," cried he, in soliloquy.

He had reached the castle-gate when it was suddenly opened by Bruff, who was showing out Mr. Apperly. In another minute Herbert was in possession of the facts testified—that Ravensbird had been in the Sailor's Rest as the time of the catastrophe.

"But, let be a bit, Mr. Herbert," continued the lawyer, in excitement. "I can't question the good faith of the witnesses, for I believe them to be honest, and Hawthorne and his wife, at all events, would be true to the Dane family; but some trickery is at work, something is up; the hands of the clock were surreptitiously put back, or some other deviltry. Ravensbird's the guilty man, and it will turn out so."

"What do you think, Bruff?" questioned Herbert, as Mr. Apperly marched hastily away, and they stood looking after him.

"Well, sir, we don't—us upper servants—know what to think. If appearances—that is, the quarrel with his master, and his revengeful threats —hadn't been so much against him, we should not have suspected Ravensbird, for he never seemed that sort of bad man. Then, again, the evidence just given has posed us; for if Ravensbird was at the Sailor's Rest, he couldn't have been here on the heights."

"Very true," responded Herbert, in a mechanical tone, as though his thoughts were elsewhere. "There appears to be some mystery over it."

"They had my Lady Adelaide before them in the hall this morning," proceeded Bruff, dropping his voice. "And put the oath to her."

"Lady Adelaide!" quickly repeated Herbert. "Why, what does she know?"

"It seems she saw the scuffle, sir, or ially saw it—as, of course, we servants suspected before, and that it was what frightened her—and the inspector thought she might have recognized the assailant."

"And did she?" asked Herbert Dane.

"Neither him nor the captain, sir. She was too frightened, she says, and knows nothing."

"Open the door, Bruff. I am going in to my lord."

Lord Dane was alone when Herbert entered the hall. His lordship gave his nephew the heads of what had transpired, dwelling much upon the testimony of the witnesses which tended to establish the *alibi*, but avowing his positive belief, in spite of it, that Ravensbird had been the man. Herbert agreed; and quitting the hall, went up-stairs to the drawing-rooms.

Lady Adelaide was alone. Herbert began speaking, in a low and cautious tone, his eyes ranging round the room, as though he feared the walls might have ears, of the catastrophe of the previous night. He was proceeding to ask what she had seen, what had caused her to scream, in the manner reported, when she vehemently interrupted him.

"Don't enter upon it! I don't speak to me! If ever you so much as touch upon it to me by the faintest allusion, I will never willingly suffer you to come into my presence again."

He gazed at her in utter surprise: he could not understand either her words or her vehemence.

"What do you mean, Adelaide? This to me?"

"Yes, to you or to any one. I will not be questioned, or reminded of the horrors of last night. I could not bear it."

Herbert Dane felt vexed, considerably chafed, and he showed it in his rejoinder.

"Does this indicate grief, inordinate grief, for the loss of your declared lover?"

"Never mind what it indicates," she answered, bursting into tears. "Now that he is gone, I feel how unjustifiable was my deceitful treatment of him. And if a promise of mine, to marry him the next hour, would recall him to life, I would joyfully give it."

"You are unhinged, my dear," whispered Herbert Dane, thinking it better to bury his annoyance and surprise, and to soothe her: but that she really was so unhinged as to be scarcely responsible for what she said, he believed. "What a pity it is," he more impetuously broke forth, "that you went near the ruins last night."

"I went there, hoping to meet you," she reproachfully interrupted.

"My dearest, I know it," he hastened to put in, in an appeasing tone. But she would not let him continue, drowning his words with her own.

"You told me in the day you should not be there, if some friends came, whom you were expecting: but you were alone, after the train came in, and I judged that they had not come. Moreover, I saw some one, as I stood at this window, going towards the ruins in the moonlight: I thought it might be you. And you reflect upon me for having gone!"

"Adelaide, what *is* the matter? What have I said or done to offend you? Are you angry because I did not go to the ruins? The two Eccingtons had given me a half promise to come over yesterday and dine, but they did not keep it: I did not much think they would. Of course I could have gone to the ruins—and *should*, had I known you would be there. I did not suppose you would go, not expecting me, and I had a reason for stopping at home. Harry Dane had said he would call in and smoke a manilla: nine o'clock was the hour he mentioned, but he was proverbially uncertain, and might have made his appearance earlier. I did not deem it expedient to be out when he came."

Lady Adelaide vouchsafed no answer. She sat with her pale face cast down, playing with the ornaments attached to her chain. Mr. Herbert Dane resumed.

"You speak and look as though you had a reproach to cast to me, Adelaide. What is the cause? How have I offended you?"

She rose up from her chair, and

Herbert noticed, as she raised one hand to push her hair from her brow, that the hand was shaking. She followed the bent of his eyes, and saw that he observed her tremor.

"I am—as you remarked but now—unhinged to-day, not fit for the society of any one," she said. "I did not intend to cast a reproach to you for not meeting me at the ruins."

And, sweeping past him, she was quitting the room, when he laid his hand on her arm, to detain her.

"A moment, Adelaide. You may surely tell to me what you would not to others—if you have any thing to tell; any thing you are concealing. Did you *not* recognize Harry Dane's adversary last night?—not by the faintest shadow of a clue? Every conjecture would point to Ravensbird, yet the man says, earnestly, that he is innocent."

Her face grew ashy white as she stood confronting him, and twice she essayed to speak, ere any sound would come from her bloodless lips.

"I was had down there this morning," she said, pointing to the floor with her hand, to indicate the hall underneath. "I was marshalled, like a criminal, before my lord, and the police, and the lawyers—I know not whom. They made me take the oath; they put to me the question that you are doing. I told them I was unable to testify to the recognition of any one; I was too terrified last night to notice, or to retain recognition. If I could not answer them, do you think it likely I can answer you? You forgot yourself when you asked me."

"Forgot myself!" repeated Herbert, wondering more and more at her strangeness of manner.

"Yes, forgot yourself; or you would not so have spoken upon the very heels of my caution. I will forgive this, I will pass it over, believing you transgressed it through forgetfulness : but never, never you attempt to open the subject to me again, for I would not suffer it with impunity."

She quitted finally the room, and

Herbert advanced to the door and followed her with his eyes. He had never seen her like this. Always gay, always light-hearted, always loving and confidential to him had she hitherto been. What had changed her? What had invoked her present dark mood? A contraction of perplexity knitted his brow, as he gazed after her; but she did not turn to look at him : at other times her nods and her smiles had been his till she was out of sight. She sped on to her own apartments, and Herbert Dane quitted the castle.

That Lady Adelaide's conduct, touching the affair, was unaccountable, all must admit, but upon none had it made so deep an impression as upon the police-inspector. After she had given her evidence, after Mitchel's remark that it might have been a woman, after Ravensbird appeared to be cleared, a most extraordinary idea flashed into the officer's mind, and grew there : was Lady Adelaide the one who had been disputing on the heights with Captain Dane?

CHAPTER VI.

THE PACKMAN—THE DEATH-ROOM.

BUT, ere long, another phase in the strange story was to be turned. As Herbert Dane was strolling down towards Danesheld from the castle, he encountered a man well known in the locality — better known than trusted, indeed. His name was Drake, and his ostensible occupation was that of a fisherman, to which he added as much smuggling as he could accomplish with impunity. He took off his blue, woolen cap, made after the form of a cotton nightcap, to salute Mr. Herbert Dane.

"A fine horrid tale I've been a hearing of, master, since our boat got in," began he. "Folks be a saying as the captain's got murdered, and his body a floating away in the sea; Davy Jones on'y knows to what part. Be it true?"

"It is an incomprehensible affair altogether, Drake, and seems to be shrouded in mystery; but I fear it is only too true. The body has not been found."

"Who was it as attacked him on the heights, master?"

"Ah! that's the question," was Herbert's response.

"They be saying, down in the village yonder, as it turns out not to have been the captain's servant, though the thing was first put upon him, and he was took up."

"I know they are saying it; at least I make no doubt they are."

"Well, now, master, perhaps I can throw some light upon this here. 'Twon't be much, though."

"You!" returned Herbert, gazing at Drake.

"Yes, me. I had been up to Nut Cape, for I wanted to have a talk with old—that is—that is, I had been up the road past the castle—"

"Never mind speaking out, Drake," interrupted Herbert Dane, significantly, for the man had got confused when he broke off. "You had been up to Nut Cape to hold one of your confabs with that old smuggler, Beecher; that's about the English of it. But if I saw you pushing in a boat-load of contraband goods under my very eyes, you might do it, for me; I have no sway in the place, that I should interfere, and I concern myself with nobody's business but my own. So go on, fearlessly."

"Well, I had been up to old Beecher's," acknowledged Drake, "but only for a yarn,—indeed, master, nothing else. I stopped there longer than I ought, and was coming back again full pelt, afraid the boat might put off without me, when I heard voices in dispute."

"Whereabouts?" asked Herbert.

"I was on the brow of the heights, had kept close to it all the way, and was just abreast o' them ruins o' the chapel, between it and the sea, when my ear caught the sound. It seemed to come from the direction of the castle, and I cut across towards it, thinking I'd spare a moment, to see what the row was. Standing about midway between the ruins and the castle were two men; the one was speaking in a harsh, commanding tone, and I had got a'most up to him when I saw it was Captain Dane. Seeing that, of course I cut away again."

"Where do you say this was?" demanded Herbert, pausing some moments before he spoke.

"Between them ruins and the castle, a trifle nearer the castle, maybe. 'Tother man was a stranger."

"A stranger?"

"Leastways he was a stranger to me; I'd never seen him afore, to my knowledge. A biggish sort of fellow, with a pack in his hand."

"A pack!" uttered Herbert again.

"Or som'at that looked like one. If 'twasn't a pack, 'twas a big parcel. I didn't take much notice of him, seeing the other was the captain. The captain was blowing him up."

"In what terms?" cried Herbert, with vivid eagerness. "Can you remember?"

"'How dare you, fellow?' I heard him say, and those were all the words I caught distinct. But I heard them both at it, railing like, as 'I steered off."

"What time was this?"

"Well, now, I can't be positive to a quarter of an hour," was Drake's reply. "'Twas past eight, and it 'twasn't near nine; I should guess it might be a quarter past eight, rather more, maybe."

Herbert Dane mused; he was revolving the information.

"Are you sure, Drake," he asked, "that it was not Ravensbird?"

"Be I a otter, master, to have no sense in my eyes?" was Drake's response. "'Twasn't no more like Ravensbird than 'twas like me or you. 'Twas a chap rising five foot ten, with broad shoulders."

"You must speak of this affair before Lord Dane."

"I was on my way to the castle now, to do it; I knows my duty. Not but what I'd rather go ten miles t'other way, than face his lordship."

Herbert Dane laughed.

"He is not so lenient to you smugglers as you would like, and you fear him. But, if you can help his lordship to trace out this assaulter of his son, it will no doubt atone for some old scores, Drake."

"Any ways it's my duty, having seen what I did see. And I'm not agoing to shirk it, master."

He proceeded towards the castle, and Herbert Dane continued his way in the direction of Danesheld. But scarcely had he taken many steps when a slight bend in the road brought him to a milestone, hidden from his view previously; and half-seated upon it, deep in thought, was Ravensbird.

"You are in a brown study, Ravensbird."

The man positively started. He had been so buried with himself as to be oblivious to the approach, and the voice aroused him abruptly.

"I was absent in last night's work, sir; that is, my spirit was," was Ravenbird's reply. "I did not hear you come up."

"Ravensbird," returned Herbert Dane, "if a man has been led into an error, the least he can do, is, to acknowledge it, when his mind opens to the conviction that it *was* an error. I regret having avowed to you my belief that you were the destroyer of your master."

A peculiar smile, somewhat cynical in its nature, flitted over the features of Ravensbird.

"I find that another attacked Captain Dane on the heights last night; at any rate, that Captain Dane and another were having a broil there together, about the time of the catastrophe; therefore it is but fair to infer that that other was the offender."

The smile on Ravensbird's face was exchanged for a look of astonishment.

"Who?" he uttered.

"Some strange man, with a pack in his hand. I should imagine it must have been a traveling hawker, or person of that class; such men have been known, before now, to commit evil deeds. He may have tried to extort money from Captain Dane, and, finding he could not, have proceeded to violence. One fact appears to be indisputable; that they were giving vent to angry passions, one against the other."

"Who saw or heard this?" asked Ravensbird. "You, sir?"

"I?" echoed Herbert Dane. "What a very senseless question! Had I witnessed it—or indeed any thing else connected with the affair—should I have kept it to myself? No, Ravensbird; had I known this, I should not have been so hasty to indulge suspicion of you."

"Then who was it?" somewhat impatiently resumed Ravensbird.

"Drake. The man stopped me a few minutes ago, to tell me what he had seen. He was on his way to the castle to declare it to my lord; and he has gone on there now."

"And he says it was a stranger?"

"A man he did not know, and had never seen before. A big, hulky fellow with a pack. Just the description one is apt to expect of those itinerant pedlers."

"Drake has been tardy in declaring this," sarcastically returned Ravensbird.

"Not at all. He could not declare it out at sea, where he has been all night. His boat is but just in—as I understand—and he knew nothing till he landed of the accident to Captain Dane."

Ravensbird did not reply. His eyes seemed to be fixed in vacancy, as if in thought. Herbert proceeded.

"When you gave utterance to the expression that you could place your finger upon the offender, I believed you were speaking in vain boastfulness, if not in deceit. I conclude now, that you must have been aware of this encounter of Captain Dane's with the stranger, and alluded to the latter when you spoke. Was it so?"

"I—I was not aware—that—that Captain Dane—I did not know of any encounter, of his, with a stranger," replied Ravensbird, in a slow, hesitating tone, his eyes still bearing the appearance of a man in a dream.

Herbert Dane scanned him searchingly.

"Possibly this man was no stranger o your master."

"Possibly not," was the reply of Ravensbird, waking from his reverie. "It is scarcely probable that a stranger would attack him to his death."

"You speak in riddles, Ravensbird. Did you allude to this man, or not, when you spoke?"

"Sir," respectfully returned Ravenbird, "you must pardon me for declining to answer."

And nothing more could Herbert Dane get from him; and the parting, in consequence, though friendly, was not to the former satisfactory.

Drake, meanwhile, reached the castle, and disclosed his tale to Lord Dane. However loose may have been the fisherman's antecedents, in the way of smuggling and other matters, bringing him under the displeasure and surveillance of the lord, that was no reason for his present account being doubted. Indeed, that he was but declaring the truth, was evident even to the lynx-eyed Lawyer Apperly, who was summoned to the conference. The police also were summoned, and Drake had to repeat his tale to them. Should he know the man again? they asked him. Drake was not sure: not by his face, he thought, for he did not take much note of it: if he knew him again it would be by his shoulders and the pack. Not very conclusive distinctive marks, decided the inspector.

A search was set on foot,—as active as could be supposed to be undertaken by village police, which is not saying a great deal. Inquiries were made at Danesheld and its environs, extending to the neighboring towns around and past them, as to whether a man, answering the description, had been seen. But all to no avail: nobody appeared to have observed any such traveler. A farm-laborer, at work about six miles off, deposed that he had noticed a man the afternoon of the accident, going towards Danesheld, a "brown man, with a sort o' box on his back."

"And big shoulders?" questioned the police-officer.

"Noa, not he," was the answer; "he didn't seem to ha' got no shoulders. A little undersized chap, it were, no bigger nor a weasel."

So that description did not tally. Neither did any other, that the police could find out, and the affair remained involved in mystery.

There is an old saying, that misfortune never comes alone. Lord Dane wrote to his eldest son to acquaint him with the melancholy fate of his brother, and requested him to return home. For years there had been an unpleasant estrangement between the brothers, but, with death, these estrangements, or rather the remembrance of them, generally end. Harry Dane had been a favorite son: Geoffry, the eldest, a cold, haughty, overbearing man by nature, had resented the partiality of his parents, his own disposition magnifying the predilection ten-fold, and he had now been for some time abroad. The handsome fortune Harry had dropped into, a young man, had also been a sore point with the Honorable Geoffry: and, altogether, he preferred to live a life of estrangement from his kindred. His letters home were few and far between, and at the present moment Lord Dane did not know precisely where to address to him: he had been in Paris, but had spoken of leaving it, for Italy, for Malta, and other places in rotation. So Lord Dane sent his letter to their banker's, in London, who was kept cognizant of the movements of Geoffry Dane, giving them instructions to forward it without delay.

They did so, and the days, nay the weeks passed on, but still Mr. Dane arrived not. Lord Dane grew angry.

"Geoffry might have written, at least," he observed to his wife, "if he did not choose to come."

Alas! he came all too soon. Not himself; but what remained of him. News arrived first: a letter written by his personal attendant, who was a native of Danesheld.

Mr. Dane had been suddenly attacked in the neighborhood of Rome by one of those fevers common to hot and unhealthy climates, and in three days was dead. The letter, written by Lord Dane, and duly forwarded by the London bankers, had never reached him (it might be traveling half over the continent after him then), and he had died in ignorance of the fate of his brother. Even then, as Lord Dane perused the unhappy letter, his body was on its way to England for interment, having been embarked on board a steamer at Civita Vecchia.

Very sad, very grievous were the tidings to Dane Castle, and the flag on it floated half-mast high,—the custom when a death occurred in the family. But a little span, since it had so floated for Harry Dane, and now it was floating for Geoffry! Lord and Lady Dane were bowed down to the very earth with grief; they were their only children; and whispers went abroad that her ladyship would not be long after them: people said they could see the "change for death" in her.

· On a gay morning in the beginning of May, a hearse, whose sable, mournful plumes contrasted unpleasingly with the world's sunny brightness, arrived at Dane Castle, having brought something inside it from Southampton. The burden was taken from within it and deposited in a certain apartment of the castle, called the death-room.

Why was it called by so unpropitious a name? the reader will inquire. Simply because it was a room consecrated to the dead. When any of the family died, they were placed there to await interment, lie in state, it may be said, and the public were admitted to see the sight. The apartment was never used for any other purpose, though occasionally opened to be aired: a large, cold, gray room it was, perfectly empty, with high windows and a stone floor. Tradition went, that when any one of the Danes was about to leave the world, that floor would become damp in patches; not damp all over, as it did in wet weather,—but they were very stupid who believed in any such nonsensical superstition.

The trestles were brought from their hiding-closet and set up in the middle of the room, and the coffins were placed upon them. Lord Dane was wheeled in, in his chair; Lady Dane glided in and stood by his side, both struggling to suppress their grief until they should be alone to indulge it. Some of the upper servants were also present, and a workman, purposely summoned to the castle, prepared to unseal the coffins.

At that moment, Wilkins, the servant who had accompanied the body from abroad, he who had written to Lord Dane, stepped forward, placed his hand on the man's tools to arrest him, and then addressed Lord Dane.

"My lord—I beg your pardon—but is it a safe thing to do, think you? May there not be danger? He died of malignant fever."

A disagreeable feeling fell upon all, and some drew involuntarily a step back. Lord Dane reflected.

"I do not fear infection," he presently said. "Let those who do fear it, retire; but I will see the remains of my son. Stories have been told, before now, of—of—others being substituted for those supposed to be dead."

Wilkins turned to Lord Dane, astonishment on his face and tears in his eyes.

"My lord, is it possible you can suspect—"

"No reflection on you, Wilkins," interrupted his lordship; "I did not mean to imply any. There is a difference between satisfaction from conviction of the mind, and satisfaction from ocular demonstration. I have no moral doubt whatever that my dear son Geoffry does lie within that coffin; nevertheless, I choose to be indisputably assured of the fact. Retire," he somewhat sharply added to the servants; "and do you," nodding to the mechanic, "proceed with your work. Had you not also better leave us?"

The last words were addressed to Lady Dane. She simply shook her head, and waited.

It was a long process, for the lead had to be unsoldered. But it was accomplished at last. The domestics had quitted the room, all save Bruff.

Lord Dane looked at him in a questioning manner.

"*I* have no fear, my lord. Allow me to see the last of poor Mr. Geoffry."

Geoffry Dane it was, unmistakably; and less changed than might have been expected, under the circumstances. A long, yearning look from all of them, a few stifled sobs from the childless mother, and the coffins were reclosed forever. Then they left the room, and the public, those who chose to come, were admitted.

A sort of fright, so to term it, took place that night in the house, one that caused some unpleasant commotion. It happened that Sophie, Lady Adelaide's maid, was suffering from a violent cough, which had clung to her some weeks, and was especially troublesome at night. She was in the habit of taking a soothing drink, for it, made of herbs, or, as she called it, in her own language, tisane, which she took regularly up to bed with her. On this night she forgot it, and would not return for it; for she, in conjunction with the rest, felt nervous when going through the long passages, considering WHAT was in the house. But Sophie's cough proved to be unusually severe. No sleep could she get; and at length she rose from her bed, determined to brave ghostly fancies and lonely corridors, and fetch the tisane. Wrapping herself up, she started, carrying a hand-lamp.

Away she scuttered down the stairs. Her road to the housekeeper's parlor, where the drink had been left, lay past the death-room. How Sophie flew by its door, how her heart beat, and her skin crept, she would not like to have told. In common with the generality of French, of her grade and class, she was given to superstitious fears touching the presence of the dead, more so than are the English of the lower orders. But there's an old proverb, "More haste, less speed," and poor Sophie received an exemplification of it; for, so great was her haste, that in passing the very spot, the dreaded door, she lost one of her slippers. With a half cry of terror at the stoppage *there*, Sophie snatched it up in her hand, did not wait to put it on, but tore on to the parlor.

The drink was inside the fender, where it had been placed to retain its warmth. Sophie took up the jug, and put it on the table for a moment while she drew breath (short with the running and the fright), and put on the refractory slipper. She was stooping down to accomplish the latter, when a noise close above her head interrupted her.

It was nothing but the striking of the time-piece on the mantel-shelf, two strokes—one, two—telling the half hour—the half hour after midnight. But Sophie's nerves were unhinged, and it startled her beyond self-control. She shrieked, she grasped the nearest thing to her, which happened to be a chair, she hid her face upon it, and she wondered how in the world she could muster courage to get back to her room.

Back she must get, somehow; for the longer she stayed, the worse she grew. "If ever I leave my tisane down-stairs again," quoth Sophie, "may a ghost run away with me, that's all!" She took up the jug, drew her cloak round her, and began to speed back again; not very fast this time, for fear of spilling the tisane.

Poor Sophie! the real fright was coming. As she gained the corridor in which was situated the death-room, her hair nearly stood on end, and her skin was as a goose's skin, quivering and cold. A perfect horror grew upon her, in that moment, of passing the dreaded door.

HERBERT DANE'S INTERVIEW WITH LADY ADELAIDE.—*See page 58.*

4

And well it might. She did gain it; how, she hardly knew; but instead of rushing past it, with her head turned the other way, some power seemed to impel her head towards it. If you ever experienced the same uncontrollable midnight terror, reader, you will understand it. Sophie's eyes irresistibly, and in spite of her will, turned right upon the door, fascinated as by the evil power of the basilisk; had her very life depended on it, she could not have kept them away. And in the same instant, a hollow, wailing sound, like a groan, broke from within the stillness of the room.

Nearly paralyzed, nearly bereft of her senses, Sophie fell against the door, and the movement caused it to open, as though it had been imperfectly latched : yet Sophie knew that the door had been securely locked the previous evening at dusk. But for the door-post she might have fallen with her head inside it; that saved her. There came another groan, and what looked like a flood of white light from the room; and the miserable Sophie, breaking into the most unearthly shrieks and yells, flew along the corridor, dropping the jug and the tisane with a crash and a splash! That those hermetic solderings and fastenings had come undone, and what they confined down had risen, and was after her, was the least of her imaginings.

Out came the terrified servants; peal upon peal rang the bell of Lord Dane; Lady Adelaide opened her door and stood at it, her face as white as her maid's.

When they gathered in the account of the shaking Sophie, some of the braver of the domestics proceeded to the death-room, and there the cause was made clear.

Kneeling on the stone floor beside the coffin, lost to all outward things, save her grief, a white dressing-gown only thrown over her night-clothes, was Lady Dane. The groans of pain, of sorrow, had come from her; and the "white light," as Sophie had described it, from her lamp. Not for a long while, a whole hour, could they prevail upon the unhappy lady to return to her own chamber: in vain they urged upon her that she would surely catch her death of cold. "What matters it?" she murmured. "Harry first, Geoffry next; both gone, both cut off in their prime : what signifies death, or anything else, that may come to me?"

Geoffry was buried in the family vault, amidst much pomp and ceremony, as befitted, according to the world's usages, the late heir of the Danes. Lord Dane was too ill to be taken to the funeral, and the chief mourner was Herbert, now the presumptive successor to the title, and to the wide and rich domains.

CHAPTER VII.

WHAT THE SEA CASTS UP—THE FLAG HALF-MAST HIGH.

THE words spoken by the servants, perhaps heedlessly, that their lady might be "catching her death," were borne out more literally than such words generally are. Whether it was the kneeling on the stone floor in the chilly night; whether it was the scantiness of the apparel she had thrown on; or the rising from her bed, hot, for that she had previously been in bed, there was no doubt, certain it is, that violent cold and inflammation attacked Lady Dane. The medical men called pleurisy ; less scientific people, inflammation of the chest: no matter for the proper term, Lady Dane was in imminent danger.

She lay in her spacious bed-room, so redolent of comfort; its fire regulated that the temperature might be of a certain heat, its little luxuries ready at hand. The servants, moving softly in their list slippers, were anxious and attentive; the doctors were unremitting; the neighborhood was concerned. Could life have been kept in Lady Dane by earthly means, they were not lacking; but when the time comes for its departure, who may prolong its stay? Lady Dane was dying; and she knew it. An eminent physician had been summoned from town; he had paid his visit that morning, and had gone back again. A rumor spread in the servant's hall—though whence originating and how *they* could have got hold of it, they themselves would have been at a loss to tell—that the great London man had pronounced it, in confidence to Mr. Wild, a case without hope.

"I said it from the first," wailed Sophie. "I knew that when two died out of the family, the third would not be long after them."

"What's that, Mam'selle Sophie?" cried Mr. Bruff.

"What's that!" sharply retorted Sophie: "it's a well known certainty to anybody who keep their eyes open. I have remarked it hundreds of times in my own country, and I dare say you have in yours, if you'll only put your recollection to work, and cast it backwards. Let two out of the same family die, pretty near together, and you may look soon for the third interment. It's safe to come, if not directly, before the twelvemonth's up."

"Nonsense," said Bruff.

"Is it nonsense? You just look abroad and take notice, if you've never noticed it before. You can begin with this household," added Sophie, tapping her foot on the floor to give force to her argument. "The captain was the first, Mr. Dane was the second, and her ladyship will be the third. When news came that Mr. Dane was dead, I said to myself, 'Then who'll be the next?'—for it came across my brain in the same minute that another there would be. And I feared it might be my lord: I never thought of my lady."

"Perhaps there'll be a fourth!" sarcastically returned the incredulous Bruff.

"Sophie's right," put in the housekeeper; "I have observed it myself many times. When two go off quietly out of a family, a third generally follows."

"If I could lower myself to think such trash, I'd never say it," rebuked the indignant butler. "Mam'selle Sophie may be excused: she's young: but when folks have lived to your age and mine, ma'am, they might know better. It is to be hoped her ladyship will recover."

"Then if she does recover, it will be his lordship that will go," persisted the undaunted Sophie. "But I don't think she is going to recover: it is not in her face. I may not be as old as you, Mr. Bruff, by twenty good years, and I shall be thirty my next birthday; but if I were you, I'd never boast of my age, until I had used my powers of observation to more purpose. Anyway, two have gone, and the other will follow. You'll see."

Adelaide Errol sat alone with her aunt, ostensibly attending on her, should she want any thing: though indeed she seemed more buried within herself and her own reflections, than thinking of Lady Dane. Since the night when she had been so terrified in the ruins, a great change had overtaken Adelaide. No longer was she the gay, careless girl of formerly: her step was languid, her spirits were unequal, her manner was subdued. In her appearance, also, there was an alteration for the worse: her brilliant color had faded to paleness, and her rounded form had grown thin. She sat in an invalid-chair before the fire (her aunt's, previous to Lady Dane's taking to her bed) her cheek was pressed upon her right hand, and her eyes were fixed on vacancy.

"Adelaide."

It was Lady Dane who spoke; and Adelaide sprang up with a start, abruptly aroused to outward things. "Yes, aunt. What can I do for you?"

"Nothing just now," feebly replied Lady Dane, whose voice was scarcely audible for weakness; and had her medical attendants been present, they would have taken care she did not try to make it audible. "Why are you looking so sad, Adelaide? What were you thinking of?"

A vivid blush rose to the cheeks of Lady Adelaide.

"It is a sad time, aunt," she answered; and the plea was too true a one for Lady Dane to suspect its evasion.

"This strange sadness—I call it strange, Adelaide, in you—has continued since the death of Harry," pursued Lady Dane. "Is it caused *by* his death?"

A blush as vivid as the previous one, but more painful. Lady Adelaide, however, remained silent.

"Child, I shall not long be here; "and I would ask—"

"Oh, aunt!" interrupted Adelaide, in a tone of pain.

"Not long," calmly repeated Lady Dane: "a few days, perhaps but a few hours. Do not distress yourself. It causes me no distress: quite the contrary: I am glad to go. I have—I humbly hope—a Friend in heaven, and he will welcome me to his Father's home. Oh, Adelaide! the world has become sad to me: I shall be *glad* to go."

Tears were raining from the eyes of Lady Adelaide. There was a pause, and then the invalid resumed:

"But I want now to speak of yourself, whilst I have power left for it. This unaccountable sadness—whence does it proceed? I do *not* think it is caused by grief for Harry's death."

"It — it — was a dreadful death, aunt," shivered Adelaide, shunning the question.

Lady Dane clasped her hands together.

"Ay, a dreadful death; a dreadful death! Still, not one to have made this lasting impression upon you; for, Adelaide, I suspect you did not love him."

"We all loved him," Adelaide was beginning, but Lady Dane arrested her words.

"Child, I am dying. If there must needs still be concealment between us, in these my last hours, at least let there not be equivocation. I believed that you did not care for Harry: I believe that you loved, and do still love Herbert—Geoffry, as we must call him now. Though I cannot quite remember to say Geoffry so soon," added Lady Dane sadly: "it puts me too much in mind of my own Geoffry who is gone."

Adelaide burst into fresh tears.

"Tell me the truth, child. Why should you conceal it now? Herbert was no match for you then: Harry was, and he idolized you: but things have changed. Herbert will succeed his uncle, and there can be no barrier to your union with him: but I should like to be satisfied how it will be, before I go. Speak the truth, Adelaide."

Adelaide Errol was visibly agitated, as she bent over her aunt, for the latter had taken her hands and was drawing her closer. Speak she must; there was no escape; but even Lady Dane, dying as she was, observed how violently her heart beat.

"Aunt, I do not wish to marry Herbert Dane."

"What!" uttered Lady Dane in her astonishment.

"I will not marry him. I—do not" —she spoke here with remarkable hesitation—"like him well enough."

Lady Dane regarded her searchingly: a suspicion came over her that Adelaide imperfectly understood; not the present conversation, but the future position of Herbert: for that Adelaide had long been wrapt up in Herbert, was her settled conviction.

"Child, are you mistaking his circumstances—his future? He will be Lord Dane."

"If he were to be King of England, I would not marry him," vehemently spoke Lady Adelaide.

"Then—is it possible?—did you really love Harry?" was the slow, doubting response.

Another flow of tears, and a softened answer.

"Aunt, if Harry could rise from the dead, I would be glad to marry him: I would rather marry him than any one else in the world."

"How I have been mistaken!" uttered Lady Dane, and Adelaide hid her face amid the bed-clothes as she listened. Lady Dane thought her manner appeared very singular, and a doubt crossed her mind whether there was not some mystery yet to fathom. Whether or not, it was not fated that Lady Dane should unravel it. During their conversation an unusual stir and noise had been gradually arising in the road; and now penetrating to the inside of the castle. Unnoticed at first, the commotion was now so great as to attract the attention, if not the alarm, of Lady Dane. Tumult like that within the well-conducted castle !

" Adelaide, go you and see what it can be. Bring me word."

Away went Adelaide : thankful, if the truth were known, to be dismissed from that bed-side. A dozen fishermen, or so, were congregated in the hall, having carried in a burden covered up, on a sort of hand-barrow. The servants were surrounding them, Lord Dane was present in his chair, stragglers, attracted by the news, made bold to push into the castle. Altogether, it was a scene of confusion. Questions were poured on the fishermen, and they were all answering at once, in their loud voices and rude patois.

Adelaide gathered in the sense of their words. What motive impelled her to act as she was doing, none could tell; probably she, herself, could not have told ; possibly, in that moment of terror, she was unconscious of her actions. A moment of unspeakable terror it evidently was to her : her lips were blanched and drawn back from her teeth, her features wore the hue of the grave : she glided amidst the crowd, laid her hand upon the barrow, and was lifting up its covering.

A fisherman darted forward, and unceremoniously pulled her back.

" It's no sight for her," he said, turning to Lord Dane, " it's no sight for women, young or old : ye may judge, my lord, that it is not !"

Then, for the first time, Lord Dane observed that Adelaide was present. .

" Go away," he said to her sadly, but imperatively; " what brought you here ?"

" Ye'd never get it out o' your sight, young madam, all yer life a'ter," spoke up another man, who had advanced to keep guard of the barrow; " and it's stark naked, beside."

" Leave the hall, Adelaide : are you mad ?" sternly reiterated Lord Dane.

The flushing crimson had come to her cheeks now, and the perspiration broke out on her brow, as she hurriedly obeyed.

" I think I must have been mad," she repeated to herself. " What possessed me ?"

Mechanically, scarcely conscious of what she was about, she re-entered the chamber of Lady Dane. The latter had contrived to struggle into a sitting posture in bed, and her eyes eagerly turned upon Adelaide their questioning light.

" What is it ? what is it ?" she uttered, for the young lady made no response to the mute questioning.

" I—I do not know, aunt."

" What is it ?" repeated Lady Dane. " You do know : I see it in your countenance."

" They said I was not to tell you," replied Adelaide—the most senseless rejoinder she could have made, proving how uncollected was her mind.

" Instinct has told me," said Lady Dane, with a gasping sob. " They have found, and brought home, the body of Harry."

" It is so, aunt," acknowledged Adelaide.

" But—at this distance of time—so long in the water—how can they recognize it ?"

" I gathered in the purport of what they were saying, aunt," returned Adelaide, evidently speaking with a painful effort, " that it was all but unrecognizable, that they knew it by the teeth and a mark on the arm. Ravensbird, who came in with them, says he could swear to it by the mark ; and they were saying that it could not have been all this time in the water."

" Ravensbird ! And Lord Dane suffered *him* to enter ?"

"There is great confusion, aunt. Perhaps he may have been unnoticed, until he spoke."

The body had been found a few miles farther off by the fishermen, and they brought it to Daneshold in their boat, never giving a thought to its being that of Captain Dane. But —as fate had it—when they reached the shore, Ravensbird happened to be strolling about there. He immediately pronounced it to be the body of his late master, knowing it, as Adelaide had said, by the teeth and the mark on the arm; and it was borne to the castle.

An inquest was held upon it, and the verdict returned was, "Wilful murder against some person or persons unknown." A rumor went about the place, and obtained credence, that had it not been for the episode, related by Drake, of the man with the pack, it might have been "Wilful murder against Richard Ravensbird," in spite of the testified alibi.

The body was buried in the Dane vault, and people mourned more truly for the Honorable William Henry Dane than they had done for the heir, the Honorable Geoffry. But, the very day of the interment, another died, to be mourned for—Lady Dane. It seemed that the flag was forever floating half-mast high now, over the castle.

All these events, following one upon another with succession so rapid, told upon the shattered frame, the broken health of Lord Dane. He was unable now to quit his chamber; and very soon, it was thought, he would be unable to quit his bed. Herbert Dane— Geoffry Dane, as he was henceforth to be called—once again, and for the third time, had to perform the office of chief mourner; and on his return from the funeral he was summoned to the presence of the old lord.

A favorite name in the Dane family was that of Geoffry. From the first creation of the barony, more than two-thirds of the lords had borne it, and it was held (superstition again!) that

those who had so borne it, had been more lucky than the rest. Herbert Dane, who was the son of the Honorable Herbert Dane, and grandson to the preceding peer who had reigned, had been christened Geoffry Herbert; his friends calling him by his second name, Herbert, that his name might not clash with that of his cousin, Geoffry, the heir. Now, however, that the succession lapsed to him, he was henceforth to be, not Herbert, but Geoffry.

He left his hat with its sweeping band in the library, and proceeded to attend the summons. He could not avoid remarking as he went in, how strangely altered and ill Lord Dane looked.

"Are you worse, uncle?" he involuntarily asked. "Don't you feel well?"

"I do not know that I am much worse, Geoffry, but as to feeling well, that I shall never do again. I may be called away at any moment, and it is necessary that I should 'set my house in order.' For this purpose—I should be more correct in saying, in pursuance of this purpose—I have caused you to come to me. According to the arbitrary decrees of fate— how capricious, how unlooked-for they are!—you will be the seventeenth Baron Dane. Geoffry, I have a charge to leave you, as such—a charge above all other charges."

"I will fulfill it, sir, if it be in my power."

The old peer stretched out his hand from his easy-chair, in which he was propped, and laid it upon the wrist of his nephew, slowly and impressively. Geoffry bent a little nearer to the anxious face.

"I charge you, by all your hopes of happiness, that you never cease in striving to bring to light the destroyer of Harry," solemnly said Lord Dane. "Spare no means, no energies, no trouble; let not idleness overtake you in your task; be not tempted by want of success to relinquish it. Should the years go on, ay, until you are an old man, and nothing have turned up, still do not flag; a conviction is upon me that search will not be always in vain. You hear me, Geoffry?"

"Oh, yes, I hear."

"Let your suspicions, your secret watchings, be directed to one quarter in particular; for, that the guilt lies in it, there is no doubt. Never suffer your surveillance to be off that man."

"Of whom do you speak, sir?" inquired Geoffry, in a tone of surprise.

"Ravensbird. Of whom else do you suppose I speak? Why do you knit your brow? why do you look displeased—incredulous?"

"Pardon me, sir, if I do not agree with you; though, if I did knit my brow, it was with perplexity, not displeasure. I cannot get over the fact that the absence of Ravensbird from the heights at the time of the occurrence has been credibly testified to; and it is a physical impossibility for a man to be in two places at once. Neither can I keep my suspicions from dwelling on that other, that packman."

"Pshaw!" returned Lord Dane, impatiently, shaking his head, "I have never attached credit to that tale of the packman. I do not say it did not take place, the encounter, dispute—whatever it may have been—as Drake describes it; but, as to that fellow's having attacked Harry to death, the notion is absurd. Some traveling bagman, passing accidentally, who importuned Harry to purchase a cotton pocket-handkerchief, or a horn-knife to cut bread-and-cheese, and Harry rode the high horse at being accosted, and drove the fellow away. It was nothing more, rely upon it. No; whoever dealt out his death to Harry, that night, had a motive in it. It was Ravensbird; I tell you it was Ravensbird, Geoffry, and I charge you look to him."

Lord Dane ceased. He appeared to have done with the subject, and a long pause ensued, each appearing buried in his own reflections. It was Geoffrey who broke it.

"What report is this, that I hear,

uncle—that Lady Adelaide goes back to Scotland?"

"It is so decided. It would not be expedient for her to remain here, now her aunt is gone. Under present circumstances, it would scarcely be expedient, a wild, random girl like Adelaide—think of her running out, mad-cap fashion, on to the ruins that ill-fated night!—but in the uncertain state of my life, it is not to be thought of. When death shall overtake me—and it is not far off: it is not, Geoffry, disbelieving as you may look—fancy what would be the position of Adelaide, were she still here. You, taking up your abode here, the castle's master, and an unprotected young lady in it! A pretty affair, that would be!"

A flush illumined Geoffry's features, symbol of his deep, passionate love for Adelaide, and he turned his face to hide it.

"It would be time enough for her to go back to Scotland then, sir—should the catastrophe occur."

"You talk like a boy," retorted Lord Dane. "Is the Lady Adelaide Errol one to be subjected to the possible comments of a scandalous world? She must quit the castle before I do."

"You cannot think, sir," said Geoffry, in agitation—he may possibly have misunderstood Lord Dane's remarks—"that I would do aught to bring scandal on Lady Adelaide? I would guard her from it with my life."

The proud old peer turned his face upon him in all its haughty severity. "What do you mean, nephew? 'If I thought you capable of bringing scandal on Lady Adelaide?' Did I deem you capable of but imagining such, I would shoot you there as you stand before me, rather than let so dishonorable a craven live to succeed to the coronet of Dane."

Geoffry felt that he was being misunderstood, and suffered the point to drop. "Where is Adelaide going to reside," he asked. "With whom? I thought she had no relatives."

"She has scarcely any. Some cousin of her late father's is willing to receive her. A Mrs. Grant, living in Worth-shire."

"Mrs. Grant," repeated Geoffry. "I have heard of her. A widow with a very bare jointure and a house full of children. Will Lady Adelaide like *that* after Dane Castle."

"Necessity has no law," observed Lord Dane. "Of course I shall take care that Adelaide is no burden to Mrs. Grant now or for the future. Were her brother what he ought to be, he might settle down and afford her a home, but Kirkdale is as wild as a March hare."

"Will Lady Adelaide like going to Mrs. Grant's?" repeated Geoffry.

"Like it, no!" returned Lord Dane. "She has never had the tears out of her eyes since the plan was mooted. But she acquiesces in its expediency, seeing there is nowhere else where she can apply for a home."

"I think—I think—uncle, will you pardon my saying it, will you sanction my saying it, that she might be happier with me?"

Geoffry spoke in a low tone of emotion, the color coming and going in his fair face. Life to him, without Adelaide Errol, would be a dreary prospect.

"Happier with you," echoed Lord Dane, in a quick tone. "In what way?"

"As my wife."

"Look you here, Geoffry; it is of no use for us to converse at cross purposes, so I will be explicit. You cannot suppose that since the death of my sons I have never cast my thoughts to the future, and to those who are left. Now, your aunt, my poor departed wife, took a notion in her head long ago that Adelaide cared for you more than she did for Harry. For my part, I deemed Lady Dane must be mistaken; I deemed it was altogether too absurd to suspect that Adelaide should do so, considering she had freely consented to be Harry's wife. But Harry went; Geoffry went; and you were left: and I told Lady Dane that if her idea was correct, you and Adelaide could now

marry. Truth to say, I would more cordially have given you my approval than I did to my son: for I do not like cousins marrying, and to you she is no blood relation."

"Well, sir?" eagerly cried Geoffry, whose eyes had been sparkling.

"Well. Two or three nights before my wife died, she told me we had all been wrong,—or rather that she had been wrong. That it was Harry to whom Adelaide had been really attached, and that she never would consent to be addressed by you. Therefore, I imagine, if you are indulging dreams of Adelaide you are nourishing a chimera."

A proud, self-satisfied smile passed over the face of Geoffry. *He* knew whom she had really loved.

Lord Dane put an end to the interview. A little thing fatigued him now, and he dismissed Geoffry.

Geoffry proceeded to the drawing-room, and there sat Adelaide. Very sad, very lonely did she look there in her mourning-robes, the only inmate of the castle save its invalid master. She rose from her seat to leave the room as Geoffry entered.

"Adelaide, am I scaring you away?"

"Oh, no," she answered, with a confused blush, and down she sat again.

"I hope you are better than you have been of late," he continued. "You have allowed me to see so little of you, that we seem like strangers."

"I have not been very well, and I have been much occupied with my poor aunt."

"I hear it is in contemplation that you should return to Scotland?"

"I believe it is."

"But it must seem strange that you should do so," he impulsively rejoined. "You may as well bury yourself alive as become an inmate of Mrs. Grant's undesirable home!"

A change passed over her face, and but for a strong effort the tears would have rained from her eyes. Purgatory itself would have scarcely seemed more terrible in prospective to Lady Adelaide than did Mrs. Grant's house.

"Adelaide," he resumed, in a low tone, "I have now come from leaving your aunt in her grave ; and to enter upon what I am about to do, may appear unseeming at such a time. It is unseemly in point of fact; but it is but a single word I would say, or ask ; and what I have heard must justify it. Give me the hope, the permission, that at a future time I may ask you to be my wife."

"It is impossible," was her low reply ; but Geoffry saw that she could scarcely speak for agitation, and that she was in fact, gasping for breath.

"Do you understand me ?" he returned.

"I believe so. You are asking me to be your wife ; is not that it ? I thank you for the—the—the courtesy—the offer—but I cannot avail myself of .it."

"Later I craved, Adelaide; that I might speak of it later."

"Neither now nor later. I beg you to drop the subject forever."

Geoffry Dane was likewise agitated, and pale as death. Were all the hopes of his later life to be thus ruthlessly blown away ?

"Adelaide, what has changed you ?" he resumed, in a deep tone. "I once thought—"

"Never mind what you once thought," she impetuously interrupted, "or what I thought either. The past is past."

"I can offer you now what I could not then ; what I never—I solemnly declare—so much as glanced at the possibility of ; I can offer to make you mistress of this castle and these broad lands."

Some emotion appeared to overcome her, for she buried her face in her hands and was shaking as though she had the ague. With an effort she looked up, and steadied her voice to speak.

"You need not enlarge upon it: I perfectly understand. You would make me Lady Dane."

"I would make you Lady Dane and

my dear wife," he interposed, in a tone of the deepest tenderness. "Oh, Adelaide, let this misery end ! What has come between us ?"

"But I cannot accept the offer," she more calmly continued, completely ignoring his last sentence, and retreating backwards, for he had made as if he would take her hands. "Geoffry Dane, *I pray you* let this subject cease, now and forever."

"Adelaide !"

"Cease, cease," she implored. "I can never give you any other answer."

"But this is inexplicable ; most strange. You must assign me the cause for your estrangement."

"No other answer, no other answer," she reiterated in a tone that savored of alarm. "The broad fact is sufficient ; why go into details ?"

"It is *not* sufficient, Adelaide. I have a right to demand its cause."

"I shall never give it you. You ask me to be your wife, and I refuse. There it must end."

"Are we to part thus—in anger ? in dissatisfaction ?"

"Not in anger, unless you choose. I thank you, Geoffry, for your courtesy, as much as though I had accepted it. And now, you must forgive me for reminding you what to-day is ; that your 'one word' has lengthened into many : and that I wish to be alone."

Geoffry Dane withdrew ; he could not well do otherwise. But, overwhelmed as he felt with disappointment, unpleasantly perplexed and puzzled though he was at her curious conduct, there was yet a hope lurking within him which seemed to whisper that a little time might set things to rights—that Lady Adelaide Errol would still be his.

CHAPTER VIII.

MARGARET BORDILLION—TIFFLE.

ABOUT half a mile from Dane Castle, standing almost at a right angle

between the castle and the village of
Danesheld, was the dwelling of Mr.
Lester, or, as he was sometimes styled
in the vicinity, Squire Lester. It was
a substantial, red-brick building,
known by the name of Danesheld Hall,
and but for its large size might have
been taken for a farm-house, surrounded as it was by out-buildings, barns,
sheds, rick-yards, poultry-yards, and
other appurtenances that a superior
farm generally possesses. Its site
was somewhat solitary, no dwellings
being in the immediate vicinity, while
the large, wild wood at the back, ranging out and extending to some distance, did not tend to render its aspect
more cheerful. The wood belonged
to Lord Dane, and was a favorite re-
sort of poachers.

Now, it may be as well to state before going on, that Mr Lester's property was not entailed. It had come
to him by bequest, not by inheritence.
A distant relative of the late owner,
he had been made the heir, unexpect-
edly to himself—the heir, upon the
condition that he should take up his
residence on the estate, and make the
hall his home. He was a dashing
young guardsman then, poor and
proud, and he scarcely knew whether
to be pleased or annoyed. The fortune was most welcome; but to veg-
etate in the country and be dubbed
"the squire,"—he winced at that.
However, we get reconciled to most
things in time, and so did George
Lester. He sold out, married, and
took up his abode at Danesheld. In
course of years his wife died, leaving
him with two children, Wilfred and
Maria, the latter four years younger
than her brother.

Mr. Lester was now nearly forty
years of age, but he did not look it.
He was a fine handsome man, rather
"fast" yet, a great admirer of beauty,
fond of society, and exceedingly popular. To say that he had become attached to Lady Adelaide, would be
scarcely a right phrase to use. He
had not suffered himself to become so,
seeing that she was engaged to her
cousin, Captain Dane. He admired

Lady Adelaide greatly, he felt that he
could love her; very delighted and
proud would he have been to make
her Lady Adelaide Lester, but for
that previous engagement to Harry
Dane.

But then came Harry Dane's death;
the barrier was removed, and Mr.
Lester's heart leaped up within him.
Not immediately did he speak; the
deaths following rapidly at the castle
one upon another, barred its propriety;
but when the rumor reached him that
Lady Adelaide was about to return to
Scotland, he threw propriety to the
winds, and besought her to become
his wife. She requested a day or two
for consideration, and then accepted
him.

Mr. Lester urged their immediate
marriage; where was the use of her
traveling to Scotland, he said; better
be married at once from the castle, and
obviate its necessity. Lady Adelaide,
as an objection to haste, put forth her
aunt's recent death. But Mr. Lester
replied that circumstances altered
cases, and he thought haste in this
instance was justifiable. Lord Dane
agreed with him. He told them both
that he felt his own life waning quickly,
and should be better content to leave
Adelaide with a legal protector. So
the usual formal preliminaries and
preparations were in their case dis-
pensed with, and the wedding-day
was fixed.

"Geoffry," said Lord Dane to his
nephew, "I cannot leave my bed and
accompany them to church to give her
away. Will you attend for me?"

It was the first positive information
Geoffry Dane had received of the forth-
coming marriage of Lady Adelaide.
Vague reports, half surmises, had
penetrated to him, but he believed
them not. A deadly pallor overspread
his face, too sudden, too intense to
be concealed; and it startled Lord
Dane.

"Be a man, Geoffry. If she won't
have you, if she prefers somebody else,
you can't alter it; but don't sigh for
her after the fashion of a love-sick
girl. Adelaide is beautiful, but she is

not the wife *I* should like to choose; she is capricious and unsteady as the breeze. Forget her, and look abroad for somebody better; there's as good fish in the sea as ever came out of it."

Geoffry's color was coming back to him, and he made an effort to smooth his brow—to pass it off lightly.

"Will you go to church and officiate for me, Geoffry?"

"No, sir," he answered in a low tone, that one that betrayed firm resolution. "If she marries George Lester of her own inclination, why—let her. But I will not take part in it."

Not only to Geoffry Dane did the projected union bring its pangs. Mr. Lester's first wife had been a Miss Bordillion, a lady of a good family, but a poor one—there was a saying in their vicinity, "Poor and proud as a Bordillion." During Mrs. Lester's last illness, which was known to be a fatal one, a very distant relative of hers, but still a Bordillion, was staying with her. They had been girls together, close and tried friends since, and Mrs. Lester besought a promise from Margaret Bordillion that she would remain at the hall after her coming death, and watch over her young daughter, Maria. Margaret Bordillion was a delicate-looking woman of two or three and thirty, and the pink hue came into her cheeks as she thought of what the world might say did she remain an inmate of the house of the somewhat gayly-inclined George Lester. But when death is brought palpably before us—and Margaret Bordillion knew that it was very near to that chamber, as she held her damp hand, and looked down at the wasted face of Mrs. Lester—minor considerations are lost in the vista of the future, which now comes so palpably before us; that solemn future where we must all be gathered together and render up our accounts, and we feel far more anxious to fulfill our duty, wherever it may lie, than to be troubled at what the "world will say." Mrs. Lester received the promise she craved, that Margaret Bordillion would—at any rate for a time

—remain at the Hall to take charge of Maria.

"And remember, Margaret," whispered Mrs. Lester, drawing Margaret's ear down, that she might catch unmistakably the low accents, "should any warmer feeling arise between you and George—it may be so—should he ever seek to make you his wife, remember that I now tell you I should be pleased with it."

"How *can* you contemplate such a thing! how can you speak of it—at this moment?" interrupted Miss Bordillion, aghast. "You, his wife, can calmly enter upon the subject of his marrying another!"

"The world and its passions are fading from me, Margaret," was the reply of Mrs. Lester. "It almost seems as if I had already left it. I feel no doubt that George will marry again; he is most likely to do so; and I would prefer that he should make you my children's mother rather than any other woman."

Mrs. Lester died, and Miss Bordillion continued at Danesheld Hall. But she kept herself very much in the background, more as though she were only Maria's governess, and declined to preside as the hall's mistress. She regulated the servants, and the domestic affairs, but she never officiated at table in the place of Mrs. Lester; when Mr. Lester had visitors, she frequently did not appear, remaining in private with Maria; and she quite as often sat in her own sitting-room, as joined Mr. Lester. Maria was only eight years old at the time of her mother's death: had she been more of a woman, Miss Bordillion would have felt her position less awkward. Some ladies might not have found any awkwardness in it; but Miss Bordillion was of an unusually sensitive temperament, exceedingly alive to the refined proprieties of life.

Two years had now passed over her head since Mrs. Lester's death, and what had they brought forth? Love. Thrown into constant contact with George Lester, who was a man of remarkably attractive manners, to Miss

Bordillion as to others; ever dwelling on the words spoken by Mrs. Lester, Miss Bordillion had, at first unconsciously to herself, become deeply attached to him. And when a woman's love has lain dormant for the first five-and-thirty years of her life, and is then awakened, it bursts into a lasting passion,—one that the young little know of. Timid, modest, retiring, she nourished it in secret, gradually giving way to the hope that she should be what Mrs. Lester had suggested, his second wife; a hope that soon grew to intensity—nay, to expectation. And Margaret Bordillion's days, now, were as one long dream of paradise.

More especially high beat her heart one morning, for her hopes appeared to be nearing their realization. It was a hot summer's day at the close of July, and as the party rose from breakfast, Mr. Lester remarked that, while the excessive heat lasted, it would be better to have the breakfast laid in the dining-room, which did not face the morning sun.

"I will tell the servants to-day," said Miss Bordillion.

Wilfred Lester was at home for his holidays, which, however, were drawing to an end. He was a high-spirited boy of fourteen, though, it must be confessed, given to be passionate and disobedient on occasions; his eyes were of an intensely violet blue, his hair and eyelashes dark, and he gave promise of being a handsome man. Maria and Edith had run out to the lawn, and Wilfred vaulted after them. A pretty little girl of eleven, was Edith Bordillion, now on a visit at the hall. She was the daughter of Major Berdillion, and niece of Margaret.

The children were gamboling on the lawn, caring nothing for the heat, and Mr. Lester stood at the window watching them. Miss Bordillion remained in her seat at the breakfast-table, reading a letter which the morning-post had brought.

"Look here, Margaret," Mr. Lester suddenly exclaimed. "Step this way a minute."

She put aside her letter and went to him.

"Has it ever struck you, Margaret, what a famous conservatory might be carried out from this end window?"

"It would be an excellent spot for one," she replied. "I think I once heard you make the same remark."

"No doubt. It has been in my mind some time. I suppose I must set about it now."

"Why now?" inquired Miss Bordillion.

Mr. Lester laughed; it was what might be called a shy laugh, and as he replied to the question, his usually free tone had a tinge of embarrassment in it.

"It is two years—more—since Katherine died; I may begin to look out soon for some one to supply her place. In that case the old house ought to be brightened up. What say you, Margaret?"

Margaret Bordillion said nothing. She stood with her eyes cast down, and her cheeks glowing. She certainly did not construe the words into an offer; she had better sense; but she did believe that George Lester's intentions pointed to herself; his embarrassment of manner may have aided the thought. *He* saw the marks of confusion; it was impossible that she could conceal them, standing facing him, as she did, in the glowing brightness of the morning; and he attributed them to displeasure; he thought she was feeling pained at the idea of Katherine's place being filled up.

"Margaret," he said, in a low, tender tone, as he gently laid his hand upon her shoulder, though neither the tone nor the action was born of tenderness for *her*, "it is not good for a man to be alone. Katherine is gone, but we are living. Ponder over what I have hinted, and try and overget your distaste to it."

Mr. Lester stepped out at the window, which opened to the ground, as he concluded, and joined the children. And Margaret Bordillion?—she remained standing as he had left her in the day's brightness, type of the brightness which had rushed over and was illumining her whole soul. "I shall be his wife, at last," she softly murmured; "his wife! his wife! how have I deserved so intense a happiness?"

The servants entered to remove the breakfast-things, and that aroused her. She called to her the two little girls, and went with them up-stairs to the study, to superintend, as usual, their lessons.

The day went on to its close, its calm varied only by an outbreak between Master Wilfred and Tiffle. Tiffle, one of the sourest of virgins, was the head-servant at the hall, and liked to rule with an overbearing hand. She was housekeeper and mistress, subject, of course, to the authority of Miss Bordillion; but Miss Bordillion interfered but little. Tiffle, if not of a desirable temper, was neither of a kindly disposition: the servants called her cross-grained, and Miss Bordillion, truth to say, felt afraid of her. When Mrs. Lester died, and Tiffle found that Miss Bordillion was to remain, Tiffle went to her master and gave warning. Mr. Lester would not take it: he fancied that the hall, deprived both of mistress and housekeeper, would inevitably come to something bad; and he raised Tiffle's wages, and told her she must stop. Tiffle ungraciously consented to a three-months further sojourn; but when the three months came to an end, and Tiffle found how little Miss Bordillion troubled her—that she had, in fact, far more sway than in the days of her late mistress, Tiffle said no more about leaving. But she hated Miss Bordillion, simply because the latter was nominally placed over her; and Tiffle was one who could hate to some purpose.

Another object of her dislike was Master Lester, and it was returned by him. That sort of repulsion must have existed between them, which two persons will sometimes entertain, one to the other, unexplainable by themselves or in metaphysics; and when Wilfred was at home there were frequent contests between him and Tiffle. On this occasion it was sharper than customary: so sharp and loud as to disturb the household: Mr. Lester was out, but Miss Bordillion, as in duty bound, interposed her authority, and ordered them both before her. It was an unusual procedure for her to make: induced possibly by a foreshadowing idea of the full and indisputable authority she might soon be vested with in that house. Miss Bordillion found that Tiffle was in the wrong—had provoked the boy unjustifiably; and she reprimanded her.

Tiffle was pretty nearly stunned with indignation: truth to say, though the fault lay on her side this time, it was as often on Wilfred's: and she withdrew, vowing vengeance in her heart against the world in general and Miss Bordillion in particular. The servants suffered from her temper that day, as they scarcely ever had suffered, and the murmurs were loud and deep.

"Let her have her fling out," cried the butler, who had been a passive listener. "It won't be for long now. I have heard news this evening."

"What's that?" cried Tiffle, turning sharply round upon him. "Did you speak of me?"

"I tell them they may as well let you have your fling out, Mrs. Tiffle," he quietly answered. "Another week or two, and it will be at an end."

"You are a fool," retorted Tiffle.

"Perhaps I am," said the man. "Perhaps master would be if he didn't set himself about remedying this. But he is going to, and to marry a wife, and to give the house a mistress—which will put your nose out of joint, ma'am."

"Is it true?" uttered one of the other servants, all of whom stood in consternation.

"It is perfectly true; otherwise I should not have repeated it. In a couple of weeks at the most, I believe they'll be married."

His accent was serious, and they knew him to be a cautious and a truthful man. Even Tiffle felt the calamity was certain, and she turned cold all over.

"It's that animal, Miss Bordillion!" she uttered, the conviction fixing itself into her mind: "it's she who has come over him, and no other. She's as sly as a cat!"

The butler only smiled; it exasperated her beyond bearing, and she flung out of the room.

"I'll go to her this minute, and tell her what I think, if I die for it!" she muttered, "and the deuce himself shouldn't stop me."

Miss Bordillion was alone in the breakfast-room; —they often sat in it on a summer's evening—it was so pleasant to be where the windows opened to the ground, and to step out when inclined. Mr. Lester was dining out that evening. The little girls were dragging a child's carriage to and fro on the lawn, in which were seated two dolls in state, Wilfred teasing them with all his might, and, altogether, making a great noise. Tiffle came brushing in, her face red. She had a long sharp nose, and gray, sly ferret's eyes: was very little in person, and generally stealthy in her movements. She was attired in an old brown silk dress and a white muslin apron.

"I lived in the family before you ever came near it, Miss Bordillion," began she, "and I think if this change was in view I might have been injected into it."

Miss Bordillion looked up, astonished at her abrupt entrance, her words, her manner altogether. Tiffle was literally panting with passion.

"Explain yourself," said Miss Bordillion.

"I say that it's a shame for the servants to have been enlightened, and for me, their head, to have been kept in the dark," burst out Tiffle. "But when things are set about in this kivert way, it don't bring much luck."

"Explain yourself, I repeat," interrupted Miss Bordillion. "What are you speaking of? You forget yourself."

"It's announced in the kitchen by Jones that you and master are going to make a match of it," shrieked Tiffle. "I suppose master told him."

Miss Bordillion was completely taken too; never had she been so much so in all her life. Tiffle's insolence was entirely merged in the news: it was that which took away her self-possession, and covered her with confusion. She blushed rosy red, she stammered, she faltered; bringing out some disjointed words that she "did not know," she "was not sure." Tiffle read the signs only too correctly.

"Lovesick as a school-girl!" she contemptuously soliloquized, and then spoke aloud. "So, as I have not been used to underhanded treatment, and can't stomach it, I'll give warning now, if you please."

And, leaving Miss Bordillion in a whirl of happy perplexity, she strode back to the servants, and boasted of what she had done.

"Good heavens!" exclaimed the butler, "you never have been such an idiot! You complimented me with being a fool just now, but you might have kept it for yourself more justly. It is not Miss Bordillion that master's going to marry."

Tiffle sat down, overcome with sundry emotions.

"Not Miss Bordillion! Who is it, then?"

"The pretty young lady at the castle,—Lady Adelaide. I should be sorry to put my foot in it, as you have done."

Tiffle said nothing in reply. She sat silent for at least half an hour, revolving in her mind the points of all she had heard and seen, and drawing her own deductions. Then she arose, and proceeded again to the breakfast-room.

Miss Bordillion sat as she had left her, in the same chair, in the same position, her eyes fixed on vacancy, and the rosy hue of happy love lighting her countenance. She was lost in the mazes of dream-land,—illusive dreamland, upon which a rude blow was now about to fall,—one that would shatter its bliss forever.

Very different was the present Tiffle, meekly standing there, from the outrageous Tiffle of half an hour ago. She deprecatingly held her hands together, smoothing them one over the other, and stole covert glances with her false eyes at Miss Bordillion.

"I am come to apologize, ma'am, for what I said just now, which I shouldn't have done but for laboring under a misapprehension. Them servants led me into it, and I should like to turn the whole lot away. I find there were no grounds for coupling your name with master's."

"Your words took me so entirely by surprise, Tiffle, that I did not meet them, or reprove you as I ought," was the quiet reply of Miss Bordillion. "I will now merely observe that Mr. Lester entertains no present intention of changing his condition, so far as I know. Do not offend again —or take up groundless notions."

"I was only mistaken in the lady, you see, ma'am," returned Tiffle, standing her ground. "I thought it had been you,—for which, as I say, I'm here to beg parding,—whereas it's somebody else. Master *is* about to marry."

Slowly Miss Bordillion gathered in the words. Had they meaning? or had they not? Her heart beat wildly, as she gazed at Tiffle.

"In less than two weeks from this the wedding is to come off," proceeded Tiffle, venturing on the unqualified as·sertion, and positively reveling in the misery she knew she was inflicting. "A dainty bride she'll make, young and lovaly as ever wore the oringe wreath ; but master—so it's said—always had an eye for beauty. You don't seem as if you had heard it, ma'am : he marries Lady Adelaide."

Misery? Ay, misery as cruel ever fell in this world. Margaret Bordillion's pulses stood still, and then began to beat with alarming quickness. All the blood in her body seemed turning to stone, her brain whirled, her heart

turned sick, the things around were growing dim to her.

"Water—a drop of water, Tiffle," she gasped out, as her sight was failing.

Tiffle whisked round to where some stood, a wicked look of satisfaction on her countenance, now that it was turned from view. She poured some into a tumbler, and carried it to Miss Bordillion, beginning to speak in a condoling tone.

"These changes is unpleasant, ma'am, when they come upon us by surprise ; but—"

Tiffle ceased ; for she saw that her words were falling on a deaf ear. Miss Bordillion lay in a fainting fit.

CHAPTER IX.

THE LEASE OF THE SAILOR'S REST.

THE indisposition of Miss Bordillion soon passed, and Tiffle withdrew in silence ; having the grace to feel that it was scarcely the moment to venture upon any more of her "condolences." The evening grew later, and the children were sent to bed ; but Margaret sat on where she was, never quitting her chair.

To say that the news had stunned her, would be to use a most feeble expression, as descriptive of the facts. Her whole mind was in a chaos ; and she was only conscious that the Rubicon, which most women must encounter once in their lives, was now passed, leaving behind it sweet and sunny plains, as of Arcadia ; stretching out before it, the way she must henceforth walk, nothing but a black darkness.

But Margaret Bordillion was one to look troubles firmly in the face, and she set herself to do so by this ; even now, in the very dawn of her agony. First of all, were the tidings true ? If so, she must decide upon her own future movements ; for, to remain in

MARGARET BORDILLION AND TIFFLE.—*See page 79.*

5

the house after the young Lady Adelaide was brought to it, his wife—Margaret bent her head with a wailing cry; she could not pursue the thought. She must, if possible, be satisfied on the point before she slept; there way only one was to accomplish it, and that was by putting the question to Mr. Lester; and she resolved to do it.

He came home about eleven o'clock, much surprised to see Miss Bordillion sitting there; for she never waited for him when he passed his evenings out.

"You are quite dissipated, Margaret," began he, in his gay, careless tones. "Eleven o'clock, and you sitting up!"

She strove to form her lips to answer, but no sound came from them. She was schooling down her manner to indifference, making an effort to speak with calmness, but it was more difficult than she had thought. Mr. Lester continued, noticing nothing.

"I am sure this is much more sensible than your dancing off up-stairs to your own sitting-room or to bed, leaving an empty room to welcome me. I have wondered why you do so, Margaret: you can't fear I shall eat you."

Margaret cleared her throat preparatory to speaking, but the self-agitation which the effort induced, was more than she well knew how to hide. Her heart was beating great thumps, beating up to her throat, her face was white and her lips were dry. She rose from her seat, and opening her workbox, which rested on a side table, stood there, apparently rummaging its contents, her back to Mr. Lester. Then she managed to bring out what she had made up her mind to say.

"I have been hearing some news to-night, and I thought I would wait and ask you if it was true. These warm evenings, too, one finds sitting up agreeable."

"What momentous news have you been hearing?" he laughed. "That the Thames has taken fire!"

"Something nearer home," she answered, dropping a reel of cotton and stooping for it. "I have been told that you are going to"—a sudden cough took her, which caused the pause —"to marry Lady Adelaide Errol."

"Now, who the deuce could have given you that information?" demanded Mr. Lester, in a joking tone.

"Tiffle. She said that Jones—at least I think she said it was Jones—had announced it to the servants, and she concluded he had authority from you."

"The notion of Miss Bordillion's listening to the gossip of servants!" was his retort; and but for his manner, still a laughing one, she would have deemed it all nonsense together; perhaps a faint hope did come across her that it might be. At that juncture the butler happened to enter with some glasses, and his master arrested him.

"So, Jones, you have been making free with Lady Adelaide Errol's name to-night—in conjunction with mine."

Jones turned crimson and purple, and Jones stuttered and stammered, but not a connected word could Jones utter.

"Pray from whom did you get your information?" continued Mr. Lester.

"Sir, I'm sure I beg pardon if—if it's not correct, or if I did wrong to speak of it," cried the man. "I got it from Mr. Geoffry Dane."

"From Mr. Geoffry Dane!" repeated Squire Lester, surprise causing him to echo the words. "How did that come about?"

"It was in this way, sir. I met Mr. Geoffry Dane in the road near the castle, and he stopped to speak; he often does, for he's a affable, pleasant gentleman; and just then my Lady Adelaide passed towards the castle, with her maid and Bruff behind her. 'She's a winsome young thing, sir,' I said, when Mr. Dane was putting on his hat again, which he had taken off to her, 'as good as a sunbeam.' 'It's a sunbeam you'll soon have near to you, Jones,' answered he; 'in a week or two's time she leaves the castle for your master's, changing her name for his.' He looked so queer when he said it."

"Queer! How 'queer?'" asked Mr. Lester.

"Well, sir, I can hardly describe—there was a funny look about his mouth; the corners of it drawn down like. It made me think he had been speaking in ridicule, but I found he had not."

The servant ceased, but no rejoinder was made to him.

"And I certainly did speak of it when I got home, sir, and I am sorry if it has given offence, but I thought there could be no harm in repeating it, as it was said openly to me. Shall I contradict it, sir?"

"Oh, dear, no," carelessly replied Mr. Lester. "You may go, Jones."

The man retired, and Miss Bordillion, who had been steadying her nerves during the colloquy, turned to Mr. Lester.

"It is true, then?"

"Yes, it is true, Margaret," he answered, his manner changing to seriousness. "I should have acquainted you with it to-morrow; the few words I said to you this morning after breakfast were intended as preparing heralds."

"And is it possible that it is so near?"

"Circumstances are compelling the haste. Lord Dane's state is most precarious, and I do not wish Adelaide to depart for Scotland."

"I think you should have told me," she returned, her voice expressing resentment. "It is a short notice for me to lay my plans and get away from the house."

"Get away from the house!" exclaimed Mr. Lester. "What are you thinking of now?"

"Nay—what are you thinking of? I may rather say."

"The house is large enough for you and for Adelaide. She will not be putting you out of your place as mistress, because it is a place you have never assumed, and never would do it. You can remain in it precisely as you have hitherto done."

"No, Mr. Lester, it is impossible,"

she answered, a sickly smile momentarily arising to her features. "Before you bring home your wife, I must leave to make room for her."

"Margaret," he returned in a low tone, "I do not forget that you promised Katherine to supply her place to Maria—to be, in a sense, the child's second mother. Are you forgetting it?"

A flush of pain dyed her face—the peculiar words called it forth.

"You are bringing home Maria's second mother, in Lady Adelaide," she said, laying her hand on her chest to still its beating.

"I should not bring Adelaide here to saddle her with the charge of a child, for whom she does not, as yet, care: and she is neither old enough nor experienced enough to fulfill the duties of a parent to one of Maria's age. When she shall have children of her own, experience will come with them. Margaret, you love Maria almost as the apple of your eye: you could not bear to part with her."

That it would bring more grief than she chose to acknowledge, was certain.

"I must bear it," was all she said.

"No, no. Margaret, by the remembrance of Katharine, for Maria's own sake, I ask you to rescind this expressed resolution, and remain with us. At any rate, for a period: say three months, six months; and then —if your sojourn be not agreeable; if you and Adelaide cannot get on well together—then it will be time enough to talk of leaving. Dear Margaret! do not desert Maria."

He had drawn close to her, and taken her hands in the earnestness of his emotion. She quietly withdrew them without reply; and Mr. Lester supposed his prayer was acceded to.

Margaret Bordillion retired to her chamber, and sat herself down to think. What should she do? what ought she to do? She was a woman greatly alive to the dictates of conscience, one who was most anxious, even at a self-sacrifice, to fulfill her duty. And conscience was already beginning to ask her whether it would be right to abandon Maria Lester.

"Should I put my own pain, my own chilled feelings in comparison with this?" she asked herself. "Terrible as it will be to me to live here when she is his wife, perhaps I *can* bear it. And I deserve punishment: yes; for I had no right to suffer myself to become so attached to him. Let me take up the punishment and bear it, as I best may."

She sat on, to the little hours of the morning, battling with her grievous trial. But no better reconciled did she get to it : and she rose impressed with the belief that she should not be able to remain. She made a kind of compromise with herself: she would not hurry away before the marriage, as was her first thought, but would remain during the month the bride and bridegroom expected to be absent on their wedding-tour (following the customs of the world), and quit it only just previous to their return.

"About Edith?" she said to Mr. Lester the following day, without touching upon other particulars. "She had better be sent back to school."

"I don't see why she should be," was his reply. "She was invited for a three-months' visit, and but a month of it has elapsed. Her remaining here will make no difference to Lady Adelaide : she will be with Maria."

Miss Bordillion offered no rejoinder. Edith could leave when she did, she thought.

A few days passed on, nine or ten, and the day fixed for the wedding was drawing very close. Lord Dane seemed to have taken a turn for the better : he still kept his bed,—from that he would never rise again,—but his general health and spirits were much improved. One morning he sent for Mr. Apperly. The lawyer express-ed his pleasure at seeing him so well.

"Yes," smiled Lord Dane : "I fancy I have taken another lease of my short span of life, and may be here a few months longer instead of a few weeks. Feeling equal to business, Apperly, I

may as well execute the will to day : I suppose it is ready."

"Quite ready, my lord, and has been this fortnight. But you were to let me know when to bring it up for signature."

"I have not been well enough to put myself to any sort of business or trouble," was the reply of Lord Dane.

"It is not well to suffer wills to remain unexecuted," remarked the lawyer. "Procrastination plays strange tricks sometimes."

"Not well, as a general rule, or when a man lies daily in danger of death," acquiesced Lord Dane. "Had I been likely to go off like the snuff of a candle, I would have signed the will the day it was made. But I do not imagine my departure will be quite so sudden as all that."

"About witnesses?" inquired Mr. Apperly : "shall I bring them with me?"

"There's no necessity. Bruff and one of the other men will do. Squire Lester may happen to be in the castle at the time : if so, he can be one."

"He marries Adelaide, we hear."

"Yes. Was it not you who drew up the settlement?"

Mr. Apperly shook his head.

"I am not solicitor to Mr. Lester. Oh, by the way," he suddenly added, "has your lordship heard that Haw-thorne is off to Australia?"

"Hawthorne off to Australia!" uttered Lord Dane, turning his eyes on the lawyer in surprise. "What should take him thither?"

"He has heard from his two brothers, who went over, as your lordship may remember, some four or five years ago. They are doing well—excellently—are making fortunes; and have written for Hawthorne to go out and do the same."

"And he intends to go?"

"Ay, and to be off in a jiffy. Since the letter came, the man has not known whether he stood on his head or his heels, his brain reeling with the golden visions it holds forth. He was with me next day, asking what he had better do about the lease of his house.

It seems he had given wings to the news, and twenty are already after it, anxious to take it off his hands,— of course subject to your lordship's approval."

"A good house is the Sailor's Rest," remarked Lord Dane; "an excellent living for any steady man. Hawthorne would do well to think twice before he gives it up."

"So I told him. But, you see that sun, my lord, its rays shining in so brightly: you might just as well try to turn that from the earth, as to turn Hawthorne from this new project. He is wildly bent upon it, and his wife is the same; she is already gone to London to lay in an outfit for the voyage."

"What do they mean to do with their furniture and fixtures?"

"Whoever takes to the house must take to them. He puts the value down at £300, altogether; furniture, fixtures, lease, and good-will; and it's not too much. One man is after it who would make a good tenant,— Mitchel."

"Mitchel?" echoed Lord Dane. "What could he do with a public house? And where's his money?"

"Your lordship is thinking of the preventive-man. I mean his brother."

"Oh, ay, I forgot him. Yes, he would be a good tenant, and could pay Hawthorne the money down. Well, I leave it to you, Apperly; but let the name be submitted to me before the bargain is actually struck. I like to approve of my own tenants."

"Very well, my lord. But I suppose I may allow the negotiations with Mitchel to go on, if he and Hawthorne so will it?"

"Yes, yes," returned his lordship, "I could have no objection to Mitchel A respectable man; a very respectable man is Mitchel."

"And at what hour shall I return with the will?" inquired Mr. Apperly. "Three o'clock? four o'clock?"

"Any hour. You won't find me gone out" responded Lord Dane, with a joking smile.

"Then I'll say three," said Mr. Ap-

perly, "and bid your lordship good-day now, hoping my visit has not fatigued you."

He had quitted the room, when Lord Dane's bell rang a hasty peal. It was to recall him.

"Apperly," cried his lordship, "I do feel somewhat fatigued, not so well as I did when you came in, and think it may be better to put off the business till to-morrow. It's not well for me to attempt too much in one day. Be here with the will at eleven in the morning."

And the lawyer, with a bow of acquiescence, turned and went out again.

When he reached home, John Mitchel was waiting to see him, the man who wished to take to the Sailor's Rest.

"Hawthorne and I have come to terms, sir," were the words with which he accosted Mr. Apperly; "and we shall want you to make out the agreement and transfer. I don't care how soon it's done."

"All very fine, my good man," returned the lawyer, who, lawyer-like, chose to throw difficulties in the way, though none really existed; "but there's a third party to be consulted in this affair, besides you and Hawthorne. And that's Lord Dane."

"I feel sure his lordship will accept me readily," returned the man. "He could not find a surer tenant; you know he could not, Mr. Apperly."

"I have nothing to say against you, Mitchel; there's no doubt his lordship might get many a worse. Well, I'll see about it in a few days."

"But, if you could manage it, sir, we should like the deeds drawn out immediately. I want to take possession next week, and Hawthorne wants to be rid of it."

"Pooh, pooh!" cried Mr. Apperly, "you can't take a bull by the horns in that way. Some men are six months getting into a house. I am busy to-day; and I shall be busy to-morrow; but you may come in again the next morning. Meanwhile, I'll contrive to see Lord Dane."

"I dare say, sir," returned Mitchel, looking hard at Mr. Apperly, "you might accept me now, if you would. It's not altogether that I am in so great a hurry to get into the house; it is Hawthorne who is in haste to get out of it: but what I want is, to make sure that I shall have it—that I shan't be put aside for another. I'd pay this, freely, to secure it, sir."

He laid down a £5 note. Five-pound notes had charms for Mr. Apperly like they have for all men, lawyers in particular. He looked at it complacently; but, true still to his craft, he would not speak the word positive.

"I have some power vested in me, Mitchel, certainly, and believe I can promise that you shall become the tenant. Subject, you understand, to the consent of Lord Dane."

"Of course, Mr. Apperly. Then it is a settled thing, for I know, his lordship won't object to me. So I'll say good-morning, and thank you, sir."

"And step in the day after to-morrow, in the forenoon, Mitchel. As to this," added the lawyer, carelessly popping the note inside his desk, "it can go into the costs."

But there was to be acting and counteracting. Somewhere about the same hour that Mitchel paid his visit to Mr. Apperly, Richard Ravensbird paid one at Mr. Geoffry Dane's. The latter looked exceedingly surprised to see him, if not annoyed.

"Sir," began Ravensbird, without any circumlocution, "report runs that, now you are the heir, my lord leaves many points of business, relating to the estate, entirely in your hands. I have come to ask your interest and influence to get me accepted as tenant of the Sailor's Rest."

He spoke fearlessly, not at all as a petitioner, more as though he was making a demand. A remarkably independent man was Richard Ravensbird.

"What! are *you* after the Sailor's Rest?" exclaimed Mr. Dane. "I have heard a dozen names mentioned; but

not yours. The man most likely to have it, they say, is Mitchel."

"I have not been after it with a noise, like the rest have, sir; but, as soon as I found it was to let, I spoke privately to Hawthorne. I must do something for a living, and have been looking out ever since I left the castle in the spring."

"Then you don't intend to go to service again?"

"Service!" returned Ravensbird. "Who would engage me, after having been taken up on a charge of murdering my former master? There may be some, Mr. Herbert,—I beg your pardon, sir, I ought to say Mr. Dane,—who don't yet believe me innocent. Not that that's the reason; I never did intend to enter upon another service, if I left Captain Dane's. The Sailor's Rest is just such a house as I should like: will you help me to it, sir?"

"Ravensbird," said Mr. Dane, not replying to his request, "it appears strange to me that you should remain in Danesheld. You have no ties in it; until you came here with your master you were a stranger to it: had a like cloud fallen upon me, however unjustly, I should be glad to get away from the place."

"No, sir," answered Ravensbird, in a quiet, concentrated tone: "I prefer to stay in it."

"To enter upon the Sailor's Rest will require money," again objected Mr. Dane.

"I am prepared with that. I have not lived to these years without saving up money. That won't be the bar—as Hawthorne knows. He has been shilly shallying, has Hawthorne," continued Ravensbird. "I knew of his intention to leave the house as soon as he did, for he read the letter from Australia to me when it came, lodging with them as I do; and I spoke up at once, and said I would take the house off his hands. He quite jumped at it,—was all eagerness to transfer it to me; but in a day or two his tone changed, and he has been vacillating between me and John Mitchel."

"Why did he change? Do you know?"

"Yes; and I have no objection to say," answered Ravensbird. "A crotchet came over him that I might not be an acceptable tenant to my lord, who still wavers as to my guilt or nonguilt."

"My lord does not waver: he believes you guilty," was on the tongue of Geoffry Dane; but he checked the words, and suffered Ravensbird to continue.

"It is scarcely likely that any reasonable man can believe me to have been the assailant, in the face of the sworn alibi; so why should his lordship nourish a prejudice against me? Will you accept me as tenant, Mr. Dane?"

"I have no power to do so: you have taken up a wrong notion altogether. I certainly have transacted business for my uncle, since I have stood, as may be said, in Mr. Geoffry Dane's place; but he has not given me authority to let his houses."

"Will you speak to him for me, sir?"

Mr. Dane hesitated.

"I would speak in a minute, Ravensbird, but I am sure it would be doing no good. Apart from any prejudice he may or may not hold against you, he is one who will not brook interference, even from me."

"You might try," persisted the man, "whatever the result should be."

"Will you undertake not to be disappointed at the result? Did it lie with me, it would be a different matter; but it lies entirely with Lord Dane."

There was a pause. Ravensbird stood in silence, as if still awaiting an answer, his piercing eyes never moving from those of Mr. Dane.

"However, as you seem so set upon it, I will speak to his lordship," resumed the latter. "But I must choose my time: it is not every day that he will allow business matters to be so much as named."

"If it is not settled between now and to-morrow night, John Mitchel

will have the place," rejoined Ravensbird, almost fiercely.

"Then I will speak to his lordship in the morning," concluded Geoffry Dane.

CHAPTER X.

THE DAMP FLAGS—THE BRIDE COMING HOME.

A JUNKET was being held in the housekeeper's parlor at Dane Castle, by the upper servants, who had invited a few friends to pass the evening. There was nothing very wrong in it: servants like moments of revelry just as much as their betters, and it would be unreasonable to say they should never enjoy them, provided they keep within bounds. Of all people in the world, who should have been smuggled into the castle, one of the guests, but Richard Ravensbird! The servants did not share in the prejudice of their lord: they believed his innocence to be an established fact, and deemed him an ill-used man. Perhaps Sophie's eloquent tongue had contributed to help them to this conviction. Wine, and biscuit, and cold punch, and rich cake, and fruit, and even ices were on the table, with other nice things; for the servants of the English nobility know what's good; and laughter and merriment reigned around.

Paying great attention to a smart damsel (smart *there*, and with a face smoothed to smiles, but who was no other than Tiffle) was the valet of Lord Dane,—an old beau, who had been in search of a wife (as *he* said) the last ten years, but had not found one to his mind. He was plying Tiffle with wine, cake, and soft speeches, when Mr. Bruff suddenly interrupted the flirtation, and recalled the valet to his duty.

"Is it not time that you should just step up-stairs, and see if my lord requires any thing?"

"My lord is sure to be sleeping

still," was the reply of the valet; "otherwise he would have rung. It's bad for him, this going to sleep at dusk, because it spoils his night's rest; but he will yield to it. Besides, my Lady Adelaide is sitting in the room. Let me alone for not neglecting my lord, Mr. Bruff."

"I wonder the young lady likes to pass her evenings in a sick chamber," grunted Tiffle.

"I know why *I* think she chooses it," responded the castle's housekeeper, dropping her voice, "and that's for the sake of company. My lord in his sick-bed is better than none. My opinion is, that she's frightened to sit alone in this great house. What she saw, or what she didn't see, that dreadful night by the ruins, I don't know; but it's certain that nobody was ever so changed in the space of time, as is Lady Adelaide."

"My faith!" ejaculated Sophie, jumping out of her chair, "if my lady didn't tell me to take her a shawl, for she felt chill, and that's an hour ago! What's my head worth?"

"And that's another odd thing," continued the housekeeper, as Sophie flew from the room. "My young lady's feeling chill, these hot nights, as soon as dusk comes on. Take her altogether, she's just as if she had some dreadful secret within her to weigh her down."

Sophie had gone from the room quick enough; but not half as quickly as she burst into it, on her return. The assembled party gazed at her in amazement, for she was evidently under the influence of some great terror, which had taken away her self-possession, and turned her face white.

"Who is in the death-room?" she panted.

"The death-room!" echoed Bruff, "why, nobody. It's locked up safe. What superstitious fancy is coming over you now, Mam'selle Sophie?"

"It's not locked up. The door's ajar."

"It is locked up," persisted Bruff. "The key's hanging in my pantry."

"I did not notice the door as I went by it," began Sophie, in explanation, "and my belief is, that it was then shut; otherwise I should never have had courage to go by it, and upstairs into the rooms by myself. But when I came back there, it was ajar. My patience! didn't I scutter on to you, my legs shaking as if they'd drop."

"Of all fanciful creatures, Mam'selle Sophie's the worst,—seeing ghosts where there are none," testily exclaimed the butler, who had a prejudice against jokes or tales being passed on the death-room. "The door's no more open than this door's open; and, to convince you, I'll go to my pantry and get the key."

He opened the door as he spoke and departed. Sophie nodding her head after him in scornful incredulity.

"If he finds the key there, I'll eat it," quoth she.

"Did you take the shawl to Lady Adelaide?" questioned the housekeeper.

"What should hinder me, when I went to do it?" returned the saucy Sophie. "My lady was asleep."

"Asleep!"

"Gone off right into a doze in the easy-chair. So I threw the shawl lightly on her knees, and came away."

"And my lord?" put in the valet, "was he asleep still?"

"For all I know. I didn't go as far as the bed. Little doubt that he was asleep, or else he'd have spoken."

At this moment Bruff returned, with a softened step and softened voice, his countenance wearing a look of perplexity.

"It's very odd," cried he, "the key's *not* in the pantry."

"So, it's Sophie that sees ghosts where there are none, and fancies doors open when they're not, and keys are in them when they're safe in their pantries!" retorted that demoiselle upon Bruff, in a tone of aggravation. "Perhaps if you go and look at the death-room, you'll find that it *is* open."

"I am going there," was the reply of Bruff. "That key is under my sole charge, and it is as much as a servant's place is worth, to take it from its hook. Whichever of them has dared to do it, shall pay the penalty."

"I wish you'd allow me to accompany you, Mr. Bruff," simpered Tiffle. "I have heard much of the death-room in Dane Castle, and have long had a curiosity to see it."

"There's nothing to see," returned Bruff; "it's a stone room, empty of furniture. But you are welcome to go, if you wish to."

"Will nobody else come?" asked Tiffle, looking round with a simper. "There's safety in numbers you know."

Example is contagious, and every one present rose to follow Tiffle and Bruff, even the scared Sophie.

Sophie was right. The door of the death-room was open—ajar, as she had termed it—and the key in the lock. But not a soul was inside the chamber. Bruff was ready to explode with indignation; that one or more of the under servants had surreptitiously obtained the key, either from the mischievous motive of annoying him, or to awaken superstitious alarm in the castle, he had no doubt, and he determined, if possible, to pounce upon the offenders.

"Why, it's nothing but a big, square dreary room, with high windows, and nothing in it!" ejaculated Tiffle, ranging her eyes around in disappointment.

"I told you there was nothing in it," said the butler. "What did you expect to see?"

Perhaps Tiffle had expected to see something in the middle, upon trestles, for she looked vexed and sour.

"I wouldn't mind going by this here room fifty times over, when the bell was tolling midnight," cried she, with a contemptuous glance at Sophie. "There's nothing here to squawk at. Where does that place lead to?"

"That's a closet," said the butler.

"What's inside of it?" demanded Tiffle.

"A pair of trestles," he replied, in a low tone.

"Oh! Could we have a look at 'em?"

"No, Mrs. Tiffle," he gravely answered. "That closet is never opened but when—when it's needful to open it."

"Well, it's a nasty, cold, dismal place!" retorted Tiffle, "not worth the coming to see. And how damp the floor is!"

The last remark caused them all to cast their eyes downwards, upon the flags. They were damp in places; capriciously damp, one might feel inclined to say; quite wet in parts, quite dry in others.

"What sort of flooring d'ye call this?" inquired Tiffle, when her eyes had taken in the effect. "Some stones give with the damp, and some don't, that is well known, but here the same stone—lots of 'em—is half wet and half dry. And whoever saw flags damp on a hot summer's night, with the weather set in for a regular drought?"

No reply was made to Tiffle. The servants were looking on the floor in ominous dismay, for the superstition relating to it was rife among them.

"It's a sign that this room won't be long without a tenant," whispered the ever-ready Sophie. "My Lord—"

"We have had quite enough nonsense for one night, mam'selle," interposed the butler, taking her sharply up. "My lord's better, and I hope he'll live many a month yet."

"I hope he will," returned the persistent Sophie. "But I have heard the Danes themselves say that this floor doesn't go damp for nothing. Ill-luck seems to be upon the family this year. After the captain and Mr. Geoffry went, I said there'd be another death, making the third—"

"And there was another,—my lady's," broke in the irritated butler. "And according to your theory, there it ought to stop. Pray what version would you give us should a fourth take place?" he cynically added.

"A fourth," debated Sophie, "well, I should say, if a fourth takes place, it would go on then to six; three and three. But death generally stops with the third."

A smile went round at Sophie's "three and three," but the butler did not vouchsafe further reply. Ravens-bird had taken no part in the conversation; his attention had been fully occupied with the apartment.

"I never was here before," he remarked; "and yet the room seems familiar to me. Where, how, and when can I have seen it."

"In a dream, perhaps," suggested Tiffle. "Strange things do come to us in dreams."

There was nothing attractive in the room to detain them, now that their curiosity was gratified, and they filed out of it. Mr. Bruff locked the door, and took possession of the key, with an air which seemed to promise that it did not get out of his keeping again. As he turned from the door, the others being by that time nearly at the end of the long passage, he saw something white gliding swiftly down it. To his intense surprise, he recognized Lady Adelaide. Her face wore a gray hue, and she positively laid hold of Bruff's arm, as if impelled by fear.

"Bruff! Bruff! something's the matter with Lord Dane," she shivered, "He looks—he looks—I don't know how he looks."

"Oh, my lady! you should not have given yourself this trouble. Why did you not ring?"

"I was frightened to remain alone," she whispered. "I dropped asleep, and when I woke, I rose to look at Lord Dane, wondering that he had not spoken or called. He was lying with his mouth open, and his face white and cold; its look terrified me."

"Perhaps he has fainted, my lady. He did have fainting-fits at the commencement of his illness."

"Bruff," she gasped, bursting into tears of nervous agitation, "it—looks—like—death."

Plenty of attendants, male and female, were soon around Lord Dane's bedside, from within the castle or summoned from without. Mr. Wild, the surgeon; Geoffry Dane; and—he had heard the rumor accidentally—Mr. Apperly.

Lord Dane was dead. He had died quietly in his bed without stir or sign, while the Lady Adelaide was in his room, not four yards from him, unconsciously sleeping. She kept shivering as she stood there now with the rest, looking on.

"Can *nothing* be done?" demanded the petrified household of Mr. Wild.

"Nothing whatever. He has been gone some time. Don't you see that he is already becoming rigid? One comfort is, he went off in his sleep, and did not suffer. I have thought this might probably be the ending."

"Then I wonder you didn't tell him so, Wild," burst forth Mr. Apperly, in a hot tone of reproof. "It was only this very morning his lordship said to me that he was not a subject to go off like the snuff of a candle."

"And why should I tell him? He was prepared for death; he knew it was coming, was very near; wherefore tell him that it might be sudden at the last!"

"No, he was not prepared for death," returned the lawyer, in a heat; "not in one sense. He had not settled his affairs."

The announcement took all by surprise. He, Lord Dane, with his protracted illness, not to have settled his affairs! Geoffry Dane smiled incredulously.

"Mr. Apperly, you must be mistaken. My uncle made his will when he was first recovering from his accident."

"I know he did; I drew it up for him; but he had a wife and children then. After they were gone, that will was of little use, and it was canceled. The second will has been drawn up this fortnight past, waiting for the signature. Upon what chance pivots things turn!" broke off the lawyer. "His lordship sent for me this morning, and appointed this afternoon for the execution. Then, feeling fatigued, said he would put it off till eleven o'clock to-morrow. And now he is gone, and the will is worth so much waste paper!"

"Wanting the signature?"

"Wanting the signature," assented Mr. Apperly. "You will be the better for it," he added, looking at Geoffry Dane, " but others will be the worse. It's a dangerous habit, is procrastination ; I don't know any thing I dislike more."

"My lord, do you remain in the castle ?" inquired the housekeeper, as they were beginning to desert the chamber.

Some of them started and looked at her. They thought she spoke to the dead lord who lay there. But no : she was addressing Geoffry, now Lord, Dane.

"Yes," he replied ; "it will, I suppose, be better that I should."

Ere the words had well left his lips, his eyes fell on Lady Adelaide,—on her look of embarrassment and her glow of color.

"Not to-night, however," he added, turning to the housekeeper. "I will see about arrangements to-morrow."

In the corridor Adelaide encountered Mr. Lester, who had that instant arrived, Tiffle having carried home the news of Lord Dane's sudden death. Without allowing herself time for reflection, for thought, she spoke words that came uppermost in the impulse of the moment :

"What am I to do now ? where can I go ? I will not remain in the castle, now Geoffry Dane is its master."

"My dearest Adelaide, why this emotion ? In a few days you know that you will be leaving it for another home,—I hope a happier one."

"But for those few days?—I cannot be the guest of Geoffry Dane ! And how can the marriage take place, right upon Lord Dane's funeral ?" was her impulsive retort.

Mr. Lester paused before he spoke.

"There is one way, Adelaide, by which to solve the difficulty, if you will consent. Be mine to-morrow. We can be married in private in this drawing-room."

The proposition nearly took away what little sense Lady Adelaide at the moment possessed. She made no reply.

"The license, which I already have, is special, so on that score there will be no impediment," pleaded Mr. Lester. " Adelaide, my darling, let it be so ! Give me a legal right to protect you in this emergency. I know that Lord Dane, could he be a party to my petition, would urge it as strenuously as I am doing."

"But—to leave the place at this moment—to go on a marriage-journey while he is lying dead—what will the world say ?"

"We can dispense with the journey, Adelaide. You must quit this house and come to mine. See you not that it is the better—nay, almost the only plan to adopt, under the unhappy circumstances ?"

"Oh, I do not know ! It is so sudden—and I am too bewildered to give proper deliberation to it. Let it rest until morning ; I shall be more collected then."

As Geoffry Dane—Lord Dane from henceforth—was departing from the castle, there stepped forth Richard Ravensbird. It appeared as though he had waited outside for the purpose.

"I must ask your pardon for interrupting you, my lord, at such a moment, especially on business," he began.

"Well," said Lord Dane.

"And I should not have thought of doing so, but I find there's not an hour to be lost.—It's about the Sailor's Rest, my lord. John Mitchel has been announcing that he has agreed with Mr. Apperly for the lease, subject to the consent of Lord Dane. You are Lord Dane now, my lord."

There was a peculiar significance in the tone of Ravensbird as he spoke the concluding sentence ; a bold, independent, almost a demanding tone. Was it possible that Lord Dane failed to remark it ?

"And you think I can grant you the lease ?"

"Yes, my lord. And I hope you will."

"Enough, for to-night," curtly responded Lord Dane. "This is certainly not the moment for the discussion of business matters."

Ravensbird respectfully touched his hat, and strode away quietly towards Danesheld. Lord Dane also proceeded in the same direction, but at a slower pace. As he was turning towards his own house, he heard footsteps behind, and found they were Mr. Apperly's, who had remained in the castle a few minutes longer than himself.

"A dreadfully sad and sudden event, my lord!" cried the lawyer. "And to think that he should not have signed the will!"

"It has shocked me much," replied Lord Dane, turning upon him his pale face—unnaturally pale it looked in the starlight. "Although we could not expect him to be much longer with us."

"I shall require instruction from your lordship upon different points," returned Mr. Apperly. "When will it be convenient—"

"I shall be at the castle to-morrow at ten," interrupted Lord Dane. "Meet me there. And meanwhile, until I shall have gone into things, let any little business matters you may have in hand, relating to the estate, rest in abeyance. Granting leases, or any thing of that sort."

"Very good, my lord. Not that any thing much is in hand just now There's that trifling affair of the Sailor's Rest; Hawthorne and Mitchel both want it got over as speedily as pens can trace parchment. Lord Dane had no objection to Mitchel as its tenant; your lordship, I conclude, will have none."

"Lord Dane's death puts a stop to negotiations for the present," was the somewhat sharp answer. "Let every thing, I say, remain in abeyance."

Mr. Apperly nodded acquiescence, wished the new peer good-night, and left him. "He'll be a martinet, unless I am mistaken," was his parting thought.

It was dusk, and the following evening; nay, dark,—as dark as we get the summer nights, when ten o'clock is drawing on. Miss Bordillion was seated alone in the handsome drawing-room of Danesheld Hall, her head running upon many things. A shadow of relief—it would be wrong to call it hope—had arisen in her heart since she heard of Lord Dane's death, for she deemed that it would undoubtedly put the wedding off for some weeks, if not longer, and there was no immediate necessity to worry her poor sad brain over her own plans for the future.

She was interrupted by the approach of a carriage, which was coming hastily towards the hall. It surprised her: they were expecting no visitors, and it was an unusual hour for visitors to come, unexpected. As it swept round the drive, past the windows, she thought she recognized it for Mr. Lester's own chariot, and she wondered, for she had not observed him go out in it. One of the servants bustled in hurriedly, to light the chandelier, and the mantel-piece branches.

"Has your master been out?" she inquired of the man. "I thought he was at the castle."

"He has not been elsewhere, I believe, ma'am. This is him, coming from the castle, now."

The man retired. A few moments, and the door was thrown open by another servant, to give admission to Mr. Lester and Lady Adelaide. Miss Bordillion rose from her seat, gazing at Adelaide: had it been the Queen of England who entered, it could not have caused her more intense astonishment. She stood as one petrified.

"How do you do, Miss Bordillion?"

She held out her hand, while Mr. Lester was taking her shawl from her shoulders, and Margaret touched it mechanically, in utter amazement. Lady Adelaide wore an evening-dress of white silk, plain, save for a little lace on its body and sleeves, a pearl necklace, white gloves, and no bonnet. Round the plait of her hair behind, was a small wreath of flowers: had Miss Bordillion looked closely, she would have seen that they were orange-blossoms. But she was too bewildered to look or to think: why should Lady Adelaide have come there, then, in evening dress? Why should she have laid aside her deep mourning? The true cause never was so much as glanced at by the unhappy Margaret.

Lady Adelaide stood right under the rays of light from the chandelier, rays that but illumined her great beauty. Never had it been more radiant, for her cheeks were flushed to crimson, and her eyes were brilliant with excitement.

"It is scarcely fair to take the house by storm in this way, is it, Miss Bordillion? But I believe there was no help for it."

What Miss Bordillion answered, she never knew. Rarely had she been scared so entirely out of her self-possession.

"Would you like tea immediately, Adelaide?" interposed Mr. Lester.

"Oh, yes."

Margaret muttered some half-intelligible words about "telling the servants to bring it," and escaped from the room. But she had not quitted it above a minute when she remembered that there were sundry toys strewn on one of the sofas, which the children had left there when they went to bed, not particularly ornamental to a drawing-room: and she turned back to get them.

She opened the door softly, for she did not care that they should take notice of her re-entrance. The sofa was close at hand, and she thought she could scramble up the things, and escape again. But her footsteps were arrested on the very threshold. Mr. Lester stood with his back to her, his tall form, handsome in its strength, bending over another which he had gathered to him. Her flushed cheek lay on his breast, and he was murmuring endearing words: words of welcome to the house, they seemed, for their sense partially struck on Margaret's ear.

Forgetting the toys, closing the door still more softly than she had opened it, Margaret Bordillion sped away, her face gray and stony with its bitter agony. Turning an angle

of the hall, into a narrow passage, she met Tiffle, and the French maid, Sophie. Tiffle glanced out of her cunning eyes, and spoke abruptly.

"What ever's the matter, Miss Bordillion? You look as if you'd been shook in the mind. Are you ill, ma'am?"

Miss Bordillion rallied herself. "Ill! why should you think that? I am very well. Mr. Lester is asking for tea, Tiffle."

"To think of this happening as it has?" continued Tiffle, standing right in front of Miss Bordillion, so that the latter could not conveniently pass. "The house not properly set in order, nor any thing; but it's not my fault, as her ladyship must know. It's as much as we've been able to do to get her rooms ready for to-night—leastways, master's rooms, which is the same thing now."

"Has Lady Adelaide come here to remain the night?" hastily inquired Margaret, more bewildered, more at sea than ever. "Here! in Mr. Lester's house?"

"My lady's come for good, ma'am; come home," responded Tiffle, winking and blinking as if the lamp near her dazzled her eyes, though in reality never taking them off Miss Bordillion's changing countenance. "She and master have just been married in the grand saloon at the castle, and he has brought her home. Sophie's come with her."

The unhappy lady did not faint at the news. She only felt that her face grew more ghastly, and she took a step backward to the wall, and leaned against it.

"Yes," she constrained her dry lips to say, making a poor effort to smile on Sophie.

"You see, miss, my lord's death last night put things about so contrarily," spoke up that demoiselle. "The new lord takes up his abode at the castle to-day, and my lady preferred to leave it. The ceremony was to have taken place this afternoon, but the minister—or what you call your English priests—he was away, and could not be had till evening. She has been dressed as she now is since three o'clock, waiting for him. And they were not quite certain that he could be found before to-morrow.

"And that's what master must have meant, then, when he said he was not sure," resumed Tiffle to Miss Bordillion. "He came home—well, it must have been near four o'clock,—and told me about setting his own rooms in order; but I was to hold my tongue about it to everybody in the hall, he said, for he was not yet sure whether they would be required to-night, or not, for Lady Adelaide. Fancy, Mam'selle Sophie, the scuffle it put me and the housemaids in!"

Miss Bordillion succeeded in getting by, and gained her own chamber. "Married! married!" seemed to be perpetually ringing in her ears.

The next day, not by her own wish, indeed in express opposition to it, for she sat in her small sitting-room, and kept the children with her, Miss Bordillion encountered Lady Adelaide. She was whisking through the hall as swiftly as possible, when she came right upon her and Mr. Lester. Lady Adelaide wore no gloves now, and the wedding-ring was fully conspicuous, as her fair hand rested on the arm of her husband. She had resumed her deep-mourning attire.

"Well, Margaret!" gayly cried he. "Where have you been hiding all the morning?"

With as hurried a greeting as she could in politeness give, Miss Bordillion quitted them. But every hour she remained in that house would be prolonged torture, and ere the day was over a message was despatched to Mr. Lester—"Miss Bordillion requested five minutes' conversation with him."

He went up at once to her sitting-room, and she hurriedly, abruptly, unfolded to him her plans. She would hire of him that small house of his that was vacant, Cliff Cottage, if he would let it her; and there she would take up her abode with Edith. Major

Bordillion would be glad that she should take charge of her as a regular thing, and would pay her well. Perhaps he—Mr. Lester—would also let her have Maria: with this help and her own income she could maintain a home.

"Margaret, why?" he inquired. "What urgent motive can you have for thus flying from the hall? Will you not tell it me?"

Tell it him! The painful crimson suffused her face, and then left it pale as marble. Did he suspect the truth, as he gazed upon her emotion? It cannot be said; but an answering rush of red came into and dyed his own face, and he uttered not one other word of opposition to her departure.

Cliff Cottage was hastily arranged for occupation, and furnished; and Miss Bordillion, within a fortnight, had taken possession of it, with Edith and Maria. Her home was henceforth to be theirs—at any rate for the present—and she would superintend their education. Another removal—or, it may be more correct to say, change—took place in the same week, in regard to the tenancy of the Sailor's Rest. Hawthorne and his wife quitted it, and Richard Ravensbird entered upon it: for, very much to the surprise of the neighborhood, very much to the inward wrath of Mr. Apperly, who would have to refund the five-pound note, the new peer had accepted Ravensbird as tenant, and declined Mitchel.

"Much good Ravensbird would do in it: he'd got no wife!" was one of the dissatisfied comments, gratuitously offered by the busy neighborhood. "Who ever heard of an inn getting along without a missis in it?"

Ravensbird soon rendered nugatory that objection, though whether to satisfy the grumblers or to please himself did not appear. He constituted Sophie its mistress, by making her Mrs. Ravensbird; and Lady Adelaide Lester had to find another maid.

And for some few years after this period no particular changes took place; therefore we need not trace them step by step. After that, changes and events came thick enough.

CHAPTER XI.

SQUIRE LESTER'S HOUSEHOLD — WILFRED.

It was the beginning of September, and stormy weather. Never had a wilder or more ominous day been experienced than the one now passing; never did the sun set with a more angry or lurid glare; the trees were swayed to and fro, as though they could not long withstand the blast; the sea-gulls flew overhead, with their harsh screams; and the waves of the sea were tossing mountains-high in their turbulence,—signs that seemed to predict an awful night.

"They will catch it at sea, to-night!" exclaimed Mr. Lester, turning round from the dinner-table, on which the dessert had just been placed, and gazing from the window, as a gust stronger than any swept past.

"I wonder you could shoot in this wind," cried Lady Adelaide, languidly lifting her head, and speaking in a languid tone. "Did you have good sport?"

"Very bad, indeed: the wind, as you say, was against it. Dane, crack shot that he is, only bagged three brace: impossible to take aim with that whirling blast in one's eyes. I don't think I ever felt the wind so high; and the beating up against it has made me dead tired. More walnuts for you, young gentleman!"

"I thought the ponies would have gone over once, on the heights," returned Lady Adelaide. "Georgie, dear, I am sure you have eaten sufficient."

"I have only had a few, mamma," responded Master Georgie, who was sitting in state by Mr. Lester. "Give me some more, papa. And, Maria, just pass me a slice of that cake."

"Did you venture on the heights with the pony-carriage?" uttered Mr. Lester to his wife, as he dropped a walnut or two into the boy's plate. "Was that prudent, Adelaide, such a day as this?"

"I soon drove off them again, when I found what the wind was," laughed Lady Adelaide. "I did not want a summerset into the sea, ponies, and carriage, and all. You say you are dead tired," she continued, after a pause; "I fancy Ada must also be. What is she doing, Maria?"

Maria Lester looked hastily down at the child on her knee. When the nurse introduced the children, four of them, a few minutes back, Maria had taken up the youngest, Ada, a pretty little girl, between four and five. The child had dropped asleep with a piece of cake in her hands. It was the same Maria Lester whom you once saw a child herself; now twenty years of age.

"I will take her up-stairs," said Maria.

"But you have not finished, Maria."

"Thank you, papa; I do not require any thing more."

Maria Lester rose, and gently gathered the little girl in her arms, without awaking her. Mr. Lester began speaking to his wife again, before Maria was out of the room.

"Dane is coming in to tea, Adelaide."

"Dane! This evening?"

The words were few, but the tone in which they were spoken betrayed annoyance and vexation. Mr. Lester smiled.

"Adelaide, I fancy you have taken a prejudice against Lord Dane. What's the reason?"

Her beautiful face—beautiful it was, still—flushed crimson, but she disclaimed the accusation eagerly. Too eagerly, Mr. Lester might have thought, had he been a keen-sighted, or suspicious man.

"I taken a prejudice against Lord Dane!" she uttered. "What a strange idea! Why should you think that?"

"You seem to be annoyed at his visits, and to receive him coldly; for-

LADY ADELAIDE'S ARRIVAL AT DANESHELD HALL.—*See page 93.*

getting, I presume, that he is, so to say, a cousin, or connection of yours. I'm sure I don't wonder at his dropping in frequently, for he must find the castle dull."

"Have you any idea *why* he comes so frequently?" asked Lady Adelaide, bending over her plate.

"Not I," said Mr. Lester, "except that our house is gayer than his. What other motive should he have?"

"None, I dare say. It was a passing thought that crossed me."

"You are mysterious, Adelaide. Let us hear the thought."

"No," she laughed. "It is not intended for the public benefit."

Mr. Lester's brow contracted.

"Do you know, Adelaide, that you are sometimes capricious? You are so now."

"I suppose it is in my nature to be so, George. Don't look cross. When you married me, you married me with my faults and failings about me, remember."

Mr. Lester said no more. But the conversation left a sore impression behind it.

Maria Lester had proceeded upstairs with the little girl. The head-nurse sat in the nursery, with two more young children, one being undressed, the other crying on the carpet; there were six in all, and the eldest, George, was but nine years old.

"Look at this child, nurse! She fell asleep on my lap directly after you brought her down."

"Tiresome little monkey!" responded the nurse. "I can't undress her yet, for I must get these two off, first. Be so kind as to lay her down in the bassinet, miss."

"Where is Susan, this evening?" returned Maria.

"Oh—Susan!—what's the good of Susan for evening work?—I really beg your pardon, Miss Lester, for answering you like that," broke off the woman, as her recollection came to her, "but I am so put out with that Susan, and my temper gets so worried, that I forget who I'm speaking to. The minute the children are

gone in to dessert, Susan thinks her time is her own, and off she goes, and will be away for two mortal hours, leaving me every thing to do. I can't leave the nursery and go after her, and I may ring and ring forever, before she'll answer it."

"Where does she go?"

"Chattering with the other servants, or gallivanting somewhere. I ought to have full control over Susan, miss, for she's under me, and I have no more over her, than I have over that wind, that's tearing round the house, as if it would tear it to pieces. I'd leave, if it were not that I am so fond of the children; I declare I would, Miss Lester."

"But, why do you not speak to mamma?"

"Oh, miss, it's that that puts me out. My lady won't hear a word against Susan, just because she's Tiffle's niece. Tiffle speaks up for Susan, as is natural, and Susan vows through thick and thin to my lady, that she's always at her post, doing her duty, and my lady believes her. The fact is, miss," continued the servant, lowering her voice, "Tiffle has managed to get the ear of my lady, and if an angel from the skies came down to try to put her off it, he couldn't do it." ·

"At any rate, Susan is not at her duty now," remarked Miss Lester, ringing the bell.

It was not answered; but in truth Maria scarcely gave time for it. She rang again immediately, a sharp, imperative peal. Of all the household, who should condescend to come up, but Tiffle!

"What's the good of your ringing like that, as if you'd have the bell down?" began she, before she had gained the room. "I won't allow—"

"It was I who rang," curtly interrupted Miss Lester. "I rang for Susan."

Tiffle stood and held her tongue, somewhat taken aback. Her manner smoothed down to meekness; false as as it was subtle.

"For Susan, miss! Does nurse want her? I have just sent her out to do a little errand for me, thinking the young ladies and gentlemen were in the dining-parlor, and that she couldn't be required in the nursery. I'll send her up the moment she comes in, miss."

"You see that she is wanted, Tiffle," gravely replied Miss Lester. "Here are three children, all requiring to be undressed at once, and it is impossible for one pair of hands to do it. Nurse tells me that Susan makes a point of being away at this hour; now, I think, you ought to speak to Susan, and order her to be more attentive to her duty. I shall speak to Lady Adelaide."

"Begging your parding, miss, there's no necessity for that, and it'll do no good; my lady has inlimited confidence in me and in Susan."

"That may be, Tiffle, but it is right she should know that the children are neglected. Send Ann here to assist the nurse until Susan shall return."

The tone was imperative. Maria, gentle and mild as she was, yet possessed that quiet, nameless power of command which few care to resist. Tiffle stood aside as she left the room, and then Tiffle shuffled on in her wake, her eyes glancing evil.

Tiffle had played her cards well. When she found that Lady Adelaide was to be her master's wife, her first thought was resentment; her intention, to depart forthwith. But when Lady Adelaide came home in the unexpected manner related, and Tiffle found that she was the hall's bona fide mistress—*Tiffle's* mistress — a mistress endowed with very different power from that invested in Miss Bordillion—then, to use a popular phrase, Tiffle began to find out on which side her bread was buttered. Lady Adelaide was young, careless, yielding, and inexperienced, and it dawned over Tiffle's mind that she might possibly still sway the household, and perhaps sway her mistress also; so Tiffle swallowed her anger, and stopped on. She felt in a rage with everybody (she generally did), and did not much care where she vented it. However,

she took care to make herself useful and agreeable to Lady Adelaide, and when Sophie quitted the hall, to become the wife of Richard Ravensbird. Tiffle succeeded her as the lady's maid, retaining also her post of housekeeper. Years had gone on since then—ten years—and how Tiffle had contrived it, was best known to herself, but she had wormed herself into the confidence of her mistress, and appeared indispensable to her comfort.

Maria passed into her chamber, and stood before the large cheval-glass while she dressed herself for walking, doing it in a hurried manner, as though she feared being stopped or interrupted. Rarely has a glass given back a sweeter-looking countenance, though it may have done one of more strict beauty. Her features were delicate and clearly defined, the cheeks wearing a healthy, damask flush, and she had soft, dark eyes, and silky hair. She was of middle height, or nearly so, of elegant figure, and in manner quiet and graceful. A truly attractive girl was Maria Lester, and gossips premised that she would be marrying early.

Ah, but there were two words to that. Some years before, when Maria was a young child, a relative of her mother's had bequeathed to her fourteen thousand pounds; but it was so left that the interest was to be enjoyed by Mr. Lester until Maria married,—not until she was of age, nothing was said about that, but until she married. So that, did Maria remain single till she was an old maid, and her father still lived, he would reap the entire benefit: she, none. This money was out on mortgage, at excellent interest, and it brought in Mr. Lester nine hundred a year. For an embarrassed man—and Mr. Lester was that now, for Lady Adelaide's extravagance and his own weak indulgence to it had rendered him so—nine hundred a-year was an enormous sum to relinquish. Mr. Lester was not a man of large income; his rent-roll produced barely three thousand a-year. This money of Maria's made it nearly four, and then it was all told; and they lived at the rate of five. Some thousands, bequeathed to Lady Adelaide by the late Lord Dane, had been spent long ago; altogether, Mr. Lester was now a man of deep perplexity and care; though, how deep, the neighbors little suspected. Be you very sure that, under such circumstances, neither he nor his wife would be in a hurry to encourage any marriage for Maria. She had only been home about a twelvemonth; that is, to reside; until then, she had remained with Miss Bordillion.

And what of Wilfred Lester? A great deal, and most of it very sad, very blamable. Wilfred was becoming, people feared, one of the black sheep of the neighborhood; and yet, he was of that unfortunate class who may be said to be as much sinned against as sinning.

At a proper age, a commission had been purchased for him in one of the crack regiments,—those whose duty seems chiefly to consist in attending upon her Majesty on state occasions. To the initiated in these matters, it is known that the expenses of such officers are enormous; almost necessarily so. Not rendered necessary by the nature of the service, or the rules of the regiment, but by that all-powerful incubus, custom—example, the doing as others do. The pay of one of these officers, compared to his expenditure, is but as a drop of water to the ocean; most of them are men of rank, possessing a weighty paternal purse to back them, and those who do not possess one in reserve, have no business to join, for they are certain to come to grief. Mr. Lester ought to have remembered this,—to have remembered how very little he could afford to allow his son.

He did not, and Wilfred entered. Careless, good-natured, attractive, and remarkably handsome, he was just the one to be made much of by his brother-officers; never was there a young fellow more popular in the corps than Cornet Lester; and—it is of no use to mince the matter—never was there one who ran more heedlessly into extravagance.

Example is contagious, and Cornet Lester suffered himself to be swayed by it,—swayed and ruined. Had Mr. Lester made him a better allowance (which, indeed, he ought to have done, or else not have placed him in the regiment), it would still have been swallowed up, though affairs might not have come to a crisis so soon as they did. Wilfred was just twenty-two when he came down to Danesheld, and laid the statement of affairs before his father. Money he must have, a large sum, or else leave the regiment.

Mr. Lester was unable to give it him. It is possible he felt that his son—his eldest son—had not been dealt with precisely as he ought to have been, and it caused him to be lenient now. Wilfred was in debt; dreadfully in debt. He could not return till at least some of it was liquidated, and what was to be done it was difficult to say. Mr. Lester was in worse debt himself, painfully short (he always was, now) of ready money, and could not assist him. One alternative indeed there was, and it was suggested by Mr. Lester, that Wilfred should sell out, and apply the proceeds of the purchase to the liquidation. Driven by pressing necessity, this alternative was ultimately adopted; but it was a cruel blow to Wilfred Lester. He saw his prospects cut off, his future blighted; and when things were finally settled, and he returned to take up his abode in his father's house, he felt like a blighted man, caring little what became of him. A sore feeling was at his heart; he knew that, but for his father's second family, for the high rate of expenditure kept up to please his father's second wife, *he* should not have suffered; and he regarded himself as a sort of sacrifice on the shrine of every thing that was unjust.

Lady Adelaide, on her part, regarded Wilfred as an unwelcome interloper. She had never liked him. Excited against him in the first instance by Tiffle (who had deemed it well that her lady's likings and dislikings should be regulated by her own), she had, even as a boy, made his home unpleasant to him, and when he returned for good, Lady Adelaide bore the infliction ill. A tacit, silent sort of antagonism was maintained between them, of which Lady Adelaide, from her position, of course obtained the best, and Tiffle did not fail to fan the flame. Wilfred occupied himself, listlessly enough, with out-door sports, hunting, shooting, fishing, as the seasons permitted, but he was devoured with ennui, and at length took to passing most of his evenings at Miss Bordillion's.

It was well he did so, at least, in one sense, for soon, very soon, the ennui was dissipated. The dispirited, listless young man, who had been ready to throw himself into the ponds instead of his fishing-line, and in truth cared little which of the two did go in, was suddenly aroused to life, and hope, and energy. Far from the present time hanging about his neck like a millstone, it became to him as a sunny Eden, tinged with the softest rapture. The dim, indistinct future, so dark, so visionless to his depressed view, suddenly broke from its clouds, and shone out in colors of the sweetest and rosiest hue,—for he had learnt to love Edith Bordillion. Not with the unstable, fleeting nature of man's general love, but with a pure, powerful, all-absorbing passion, akin to that felt by woman.

A few months given to dreamy happiness, and then he spoke to Mr. Lester. The appeal perplexed Mr. Lester uncommonly. He could have no objection to Edith; she was of as good family as his son (it may almost be said, of the same), and there was no doubt she would inherit a snug fortune at the colonel's death, for she was his only child. Colonel Bordillion had been in India now for many years, spending little, and making money. What perplexed Mr. Lester was *his* share in the affair. Wilfred, in his eagerness, protested they could live upon nothing,—as good as nothing. He did not wish to cripple his father; let him allow them ever so small an income, and they would make it suffice. Edith said they would. Mr. Lester pointed out to Wilfred that what he *could* allow would be very small indeed, but if the colonel would come forward with present help to Edith, he would add what he was able to spare. These statements were drawn out, and particulars written to Colonel Bordillion.

The only one who protested against the match, was Lady Adelaide Lester. Not openly: in private, to her husband. It was the most imprudent thing she ever met with. What did a young fellow like Wilfred want to marry for? Better get him an appointment under government, or despatch him somewhere abroad. Mr. Lester listened, and inquired why. They were bent upon marrying, he said. Edith was a very nice girl, and if they would be contented to make a moderate income suffice, they might as well marry. *He* could give but little; but the colonel would most likely come down with four or five hundred a year.

"Suppose he should refuse to come down with any thing?" returned Lady Adelaide.

"Then the affair would be at an end," emphatically replied Mr. Lester. "In that case, I would never give my consent."

Meanwhile, Wilfred and Edith lived on, looking forward to the answer of the colonel, and reveling in the golden visions of dream-land. Are such ever realized? I never knew them to be. In due course the reply of the colonel came. It was addressed to Wilfred, and inclosed a short note for Edith.

Have you ever passed from the broad light of day into the gloomy darkness of a subterranean dungeon? If so, you may remember the utter chill that seemed to overwhelm your feelings, both mental and bodily. Just so did the news from India plunge its recipients from the sunny brightness of expectancy, to the blackness of despair; but, whatever your own experience of a chill may have been, it was as nothing compared to that which shivered the frames and hearts of Wilfred Lester and Edith Bordillion.

The colonel would have been delighted with the union, and cordially given them his blessing ; nay, he gave it them still, should it be carried out; but of help, of money, he had none to give. The Calcutta Bank, the one in which he had hoarded the savings of years, no inconsiderable sum, had just gone smash, and left him penniless. The public newspapers would supply them with details.

Wilfred put up the letter, and sat on, buried in a gloomy reverie : Edith sat opposite to him, not weeping, but looking much inclined for it.' The letter had come in by the evening's post addressed to him at Miss Bordillion's, and it happened that they had received it alone, for that lady was out.

"I have decided what we must do," Wilfred said, after a while. "Edith, you were—you are—to be my wife ; will you be guided by me in this business ?"

"Of course I will," she answered.

"And you would not like—after all our fond hopes and plans—that we should be separated forever ?"

A passing shiver, and a faint answer.

"No, I should not."

"Then, my darling, before this week is over, you must be mine."

She looked up with a start of surprise, thinking he was jesting.

We must be married privately, and declare the fact after it is over. Otherwise nothing in the world will prevent their separating us : I foresee it. Don't look scared, Edith ; it will all come right in the end. Say nothing yet about this news."

"But how are we to live ?"

"My father, when he knows we are married, will allow us something, and we must economize till brighter days turn up. Shall you be afraid of it ?"

"Not of the economizing. But—"

Wilfred stopped her : he deemed it more politic to drown objections than to combat them. And he managed, wonderful to say, to obtain her consent to the plan.

It was strange that he should be able to do so ; but far more strange was it, that Tiffle obtained an inkling of what was going forward. She poked, she pried, she ferreted ; it was her daily habit; and in ordinary cases no wonder that she succeeded in unearthing secrets, though how she managed to scent this one, was in truth a marvel. The very day before that fixed for uniting them—and no soul knew of it, as they believed, but themselves—Tiffle went mincing into Lady Adelaide's room, her hands meekly folded, and the whites of her eyes turned up.

"Oh, my lady! such dreadful inhiquerty that has come to my knowledge ! I have been turned upside down to think how you and dear master's being deceived."

"What is the matter now ?" asked Lady Adelaide.

"Them two mean-spirited weasils are going to get married on the sly. I mean Mr. Wilfred and his sweetheart," added Tiffle, perceiving her lady's puzzled look. "Without saying a syllable, or letting any soul know it, my lady, they are going to ignite themselves together in secret till death do them part."

"But why in secret ?" demanded the amazed Lady Adelaide. "They are to be married when news arrives from the colonel, and it is expected daily. There is no motive, no inducement for them to do in secret what they may soon do openly. You must have found a mare's nest for once, Tiffle."

"My lady—craving your parding—are the nestesses I find ever mare's nestesses?" responded Tiffle. "I know my place, and what's due to your ladyship too well, I hope, to bring you tales of news that could turn into mare's nestesses. They have got quite motive enough—let them alone for that : and the motive is, my lady, that they *have* heard from Injia, and the colonel can't help them by as much as a shilling a year, for he has lost every ioter of his fortune. The place where it was kept has gone bankript, my lady."

"Is this true?" uttered Lady Adelaide.

"It's gospial true," returned Tiffle. "And, those two sly ones, thinking there's no chance now of Mr. Lester's consint, are going to take French leave, and marry without it. I can't quite come at the precise time it's to be, but I'm sure many days won't go over first."

"How did you come at it at all?" interrupted Lady Adelaide. "How do you come at things?"

Tiffle's countenance became very innocent.

"I keep my eyes and ears open, my lady."

"You must listen at doors, and behind hedges, Tiffle."

"My lady, whatever I do, it's out of regard to your ladyship,—that you should not be hoodwinked by designing serpints. And I tell you for a truth, and you may believe me with conferdince, that he's going to convert that girl into Mrs. Wilfred."

Lady Adelaide laughed,—a laugh that sounded more like derision than mirth.

"That is soon stopped," she said. "Give me that shawl, Tiffle."

She was throwing a shawl over her shoulders, to proceed to the dressing-room of Mr. Lester—for he, like herself, was dressing for dinner,—when Tiffle placed herself in her way, and spoke demurely:

"If I might venture to segest to you, my lady, I'd just let 'em do it, and I'd not stop 'em. If it comes to Mr. Wilfred begging consent of his father, there's no answering but he may get it, and a yearly allowince with it. But when master finds out that they have gone and done it of themselves, in defiance of him, as may be said, then the fat 'll be in the fire. Master won't look at 'em, or give 'em a farthing, and it 'll be exactly what they deserve."

Lady Adelaide, it must be presumed, found this advice good, for she kept the tidings to herself, and let things take their course. The consequence was precisely what Tiffle had sug-gested. Wilfred married, and — to borrow her own words—the fat was in the fire. In no measured degree, either. Wilfred purposed telling his father in the course of a few days after the event, but Lady Adelaide forestalled him, and her manner of imparting the news was in the highest degree calculated to anger and inflame Mr. Lester. A furious interview succeeded between father and son. And Mr. Lester cast him off, declaring that he should never have assistance from him during his own life, nor would he leave it him after death.

"And that's glorious news," cried Tiffle, to her mistress; "worth a choris of hallclugiers. It's your ladyship's own dear child, Master George, that will inherit, as is but right he should."

"Nonsense, Tiffle!" But Tiffle saw the beaming look of satisfaction which, in spite of the "nonsense," overspread the features of Lady Adelaide at the suggestion.

Months had elapsed now since the marriage, nearly twelve, which brings us again to the present, and to Maria Lester dressing herself for her evening walk. As she turned from the glass, she stood for a moment at the window contemplating the weather, listening to the howling wind.

"It is certainly an unusually boisterous evening," she soliloquized, "but I would rather encounter it than remain at home to meet Lord Dane." With that, she descended to the hall, and as she crossed it she addressed a man-servant :—"James, should I be inquired for in the drawing-room, say that I have gone to take tea with Miss Bordillion.

CHAPTER XII.

SHAD.

SCARCELY had Lady Adelaide reached the drawing-room, Mr. Lester lingering still at the dessert-table, when Lord Dane was announced. He had altered far more than Lady Adelaide. Could it be, that that tall, stern man, with the gray hair mixing with his luxuriant locks, was the former slender stripling, Geoffry Herbert Dane? His age was but eight-and thirty yet, but he looked older than his years. Handsome he was still, and handsome he ever would be, for he had the prominent, well-shaped features of the Dane family, but there was a fixed expression of care upon his brow. High in position, wealthy in means, possessed of all the extraneous accessories to make life happy, one might wonder how the care got there,—like the flies in amber.

Lady Adelaide stood in her evening-dress of white brocaded silk, jewels in her hair, on her neck, on her fair arms. Highly extravagant was she in her attire, as the family income knew to its cost; but dress she would, and dress she did. As Lord Dane greeted her, he could not help thinking how little she was changed; charming and attractive did she look, almost as much so as when she was his young love.

"What a terrible night!" she exclaimed.

"Yes, it is blowing great guns," replied Lord Dane. "I hope there will be no disasters at sea."

"Did you come on foot?"

"On foot! This little way! oh, yes," he laughed.

"Nay, not for the distance," she said. "I was thinking of the weather."

"I have become inured to that, whatever it may be : my nine year's travel did that good service for me."

"I cannot imagine what attraction you could have found, to keep you so many years. And you never remained long in one place, you say."

"No. I went everywhere, everywhere in Europe, not out of it. By the way, though, yes, I did go out of it, for I explored Turkey in Asia."

"And your attraction, I ask, Lord Dane?"

"I had none. The very restlessness would imply the want of that.

I have found that since my return. It is here, at home."

She lifted her eyes inquiringly towards his.

"An attraction that, when a consciousness first dawned over my spirit, I strove to combat; but the more I strove, the less would it take its departure. I believe I have no resources but to yield to it. Adelaide,—forgive me, that I speak to you in the familiar terms of former years,—will you be my advocate? will you hear me with favor?"

He spoke in the low, tender tone that had once been as the sweetest music to her ear,—he took her hand in his pleading earnestness. Will you excuse Lady Adelaide for the error she fell into? remembering old days, it was perhaps a natural one. She thought he was pleading for *her* favor : not for her influence with another. A crimson blush overspread her face ; but it was succeeded by a deadly paleness.

"Have you forgotten who I am?" she asked, in a low, proud tone, not so much in resentment, but as though she thought he really had forgotten it. "You forget yourself, Lord Dane : I am the wife of Mr. Lester; the mother of his children."

Lord Dane released her hand, and broke out into a half laugh : its derision was not so wholly suppressed, but that it jarred on the ear of Lady Adelaide.

"You threw me away when you married Mr. Lester, Lady Adelaide, and I fully understood that I was thrown away forever : I have not allowed myself to contemplate it in any other aspect. I ask you ten thousand pardons for having expressed myself badly, which I conclude I must have done. The attraction I alluded to, as drawing me to this house, is Maria Lester."

A burning, passionate suffusion of shame dyed the brow of Lady Adelaide. Never did woman fall into a more awkward or humiliating error. She could have struck herself; she could have struck Lord Dane : she opened her lips to speak, but no appropriate words would come—none that would not make the matter worse. That Lord Dane should enjoy her confusion was but natural: perhaps he felt half repaid for what she had made him suffer in days gone by.

"I have led a roving life long enough," he continued, in a calm, matter-of-course tone, assumed possibly to put her at ease; "and it is time I settled down. I did not think it could have escaped your observation that I have been striving to win Miss Lester. I never met with any one I so thoroughly esteemed," he emphatically added; "and my motive in speaking to you is, to crave your influence with Mr. Lester that he will allow me to make her Lady Dane."

That Lord Dane had been marked in his attention to Maria had certainly not eluded the observation of Lady Adelaide, and a suspicion had crossed her mind that it might bear a serious meaning: this had been in her thoughts that very evening, when she had, somewhat mysteriously, inquired of Mr. Lester whether he had any idea why Lord Dane came so frequently. How was it, then, that she had forgotten this, and jumped to that other idea, touching herself? Her face burnt still. But she essayed to turn it off defiantly, and threw back her head with a haughty gesture.

"Why do you not apply to Mr. Lester yourself, Lord Dane?"

"Because I prefer to apply, in the first instance, to you," he answered, in a courteous tone, as he took a seat near her. "I would ask it of your kindness to intercede with Mr. Lester. It has been told to me that he will not regard favorably any suitor for his daughter."

What was Lady Adelaide to reply to this? Mr. Lester would have no objection in the abstract to Maria's marrying; Lady Adelaide, on her part, would have been glad to see the day that removed her from the hall; but what they both did object to, and would find most inconvenient, was the resigning nine hundred a year. In short, they were unable to resign it, and the only alternative was, to keep Maria. Lord Dane, however, could dive into motives as quickly as most men, and he had formed his resolution.

"I scarcely need mention that, in seeking Miss Lester for my wife, I seek but her," he resumed. "There is, it occurs to me that I have heard, some trifling, paltry income that was bequeathed to go with Maria when she marries, but the large revenues of the Dane estate, the settlements I am enabled to offer, preclude the necessity of her bringing money to add to them. Will you, dear Lady Adelaide, tell Mr. Lester that I wish to take Maria alone; that any little fortune of hers, I shall beg him to retain."

"But why not tell him yourself?" repeated Lady Adelaide in a far more gracious tone.

"Mr. Lester is a man sensitive on pecuniary matters," smiled Lord Dane, "and will receive that part of the communication better from you than from me. Legal arrangements, of course, can be called in, to bind the bargain. May I count upon your interest with Maria?"

Some stifling weight seemed to oppress her, and she made no immediate reply. She rose from her seat, in agitation that she could not wholly hide, walked to the window, and drawing aside the blind, stood looking out on the boisterous night. Lord Dane watched her. Was her strange manner caused by any lingering tenderness for him on her own part? He could not think that; but he wondered, and he fell to speculating on its cause. Lady Adelaide came back, and interrupted him.

"I prefer to remain neutral in this affair, Lord Dane," she said. "I will not second your efforts to gain Miss Lester, but I will not impede them. All I can do is to repeat to Mr. Lester, impartially, what you have said, and then the matter must progress, or the contrary, unbiased, uninterfered with by me."

"You will not be against me with Maria?"

"I have said I will not. I shall remain wholly and entirely neutral."

Lord Dane bowed.

"She is at home, I presume."

"Yes," replied Lady Adelaide, ringing the bell. "Tell Miss Lester that the tea is coming in," she said, to the man who answered it.

"Miss Lester is gone out, my lady."

"Out! This turbulent night!"

"She has been gone this half-hour, my lady. She is taking tea at Miss Bordillion's."

"Maria does do things that nobody else would think of," observed Lady Adelaide to Lord Dane, and at that moment Mr. Lester entered.

And now to follow Maria. As she sped along from the hall, the wind nearly took her off her feet, but she kept up bravely, and laughed as she laid hold of objects to steady herself by. By the road, Miss Bordillion's house was about ten-minutes' walk from her own house; but there was a path through the wood, half as long again: a quarter of an hour say, it would take her that way, and Maria chose it as being the most sheltered.

The shades of evening were drawing on apace, and the wood struck a gloom upon her as she turned into it. There the wind did not impede her; though, as it moaned and shrieked overhead, and shook the trees to their very centre, imparting a weird-like, ghastly loneliness to the scene, Maria began thinking of the supernatural stories she had read of the old German forests; and as some object suddenly struck out from the trees, and stood in her path, she positively could not suppress a scream. The next moment, however, she was laughing.

"How stupid I am; But you should not have startled me, Wilfred."

A tall, slender young man of four-and-twenty, wearing a shooting-coat, and carrying a gun in his hand. His face was almost delicately beautiful, and his dark-blue eyes, deeply set, were shaded by long, black lashes. His forehead was broad and white, and his hair was black, like the lashes. Such was Wilfred Lester.

"I did not intend to startle you, Maria: who was to think you would be in the wood to-night?" he said as he turned to walk beside her. "Where are you off to?"

"Miss Bordillion's. How—how—is Edith?" she added, with much hesitation.

"What! I suppose it is high treason even to inquire after her," returned he, noting the timid tone. "Have they forbidden you even her name? Come, Maria, confess; you can't say more than I guess; perhaps not so much."

"Something very like it," she replied.

"Of course. Perhaps they have interdicted your speaking to me, if we happen to meet?" he pursued.

"No, Wilfred. They have not done that yet."

"Yet! That's to be the next thing. I suppose you live in daily expectation of it."

"How are you getting on?" she returned, evading his question. "Is Edith better?"

"We are not getting on at all, Maria; unless going backwards is getting on. It's backwards with us, generally, and backwards with Edith."

"Is she not getting strong?"

"No, and she never will, and never can, while things are as they are. If there's justice in heaven—"

"Hush, Wilfred! It will do no good."

"And no harm—but have it as you like. You have not answered my question, Maria. I say you live in expectation of an order to pass me when we meet. Is it not so?"

"Should it come, Wilfred, it will be partially your own fault."

"No doubt of it. I am all in fault, and they are all in the right. But I did not expect to hear *you* say it!"

"You are too petulant with me without a cause, Wilfred," she said, turning her kind face upon him full of anxious expression. "You know that I care for you more than I do for any one in the world. Even papa, I am not sure that I love and care for as I do for you," she added, in a tone of apology, "if it be not wicked to say it. But I have not seen much of him of late years, and—"

"And he has been so exclusively occupied with his lady-wife, with his children, to the neglect of us, that it would be little wonder if all your love for him had faded and died," interrupted Wilfred Lester. "Speak the truth out fearlessly, Maria. Do you deem that, under such circumstances, they have a right to forbid our intercourse? I speak of you and myself," he added, dashing his hair from his brow, "not of Edith."

"If they did forbid it, I am not sure that I should obey," she steadily answered. "I have debated the point with myself much lately, and I cannot tell what would be my course of action. I hope it will not be put to the proof. But I repeat that it will be partly your fault if it comes. What are these tales that are going about respecting you?" she asked, lowering her voice.

"Tales!" uttered Wilfred.

"That you are taking to ill-courses—to poaching for game and fish—to stealing out at night with evil men! Wilfred," she shivered, "you know of the attack on Lord Dane's keeper?"

"I should think all the world, for ten miles round, knew of that," returned he, carelessly. "Well?"

"They say that—that you were one of them, disguised."

"Oh, they do, do they! Give a dog a bad name, and hang him! I wonder they did not bring in my wife as well, and say she accompanied me. Who carried this precious news to you, Maria?"

"I don't know how it reached the hall; I was too sick and terrified to inquire; I have some idea it was through Tiffle,—that she communicated it to Lady Adelaide. Papa walked into his own room when it told him, and I saw him shaking like a leaf. Wilfred, I know you are forbidden the hall, but, accused of such

a crime, you should brave the mandate. Go into my father's presence and deny it,—that is, if you can deny it."

"If I can deny it! What do you mean, Maria? Do you think I go out by night to murder gamekeepers?"

"Then you will, for once, come to the hall and disclaim it," she eagerly said.

"No. If I did commit murder, it would be my father and his wife who have driven me to it; let them enjoy the doubt as they best may."

"But, Wilfred, is it true that you go out poaching!"

"I! poaching! How has your mind been thus poisoned against me? I have my game license."

"But they talk—they talk of gins and snares," she whispered; "of the entrapping game, wholesale, to—Wilfred! what's that?"

The hasty, startled tone in which the last words were uttered, caused Wilfred Lester to lift his head and peer around him. He saw nothing.

"There was some one watching us," she breathed. "There; where the trees are thick. How strange!"

"It must have been your fancy, Maria. Who would be likely to watch us? To what end?"

"I am quite certain it was not fancy. I saw a face bending towards us, trying, as it seemed, to hear what we were saying. I was not quite sure at first, and I looked steadfastly, and then it moved away. It seemed about the height of a boy, and it was like a boy's face. Wilfred, you need not doubt me."

Wilfred Lester strode to the spot indicated, and pressed through the trees. Not any creature was in sight, human or inhuman, but there was a narrow path striking off farther into the wood, favorable to escape.

"Some wandering thief of a youngster, come to hunt if there might be a stray partridge dropped," he remarked. "The sight of us has scared him away."

"What his motive may have been, or what he came for, I know not; but there he certainly was, and watching us," returned Maria.

They emerged from the wood. To the right lay the residence of Miss Bordillion; to the left, the little cottage inhabited by Wilfred Lester; the latter not many yards off, but an angle of the road hid it from view. As they stood, talking yet, before branching off on their separate paths, a very curious-looking lad came running past. Slim to a degree, with restless, wriggling movements, he was not unlike a serpent; he had that old, precocious face sometimes seen in the deformed, and sly, sly eyes. Not that he was deformed, only very stunted for his years, which were near fifteen. An ordinary spectator might have thought him ten.

"Hallo, Shad," cried Mr. Wilfred Lester, "where are you scuttering off to?"

The boy stopped. Rejoicing in the baptismal name of Shadrack, he had never, in the memory of the neighborhood, been called any thing but Shad. His other name nobody knew, and it did not clearly appear that he had one. Nearly fifteen years ago, he was first seen at the hut of old Goody Bean; she said he was her daughter's who had been many a year away from home; but Goody Bean was not renowned for veracity. To whomsoever he belonged, there he had been from the first day to this.

"Please, sir, I'm a going home; and I've been getting some sticks for granny."

He spoke more like a boy of ten than of his own years; but, looking at his sharp face, it might be doubted whether the simplicity was not put on. It was one of two things: that he was a very unsophisticated young gentleman, or else one of rare and admirable cunning.

"Have you been in the wood to get those, Shad?" demanded Miss Lester, looking at the few bits of faggots in the boy's hands.

"I've a been o'ny on tother side the hedge, miss; I doesn't like the wood, when the trees moans and shakes."

"Have you *not* been in the wood?" she returned, looking keenly at him.

"I was there yesterday, miss."

"I spoke of this evening."

"No," he said, shaking his head from side to side, something like the trees. "Granny telled me to go into the wood, and bring her a good bundle, but I wouldn't when I heard the wind; and I expec's a whacking for it."

He shambled off. Miss Lester turned to her brother. "Is he to be believed, or not? It may have been he who was watching us."

"Very likely. It is of no consequence if he was. As to believing him, I think he is even less worthy of credit than his grandmother; and that's saying a great deal. Why! what does *she* want?"

A decent-looking woman, with a sour face, was coming full pelt towards them from the direction of Wilfred's cottage, calling out as she ran, "Master! Master!"

Wilfred took a step forward to meet her.

"Is the house on fire?" quoth he.

"Sir," returned Sarah,—for that was the name she bore, and she was his servant,—"my mistress is lying like one dead; I'm not sure but she's gone."

A moment's bewildered hesitation, and he started off; but arrested his steps again, and turned to Maria:

"Will you not come, in the name of humanity? Your entering my house to say a word of comfort to Edith— dying as she may be, as I fear she is, for the want of countenance, of kindness—will not poison Mr. and Lady Adelaide Lester. Judge between me and them, Maria."

He waited for no answer, but sped on. The appeal was successful, and Maria followed with the maid.

Edith, who had been for some weeks in a very precarious state of health, had fallen on the floor in attempting to move from the sofa. Sarah heard the noise and ran in; her mistress looked so still and deathlike, for she had fainted, that the woman was frightened, and as speedily ran out again, hoping to get assistance; and in the road she saw her master. They lifted her up, and she revived; but she could not talk much to Maria. The latter, who had not seen her for many, many weeks, interdicted, as she was, from going near her brother and his wife, was shocked at the change, and surely thought she would not be long in this world.

"Sarah," she exclaimed to the servant, with whom she was alone a few moments, ere departing, "what a terribly weak state your mistress appears to be in! what can cause it?"

"It's just famine," bluntly returned the woman, "and nothing else."

Maria was shocked and bewildered at the answer, and could only stare at the speaker.

"*Famine!*" she uttered, feeling ready to faint, herself. "Oh, Sarah! things cannot be as bad as that with my brother!"

"They ain't much better, and haven't been for some time, so far as missis is concerned, Miss Lester. Me and master, we can eat hard food; bread-and-cheese, or bread-and-bacon, or a bit o' meat and a heap o' potatoes and onions made into a Irish stew, and we can wash it down with water and thrive upon it. But missis—she can't: she could no more swallow them things than she could swallow the saucepans and gridirons they're cooked in. When folks are delicate and weak in health, they require delicate food. Beef-tea, and jellies, and oysters, and a bit o' chicken, or a nice cut out of a joint of meat, with a glass or two of good wine every day; that's what Miss Edith wants. And she's just going into her grave for the want of it."

Maria turned from the door on her way to Miss Bordillion's, feeling that her brain was as a chaos. Suffering —dying, from want of proper food! Maria had never been brought into contact with these hard realities of life;

had never glanced at the possibility of their touching her own family.

Miss Bordillion—a gentle lady now, in a close cap and white hair, was surprised to see Maria come in. She had not expected her through such a wind, and, it was later than Maria's usual hour. No trace of the heart-conflict she had to do battle with for years, and to conquer, was discernible on her features—always excepting the hair: that had turned white before its time.

Maria threw off her shawl and bonnet, and sat down to the tea-table, in the middle of which meal she had disturbed Miss Bordillion. The latter rang the bell, and the maid brought in a cup and saucer.

"Some butter," said her mistress.

"You never were taking your tea without butter!" exclaimed Maria. "Eating dry toast!"

"It is well to abstain from butter sometimes, if we are bilious," said Miss Bordillion.

But Maria observed that she got quietly up, and, surreptitiously taking the sugar-basin from the sideboard, placed it upon the table. So that she was also abstaining from that—and Maria had never heard that sugar would do good or harm to bile. An inkling of the truth flashed over her.

"You are abstaining from motives of economy!" she said in a low tone.

Miss Bordillion would have smiled off the subject with a jest, but Maria was eager and persistent.

"Why should you treat me as a child, or a stranger?" she continued. "Dear Miss Bordillion, I have just been initiated into the necessities of one household; let me hear what is amiss in yours."

"You have mentioned the word, Maria—necessities," was the reply of Miss Bordillion. "My household and luxuries have nearly parted company. Since you and Edith left me, I have been thrown entirely upon my own income: and that, you know, is little more than a hundred a year."

"But, to go without sugar and butter !" repeated Maria, unable to lose sight of the phase of the question practically before her.

"No great deprivation to me," smiled Miss Bordillion. "And considering I do not pay rent for my house, which your father has never yet permitted me to do, I could make my income suffice for my moderate wants : but, alas, Maria I two families have to be kept out of it."

"Two !" uttered Maria.

"Can I see your brother and Edith starve ?"

Maria made no reply. Her heart was beating.

"How do you suppose they have lived ?" proceeded Miss Bordillion. "For a few months after their marriage, I remained very angry, and did not see them ; I thought it so imprudent, so unjustifiable a step to have taken, and I joined Mr. Lester in his blame. They were positively without resources, without any, and during that period they parted with all their trifling valuables, and also got in debt. Of course that stopped their credit ; that, and Mr. Lester's known displeasure—"

"The tradespeople might safely trust them," interrupted Maria. "Wilfred is my father's eldest son, and the estate will descend to him some time."

"Have you forgotten that the estate is not entailed ?" asked Miss Bordillion, striving to speak in a careless tone. "Not an acre of it need come to Wilfred, not a single shilling : he may find himself as penniless at his father's death, as he is now."

"Oh, Miss Bordillion I do not hint at any thing so unjust."

"A few weeks ago, Edith's baby was born, and died. She was very ill, and they sent for me. I deliberated whether or not to go ; my own heart was inclined to forgiveness, but I did not like to do what would displease Mr. Lester. However, I went. Apart from Edith's state, I found things very bad. The rent of the cottage was in arrear, and they had nothing What could I do, but help them ?"

"And you help them still ?"

"My dear, but for me, they would never have a meal. And all out of my poor little income. So don't wonder," she added, with an attempt at merriment, "that my butter and sugar are too costly to be approached lightly."

Maria fell into a most unpleasant reverie. She was revolving all she had heard and seen, all she feared. The part of the whole which she most shrank from, was the rumor touching the ill doings of her brother. Urged on by the necessities of home, of Edith, what might he not do.

"Have you heard the whispers about Wilfred ?" she asked, aloud, flying from her own thoughts. "That he—that he—has been seen out at night, on Lord Dane's lands ?"

"Hush !" interrupted Miss Bordillion, glancing round her with a tremor that seemed born of fear.

CHAPTER XIII.

AN AWFUL NIGHT—AND AN AWFUL SCENE.

RARELY had such a night been known within the memory of the oldest inhabitant of Danesheld. The storm of wind was terrific : now, it swept through the air with a rushing, booming sound ; now, it shook old gables and tall chimnies, unhinged shutters, and crushed down out-houses; and now it caused men and women to stagger as they strove to walk along. But for the wind, the night would have been nearly as bright as day, for the large, clear moon was at the full ; but the clouds that madly swept across its face obscured its brightness, causing a dark shadow to fall upon the earth. Even the fitful gusts, when clouds were absent, seemed to hide the moon's rays, and dim them.

A knot of men were congregated in the tap-room of the Sailor's Rest. Richard Ravensbird, looking not a day older than when you saw him last, hard, composed, phlegmatic as ever, was waiting on them, or joining in their converse, as the case might be. Sophie was in the bar-parlor. She did look older. Somehow, Frenchwomen, after they pass thirty, do age unaccountably. Not that Sophie had changed in manner; she was free of tongue and ready at repartee, like she always had been.

"How's Cattley getting on? Have ye heard?" asked one of the men of Ravensbird, taking his pipe from his mouth to speak.

Ravensbird had handed a fresh jug of ale to another of the company, and was counting the halfpence returned into his hand.

"Cattley may be better, or he may be worse, for all I know," returned he, when he had finished counting. "It's no concern of mine; I don't meddle with other folk's business."

"'Tain't much meddling, landlord, to hear whether an injured man's getting on his legs again, or whether he's a going to have 'em laid out stiff," retorted the questioner. "I ha' been at sea three days, and 'tis but natural to ask after a poor fellow as have been a'most murdered when one gets to shore again."

"A fine trouble your boat had, to get home," put in a man, before any one else could speak. "I was down the beach this afternoon, and see it a-laboring."

"Trouble!" echoed the other. "I never hardly was out in such a gale—and the wind blowing us right ashore. It took our best management, I can tell ye, to keep her off it. Does nobody know any thing of Cattley?"

"Cattley's better," answered one who sat in a corner. "I saw Mr. Bruff to-day, and asked him. He said he was going on all right. My lord's downright savage, though, because the fellows are off."

"What fellows!" cried the sailor in a quick tone. "Not Beecher and Tom Long?"

"Beecher and Tom Long. Cattley was well enough to be taken into the hall yesterday, from his bed: they wrapped him up in blankets, put him

in a chair, and carried him in; and Beecher and Tom Long were brought up from the guard-house in charge of the police. But Cattley couldn't swear to them: he said he had no moral doubt that they were the two, but could not speak to it with certainty. Of course that put a stop to all chance of conviction, and Lord Dane was obliged to liberate them. Such a lecture as he read them first!"

"Did he?"

"Bruff heard it. He was present during the time, close to my lord's chair, and he said his lordship was as vexed and snappish as could be. Old Beecher came forward, with all the brass in the world, and said he'd take an oath his son was in bed at home the night the row happened. Lord Dane told him his oaths went for nothing, and he regretted the evidence was not more conclusive."

"But there was a third, engaged in the attack," resumed the sailor.

"Said to be. Cattley speaks of another, who was watching from a short distance. He did not join in the attack."

"That was Drake, then; not a doubt on't. Smuggling or poaching, it all comes alike to him. I'll lay any money it was Drake."

"You'd lose it, then. The third fellow was a tall, thin man. Drake's short and stumpy. I say, landlord, what's your opinion of it all?"

"Haven't I just told you that I mind my own business?" returned Mr. Ravensbird. "If everybody did the same there'd be less contention in the world."

"Richard, Richard," a voice was heard calling out, "step here a moment."

It was that of Mrs. Ravensbird, and her husband proceeded to the room where she was sitting. She had a candle in her hand, and appeared as though she had just been up-stairs.

"I'm afraid, Richard," she said, "I protest I am: the very house seems to rock. I shall not go to bed to-night."

"Nonsense!" returned Richard Ra-

THE MEETING IN THE WOOD.—*See page 107.*

7

vensbird. "Folks sleep best in windy weather."

"If they can get to sleep. It's what I shan't try at to-night. You just go up to our bedroom, and see what the wind is there : the bed itself's shaking."

"They are calling for more ale in the tap-room," cried a very smart maid, entering at this juncture. "Am I to serve it, sir? The clock wants but two minutes of eleven."

"Oh, for goodness sake let them stop on as long as they like to-night," put in Sophie to her husband. "Better be in danger in company, than alone."

Richard Ravensbird looked at her in surprise.

"Danger!" he repeated : "why, what is the matter with you, Sophie? You are surely not turning coward, because the wind is a little higher than ordinary?"

"The wind is worse than I have ever known it since I lived in the Sailor's Rest," she responded. "It's awful enough to make the bravest think of danger."

Ravensbird returned to the tap-room, and told the company it was eleven o'clock. They did not, however, seem inclined to move : and, whether it was the wind howling without, which certainly does induce to the enjoyment of comfort within, or whether in compliance with his wife's words, Ravensbird proved less rigid than usual as to closing his house at eleven ; and suffered more ale to be drawn. The servant was bringing it in, when a fresh customer entered. It was Mitchel, the preventive-man. He took off an oil-skin cape he wore, and sat down.

"Why, Mitchel! is it the wind that has blown you here?" were the words Ravensbird greeted him with. "I thought you were on duty to-night."

"The wind won't let me stop on duty, Mr. Ravensbird, so it may be said to have blown me here," replied Mitchel. "I saw you were not closed through the chinks in the shutters. It's an awful night."

"Not much danger of a contraband boat-load stealing up to the beach to-night," laughed one of the company.

"No, the Flying Dutchman himself couldn't bring it up," said Mitchel. "What with the security from that sort of danger, and the non-security from another, namely, that we might get whirled off the heights into the sea, and be never more heard of, the supervisor called us off duty. What a sight the waves are, to be sure!"

"The men have not been on duty below all day."

"Couldn't have stood it," answered Mitchel, "the sea would have washed them away. It's great rubbish to keep men there at all, now they have put us on to the heights. I'm afraid of one thing," he added, lowering his voice.

"What's that?"

"That there's a ship in distress. My eyesight's uncommon good for a distance, as some of you know, and I feel sure that I made her out, and even her very lights. The worst was, the gusts whiffled one's sight, and steady for one minute, one couldn't stand. I pointed the ship out to Baker, when we met, but he could see nothing, and thought I was mistaken."

"But—if it is a ship—why do you assume that she must be in distress?" inquired Ravensbird.

"Could a ship be off the coast, in such a storm as this, and not be in distress?" was Mitchel's answer. "And the wind blowing dead inland! Mark me! if that is a ship, she'll be on the rocks to-night."

"Mitchel," cried one of the company, "you were always one of them given to croaking. And croaking don't help us on in the—"

The man's voice stopped abruptly, and the assembly simultaneously started to their feet. A heavy, booming sound had struck upon their ears. Mrs. Ravensbird rushed into the room.

"It is a cannon!" cried she.

If it was a cannon, it was firing off quick and sharp strokes, one after the other, as no cannon ever had been known to do yet. Some of those startled listeners had heard that sound before; some had not.

"It is the great bell at the castle!" uttered Mitchel, "I am sure of it. The last time it rang out, was for that fire in the stables, before the old lord died. What can be the matter?"

They moved in a body to the house door, and stood in the road outside, listening and looking. Though the Sailor's Rest stood alone, somewhat apart from any dwelling, they could see that the alarming sound had brought others to their doors, and night-capped heads to windows.

"The castle must be on fire," exclaimed one, drowning the chorus of voices: "we ought to set off to it."

"I wish you would all be still for an instant," interposed Ravensbird. "Listen: as keenly as the wind and that heavy bell will allow you."

They hushed their clamor and bent their ears in obedience to the injunction. And then they caught what the noise in the tap-room had prevented their hearing before: a minute-gun fired from the sea.

"It is the ship in distress," eagerly uttered Mitchel, "I knew she would be. She's signaling for help. And the castle-bell is giving notice of it; it used to in the old times."

Before they decided what to do, or whether to do any thing—some being for rushing off to the castle, others to the beach,—one of the footmen in the Dane livery, white and purple, came flying towards them.

"A large ship in distress!" he exclaimed. "We think she may be an Indiaman, with home-bound passengers. Is the sea too bad for help to go out?"

The man spoke in agitation; it is an agitating moment, when the lives of our fellow-creatures are at stake within sight. That the lives of those, now in danger, must inevitably be lost, appeared only too sure. Somebody inquired of the servant, what Lord Dane thought.

"My lord's not at home," was the man's reply. "Some of us fancied we heard signals of distress from sea; and we went up to the turret-chamber, and there made out the ship, and saw quite plainly the flash of her minute guns, though the wind deadened their sound. Mr. Bruff gave orders then for the alarm-bell to be rung, to arouse the village: first of all sending a messenger to my lord, that he might not fear it was any thing amiss at the castle itself."

"Is he far away?"

"Who? my lord? He is only spending the evening at Mr. Lester's."

The company got their caps, which they tied down firmly on their heads: those who possessed no caps tied on handkerchiefs, for their hats would be useless on the beach, and they left them at the Sailor's Rest, and hastened down. The news had spread. The ship, drifting gradually in shore with the wind, was nearer now, and her guns were louder; and all Danesheld was flocking towards the beach.

They could discern her very plainly in the snatches of bright moonlight— a noble ship. One old sailor, who possessed fine eyesight, keener than even Mitchel, professed to make out her build, and declared she was an American. Whatever she might be, she was certainly drifting on rapidly to her doom. She had probably been at anchor, and the chain had broken.

Her position was a little to their left hand as the people stood, and she would most likely strike just beyond the village, towards Dane Castle. The wind was as a hurricane, howling and shrieking, buffeting the spectators, and taking away almost their life's breath: the waves rose mountains high, with their hoarse roar; and the good ship cracked and groaned as she bent to their fury.

Oh! the scene on board!—could those watchers from the shore have witnessed it! Awful indeed seemed the jarring elements to them: what, then, must they have been, to those who were hopelessly in their power!

Reader, we may assume that it has never been your fate to be on board one of these ill-fated ships at the moment of its doom. No imagination, however vivid, can picture the awful bearings of the scene. Bewildering confusion, sickening distress, unbounded fear. Almost as terrible is it as that Great Day, pictured to us of what shall be the last judgment: for that Great Day, for them, is at hand—time is over—eternity is beginning—and all are not prepared to meet it !

Two gentlemen came together, arm-in-arm, and the crowd parted to give them place. They were Lord Dane and Mr. Lester. Mr. Lester carried a night-glass, but the wind would render it almost useless.

"Why, she's nearly close in shore !" uttered Lord Dane, in an accent of horror.

"Another half-hour, my lord, and she'll be upon the rocks," responded a bystander.

"Mercy ! how fast she's drifting ! One can see her drift !"

"My men," said Mr. Lester, addressing himself more particularly to the fishermen and sailors, many of whom had congregated there, "can nothing be done ?"

One unanimous, subdued sound was heard in answer: "No !"

"If one of 'em, any crack swimmer, could leave the ship, and come ashore with a hawser, that's their only chance," observed an old man. "Not that I think he'd succeed : the waves would swallow him long before he got to it."

"There's the life-boat," cried Lord Dane.

The crowd shook their heads with a smile.

"No life-boat could put off in such a sea as this !"

Never, perhaps, had been witnessed a more hopeless spectacle of prolonged agony. Once, twice, three times, a blue-light was burnt on board the ship, lighting up more distinctly than the moon had done her crowd on deck, some of whom were standing with outstretched hands. And yet those on shore could give no help. Men ran from the beach to the heights, and

from the heights to the beach, in painful, eager excitement; but they could do nothing.

On she came,—on, on, swiftly and surely. The night went on : the hurricane raged in its fury ; the waves roared and tossed in their terrific might ;—and the good ship came steadily to her doom. In two hours from the time that the castle-bell boomed out she struck ; and, simultaneously with the striking, many souls were washed overboard, and were battling their own poor might and strength with the water as hopelessly as the ship had done. The agonized shrieks of woe were borne over the waters with a shrill, wailing sound, and were echoed by the watchers : some of whom—women—fell on their knees in their nervous excitement, and prayed God to have mercy on the spirits of the drowning.

"She'll be in pieces ! she'll be in pieces ! and no earthly aid can save her !" was the cry that went up around.

As it was being uttered, another dashed into the heart of the throng,—one who appeared not yet to have been among the spectators. It was Wilfred Lester. He wore his sporting-clothes, as he had done when Maria met him in the evening. Pressing through it to the front with scant ceremony, he leaned his arms on the rails of the little jetty, and contemplated the beating vessel.

"Good heavens !" he uttered, after a few moments' steadfast gaze ; "she must have struck !"

"This five minutes ago !"

"What is that in the water ?" he continued, after another pause.

"Human beings drowning. They are being washed off the ship fast !"

All that Wilfred Lester possessed of excitement was aroused within him.

"Human beings drowning !" he repeated, his voice harsh with emotion. "And you are not attempting to rescue them ! Are you mad, or only wicked ?"

One by his side pointed to the foaming sea.

"Let that answer you."

"It is no answer," said Wilfred Lester. "Where's the life-boat?".

Mr. Lester drew away to hide himself amidst numbers: he had not cared lately to come in contact with his son. But Lord Dane pressed forward.

"You are excited, Lester," he observed to Wilfred; "and I acknowledge the sight is sufficient to excite the most stoical man on earth. You might as well talk of a balloon as a life-boat: the one could no more get to the ship than the other."

"The effort might be made," returned Wilfred, eagerly.

"And the lives of those making it sacrificed," rejoined Lord Dane.

Wilfred turned to where a knot of fishermen were congregated. He was familiar with them all, and had been from boyhood.

"Bill Gand, where's the life-boat?" he said, to a weather-beaten tar, who looked sixty at the least, to judge by the wrinkles on his face. "Is she ready?"

Bill Gand pointed with his finger to a small and snug creek at some little distance: he was not a man of fluent words. The life-boat was moored in the creek, and could be out at sea (wind and weather permitting) in a few minutes.

"Was made ready when the castle-bell tolled out, Master Wilfred," answered he.

"And why have you not put off in her?" demanded Wilfred, in a tone of command.

"Couldn't dare, sir. And the sea be higher now nor it was then."

"Couldn't dare!" scornfully echoed Wilfred Lester, whose anger, like that of the waves, seemed to be rising. "I never knew a British sailor could be a coward until now: I never thought 'couldn't dare' was in his vocabulary. I am going out in the life-boat: those of you who can overcome 'fear' had better come with me."

He turned to quit the spot and make for the creek, but fifty voices assailed him. "It would be sheer madness to attempt it." "Did he mean to throw away his life?" "He and the life-boat would be swamped together!"

"Then swamped we will be!" retorted Wilfred. "Do you see there?" he added, waving his hand in the direction of the ill-fated ship; "when your fellow-creatures' lives are being swamped wholesale, when you see them buffeting with the pitiless waves, does it become you to hesitate attempting their rescue 'for fear' yours should be?—and you brave seamen! Come on, my men! if there be any of you who deserve the name."

How contagious is example! How valuable a little sterling encouragement! How effective a spice of stinging ridicule! Several "good men and true," acted on by the words, declared themselves ready to man the life-boat; and pretty nearly the whole crowd trooped off in the wake of Wilfred Lester.

He was long of leg and fleet of foot, and was already busy with the boat when they gained him. A voice called out that if she must go out, Mr. Wilfred had best not be one to man her: he was no sailor. Wilfred Lester caught the words, and turned his handsome face towards the sound; very pale looked his features in the moonlight; pale, but resolute.

"Who said that?" he asked.

It was old Bill Gand.

"You are not yourself, Bill Gand, to-night. Would I urge others on a danger that I shrink from?"

"Venture in that there boat, Master Wilfred, and you wunna reach the ship alive," cried Bill, "let alone come back. Nor the rest, nor the boat neither."

"It is possible; but I think we may hope for a better result. We are embarking in a good cause, and God is over us."

The last words told; for, of all men, a sailor has the most implicit trust in God's mercy,—a simple, childlike, perfect trust, that many who call themselves more religious might envy. They were contending now who should man her, numbers being eager; and there appeared some chance of its rising to a quarrel.

"This is my expedition," said Wilfred Lester; "but for me you would not have attempted it; allow me the privilege, therefore, of choosing my men. Bill Gand, will you make one of us or not?"

"Yes," answered the old sailor, "if it's only to take care of you. My wife's in the churchyard, and my two boys are under the waters: I shall be less missed nor some.".

The twelve were soon named, and they went into the boat. Wilfred was about to follow them, when some one glided up, and stood before him.

"Will it prove availing if *I* ask you not to peril your life?"

The speaker was Mr. Lester. Wilfred hesitated a moment before he answered:

"I could not, for any consideration, abandon the expedition; nevertheless, I thank you, I thank you heartily, if you spoke out of interest for my welfare. Father, this may be our last meeting: shall we shake hands? If I do perish, regret me not; for I tell you truly, life has lost its value for me."

Mr. Lester grasped the offered hand in silence, a more bitter pang wringing his heart than many of the bystanders would have believed. Wilfred leaped into the boat; and it put off on its stormy voyage, the spectators tearing round again to the spot, whence they could see the sinking ship.

What a fine picture the scene would have made! could it have been represented both to the eye and the ear—not unlike those old Dutch paintings of the Flemish school. The doomed ship and her unhappy freight of human life, soon to be human life no longer; the life-boat, launched on her perilous venture, making some way in spite of the impeding wind—now riding aloft, now engulfed under a huge wave, now battling with the furious sea for mastery; the anxious faces of the spectators, and their hushed, breathless interest, as they watched the progress of the boat, or the dim and dreadful

spot farther on; with the bright moonlight lighting up the whole, and the night sky, over which the clouds were racing; while, ever and anon, the faint tinkle of a bell might be heard from the ship, and the heavy bell at the castle still boomed out at intervals!

Would the boat reach the ship? Those in the boat, as well as those on shore, were asking the question? Bill Gand, the oldest of them, declared he had never wrestled with a gale so terrific, with waves so furious. The mystery to Bill then—and it would remain a mystery to him throughout all his after life—was that they *did* wrestle with them. Minute by minute, as they strove to labor on, and the angry sea beat them back, did he believe would be their last; that the next must see them in eternity: all who were with him believed so, including Wilfred Lester. How was it that they did escape? It appeared nothing less than a miracle—an impossibility effected; and they could not account for it, unless Wilfred Lester's words on shore could do so: It was a good cause, and God was over them.

But they did not reach the ship. No: too many poor wretches were struggling with the waves, nearer to them; and they picked up what they could—picked up until the boat could hold no more. Shouting out a cheering cry of hope to the wreck, they turned in shore again.

The going back was less labor, for they had the wind with them, but it was not less dangerous. Some of the men, powerful, hardy sailors that they were, felt their strength drooping; they did not think they could hold out to the shore. Wilfred encouraged them, as he had done in going, cheering on their spirits, almost renewing their physical strength. But for him, they would several times have given up the effort in despair, when they were first beating on for the wreck.

"Bear on with a will, my brave lads," he urged; "don't let the fatigue master you. I and Bill Gand are good for another turn yet; but we'll leave you on shore to recruit force, and bring others in your stead. You shall join again the third time. Cheerily on with a will! I wonder how many times it will take, to save them all?"

One of the rescued spoke up to answer. All could not speak, for some were lying, hurt or senseless, in the boat. He was an able-bodied seaman.

"It would take several times, master; but you'll never get the chance of going to her a third time, if you do a second. She was parting amidships."

"Parting amidships!"

"I think so; and so did the captain. She must have struck upon a rock, and was grinding and cracking awfully."

"Whence does she come?"

"From New York. A passenger-ship. A prosperous voyage we have had all along from starting, and this is the ending! A fine ship she was, spick and span new, eleven hundred tons register, her name 'The Wind.' I didn't like her name, for my part, when I joined her."

"Many passengers?"

"Forty or fifty; about half a dozen of them first-class; the rest, second."

"Did you jump overboard? hoping to swim for your lives?"

"No, no; who could swim in such a sea as this? All you saw in the sea were washed off. Some had sunk when you got to us."

Of course the above conversation had only been carried on at intervals, as the struggling boat permitted, and now it ceased altogether, for every energy had to be devoted to the boat, if they were to get her to the shore.

A low, heartfelt murmur of applause greeted their ears as they reached it; it might have been louder, but for remembrance of what the brave adventurers had yet to do, and the little chance there was of its being done—the very small portion these few saved formed of those to be saved. As Wilfred Lester stepped ashore, his face white with exertion, and the salt foam dripping off him, it is possible

he looked for a father's hand and a father's voice to welcome him. If so, he was mistaken. Mr. Lester was still there, but did not advance. What he might have done alone, it is impossible to say, but his wife was now with him. Strange to relate, Lady Adelaide had ventured, in her curiosity, down to the beach, and stood, braving the wind, supported between her husband and Lord Dane. Perhaps Mr. Lester did not choose to notice Wilfred in the presence of his wife, for he knew how much at variance they were; or perhaps he already repented of his late greeting. Wilfred saw her standing there, and turned again to the life-boat.

"These poor creatures must be conveyed to warm beds, and warm fires," he exclaimed, looking at some of those he had helped to rescue, "or they may soon be no better off than they would have been if left in the water."

"I can receive two or three," exclaimed Richard Ravensbird, pressing forward. "I have not been able to do any thing towards saving, but I can towards sheltering."

"Two vehicles were waiting, having come down to be in readiness, if wanted, and they were brought into requisition, one of them taking its way to the Sailor's Rest. It contained a man who was too exhausted to speak much, or to notice any thing, and a young man who appeared to be in attendance upon him, probably a friend.

"That we owe our lives to you this night, under God, there is little doubt," the latter cried, grasping Wilfred Lester's hand. "The time to thank you, I hope, will come."

Wilfred began mustering his second crew. Old Bill Gand insisted upon being one.

"Not you, Dick," cried Wilfred to another; "I won't have you; you could not stand the labor."

"I'm as strong as I was before my illness, sir," pleaded Dick.

"I will not admit you, I say. Stand back. We have no time to lose."

Scarcely had the words left Wilfred Lester's mouth, when a prolonged, dreadful shriek, only too palpable to the ear, arose from the wreck. It was some minutes before those on shore could make out its cause. But, when they did; when they discovered what had happened—alas! alas! The rescued sailor's words had been too surely and swiftly verified. The vessel had parted amidships, and was settling down in the water.

Oh, for the life-boat now! One more voyage, and it may yet save a few of those now launched into the water. Before it could take a third, the rest will have been launched into eternity.

And the life-boat hastened out amidst cheers to force its mad way, but it rescued none. The hungry waters had made too sure of their prey.

CHAPTER XIV.

THE RESCUED.

BUT three passengers had been rescued. The two conveyed to the Sailor's Rest, who had been chief-cabin passengers, and a steerage passenger; the rest saved, were seamen; not one of the officers, all had gone with the ill-fated ship.

Messengers had been dispatched to Sophie, and when the fly got there, she had warm beds in readiness, and hot flannels, in case rubbing should be necessary. One man, it was he who had seemed so exhausted, had nothing on but his shirt and drawers. A large cloak had been thrown over him as they raised him out of the life-boat; and then he spoke a few words.

"My head. I am cold. Get a shawl for my head."

Shawls were not plentiful on the beach, for none had been brought down, but a large neck-handkerchief was found in somebody's pocket, and the man's head was enveloped in it. He feebly pulled it far over his face,

as if to shield it from the cold. Little could be seen of his features when he got to the Sailor's Rest, but Sophie jumped to the conclusion, by some reasoning process of her own, that he was a man of fifty, or hard upon it. His wet hair hung about his face,—nearly white hair. He declined all assistance, shut himself into the chamber prepared, dried himself by the fire, got into bed between the warm blankets, and then rang the bell.

It was for a large basin of hot gruel with a glass of brandy in it.

When the maid took it up to him, she said that the young man, his fellow-passenger saved, wished to know if he could come in, or do any thing for him.

No, was the answer. And the young man had better lose no time in getting to bed himself. He might come in in the morning; and nobody else was to disturb him till he had been in, unless he rung.

Sophie did not go to bed that night; she had said she would not, and was glad of the excuse of being busy. One of the rescued sailors had by some means got his head much cut; besides the two cabin passengers he was the only one taken to the Sailor's Rest, the others had found refuge elsewhere, and Sophie busied herself in attending to him, and in drying the younger passenger's clothes—for he, when saved, had been completely dressed.

About eight in the morning, Sophie was in her parlor, when the passenger, mentioned, entered, attired in the said dry clothes. Sophie turned hastily, and thought, in that first moment, that she had never seen so prepossessing a man. He appeared about four-and-twenty, tall, and of lofty bearing, with clearly-cut features, dark hair, and a most attractive countenance.

"Are you a clever needle-woman?" asked he, with a very winning smile.

Mrs. Ravensbird, won by the good looks, the courteous manner, and the pleasant voice, began protesting that she was famous, nobody more clever than she. She had been out-door pupil in a convent in France for seven years, and let the Sisters alone for making girls into expert needle-women. Did the gentleman want a button sewn on?"

The gentleman smiled again. Had it been only that, he thought he could have managed the job himself without troubling her, provided she had supplied him with needle and cotton. "No," he continued, "it is something that requires more skill. I want a shade made for the eyes."

Sophie raised her own to the eyes looking at her; clear, bright eyes they were, of a dark gray, and she wondered what they could want with a shade.

"It is for my fellow-passenger," he proceeded to explain. "I have been to his room, and all his cry is for a shade for his eyes. He suffered with them during the voyage, I observed, and the light of the room this morning effects them much."

"Oh, I'll soon make that," said Sophie. "Who is he, sir?"

"You must ask himself that question," was the reply. "A large shade, he said, made of thin card-board, covered with dark blue or green silk, any color, in fact, and tapes to tie it on with."

"Tape!" ejaculated Sophie; "you mean ribbon, sir."

"Any thing. He will not care what the materials are, provided his eyes are shaded. I asked him about breakfast, but he seemed only anxious for the shade."

Sophie soon got her necessary materials; a sheet of card-board, which she fished up from somewhere, and some purple silk, the remnant of a dress; and set to work. The gentleman sat himself on the arm of an old horse-hair sofa opposite, and watched her fingers. His orders were, he said, laughingly, not to go up again without the shade.

"And so you and he met on board as fellow-passengers!" cried Sophie, as she worked. "Strangers, I suppose, to each other until then."

"We were on board, fellow-passengers."

"It's strange how intimate people grow upon a sea-voyage!" resumed she, "just as if they had been friends for years. The old gentleman seems ill."

"Very ill. Very ill, indeed, he has been all the voyage."

"What is his name? what was he coming to England for?" proceeded Sophie. "I suppose he's an American?"

"His name—his name?" deliberated the gentleman, as if casting back his thoughts. "I am not sure that I heard his name mentioned during the time we were in the ship. As to his motive for coming to England, I cannot speak. Gentlemen travelers do not unceremoniously inquire into each other's private affairs, Mrs. Ravensbird."

"I hope you will let me have the gratification of knowing your name, sir," continued Sophie, nothing daunted. "I'm sure it's a pleasant one."

"Do you guess so?" laughed he. "I do not discern much in it myself. Lydney."

"Lydney!" repeated Sophie, after him. "And are you an American, too, sir? And have you come over on business?"

"I have come over on pleasure—to look about me, never having had the honor of seeing old England before," answered he, good-humoredly. "How many more questions would you like answered, Mrs. Ravensbird?"

"Ah, hah! it's my French nature, and I ask you to excuse it. I am not English; you may tell that by my tongue; and we Gauls are always curious. Do you speak French, Mr. Lydney?"

"Quite as well as I do English. My mother was a French woman."

Sophie's eyes sparkled with delight; her heart had warmed to him at first, she said, and forthwith she commenced a rattling conversation in her native tongue. He sat there till the shade was finished, and then went up-stairs with it.

In the course of the morning Lord Dane walked into the Sailor's Rest, to inquire after the rescued. Richard Ravensbird was not in the way at the moment, but Sophie was quite equal to receiving his lordship. In earlier days, when he was plain and poor Herbert Dane, she had been rather fond of chattering to him, or he was to her; and her manners to him still retained far more of ease than did those of some of the inhabitants of Danesheld. Sophie began pouring into his ear all the news she had been able to collect, as regarded the two passengers, coupled with her own additions; for she was one of those who form conclusions according to their active imagination, and then assume them to be facts.

They were both Americans, from the United States, she said; the old gentleman travelling over here for his health, especially for a weakness in the eyes; and the young one for pleasure. They had first met on board, and got friendly together. The old gentleman's name she had not come at yet, but the young one's was Lydney. Such a pleasant young man!—spoke French like an angel—and as rattling and free as my lord himself used to be, in the by-gone days. And Madame Sophie cast a half-saucy glance to my lord when she said it.

"Are they gentlemen?" inquired Lord Dane. "Or people in business, merchants, and that sort of thing?"

"The young one's a gentleman, if ever I saw one," returned Mrs. Ravensbird, warmly. "In looks and manners he is fit, every inch of him, to be what you are, my lord—a British nobleman. There's no mistaking him for any thing inferior. And, do you know, his face puts me in mind of somebody, but for the life of me I can't tell who. As to the other, the old man, I don't know whether he's a gentleman or not; I have seen little of him, except his shoulders and his purple shade,—the one I made him; for there he lies, buried in his pillow and the bed-clothes, his face to the wall, and his back up; and all you can discern of him, barring the shade, is his white hair. When we go in with a tray of refreshment, he tells us to put it on the table by the bed, and helps himself when we are gone."

"The younger one is up, I suppose," remarked Lord Dane.

"Oh, up hours ago, my lord; up and out. He seems in a fine way about some box being lost that was on board, and is going towards the wreck to hear if there's any chance of things being got up. Does your lordship think there is?"

"A few things may be, perhaps; I cannot tell. I wish to send a message to this old gentleman, if you will convey it to him," continued his lordship, "Say that I, Lord Dane, shall be happy to render him any assistance, and if he would like me to pay him a visit, I can do so now."

Sophie ran up the stairs to the invalid's chamber, and came back again, shaking her head.

"I'll lay any money he's a cross-grained old bachelor," cried she, " he speaks up so sharply. He answered me quite rudely, my lord. 'My service to Lord Dane, but tell him I am a private individual, seeking only repose, and am not desirous of forming acquaintance, even with his lordship.' You might speak it more civilly, I thought to myself, as I took it from him."

"Oh, very well," said Lord Dane. "When these disastrous circumstances occur, it is due from my position to show courtesy to the sufferers; but if it be refused, of course the obligation is at an end. It is the last time I shall trouble your old gentleman, Mrs. Ravensbird."

The wind was less violent this morning, and many people were gathered on the heights, watching the spot where the wreck had been. At low-water part of the ship could be seen, and she lay with her larboard side to the rocks. Quantities of chips were floating about, and pieces of iron might be discerned on the beach. The masts and yards were gone, and there was no symptom of a bowsprit. Something more appalling than wood or iron floated in occasionally—a human body; not near enough, however, to terrify away the watchers on the heights, some of whom were ladies.

Standing most imprudently on the very edge of the heights, in their eager sympathy, their sad curiosity, were Miss Bordillion and Maria Lester. The latter, who was a little apart, bent forward to look at some bustle right underneath, when a gust of wind, more furious than any they had experienced that morning, suddenly swept over them, swept over Maria, and—

"Take care, Maria!" shrieked out Miss Bordillion, in an agony of terror.

Whether Maria could have "taken care," must remain an unanswered question. Certain it is, that the wind shook her, and she had all but lost her balance, when, at the very moment of peril, just as Miss Bordillion called out, a strong arm was thrown round her, and snatched her into safety. She had felt her own danger, and her face was perfectly white, as she turned it to her preserver.

She saw a stranger. A young aristocratic man, who had "gentleman" stamped on every motion and lineament.

"I thank you very greatly," she said to him, from between her agitated lips. "I did not know the wind was still so high."

Miss Bordillion, in her gratitude, laid hold of the stranger's hand.

"Let me thank you! let me thank you! I do believe you have saved her from destruction! Ah, Maria! you may well weep!" she added, as Maria, overcome by the fear and agitation of the moment, let fall a few hysterical tears. "How could you be so imprudent?—how could you advance so near? Thank him better, child, for there's no doubt he has saved you from death!"

"Not from death so certain as I was saved from last night," he smiled, hoping to reassure Miss Lester. "I was a passenger in that ill-fated ship,"

he said, in answer to the inquiring looks of Miss Bordillion, "and was one of those rescued by the life-boat."

"Is it possible?"

"But for a gentleman who took command of that life-boat, and shamed the sailors—as I hear—into manning her, sharing himself the danger, we should all have perished," he proceeded. "He was but a stripling, no older than myself; but he showed a braver heart than the inured-to-danger sailors."

Maria's face was glowing as a damask rose, and the tears rested on the eyelashes.

"Shall I tell you who that was?" she said. "It was my dear brother, Wilfred Lester."

And in a few minutes it seemed as though they had been conversing together for years. There are certain events that break the barriers of restraint more effectually than time can do.

"We must not part without hearing your name," said Miss Bordillion.

"William Lydney."

"And I am Miss Bordillion. And this is my address," she added, giving him a card, for she, like many other old-fashioned ladies, kept her card-case in her pocket. "I hope, Mr. Lydney, that you will call upon us."

"That I will be sure to do," he answered, a gratified expression lighting his countenance. And he lifted his hat as Miss Bordillion and Maria moved away.

The chamber in which the invalid lay, at the Sailor's Rest, was a commodious room, the bed at the farther end of it, opposite the door, and the fire-place in the middle, between the two. It was very comfortably furnished: a sofa, a centre-table and side-tables, besides the requisite furniture for a sleeping-room, but its space afforded good accommodation. On this same evening at dusk, Mr. Ravensbird himself was in the chamber, attending to the fire, when the sick gentleman suddenly addressed him:

"What sort of a neighborhood is this?"

Mr. Ravensbird probably wondered in what light he was intended to take the question, whether as to its natural, its social, its political features, or any others. But he did not inquire.

"It's a dull neighborhood rather," said he. "Except when it gets enlivened by any such event as that, last night, or by a poaching or smuggling affray. Lord Dane's having abandoned it for several years did not tend to make it gayer."

"He is your great man of the locality, I conclude, this Lord Dane?"

"Oh, yes, sir. The Danes have been the lords of Danesheld from times unheard of. And plenty of state they have kept up. But, to have the castle closed, or as good as closed, has been like a blight upon the place.

"The present Lord Dane has been absent from it?" questioned the invalid.

"He went abroad almost as soon as he came with the title, within two or three months of it, and has not long returned. Eight or nine years he must have been away."

"Is he married?"

"No, sir. His sister is with him at the castle at present,—Miss Dane. And will stop, people surmise, unless his lordship should give it another mistress."

"Perhaps you'll inform me what you are talking of," cried the invalid from the bed. "Lord Dane has no sister."

"Yes, he has, sir. And she is with him, as I tell you, at the castle."

"Then I tell you he has not a sister," was the sick man's irritable answer, but delivered in a subdued, quiet tone as the rest of his conversation had been, as though the voice stuck in the throat. "Some years ago I was in this part of the world and knew all the Danes. The present lord I knew very well: there was no sister then."

Richard Ravensbird thought it as well to drop the contention and suffer the stranger to have his own way, for he did not appear one likely to relinquish it. He stretched his head up to get a sight of the sick man's face,

but did not succeed: the upper part was under the purple shade, and the lower part under the bed-clothes.

"Yes, I knew a good bit of the Danes then," went on the invalid. "My lord and my lady, the two sons, the cousin,—in short, all of them. Has the younger one, William Henry, ever been heard of?"

"How do you mean, sir?" quickly cried Ravensbird, who began to doubt whether the stranger was cognizant that he, Richard Ravensbird, had been suspected of, and charged with the murder,—a point upon which he was sensitive. "He was heard of so far as that his body was found, and was buried in the family vault."

"How did they recognize it?"

"By certain marks," replied Ravensbird. "I recognized it myself. I was Captain Dane's servant."

"It was a nasty pitch-over, that fall from the heights," soliloquized the stranger: "it took place while I was in Danesheld—"

"I beg your pardon, sir, you are never Colonel Moncton?" breathlessly uttered Ravensbird.

"What if I am?" coolly asked the stranger.

Ravensbird paused. He did not know "what," but felt in much doubt and surprise. Convinced, moreover, also that, whoever it might be, whether Colonel Moncton or another, his own suspected share in the affair was known. He therefore set himself to speak of it calmly and openly, as he always did, to those aware of the struggle; otherwise he preferred to maintain a complete reticence on all points relating to that night.

"Yes, it was a fatal fall, a nasty struggle," Ravensbird observed: "and who the adversary was, remains a mystery to this day. Two or three were suspected. I, for one, and was taken up on suspicion; and a packman, for another, who was seen in angry contest with the captain on the heights, that same night: but I, in my own mind, suspected somebody else."

"Pray whom did you suspect?"

"I should be sorry to tell," answered Ravensbird.

"What were the grounds for suspecting you?" inquired the invalid, after a pause.

"That quarrel I had with Captain Dane—which I suppose you heard of, if you heard of the rest. It occurred in the morning, when he kicked me out of the castle, and the catastrophe took place in the evening. People's suspicions—and naturally enough, I acknowledge—flew to me. But they were wrong. I would have saved my master's life with my own: I would almost bring him back to life now at the sacrifice of my own, were it in my power. I was much attached to him, and I am faithful to his memory."

"In spite of the kicking-out?" put in the stranger.

"Pshaw!" returned Ravensbird. "A dispute of a moment, in which we both lost our tempers, could not destroy the friendship of years. Yes, sir, I presume to say it—friendship. He was the Honorable Captain Dane, and I but his servant; and though he never lost his dignity any more than I forgot my place, there was a feeling between us that might be called friendship."

There ensued a long silence. The gentleman broke it.

"What has become of Herbert Dane? He was to have married Lady Adelaide Errol. There was some—some—some talk of such a thing, I fancy."

"He did not marry her. Ah! that was another mystery. She would not have him, after all; and she married Mr. Lester. She has a whole troop of children now."

"And where is Herbert Dane? What has become of him?"

Ravensbird turned round to the bed in astonishment.

"He is at the castle now, sir; I have just said so."

"He at the castle! What for?"

"The castle is his home, sir," replied Ravensbird, beginning to wonder whether the sick man was in his right mind.

"Whose home? I am speaking of Herbert Dane. What should bring the castle his home? Does Lord Dane tolerate him there?"

"Why, sir, is it possible you do not know that Herbert Dane—that was—is the present Lord Dane?" uttered Ravensbird. "He succeeded the old lord."

The stranger raised himself on his elbow, and peered at Ravensbird under the purple shade.

"Then what on earth has become of Geoffry?—the eldest son? Where was he—that Herbert Dane should inherit?"

"He died at the same time as his brother," answered Ravensbird, shaking his head. "Before the body of my master was found, the remains of the other were brought home, and interred in the family-vault."

"Where did he die? What did he die of?" reiterated the invalid, who appeared unable to overcome his shock of astonishment.

"He died of fever, sir. I can't take upon myself just to say where, for I forget; but he was put on board at Civita Vecchia. My lady went almost as quick; and the old lord did not live above a month or two."

"I know; I know," cried the stranger with feverish impatience, "I saw their deaths announced in the newspapers; and I saw the succession of the new peer, 'Geoffry, Lord Dane.' Not of Herbert."

"His name is Herbert Geoffry, sir. As soon as he became heir, he was no longer called Herbert, but Geoffry. It is a favorite name with the Lords Dane."

The invalid laid down and covered his face. Ravensbird was about to leave the room, when he spoke again.

"This Herbert,—Lord Dane, as you tell me he is,—is he liked?"

"He has not given much opportunity to be liked or disliked, sir, stopping away so long," was the rejoinder of Ravensbird. "He behaved generously in the matter of my lord's will. The will left presents and legacies to servants, and fifteen thousand pounds to Lady Adelaide Errol, but my lord died before he signed it ; consequently it was void. The young lord, however, fulfilled all the bequests to the very letter, as honorably as though he had been legally bound to do so."

"Why did he not marry Lady Adelaide ?" sharply put in the invalid.

"She turned round, sir, as I tell you, and would not have him. It was exactly like a sudden freak, a change of mind that nobody could account for. My present wife was maid to her at that time, and I heard of her refusal : but it was not generally known that there was any thing between them."

"Perhaps there never was any thing between them," remarked the invalid.

"Oh, yes there was, sir ; when he was plain Herbert Dane," significantly replied Ravensbird. "Ah! he little thought then to be what he is now—the Lord of Danesheld !"

The stranger turned his face to the wall, and put up his back ; and nothing could be seen of him but his white hair, and the purple shade.

CHAPTER XV.

THE JAPANNED BOX.

THE days went on, and the divers were busy, striving to fish up articles from the wreck. The coast presented an unusually stirring appearance, so many idlers flocking constantly to the scene,—the preventive-men being in charge, so that no depredations could take place. As the divers' exertions, however, appeared likely to meet with but poor reward, the idle spectators got tired of thronging to the spot, and the operators and coast-guard were left comparatively in peace.

One visitor they constantly had, and that was the young stranger, Mr. Lydney. He expressed himself as being most anxious to recover a certain box, describing it as one of middling size,—a tin one, japanned. Wil-

fred Lester, between whom and Mr. Lydney an intimacy was springing up, laughed at him one day, and rallied him on his disquiet.

"One would think all your worldly wealth was entombed in that chest, Lydney," he observed.

"And it is—in a measure," was the answer, "for it contains valuable deeds and documents, without which my worldly wealth will be of little value to me."

"Suppose it is gone forever ?" returned Wilfred. "Would the loss be totally irremediable ?"

"Upon my word, I cannot say," replied Mr. Lydney. "Some of its documents might be replaced, but others,—I would rather not dwell on that possibility : I am of a hopeful nature."

And he appeared, in this instance, not to be of a hopeful nature in vain. One morning, a fortnight after the night of the wreck, Mr. Lydney found, upon going down, that the divers had brought up several things. They were of various and opposite kinds, as you may well imagine. A part of a beam of wood ; a gold Albert chain ; a small cask which contained salt meat; a sealed case, holding letters ; and there were divers boxes. Once, they thought they were hauling up a poor little baby, but it proved to be a huge, wax doll, dressed in lace and satins ; its young mistress was colder and more lifeless now than the doll.

With an eager step, when he saw the recovered things, did William Lydney hasten to inspect them. Owners had been found for none ; not for one of those articles lying on the beach. The owners had gone with the wax doll's little mistress, and would awaken no more in this world.

"Is it among 'em, sir ?" asked Mitchel, the preventive-man, coming up as Mr. Lydney stood over the boxes ; for his anxiety to recover the chest was no secret. "There's one tin case, you see, sir, but I fear it's larger than you describe yours to be."

William Lydney lifted his head,

and his face expressed keen disappointment.

"It is not among them," was all he said.

"What's this?" rejoined Mitchel, turning round to speak as he was walking away, for he perceived that something else was coming up, to be added to the relics.

It was a japanned box, about two feet square, with the initials "V. V. V." surmounted by a Maltese cross, studded on it in brass nails. Mitchel scarcely need have asked what it was had he glanced at the countenance of Mr. Lydney: the eager, trembling expectation, the intense joy that lighted it up, proved it was the much-wished-for chest. In the moment's excitement he took it, he alone, from the grasp of the men who bore it. William Lydney was a strong man, but not strong enough to lift that heavy case in ordinary moments.

"It's the one ye've been looking out for, ain't it master?" asked one of the bearers, as it was deposited on the beach.

"Yes it is," replied Mr. Lydney. "I will reward you and the divers well."

"But them letters don't stand for your name, sir," cried Mitchel, as the men moved away again.

"I have not said they did," laughed Mr. Lydney. "But now, to get it up to the Sailor's Rest. I'll leave you guard over it, Mitchel, while I go and find somebody with a truck or barrow; or get Ravensbird to send. Mark you, my good man, it's very precious."

"I'll take charge of it, sir," smiled Mitchel; "it's all in my duty and my day's work. Where you leave it, there you'll find it, untouched."

You spoke there without your host, Mr. Preventive Mitchel.

Hardly had Mr. Lydney quitted the beach when Lord Dane appeared on it. He was in sporting attire; but underneath his black velvet coat, linen shone out of the finest and most costly texture. His keeper—not the one who was wounded—had gone to the preserves with the guns and dogs, and

Lord Dane had been following him, when a rumor met him that the divers were now beginning to find. His lordship turned off his way for a short visit to the beach. There stood Mitchel, keeping watch over the things, in pursuance of his promise to Mr. Lydney—and also in pursuance of his duty.

"Is this all they have got up?" uttered his lordship to Mitchel, in a tone of surprise. "I thought it must have been half the ship full. Young Shad came grinning up to me, and said the beach was covered."

"A light-fingered young monkey!" apostrophized Mitchel. "I drove him off from here, for it would require a man with ten eyes to watch him. No, my lord, they have not got up much, and I don't expect they will; though they have been more fortunate the last few hours than they have been all along. That box has turned up at last, my lord, that the young gent has been so worried after."

"What young gent?" asked his lordship.

"That fine young man who was saved in the life-boat, and is stopping at the Sailor's Rest," replied Mitchel. "How anxious he have come here, day after day, a watching and waiting, all for this japanned box! Had it been crammed full of thousand-pound banknotes he couldn't have been more eager. That's it, my lord, behind you."

Lord Dane was standing with his back to the box, and turned round at the words. What could he find in it to attract his notice? Something, apparently; for he remained gazing down at it. Like one transfixed stood he: and when he did rouse himself and lift his head, it was only to walk round the box, survey it on all sides, touch it, shake it, and, in short, look like a child does at a new toy, as if he would very much enjoy the pulling it to pieces to see what was in it.

"Who do you say this belongs to?" cried he presently to Mitchel.

"That young American, my lord, who was brought ashore in the life-boat. Your lordship must have seen

THE RESCUE ON THE HEIGHTS.—*See page 124.*

him many times : a fine, handsome man he is, pleasant to speak to. I mean Mr. Lydney."

" Is it his chest ?"

" It can't well be anybody else's," returned Mitchel, " as your lordship would say, if you had seen his anxiety over it. When it came up this morning it was just as if he had found a treasure : all a-tremble he was with delight."

" Lydney ? — Lydney ?" repeated his lordship to himself, as if oblivious of the presence of Mitchel. " Lydney ? Have I heard that name ever ? It does not strike upon my memory. Neither does it answer to—to—"

Lord Dane stopped ; he was looking down at the initials on the box, and Mitchel spoke up, possibly believing he discovered the drift of the peer's thoughts.

" The letters don't stand for his own name, my lord, as I remarked to him just now ; and he answered me, merrily like, that he had not said they did. He is gone to send down some men to remove it to the Sailor's Rest."

Lord Dane stepped to the rest of the things and glanced keenly at all. " Does any of this belong to him ?" he questioned of Mitchel.

" Nothing else, my lord ; nothing but that japanned box that seems so precious to him. He has not appeared to care at all about any other part of his luggage being found, though he says he had a good bit on board."

Lord Dane walked away without saying more, and Mitchel remained in charge. Presently, somewhat to the surprise of the latter, his lordship reappeared, followed by an empty cart and two men. The cart belonged to a miller on the Dane estate, and was on its way to fetch wheat to be ground. Lord Dane encountered it as he turned off the beach into the road, and commanded it into his own service, for what purpose you will see.

Down came the cart, its two attendants, and his lordship, and halted close to Mitchel and the recovered

things. Lord Dane pointed to them with his finger. " Hoist them in," said he.

The men did so, to the wondering surprise of Mitchel, and made short work of the process. None of the articles were heavy, save the japanned box. That went in with the rest ; but the barrel of pork and the beam of wood his lordship told them they might leave on the beach. Then the cart and its contents proceeded to move away again.

" My lord," uttered Mitchel, in a perfect ecstacy of consternation, "they must not take off the things, especially that tin chest. I am left here to see that nobody does do it."

" I have ordered them to the castle for safety," replied Lord Dane.

" But that tin case, my lord,—its owner is coming down for it directly. And I passed my word that he should find it here safe and untouched. If he complains to the supervisor I may lose my place, your lordship."

" Lose your place for yielding the authority vested in you to mine !" returned Lord Dane, in a good-humored tone, which seemed to chaff at Mitchel's simplicity. " We don't know yet to whom these things may belong, and they will be in safety at the castle."

" But—I hope your lordship will pardon me for speaking—this tin box has got its owner," persisted Mitchel. " When the gentleman returns for it, what am I to say to him ?"

" Mitchel," said his lordship, quietly, "you must understand one thing which you do not yet appear to be aware of. As lord of the manor, I possess a right to claim all and every thing fished up from that wreck, whether the original owners be saved or not. I do not wish to exert this privilege ; I should not think of doing so ; but I do choose that these things shall, for the present, be placed in the castle, that they may be in safety You may say that to Mr. Lydney."

Lord Dane strode off after the cart, and Mitchel remained where he was, as still as though he had been changed to a petrifaction. The procedure did not meet his approbation; and, in defiance of Lord Dane's assurance, he feared he might get into trouble over it. He neither spoke nor moved, but just remained staring and thinking. Neither did he when, some time after, Mr. Lydney appeared. Ravensbird came with him, and a man with a truck.

"Why, where's the box?" exclaimed Mr. Lydney, gazing round. "Mitchel, what have you done with the box?"

"I don't know," replied Mitchel, speaking helplessly. "I have not done any thing with it. Lord Dane came down, and sent it away, and the other things also."

"Sent it where?" asked Mr. Lydney.

"Up to the castle, sir. He was lord of the manor, and possessed a right to claim what was got up from the wreck, he said. Not that he should think of claiming them, but they must be put in the castle for safety till the owners turned up—which, of course, they are never likely to do: but perhaps he meant their friends."

"The owners of that japanned box had turned up," cried Mr. Lydney. "His lordship had no business to interfere, so much as to put his finger upon it. How could you think of allowing it, Mitchel. You are to blame."

"If you were not a stranger here, sir, you would never ask how we can think of allowing sway to Lord Dane," was the reply of the preventive-man to Mr. Lydney. "He is master of every thing; of Danesheld and the people in it. I had no more power to keep your box back, when Lord Dane said it was to go, than I have to stop that sea from flowing."

"Nonsense," said Mr. Lydney, who appeared much provoked. "Lord Dane cannot be allowed to play the martinet over all the world."

"Well, sir, I assure you it was no fault of mine. But if you go to the castle, of course he will give the box up to you; it can't be of no use to him."

Ravensbird looked round at Mr. Lydney. "I don't think you'll get it, sir," he said. "At any rate you must go cautiously to work."

With a haughty toss of the head and contemptuous curl of the lip, not directed at Ravensbird,—but ill or underhand doing always excited the scorn of William Lydney,—he proceeded immediately to the castle, the man and the truck following in his wake. Not Ravensbird; it was rare, indeed, that he troubled the castle. He rang a sounding peal on the bell, just as Mr. Bruff, who was quitting the house, opened the gate.

"I wish to see Lord Dane," said Mr. Lydney. And Bruff thought that no man had ever appeared at that castle yet, possessing more of the bearing and tones of a chieftain. He bowed low.

"His lordship is out, sir."

"I was informed his lordship had just returned, in charge of some property got up from the wreck."

Bruff looked curiously at the visitor. Who could he be, presuming to speak in those scornful tones, palpably directed towards Lord Dane and his doings? Bruff did not resent it, but he felt convinced that the gentleman before him *was* a gentleman, and an honorable man.

"My lord did return here, sir, with the men who brought up the things. But he has gone out since."

"Amongst those things was a box, which I claim," proceeded Mr. Lydney. "I must request you to deliver it to me."

"It is not in my power, sir. I dare not meddle with any thing against the orders of Lord Dane."

"I say that I claim it," quietly returned Mr. Lydney, "and I must have it given up to me."

"I am sure, sir, when you remember that I am Lord Dane's servant, you will see how impossible it is that I can meddle with any thing, contrary to his lordship's orders."

"The things are in the castle?"

"Certainly they are, sir. His lordship had them put in the strong-room, that they might be in safety: he gave me the key, and charged me not to let them be touched: the death-room we used to call it; but the name, not being an agreeable one, has been changed."

"Do you know that you may do me an irreparable injury—an injury that can never be removed—by refusing to deliver up that property?" pursued Mr. Lydney.

"I am sorry to hear you say so, sir; and if it depended on my will, you should have it this instant; but this is a matter of duty to my lord, which I, receiving his wages and living under his roof, must not violate."

Mr. Lydney silently acquiesced in the good faith of the reasoning, and perceived how useless it would be to argue the point further.

"Is there any one who holds authority at the castle, to whom I can apply?" he inquired.

"Miss Dane is at the castle, sir: my lord's sister; but as to authority, —you can see her, if you please, sir."

The visitor motioned with his hand in reply, and Bruff led the way to the drawing-rooms.

"What name, sir?" he asked, pausing, with his hand on the door.

"Mr. William Lydney."

Miss Dane rose at his entrance. She was older than her brother; in fact, in her forty-second year; but she assumed the dress and the manners of a girl of twenty. She had small and rather pretty features, a delicate complexion, and a soft rose-color on her cheeks,—altogether looking very much more youthful than she really was. Her dark-brown hair, beginning to be sprinkled with silver, was worn, as carelessly as a child's, in a profusion of long ringlets all round her head; and her blue eyes had a habit of shyly sinking from the gaze of other eyes, especially those of gentlemen. Putting her vanity and her affectation aside, Miss Dane was not to be disliked. She was simple and kind-hearted—not overburdened with strong intellect;

and the most marked peculiarity about her was, that she fancied every stranger fell in love with her at first sight. Danesheld called her an old maid: Miss Dane would have been mortally offended, had she heard them. She was attired in a light-blue silk, and jacket to match, jointly set off with many trimmings and silver buttons.

"I have the honor of speaking to Miss Dane?" began Mr. Lydney.

Miss Dane curtsied and simpered, and simpered and curtsied again.

"What an attractive man!" quoth she to herself; and forthwith fell right in love with him, and fondly hoped that he was returning the compliment. Mr. Lydney, however, was too much engrossed by his tin box and its abstraction, to admit softer impressions just then, even though he had been as susceptible as the lady. He gave her a concise history of the affair, and inquired whether she would not give orders that his box should be restored to him.

"I never heard of such a procedure," cried she, in a pretty little weak voice, and shaking her ringlets affectedly. "Geoffry—my brother—went down to the beach, and ordered the recovered things up here, you say? What did he do it for? what did he want with them?"

"That is precisely what I should be glad to know, Miss Dane?"

"I don't think they can have come here, dear sir; I fancy there must be some error. Allow me to wring for Bruff."

She tripped to the bell before Mr. Lydney could forestall her; and Bruff —who for some reason, best known to himself, had delayed the errand he was departing upon when Mr. Lydney appeared at the castle-gate—came in answer to the summons.

"Bruff," asked Miss Dane, "have any boxes and things been brought here this morning, belonging to that wrecked ship?"

"Yes, miss," answered Bruff. For Miss Dane, though living at the castle as its mistress, never would submit to be addressed as "ma'am." In her opinion it would have taken from her appearance of youth; and woe be to the servant who transgressed, for he fell under her stern displeasure : at least, as stern as simple Miss Dane could show.

"Is this gentleman's box here, then ?" she proceeded.

"I can't say that, miss; I did not remark particularly what came. It was all put in the strong room. If the box was in the cart with the other things, it's here."

"It is of the very utmost consequence that I should have it, Miss Dane," struck in Mr. Lydney. "Lord Dane would surely not object to its being returned to me, were he at home."

Of course not, sir," warmly acquiesced Miss Dane. "Bruff, you cannot do wrong by giving up to this gentleman his own property."

"My lord's orders were that the things should not be touched, under any pretence whatever, miss," remonstrated Bruff.

"Yes, I can understand that; when there were no claimants for them, he naturally would cause them to remain in security. But this gentleman claims his box and requires it : so you must give it to him."

"Not upon my own responsibility, miss," returned the butler. "If you order me to do so, that of course alters the case."

"Dear me, Bruff, how tiresome and precise you are !" ejaculated Miss Dane, with her childish simper. "It stands to reason that his lordship, in taking possession of the property, could only have had regard to the interest of the owners; therefore I cannot do wrong in desiring that what belongs to this gentleman should be given up to him."

Mr. Lydney rose. "It is a japanned box," he said to Bruff, "with initials and a cross on the lid in gilt; you cannot mistake it. But I may as well go with you, and point it out."

Bruff seemed to hesitate still, and at length turned to Miss Dane.

"Miss," he said, "you know what my lord is, if he is disobeyed. Now I really dare not do this of my own accord—though I'm sure I ask pardon for saying so, in the face of your orders. Perhaps, miss, you would not mind coming to the strong room, and delivering up the box yourself, as it were."

Miss Dane did not mind it at all : she rather liked the expedition, especially when the handsome young stranger gallantly offered his arm as an escort. Down-stairs they went, through the passages to the strong room, she mincing and chattering by his side. Bruff produced the key, and unlocked the door.

When the reader first saw that room, it had trestles standing in its middle, bearing something cold and heavy. Now the trestles had disappeared, and in the same place, thrown in a hasty heap on the floor, were the relics fished up by the divers. Mr. Lydney released Miss Dane, and stood an instant, his eye rapidly scanning them one by one. A look of angry perplexity rose to his face.

"My box is not here," he exclaimed with sternness.

It was a contretemps that neither Miss Dane nor Bruff had expected—perhaps the latter felt rather relieved than otherwise. Certainly no japanned chest was amongst the articles. Mr. Lydney turned to Bruff.

"Where has it been put to ?" he inquired, his quiet tone carrying more command with it than many a louder one.

"If it is not here, sir," promptly replied Bruff, "it was not brought to the castle. The things were removed from the cart straight to this room, and I can be upon my word that nobody has been near them since."

"It was brought to the castle safe enough," returned Mr. Lydney. "If you saw the things taken out of the cart, you must remember it."

"A japanned box, you say, sir," cogitated Bruff, casting his thoughts back. "I cannot be certain that I did see it; I took no particular notice what the things were, though I can attest that they were all placed in this room."

" Then it has been removed since," replied Mr. Lydney.

Bruff shook his head. " I can equally attest, sir, and in the most positive manner, that that could not be. The key has not been out of my possession."

Mr. Lydney felt sure that the box had been removed, and he began casting round his eyes for hiding-places. They fell upon the door of a closet, and he pulled it open, for the key was in. A dark closet, with nothing in it but some trestles, which leaned against the wall. There were no signs of the box.

" It is like magic," observed Miss Dane. " If the box was positively brought up in the cart, as you affirm, dear sir, the cart must have taken it away again ; that's the only solution I can come to. My brother, hearing it was yours, may have sent it to your lodgings."

But this hypothesis was destroyed by Bruff, who declared that when the cart drove away from the gate it was perfectly empty. Mr. Lydney appeared to be thrown up. He inquired at what hour he could see Lord Dane.

" He would probably not be home before the dinner-hour," Bruff rejoined, —" six o'clock. His lordship dined at six when in the country."

" But, my dear sir," interrupted Miss Dane, as Lydney was wishing her good-morning, " if the box has been so long in the water, its contents must be saturated and useless. You may be disturbing yourself for nothing."

" I expect the contents are intact," was the reply. " The box contains another, which is hermetically sealed, and is impervious to fire and water. I have the honor, madame, for the present, to wish you good-day."

Outside the castle, Mr. Lydney paused to consider what he should do in the emergency. He came to the determination to seek out the men belonging to the cart, and proceeded to the beach to inquire of Mitchel who they were. Mitchel gave the necessary information, adding (when he heard the box was missing) *that it did go away in the cart*. And Mr. Lydney found the men.

But it afforded him very little service. They were a couple of dull, stupid clodhoppers, of that species of rustic whom we are apt to marvel at—to question, almost, whether they can be human beings. They had just sufficient brains to get through their day's work at the miller's, and that was all.

"A tin box, japanned, wi' gilt marks outside on't ? They didn't know : my lord telled 'em to pick up the things what laid on the shingle and take 'em to the castle, and they did so. There couldn't be no box missing out of 'em, 'twarn't likely."

" But I tell you that it is missing," said Mr. Lydney ; " and, as to your not recollecting it, if you lifted it into the cart, and then removed it from the cart to Lord Dane's strong-room, you must have observed it. It was a peculiar-looking box."

The men scratched their heads. They moved the things for sartain themselves, but they didn't mark one thing more nor another—

" Was the box taken from the cart between the beach and the castle ?" impatiently interrupted Mr. Lydney.

The two fellows stared, evidently considering it a foolish question. Not it, they answered. They had drove right from the beach to the castle, the one walking by the cart, t'other behind it : where should they be likely to leave a box, when my lord had ordered 'em to the castle ? By token, my lord hisself was near 'em, and must have kept the cart in sight, and could say whether they had stopped or not.

"And you left *all* the things at the castle ?"

They left 'em all, and come away with the empty cart to fetch their sacks o' wheat.

And nothing more satisfactory than this could Mr. Lydney get out of them.

Though he believed they were too stolid to tell any thing but the truth.

CHAPTER XVI.

THE SEARCH.

MR. BRUFF entertained an idea that there was no policy like that of taking the bull by the horns. Accordingly he quitted the castle, and contrived to cross that portion of the Dane preserves where he deemed it most likely Lord Dane would be. Upon seeing him, he went boldly up and told his tale of the occurrences of the morning, deprecatingly dwelling upon the fact that the room had been opened by Miss Dane's orders, against his own will.

Lord Dane was sitting on the stump of a tree, solacing himself with a sandwich and something good from a flask. Bruff stood humbly before him, expecting little less than that his head would be snapped off. Few peers visited disobedience of orders more sharply than he of Dane.

"As a general rule, Bruff, you know that what I say is law, and may not be violated with impunity," cried his lordship, with his mouth full. "In this instance the matter was not momentous; but I shall speak to Miss Dane, who appears to have been more in fault than you. Did you give the young man his box?"

"The box was not there, my lord; leastways the one he said he was looking after," replied the amazed and relieved Bruff. "A tin box, japanned, with gilt initials outside, he described it to be: there was nothing answering to the description, your lordship"

"Then what brought the fellow intruding after it?" cried his lordship, testily. "That's just what I expected it would be,—that every man, woman, and child, who might have ever so remote an interest in the ship, would be poking themselves up to view the relics; and therefore I ordered you to

keep them closed. Let them go down with the divers and hunt there."

"The young gentleman says the box was found and brought to the castle, my lord," returned Bruff, believing Lord Dane was taking a wrong view of the facts. "But, as I told him, if the box came with the other things, there it would now be, with them."

"Rubbish!" returned Lord Dane. "The box could not vanish through the floor. Perhaps you overlooked it, Bruff."

Mr. Bruff thought not; and subjoined the information that the young gentleman had announced his intention of calling at the castle, to see Lord Dane upon the point.

"He is welcome," said his lordship.

Mr. Lydney so timed his visit as to see Lord Dane just before his dinner-hour. He was received with politeness.

"My butler has been telling me some rigmarole story about a box vanishing out of the strong-room," began his lordship, in a free, frank tone. "But the thing is impossible: if the box was placed in the strong-room, it must be in it still."

"The box was certainly put in the cart to be brought to the castle,—to that Mitchel can testify," returned Mr. Lydney, in a tone as free as his lordship's, though somewhat more haughty. "The question is, where was it put after it reached the castle?"

"Did Mitchel take notice of the box?"

"Yes," emphatically replied Mr. Lydney. "And Mitchel says that your lordship also took notice of it, and remarked that the initials on it were not those of my name."

"Is it that box which is missing? the one with the three gilt V's upon it?" exclaimed Lord Dane. "Oh, that was certainly placed in the cart: I saw the men put it in."

"May I inquire why your lordship should have meddled with the box at all—"

"I had the things brought up for security," interrupted Lord Dane.

"But I had claimed that particular box, and had left it in Mitchel's care, while I went for means to remove it," said Mr. Lydney. "It appears to me that it could not be any concern of your lordship's. As to safety—Mitchel, I say, was in charge."

"Were you accustomed to see much of wrecks, which I do not suppose you are, you would know how next to impossible it is for any preventive-men to stop the pilfering of the marauders that infest the coast," rejoined Lord Dane. "It was my duty, as lord of the manor, to take care that the things recovered remained intact. You are at liberty to claim your property, and remove it from the castle."

"But where is my property?" asked Mr. Lydney. "Your servant showed me the things brought here from the beach, all the things, he said; and it was not with them."

"Sir, to reiterate such an assertion makes me quite angry," tartly rejoined Lord Dane. "A box locked up safely in a strong room could not vanish from it: it must be there still."

Lord Dane rang the bell for the key of the strong room as he spoke, and Bruff brought it to him. He and Mr. Lydney then proceeded thither.

"Your lordship must perceive that the box is not here," said Mr. Lydney, pointing to the things as they lay on the floor.

Lord Dane glanced at them with a keen and curious eye: and when he found beyond doubt that the box really was missing, he appeared on the point of losing his temper. "It is most strange, most singular!" he uttered; and, striding to the door, shouted out for Bruff.

The man came in hasty answer to the summons, and Lord Dane abruptly addressed him:

"Whom have you dared admit to this room? Somebody must have entered and removed the box."

"I declare to goodness, my lord, that not a soul has entered it," cried the unhappy Bruff, "saving this gentleman and Miss Dane. The key never was out of my personal custody." And Lydney felt convinced that the man was speaking the truth.

"The box must have been conveyed to some other room when brought to the castle, not to this one at all," he observed, but Lord Dane interrupted him.

"I give you my honor, sir, as a peer of England, that the things brought in the cart were placed in this room, and in this room only. The men had no opportunity of entering any other, and did not enter one."

"I can bear my lord out in that," interposed Bruff, turning his honest face upon the stranger. "The things were brought straight to this room through the outer passage, not the inner one: had the men wished to go into another room, they could not. Besides, I was with them all the time, and my lord also was looking on. I'm sure it's like magic."

"I can surmise how it is," said Lord Dane; "the men must have omitted to remove the box from the cart."

"No," said Mr. Lydney. "I have questioned the men, and am satisfied that it was brought into the castle."

"My lord," put in the butler, "I watched the cart go away from the gates, and it was quite empty."

"It is inexplicable," exclaimed Lord Dane. "But I hope," he added, turning to Mr. Lydney, with a frank smile, "that it will soon be explained, and the box found, for you appear to set store by it."

"It shall be found, if there be law or justice in England," warmly spoke the young man.

"Nay," said Lord Dane, "you would seem to cast blame to me; but that is not just."

"My lord," returned Mr. Lydney, "it is against my nature to act, or suspect, in an underhand manner, and therefore I candidly avow my opinion that your lordship has custody of the box. Had it been lying on the beach unclaimed, as the other things were, and you had ordered it to the castle, I could have understood it; but that you should do so in the face of Mitchel's assurance that it was mine, and that I was then bringing assistance to remove it, does appear to me to be a procedure fraught with doubt. I can only believe that your lordship did so to obtain possession of the box."

"Why! what do you suppose I wanted with the box?" uttered Lord Dane.

"I am unable to say."

"You are smarting under this loss, young sir, which I confess is a vexatious one, and therefore I excuse your language," equably returned Lord Dane. "I will even condescend to point out how totally absurd your suspicions are. That the things were all brought to this room I have testified to you; my servants have done the same, and you can also question the miller's men. Now, this room is some distance removed from any other room in the castle, and I ask you how it would be possible for me to carry a heavy box, which most likely I could not even lift through the passages to them? You may be capable of deeming that my servants helped me, or carried it by my orders: but I give you hearty leave to question them all. No, Mr. Lydney; I will swear to you that not a thing went out of this room-door again after it was brought in at it: I locked the door upon the things immediately, and handed the key to Bruff. Since then it lies with him."

Bruff looked up deprecatingly, but did not again defend himself. That there was point in what Lord Dane advanced Mr. Lydney could but acknowledge, and perhaps he began to doubt whether his suspicions were correct. He returned with Lord Dane to the reception-room, for he had left his gloves there, and then took his leave. Standing at another door, as he passed through the corridor, was Miss Dane, apparently calling to her little pet dog; in point of fact, watching for the departure of the handsome stranger. Her ringlets were more elaborate, now they were arranged for dinner, and were ornamented with sundry bows of sky-blue ribbon; her white dress, made after a girlish fashion, was also decorated with blue.

She gave a little start, as of surprise, when Mr. Lydney approached, and put down her arms like a timid child. "You here again? How nice! Oh, I hope you have found your box."

"It cannot be found," was the answer. "It appears to have vanished in some unaccountable manner from Lord Dane's strong room."

"Vanished as the ghosts do," simpered the lady.

"Not exactly. The days of ghosts are over, Miss Dane."

He quitted her to depart. As she watched his receding figure, Lord Dane came up whistling, his hands in his pockets.

"What are you looking after, Cecilia?"

"That handsome young man," avowed Miss Dane. "I never saw one so good-looking before."

"H—m," returned Lord Dane in a tone of dissent. "Not a bad figure, though."

"Geoffry, who does he put you in mind of?"

"Not any one," answered Lord Dane, resuming his whistling.

"Ah, you never can see likenesses as I do. He is exceedingly like old Lady Dane."

Lord Dane stared at his sister, and then laughed slightingly. "You take queer fancies in your head, Cecilia. That man is no more like Lady Dane than he is like you or me. I should be sorry if he were."

"Why?"

"Because a suspicion is drawing over my mind that he is not what he assumes to be,—that he is not a good character: an adventurer, in short who is bent on nefarious purposes."

Miss Dane gave vent to a scream of genuine mortification. If her brother said so she feared it must be the fact, for she knew how clear-sighted Lord Dane was.

Bruff, meanwhile, was showing out the same—gentleman, or adventurer, or whatever he might be. They stood for an instant to converse beyond the gate.

"I hope, sir, you will not attribute

this loss to any fault or carelessness of mine," spoke Bruff.

"No, I do not," was the ready answer. "But, you must admit that it is strange in the extreme."

"I can't make it out in any way, sir; turn it about as I will there's no opening for a probability to creep in at."

"Lord Dane delivered the key to you immediately?"

"That he did, sir. When the men had carried in the things I went to the door with them, and saw them drive off with the empty cart. Then I turned back along the passage to the room, and there stood my lord waiting for me. He locked the door fast in my sight, gave me the key, and ordered me to keep it locked, and to allow no one to enter. Then he went out, and returned but just now. Now, sir, even allowing that my lord had an inclination to remove that box elsewhere, as you seemed to suspect, he could not by any possibility have had the time, either to do it himself, or to get it done: and my own moral persuasion is, that the box never did come into the castle. Halloa! you young eaves-dropper? what do you do here?"

The latter words were addressed to Mr. Shad, who was standing in close proximity. Mr. Lydney turned hastily, and thought he had never seen so strange-looking a boy. The butler pointed his finger in authoritative warning, and the lad shuffled off.

"Had the box been of light weight I might have thought that young reptile had pilfered it from the cart," observed Bruff to Mr. Lydney. "He must have stolen after when the cart came up here from the beach, for I saw him hovering close by when the men were taking the things from it. A box of that weight, of course he could not take."

Mr. Lydney strode away, overtook Shad, and laid his hand upon his shoulder. "What is your name?" asked he.

"Please, sir, it's Shad."

"Shad—what?"

"I doesn't know."

"The drivers recovered some things this morning from the wreck, and a cart took them up to Dane Castle. You followed, I believe, Mr. Shad. Did you see the cart unloaded?"

"I didn't finger nothing," was the response of the boy.

"That is not what I ask you. *Can* you speak truth?" proceeded Mr. Lydney, doubting whether much truth could come from a mortal, possessing a countenance like the one he gazed on.

Shad only grinned.

"You see this sixpence," said Mr. Lydney, taking one from his pocket. "I am going to ask you a question or two; answer me with strict truth, and it shall be yours. Equivocate only by a word, and instead of the sixpence, you shall get something not so pleasant."

"I know what you'd ask me," burst forth the boy, forgetting his usual *role* of 'simpleton,' in the eager fascination the sixpence bore for him; "it's about your lost box, that a row's being made over, him with the three letters on it. I see it took in to the castle."

"You did?"

"I see it with these two eyes o'mine," avowed Shad, lifting his sly orbs, sparkling now, to the face of Mr. Lydney. "It was a'most the last thing left in the cart; the two millers carried of it in, and Mr. Bruff went a'ter 'em up the passage."

"Where was Lord Dane then?"

"I didn't see him. I think he was agone into the castle afore."

"You saw the cart drive away, no doubt; was it quite empty?"

"Yes; there warn't nothing left in her. Master, I'm telled the truth, and now, please, for the sixpence."

"Should I find later that you have not told the truth, it shall go hard with you," said Mr. Lydney, dropping the sixpence into his hand. "But if you could only learn, Shad, how much easier it is to speak truth than the contrary, what a vast amount of trouble it saves, you would never say another false word again."

Shad's only reply was to amble off, his arms flinging themselves about in wild delight at the possession of the sixpence.

It was somewhere about this hour, or a little later, for the shades of night were gathering on the earth, that Miss Lester and her brother were walking through the wood-path, already mentioned. Once more Maria had transgressed home orders, and had been to see Edith, for the accounts she heard of her state of health grew more dark day by day. The visit paid, she was now returning home, Wilfred escorting her through the wood. In more open parts, Maria would scarcely have dared to be seen with him, fearing it might get reported at home, and that unpleasantness would be the consequence. They had walked at first in silence, but Maria's thoughts were gradually winding themselves up to a pitch of excitement, and she suddenly broke it, clasping her hands as she turned to her brother.

"Oh, Wilfred! is there nothing that you can do. Try any thing. Look out for a situation; no matter what, so that you can but earn a trifle. Throw pride to the winds."

"Pride! Gad, I don't think much of that stops by me, Maria," was his reply. "What would you suggest that I should do? I know of nothing. I cannot go and open a general shop in Danesheld, wanting funds; I cannot engage myself as keeper to Lord Dane; I don't suppose I should get hired if I offered myself as footman to my father, to replace the one I hear is leaving."

"How can you thus turn what I say into ridicule? and Edith in the state she is!" rejoined Maria, with displeasure in her voice, but tears in her eyes.

"Not ridicule, Maria," he quietly replied. "These subordinate situations being closed to me, are a proof how much more closed better ones would be. It was in that light I spoke."

"But you are wrong. You draw a wrong deduction," she argued. "These mean sort of situations for making money, are of course closed to you; but there are others, suitable to a gentleman."

"I don't know how a gentleman, entirely devoid of means, could put himself in the way of obtaining such. Maria, it is of no use to finesse longer, and to play at pride and propriety. You see these clothes?" pointing to the velveteen suit he wore. "They are all I possess."

"Where are your others?" she uttered, breathlessly; "your better suits?"

"Pledged. Pledged for food. I may have to put in this coat also, for some pressing necessity, and to go about, astonishing Danesheld, in shirt-sleeves. It is not very likely that I could take any situation appropriate to a gentleman."

The crimson had flushed into Maria's face; it seemed that she was at a loss for words. They were drawing near to the wood, and Wilfred stopped.

"I shall not go any farther, Maria. But, before we part, I wish you would tell me whether there's truth, or not, in a report I have heard. Rumor runs that you are to marry Lord Dane."

Maria turned away her head, and remained silent.

"I see," said Wilfred, "it is so. Think well what you are about, Maria; remember he was once the choice lover of Lady Adelaide; and she his. That is, if tradition tells true."

"Do not allow yourself to repeat such stories," remonstrated Maria. "Lady Adelaide is papa's wife. And disabuse your mind upon another point, Wilfred; I do not wish to marry Lord Dane."

"Oh! Is the wish, the liking, all on his side?"

"It is not on mine. I do not dislike Lord Dane, but I shall never like him well enough to marry him. There is only one thing—"

At this moment an interruption occurred. It had pleased Mr. Lydney, buried in deep thoughts, to take a circuitous path from the castle to the Sailor's Rest, which path led him through the wood. He had scarcely entered it when his eye caught sight of young Mr. Shad, twined, something like a snake, round the thin trunk of a tree, and evidently in the act of listening. At the same moment, his ear caught the sound of voices. He went gently forward, laid his grasp upon the gentleman, and drew him out before the astonished gaze of Wilfred and Miss Lester.

Young Shad whined out—

"What had he done? It was hard a poor little fellow couldn't be watching an ant's nest, but he must be pounced upon and took up, as if he was a bird or a rabbit."

"I hope you were saying nothing that all the world may not hear," said Mr. Lydney, addressing them, "for this boy was certainly listening."

"No, I wasn't," sniffed Shad, trying to squeeze out a tear. "I never heard nothing. I was looking at the ant's nest."

"You young dog, you'll come in for my stick some of these days," cried Wilfred Lester, shaking his cane menacingly at him. "You are always up to your tricks. I don't believe there's an ant's nest there. No, there is not," he added, going to the spot, and examining. "Now, what do you deserve?"

"I never said as there was," wailed the incorrigible Shad. "I said as I was a looking for him. Granny al'ays tells me to look out for the ants' nests."

Finding himself at liberty, he scampered away at the utmost speed of his legs; but only to double back again when he was beyond sight and hearing. Dodging stealthily amidst the thick trees, he got as near to the spot as he dared, his ears all awake. Finding himself balked, for by that time the three were dispersing, he solaced his inquisitive mind by dodging the further movements of Mr. Wilfred Lester.

"As shrewd a young spirit as ever crossed my path, that Master Shad,"

exclaimed Mr. Lydney. "One to be guarded against, unless I am mistaken. Who is he? He told me he did not know his name."

"I don't think he does know it, or anybody else in this neighborhood, except the old woman he calls granny," replied Mr. Wilfred Lester. "Shad's parentage remains amidst the things untold. He is a sly young imp of mischief."

"He has an evil physiognomy, and a cunning one," returned Mr. Lydney. "Bad qualities, both; doubly bad when they go together."

"The gossips are engrossed with the tale of the loss of your property, the box brought to light by the divers," resumed Wilfred. "Is it found?"

"No! It is the most extraordinary, the most unaccountable—however, I will say no more till I call in the aid of the police," Mr. Lydney broke off. "Is Lord Dane a man of veracity?" he added, abruptly.

"I know nothing to the contrary," replied Wilfred Lester. "I cannot say that he is a favorite of mine; we all have our likes and dislikes; but— a man of veracity? Yes, I should deem him to be that. But I must leave you, for I have an appointment, and shall be late for it. Good-night. Lydney, just see my sister the few steps to the end of the wood."

He sped off unceremoniously, and Mr. Lydney turned to walk by the side of Miss Lester.

"Were the contents of this lost box of very much consequence?" she inquired.

"Of the very utmost consequence," he answered. "Strictly speaking, neither the box nor the contents belonged to me, but they were in my charge; and I would rather give every shilling I possess in the world than lose them."

"Are you going to make a long stay in Danesheld?"

"I cannot tell how long it will be. Hitherto I have been hoping for the box, which this morning brought up. Now it is gone again, and I am no more forward than before."

"Its disappearance certainly appears to savor of the marvelous," observed Maria. "But, rely upon it, it never was placed in the death-room."

"In the what room?" echoed Mr. Lydney. Maria smiled at his surprise.

"They call it the strong room now; but until the return of Lord Dane from abroad, it was known as the death-room, being the apartment where the Danes, after death, lie in state. Except in Lord Dane's presence, most people call it the death-room still."

"I fancy—now you speak of it—that Lord Dane's butler called it the death-room to-day; but it nearly escaped my notice," observed Mr. Lydney.

He conducted Maria to the door of the hall, and then wished her good-evening. From some cause they had dined earlier than usual that day, and Maria supposed that tea would be waiting. It was not, however, and she proceeded to the study of her father, where he sat alone. Mr. Lester was reading a newspaper; Maria waited till he looked up.

"Papa," she said, untying her bonnet-strings, "there has been an understood embargo, more implied than expressed to me, that I should not go to Wilfred's house."

"Of course," replied Mr. Lester; "it could not be permitted."

"I have come to tell you that I have transgressed it, and have been there, twice. The first time my going was, if I may so express it, involuntary; the second, this evening, I went in deliberation. It would not be right if I kept it from you, papa."

"And what took you there?" angrily demanded Mr. Lester, after surveying Maria for some moments in silence.

"I went to see Edith. Papa, I think she is dying."

Mr. Lester made no reply,—only let fall the glasses that rested across his nose. Their gold chain went down with a chink.

"And she is dying of hunger," Maria continued, catching up her breath with a sobbing sigh. "Dying of hunger, papa."

"Don't talk absurdly," reproved Mr. Lester.

"Papa, it is so. She cannot eat the coarse food they can alone procure, and she is sinking for want of the delicacies necessary for her condition. Miss Bordillion has helped them till she has little left for herself. Oh, papa, my heart feels as if it would burst."

"Why do you tell me this?"

"I could not be disobedient without telling you. Dear papa, will you not assist them? Just a little, to get Edith a few things until she is stronger."

"I will not," affirmed Mr. Lester, in a deliberate tone. "Your brother and his wife have brought this upon themselves, and they must abide by it. You cannot go near them again."

"Papa, I pray you do not impose that command upon me," she implored in agitation. "I am not sure,—dear papa, pardon my saying so,—but I am not sure that I could strictly obey it. He is my brother; he is deserted of all. I fear it may be my duty to stand by him, even though you bade me not. Do not bar all intercourse; I will promise very rarely to go; never, unless occasion should seem to require; and if you like, when that shall happen, I will tell you that I have been. Our mother is dead; you have other ties; but Wilfred and I are alone."

No reply made Mr. Lester. Maria waited, but none came; and she turned and quitted the room with a slow step.

CHAPTER XVII.

A THOUSAND POUNDS REWARD.

HAD Miss Lester quitted her father's study with a hasty step instead of a slow one, she would probably have run over Tifle; for that damsel had had her ear glued to the door throughout the greater portion of the interview. Tiffle proceeded to Lady Adelaide's dressing-room, closed the door with a mysterious air, and turned up the whites of her eyes.

"Such treason and plots as is being hatched, my lady; that of Guy Fox's was nothing in comparison. There's Miss Lester been shut up with master till this blessed minute, a pleading for them two married ones, and declaring that she has been to see 'em, and is going again."

"Impossible," returned Lady Adelaide; "Miss Lester would not disobey expressed commands."

"She has disobeyed 'em, my lady. And she has been a-making up a tale to her pa, that them two are famishing, and ought to be helped. My lady, if you don't mind, master will take 'em into favor again, and allow 'em a income—to the wrongs of the dear little cherybums at home, your ladyship's own. I—I—I'd let 'em famish, if it was me," emphatically added Tiffle.

"They deserve nothing better," said Lady Adelaide. "Does he go out at night still?"

"Oh, don't he?" replied Tiffle. "Last night as ever was, he and that Drake, and young Beecher was on my lord's grounds," she continued, sinking her voice. "Let it go on a bit, my lady; he'll be dropped upon."

"Where do you get your information, Tiffle?" demanded Lady Adelaide.

"My lady, I do get it, and it's for the good of the family I'm proud to serve. If I pay all my wages away in bribes, I don't regret it, so long as I can render service to your ladyship, and the precious little ones. But to say precisely how, when, and where I do get the information, is beyond me, and your ladyship must ixcuse my saying so. Let them two once get the upperhand of master, and they'd be for turning us out of house and home."

Before more was said, a loud knock, as of a visitor, was heard at the hall door. Tiffle—who seemed to make it her business to watch everybody's business in the house, as keenly as a cat watches a mouse—left the room with a spring, and planted herself where she could see down into the hall. The visitor admitted, she came back.

"Is it Lord Dane?" inquired Lady Adelaide.

"Not at all, my lady. It's that young man that is lodging at the Sailor's Rest; that Mr. Lydney who was hooked up in the life-boat. I saw Miss Lester walking with him just now, so she has invited of him to tea, no doubt."

"Saw Miss Lester walking with him! invited him to tea?" reiterated Lady Adelaide. "What are you saying, Tiffle?"

"Oh, my lady, they have growed to be upon quite close terms of friendship," carelessly replied Tiffle. "Miss Lester is forever meeting of him at Miss Bordillion's, where he have got intimate."

Mr. Lydney, however, had not come "to tea," or to visit Miss Lester. His business was with Mr. Lester, and into his study was he shown. Not many minutes had he quitted Maria when it occurred to him that Mr. Lester, in his magisterial capacity, might be of service to him. Mr. Lester received him cordially; a speaking acquaintanceship had grown up between them since the night of the wreck, and he liked young Lydney much. Miss Bordillion had also informed him of the service he had rendered Maria. "Saved her life," Miss Bordillion expressed it; but Mr. Lester laughed at that.

"I must ask you to pardon my calling upon you at this unseasonable hour,—unseasonable for business," began Mr. Lydney, as he took the chair placed for him. "You are, I believe, in the commission of peace for the county?"

"I am," replied Mr. Lester.

"Then will you allow me to request you to grant a warrant to search Dane Castle?"

Had Mr. Lester been applied to for a warrant to search his own house inside and out, he could not have evinced more surprise.

"Search Dane Castle?" he echoed.

"You probably have heard, Mr. Lester, the details of the loss of my box this day; for Danesheld is a small place, famous for tale-bearing; and a transaction taking place at one end of it at ten in the morning, would be known at the other by ten minutes past—"

"That is so," interrupted Mr. Lester with a laugh. "And I believe I am as cognizant of the circumstances attending the loss of the box, as you can be."

"Then, Mr. Lester, I will go on. That box, rely upon it, is in Dane Castle; and I must have it found."

"What grounds can you possibly entertain for coming to that conclusion?" slowly uttered Mr. Lester. "Lord Dane can have no motive for detaining or concealing the box : he would only be too glad to hand it over to you,—you being the owner."

"I draw my deductions from facts," returned the young man. "What right—nay, I will say what motive—had Lord Dane to interfere with my box at all? Mitchel told him it was mine, and that I was about to remove it."

"I do not myself see any necessity there was for his doing so," reflectively replied Mr. Lester. "As to his motive, it must have been zeal—over zeal that no harm should come to the things,—your box among them. Were I to conjecture, I should say the box fell from the cart, unseen, on its way to the castle."

"I think that would scarcely be your conjecture did you know how heavy the box was, Mr. Lester. It could not well fall unseen or unheard; and one of the men walked behind the cart. Besides, it was seen to be carried into the castle."

Mr. Lester pricked up his ears. The last little bit of information was new to him.

"By whom?" he eagerly asked. "I

understood it had not been observed whether it was positively taken in, or not."

"A somewhat noted young gentleman of your vicinity, Shad by name, saw it go in—"

Mr. Lester interrupted with a burst of laughter; and it was some moments before he recovered himself, so entirely did the avowal excite his mirth.

"Excuse me, Mr. Lydney, but the remark proved how great a stranger you are to our village politics and to Shad. Why, he is the falsest boy you can conceive; he tells more lies in an hour, than another lad would in a lifetime. I doubt if he ever spoke a word of truth yet, knowing it to be truth."

"I agree with you in all that," replied Mr. Lydney, who had sat perfectly composed until the laugh was over; "from my limited observation of the boy I should judge him to be an exceedingly bad boy, an habitual and systematic deceiver. Nevertheless, I avow to you my belief that in this one instance he has told me truth. Depend upon it, he can tell truth, if it suits his purposes of self-interest. He said the two men carried the box into the castle, it being nearly the last thing taken out of the cart, and that Lord Dane's butler followed them in. I repeat to you, Mr. Lester, my conviction that this account was in accordance with fact."

"Can you suspect any of the servants of having cribbed it?" hastily asked Mr. Lester. "Bruff is as honest as the day—a most respectable man—was butler to the old Lord Dane."

"No: I cannot suspect the servants; by what I hear, they never went near the box." And this was an unlucky admission of Mr. Lydney's, for it took away all semblance of a plea for the grant of the search-warrant; that is, according to the opinions or the prejudices held by Mr. Lester.

"Whom do you suspect?" he inquired of his guest, fixing his eyes searchingly upon him.

"It is a question, Mr. Lester, that I cannot answer you. I believe the box to be in the castle, concealed by some person or persons, either intentionally, or—it is just possible—inadvertently, the result of an oversight; therefore, I apply to you to grant me a search-warrant."

"I am sorry to refuse," he said, at length, "but I am really not satisfied that the law would justify me in doing so. The only direct evidence that the box did go into the castle comes from that Shad; scarcely one upon whose word we could venture to thrust the insult of a search-warrant upon Lord Dane."

He spoke the last sentence in a sarcastic tone. Mr. Lydney's voice rose courteously in answer.

"I thought it might prove so. I felt that you would be chary of granting a search-warrant against Lord Dane, who is your intimate friend. Well, Mr. Lester, I can hardly blame you; perhaps in your place I should not be any the more willing."

"Nay, nay," interposed Mr. Lester. "don't put the refusal upon friendship. I do not see that the grounds are sufficient to grant a search-warrant."

"I must apply to another magistrate," observed the young man.

"Of course that is entirely at your option. I do not think you will find another more willing to grant it than I. If you do, I am not sure that it would serve you."

"Why not?"

"Lord Dane is higher in the commission of peace than we are; we are but county magistrates; he is the lord-lieutenant; as such, we are under his authority,—under his thumb. Were a warrant to search his house issued by one of us, I am not sure but he has the power to draw his pen down it, and render it null and void. I say that I am not certain of this, Mr. Lydney, for I would not willingly mislead you; but I fancy it would prove to be the fact."

Not a very consolatory suggestion for William Lydney. He rose to leave. Mr. Lester rose also.

"Will you spend an hour or two with us this evening, and be introduced to Lady Adelaide?" said the latter. "We are just going to tea."

"I shall be very happy," was the answer. "I have thought once or twice that I should like to know Lady Adelaide."

But no sooner had Mr. Lester given the invitation than he repented of it, for it occurred to him how exceedingly awkward it would be did Lord Dane come in, as he mostly did now of an evening. It might be any thing but pleasant for two men to meet in social intercourse, one of whom was applying for a search-warrant against the other. Mr. Lester accordingly sat upon thorns, but his guest spent a remarkably pleasant evening, completely gaining the favor of Lady Adelaide. Lord Dane did not make his appearance.

Bearing in mind the doubt expressed by Mr. Lester whether Lord Dane might not quash any warrant issued by a magistrate, Mr. Lydney determined to apply direct to the police, and on the following morning proceeded to the station. The inspector was not there; one of the subordinate officers heard the story, and then asked what it was that he required,—what was the object of his application.

"I want the assistance of the police to aid in discovering this box," was the reply. "I wish Dane Castle to be searched for it."

The policeman gave a slight shake of the head, which seemed to argue rather unfavorably for Lydney's demand. He could not take any such responsibility upon himself, he observed, but he would report the application to his superior, and the gentleman had better call again.

Little indeed was Mr. Lydney acquainted with the usages of the neighborhood, and with Lord Dane's sway in it, if he supposed the police could receive such an application and not make his lordship acquainted with it. The inspector himself carried it to the castle in the course of the day, and Lord Dane accorded him a private interview.

"Search the castle, forsooth!" ironically ejaculated his lordship. "It were more to the purpose that he permitted himself to be searched; that he declared who and what he is. Look at the facts, inspector. Here's a young man saved from a wreck with what he stands upright in, taken up his abode at a public house, and worms himself into the best houses of the neighborhood, on a footing of equality. He is obstinately silent as to his antecedents: that he has been asked of them, I know, but he does not answer. How can we tell that he is not an adventurer, a chevalier d'industrie? For my own part, I believe him to be one, and that it will turn out so in the end; I have my reasons for thinking so. He spent last evening at Squire Lester's."

"Did he, indeed, my lord?" returned the inspector, in a tone of dismay, taking his cue from the peer.

"At Miss Bordillion's he is intimate; at other houses he is intimate; he has contrived to scrape acquaintance with my own sister,—places, all, where he has insinuated himself. Yesterday evening he was actually walking in the wood with—with"— Lord Dane arrested the words on the tip of his tongue, and then substituted others—"with a young lady; a young lady of the highest consideration."

"Why, there's no knowing what it may end in, if he really is an adventurer," cried the inspector.

"It will end in the neighborhood's having cause to repent its folly, its credulity," returned Lord Dane. "With regard to the box he claims—and I dare say it is just as much his as it is yours or mine—." But here his lordship summoned Bruff and the key, and marched the inspector to the strong room.

"Here they are, the things that came from the wreck," continued Lord Dane, pointing to the articles which lay on the floor, just as they had done the previous day. "Does it stand to common sense that if the box had been brought to this room it could have vanished out of it, the door being secured fast? Why that box more

than any other? No, Mr. Inspector, if the box had been here at all, here it would be still. Who is to know that he did not contrive to get it from the cart himself, and is making this fuss to put you police off the scent that he has got it?"

"A not-improbable supposition, if he forked what did not belong to him," cried the inspector. "A pretty fellow he, to talk of a search-warrant for the castle!"

"I'd see him hanging from the yard-arm of the tallest ship in the harbor before he should execute it," haughtily spoke his lordship. "But I am far from imposing the same impediment upon you, inspector. If you choose, for your own satisfaction, to go through every room and examine every nook and corner of the castle, you are at liberty to do so. Bruff will guide you, or you may go alone, as you please. Here's the trestle-closet: begin with that."

"My lord, for my own satisfaction I should certainly not need to do so: if it would be for your lordship's satisfaction, I will. You do not cast a doubt to any of the servants?" he added, lowering his tone.

"The servants?" echoed Lord Dane, with a pause and a stare, as though the idea to suspect them had not before occurred to him. "No, I don't; what should they want with the box? But—there, you had better go through the castle: it will set the matter at rest."

Accordingly the inspector did go through the castle, searching it thoroughly, but found no trace of the lost box. Lord Dane's manner had changed to one of chilling hauteur when the officer rejoined him.

"And when this man—Lydney, or whatever his name is—shall presume to speak to you again of a search-warrant for Dane Castle, inquire a little as to who *he* may be, and what he may be doing here, and where he comes from," said his lordship. "Understand me, inspector; you have my orders to do this: find out what you can, and report to me."

"Very good, my lord," said the inspector; and, bowing low, he backed out from the presence of Lord Dane.

The inspector was much occupied that day, and it was not till evening that Mr. Lydney succeeded in finding him. The inspector did not at first tell him that he would not accord his application; he fenced with the question. He went to work in his own cautious manner, every eye and ear open to gather what he could of the applicant and his belongings.

"Am I to understand," he demanded, "that you accuse Lord Dane of stealing the box?"

"No; I do not accuse him of that, not feeling sufficiently sure of my grounds," was the bold answer. "That Lord Dane had the box taken away in the cart is indisputable; that it must have reached the castle appears almost equally indisputable; and also, in my opinion, that it entered it. Where, then, is the box? Lord Dane does not give it up; he either cannot or he will not, one of the two; and the only course of action left to me, the only approach to redress, is to have the castle searched by the police."

"Were those proceedings adopted they would carry with them an outrage, an insult upon Lord Dane," urged the inspector. "You must remember who and what he is—a peer of Great Britain; lord-lieutenant of the county; lord of the manor; a man of high character—"

"High character?" interrupted the young gentleman.

"Yes; high character," warmly repeated the inspector, "and very high character, too. What, to the contrary, has ever been breathed against Lord Dane? But it's of no good wandering from the point like this. The fact is, sir, to speak plainly, before we can listen to any charge or slur on Lord Dane, we must know who it is that would prefer it."

"What difference does that make?" inquired Mr. Lydney.

"It makes all the difference," said the keen inspector. "A worthless fellow, a known poacher or smuggler,

might come to us with some trumped-up, imaginary complaint against his lordship, and we should show him out at the door for his temerity. But were a gentleman of position and character, such—let us say, for example—as Squire Lester, to bring forward any charge against his lordship, it would carry weight. Now, do you see the distinction?"

"I am a gentleman, if you require that assurance," returned Mr. Lydney, "one entitled to position."

"Can you prove it, sir?"

"You have my word for it," was the haughty answer; "a word that never was doubted yet."

The inspector smiled somewhat broadly. "Words don't go for much in law," said he; "proofs are better. You are an American, I have heard.

"I am an Englishman. That is, of English descent, though born in America. My father's family are of reputation in England, and know how to hold their own."

The inspector's ears were opened an inch wider, and his tongue was ready. "Where do they live? in what part of England? Lydney? Lydney? the name is not familiar to me as borne by any family of note."

"I cannot give you further information. It is as I have told you, and you must trust to my word."

"But where can be the objection to speak out?" urged the officer.

"That is my business," was the cold, stiff answer.

"Very well, sir," returned the inspector; "you have said just as much as I expected you to say, and no more. You assert that you are somebody grand and great, and when I ask for corroborative proof you decline to give it. Now, *do* you think that any charge from you against my Lord Dane would be listened to?"

Lydney regarded him in silence.

"Perhaps you'll tell me whether you followed any business in America?" pursued the officer.

"I have told you I am a *gentleman*," was the quiet but emphatic answer.

"Will you tell me, then, what your business may be in this neighborhood, and how long you intend to stop in it?"

"My business in the neighborhood!" echoed Mr. Lydney. "Why, did not the sea cast me upon it? As to my remaining, if I choose to remain in it for good, I believe there is no law to prevent me. I can promise you one thing, I don't quit it till the box is found."

"Our conference is at an end, sir," said the inspector. "My time is valuable."

"Am I to understand that the police refuse their assistance to me in my efforts to recover the box?"

"Not at all," more cordially replied the inspector: "we should be very glad to find it, for our own satisfaction. What we decline to do, is, to act in any offensive manner towards Lord Dane. Especially," he pointedly added, "when an unknown stranger, and one who won't declare any thing about himself, urges it. But now, sir, I am not ill-natured, and if it will ease your mind at all to know it, I can testify that if you did get the search executed, it would be fruitless, for the box is not in the castle."

"You cannot know that it is not."

"I never testify to a thing that I don't know," coolly returned the officer. "I searched the castle myself for it this day."

"You!"

"I did: searched it effectively and thoroughly: there was not a space the size of that," holding up two fingers of his hand, "that I did not go into. I did it by Lord Dane's wish—for of course it was not an absolute impossibility, though next door to it, that the servants had not made free with the box. It is nowhere in the castle."

To say that Lydney was completely astonished at the information, would be saying little. He had fully made up his mind that the box *was* in the castle.

"Then where can it be? what can have become of it?" he exclaimed aloud.

"I can't say: to my mind, it's a queer business altogether. I don't much like the fact of that Granny Dean's Shad having been close to the cart when it was unloading. That imp would lay his hands on any thing he could; and a japanned box, got up from a wreck, would be the very treasure he'd like to finger. Still, that idea does not go for much with me; that he did not carry it off himself, is certain; first, because he could not, from its weight; next, because I have evidence that when the cart went away empty, he shambled, empty handed, after it."

"You have been collecting evidence upon this loss, I perceive."

"Undoubtedly. When losses take place, whether mysterious or otherwise, it is our business to do so. We were yesterday in possession of all the facts,—so far as they go."

"And what are your deductions?" was the next eager question. "Can you give a guess at how or where the abstraction took place?"

"Not the faintest. It's as uncertain a case as ever came under our care. We shall keep a sharp look-out. It is your own box, I think you said?" the inspector carelessly added, with a keen, rapid glance of the eye.

"I did not say so," was the unexpected answer. "It was in my charge, and I have authority to claim it; but neither the box nor its contents belonged to me."

"May I inquire whose it was?"

"When the box shall be found," was Mr. Lydney's rejoinder, suppressing a peculiar smile. "You may ask then, and will be satisfactorily answered. Would it be of any use," he resumed, as though the thought had that instant struck him, "to offer a reward?"

"Well, it might," said the inspector. "Particularly if any customer, like that young Shad, should have got hold of it. Yes: a reward might bring the box back."

"Then be so good as to take the necessary steps to announce it. Spare no trouble, no time, no expense: you shall be well repaid."

"Very good, sir. What shall we say?—five pounds?—ten pounds?—for the reward, I mean?"

"Offer a thousand pounds," quietly rejoined Mr. Lydney. "A thousand pounds to be paid to any one who shall restore the box intact."

Surprise and the munificent amount both combined, sent the inspector staggering backwards.

"A thousand pounds!" he stammered. "The box must be valuable, sir, and you rich to offer that."

"The box, to its owner, is invaluable," replied Mr. Lydney. "And the reward I offer would be paid from his pocket, not from mine."

He quitted the station-house as he concluded, and the inspector followed him to the door, and looked after him down the street.

"I said it was queer, and it is," was his mental comment. "A thousand pounds!"

———————

CHAPTER XVIII.

A BATTLE ROYAL—A WOOD.

MR. LYDNEY walked down the street slowly, his brain working. The inspector's information of having searched the castle by Lord Dane's orders, astonished him much; and he began to ask himself whether he was justified in assuming that Lord Dane had been the willful delinquent. The train of thought led him to glance at others connected with the affair, especially young Shad. Could it be that that young gentleman had succeeded in blinding him, and was he the real thief? or the assistant of the thieves? Verily he began to doubt it.

Somewhat impulsive in what he did, he determined on the instant to seek out Shad, and question him again. A glance too cunning, or a word too sharp, might betray Shad's share in it. He was not quite sure of the road that would conduct him to Granny Bean's, but believed it was the one that skirted the wood, leading past the cottage of Wilfred Lester, and he took it.

"I believe now I ought to have turned down by Miss Bordillion's," he soliloquized, as he arrived opposite Wilfred's residence, and halted. "Suppose I ask?"

Opening the gate, he walked up the little garden, where something occurred that startled him considerably. The door was stealthily unlatched, and he was pounced upon by a tall female, and dragged towards the dark passage.

"Thanks be to the stars that you're come!" apostrophized she, in a covert whisper. "Now it's of no use your being angry and struggling to get off. I've had you in my arms when you were a baby, and I know what's right and what's wrong. There's a whisper abroad that the poachers are out tonight, and if the keepers have got an inkling of it, there'll be a conflict. You shan't go, then, master; you are killing your wife outright,—sooner a deal than she'd go of her own natural ailments, for she is beginning to suspect, and lies in dread. Have you no pity for her, Mr. Wilfred? Come in, and let me bar the door, and then you, at any rate, will be in safety."

"My good woman," he exclaimed, as soon as he had breath to speak, for she had held him in a tight grip, "for whom do you take me? I am Mr. Lydney. Is your master at home?"

The servant fell against the wall like one turned stupid, and he had to repeat his question.

"I'm just a fool and nothing else!" cried she, speaking in a light tone, to cover, Lydney thought, her agitation. "I was expecting a friend to call upon me, and thought it was him; and I'm sure I ask your pardon, sir. Master? no, sir; I don't think he is in."

"Never mind: I merely troubled his house to ask a question. Which way will take me to the hut of Granny Bean?"

"Straight on, sir, to the right. When you come to the triangle, turn down the field, and you'll see it,—a little low cottage, all by itself, at the back of the wood. Once again, sir, I beg your pardon, and I hope you'll never talk about the mistake, or what I said or did ?"

"Not I," laughed Mr. Lydney. "Make my compliments to your master."

So he had been on the right road, after all ; and a few minutes brought him to Granny Bean's cottage. It appeared to be closely shut up, and he might have imagined its inmates, Granny and Shad, had retired to rest, but for the commotion that was taking place within. Now rose an old woman's voice in shrill shrieks of rage ; now Shad's in shriller whines. Mr. Lydney knocked, on the door and on the shutters, but little chance was there of his being heard while the noise lasted.

"You infamous young dog," raved she, with a profuse sprinkling of worse language, which the reader may imagine if he pleases, but which certainly will not be transcribed : "to go and rob your old granny of her hard-earned savings ! You'll come to the gallows, you will."

"'Taint yourn," returned Shad, his denial intermixed with similar embellishments of speech. "The new gemman give it me for telling him about the box, and I'll take my oath to it. Come, you ! hand it over."

"Oh you wicked sarpint ! as if any gemman 'ud go and give *you* a whole silver sixpence ! Now, will you be off ? You ought to have been on the watch a good half-hour ago."

"No, I wun't," said Shad's voice. "I wun't go on the watch, and I wun't stir anywheres till I gets my sixpence."

The old woman appeared to be beating him, or he her, by the scuffling sound and the shrieks. "I'll tell Miss Tiffle ! I'll tell Miss Tiffle !" the old voice reiterated.

"Miss Tiffle may be hanged, and you with her !" gasped Shad, as the commotion grew worse and worse. Mr. Lydney had no doubt they were fighting and struggling for possession of the sixpence. He feared some injury might be done, and he gave a thundering peal at the shutters, enough

to awaken their alarm, just as a loud shout of triumph from Shad seemed to proclaim that victory and the sixpence had declared themselves for him.

Total silence supervened : the knock had startled them. Mr. Lydney thundered again. But still he remained unanswered. He could hear some stealthy movements inside, accompanied by the hasty shutting of a door, and he knocked once more, louder than ever.

It brought forth the head of the woman to a window on the right. The cottage had two rooms, both on the ground-floor, a window in each. She opened the shutters, and thrust her face through the aperture, reconnoitering—a red and wrinkled face, surmounted by a cap in tatters, probably (the tatters) the result of the recent conflict, the whole shaking as if suffering from palsy.

"Have you been committing murder here ?" demanded Mr. Lydney.

"I was a saying of my prayers out loud, if that's murder," returned the dame. "What now ? what do you mean ?"

The bold assertion took away his self-possession for a moment. Where was the profit of bandying words with such a woman ? "I want Shad," he resumed.

"Shad ! I can't go for to disturb him from his rest to-night. Shad's abed and asleep."

"Why, you audacious old creature !" he could not help exclaiming. "I wonder you don't fear a judgment for falsehoods so deliberate. You and Shad have just been at it, tooth and nail, fighting after a sixpence. Let me tell you the sixpence is his, for I gave it him."

"Now, did you, indeed, sir ?" was the bland answer, the tone changing as if by magic : "what a dear, good, generous gentleman you must be ! You haven't got another about you, to bestow in charity upon a poor, lone, wretched, half-starved widder, have you ? I'd remember you in my prayers ever after, I would."

"If I had fifty, I would not give you the shadow of one ; and I don't imagine your prayers will do yourself much good, let alone anybody else. I want Shad, I say."

"Oh, sir, dear sir, you are a joking ; perhaps another time you'll remember me. I'd be everlasting grateful, if it was only a few poor coppers."

"Do you hear me ask for Shad ?" interrupted Mr. Lydney. "Send him out to me ; or open the door that I may get to him."

"Shad's abed and asleep, which I'll swear to, and I daredn't break into his night's rest," was the impudent answer. "A delicate child, as he is, and the stay and staff o' my life—if I was to lose him, I should die of grief. Come any time in the morning, sir, when his night's rest's over, and you're welcome. I tucked him up, the darling, a hour ago in his little bed, and a sweet sleep he dropped off into."

"Of all the extraordinary characters, I think you must be the worst !" uttered Mr. Lydney. "Shad's no more in bed than I am. I heard your conflict, I tell you. These false assertions sound perfectly awful from a woman at your time of life."

"Strange noises is heard outside this hut, at times,—folks have said so afore. It's the witches a playing in the air, I fancy ; and it's them you must have heard,—unless it was me at my prayers."

"Will you send out Shad ?"

"I'm sure I'd obleege you in any ways but that, such a nice gentleman as you seem to be ; but I wouldn't wake up my poor sickly gran'child for any thing—no, not if you offered me fifty sixpences."

Giving a good-night to Granny Bean, more emphatic than polite, Mr. Lydney strode away. He must put off seeing Shad till the morning. He did not return to the road, but went to the back of the cottage, where he believed he should find a path leading through the wood, and that would be the nearest way to the Sailor's Rest. Curiosity induced him to turn round and look at the cottage, and there he saw a door ; so Master Shad and his granny had ingress and egress by back and by front.

Pursuing the path, which was there as he had expected, Mr. Lydney sped on with a smart step, buried in thought. It was a starlight night ; though few stars penetrated to the wood-path ; nevertheless, it was not wholly dark. He had arrived at about the midst of the wood, where the trees were thickest, when a sound, as of one pushing through the thick brambles, caught his ear. Having been told that certain suspicious characters did sometimes lurk in that wood, Mr. Lydney drew close to the trees, to see who might be approaching.

It was Wilfred Lester. Panting, eager, excited, he came tearing on, at a right angle with Lydney, where no path seemed to be. He crossed the path by a bound, penetrated the trees on its opposite side, and went pushing on, as though he were making straight for home, and clearing a way to get to it.

Mr. Lydney remained immovable. Not looking after him, for the trees prevented that, but wondering what his appearance could mean. That Wilfred was in excessive agitation was apparent, and involuntarily certain mysterious words, spoken by the servant when she had so unceremoniously made a prisoner of him, rose to the recollection of Mr. Lydney. He was, as the saying runs, "putting that and that together," and by no means liking the appearance of things, when another movement, one far more stealthy, attracted his attention.

Stealing out into the path in the trail left by Wilfred Lester, came Mr. Shad, like a young hound scenting its prey. Once in the path, he made a dead stoppage, unconscious that any eye or ear was near him.

"He's tored home to his lair," soliloquized he, aloud, looking at the spot where Wilfred Lester had disappeared. "No good to track him again to-night. I'll go and tell her now."

Mr. Lydney had stretched out his hand to lay it on the boy, but a second impulse prompted him to hesitate. Far better, himself, track this erratic gentleman, and discover if possible, what treason was being hatched. That some plot was agate against Wilfred Lester, and probably against others, Mr. Lydney felt convinced. He also felt pretty nearly convinced of another thing : that Wilfred was hatching enough mischief, of his own accord, against himself; but that was no reason why Shad should augment it into more.

Shad flew along the path, in the direction opposite to Granny Bean's, and when near the end of the wood struck among the trees to the right; a minute or two brought him to the wood's edge, and close to the back of Squire Lester's. Mr. Lydney followed him : tall and slender, he could penetrate the trees as well as Shad, and when Shad stopped he stopped.

Shad was in his favorite attitude, twined, just like a snake, round one of the outer trees thin stem, gazing in expectation at the open space before him. Mr. Lydney halted sufficiently near to see and hear : he wondered who the " her " was to whom Shad was bound. Having had experience by this time of the insatiable nature of Madame Ravensbird's curiosity, a half suspicion crossed his mind that she might be the audience expected by Shad. Not so, however.

A female of stealthy and ambling gait, not unlike Shad's own, appeared, somewhat mysteriously, in that open space. She could not have sprung from the ground, like the spirits do in pantomimes, therefore it was fair to infer that she had emerged from some back-door of Squire Lester's. Shad gave a soft whistle, and the lady came tripping up to it. It was Tiffle.

" Well?" cried she.

" He's agone right home," answered Shad. " When I got up to 'em, they was a having hot words, him and Beecher and Drake, and another; I thought it were Ben Nicholson, but I wouldn't swear it. He was a blowing of 'em up—"

" Ben Nicholson was blowing 'em up?" interrupted Tiffle.

" How stupid you be !" snapped Shad. ". Lester. He was a blowing the three men up for wanting to go right where they know'd the keepers 'ud be, and he got in a passion, a swearing he wouldn't jine in nothing that might bring bloodshed, and back he went, a cutting right through the thick of the bushes I followed after him till he cut over the cross-path, our'n, and into the bushes ayond it. I know'd then that gone home he was for sartin. I say, where'll be the pull o' my dodging him, if he's a going to take to shirking ?"

Tiffle had listened in silence.

" How did they ferret out where the keepers would be ?" asked she.

" Can't tell," said Shad. " I only got up at the tail o' their confab. I didn't hear nothing of what they'd been a saying afore."

" Then you were late; and a wicked, inattentive, good-for-nothing—"

Shad began to whimper.

" If I was late, it were granny's fault, Mrs. Tiffle. She set on me and a'most killed me. You should be hid in the oven or somewhere, and see her in her tantrums, you'd not believe it was any thing but Old Nick's mother let loose. Look here ! here's where she bited me, and here's where she kicked at me, and here's where she scratted me, and clutches of my hair she tored out by han'fuls."

Shad exhibited various damaged spots about his face and arms, and let fall a shower of dolorous tears. Tiffle —somewhat to the surprise of Mr. Lydney, who had recognized her for Lady Adelaide's maid—was remarkably demonstrative in her condolences. She grasped Shad tenderly in her arms, and kissed the places fervently with her own lips.

" Granny's a regular hyenia when she's put up," cried she. " But I'll be even with her. What did she do it for ?"

"She have got the nastiest, slyest ways," returned Shad, who appeared not to relish the embrace so much as Tiffle did, and wriggled himself from it as soon as he possibly could. "She dives into my pockets and into any thing, she do, and to-night she found a sixpence in 'em, and she set on and swored it were hern, and that I robbed her on't, and she grabbed it from me, and—my ! warn't there a shindy ! and such a row came to the shutters amid it. I grabbed it again, though," concluded the gentleman, with glee, as he took out the bright sixpence and exhibited it to Tiffle.

Tiffle did not look at it with equanimity. She took the same view of its possession that Granny Bean had done,—though whether granny had really believed that it was stolen from her, or that she put forth the plea to gain possession of it, cannot be told.

"You little divil !" apostrophized Tiffle, her affectionate mood changing. "If you begin to bone money, you'll end your days a-working in gangs and irons. Now, you tell me where you stole that ?"

"If ever I see the like ! You're as bad as granny," whined the boy. "I might as well be a dog what's mad, and roped-up at once ! That there sixpence was given me by a gemman; gived out and out."

"Give for what ?" sharply responded Tiffle.

"Give for telling about his box. It's that one what's stopping at the Sailor's Rest. He asked—did I see the things took up to the castle-gates, and I said I see 'em; and then he said if I'd tell him the truth and no lie, whether the box went into the castle or not, I should get a sixpence, and I did, and he give it me."

"Did you see the box took in ?" quickly asked Tiffle.

"What should ail me ?" responded Shad. "I were a watching."

"And it was took right in ?"

"It was took right in," answered Shad, his eyes glistening, "as right in as ever any thing was took into that castle yet. Them two miller's chaps carried of it, like they did 'tother lots, and that big Mr. Bruff a follered of 'em. Not as he seemed to be taking much heed hisself. I telled the gemman this, and he give me the sixpence."

"Shad, you must keep your eyes open upon him, that Lydney, as well as upon Will Lester," was Tiffle's next remark. "Ferret out all about him, where he goes, and what he does; he's in this wood sometimes, I know; find out what for. He looks like a gentlemin ; but he may be one of them gentlemin what comes to places to be after watches, and chains, and rings. You find out. I've got my reasons. And be sure, mark it if you see him with Miss Lester."

Mr. Lydney, from his hiding-place, felt infinitely obliged to her.

"And now, there's no more to be done to-night, as he has hooked it off home," proceeded the refined Tiffle. "So you get back again as quick as you can, and get to bed."

She turned away towards the hall : Shad turned towards the path that would lead him to Granny Bean's ; and Mr. Lydney remained where he was till the echo of their footsteps should die away.

Scarcely had Tiffle gone many yards, however, when she met Lord Dane, in the angle made by the side of the hall : to the right was the back-entrance ; to the left, the front. Tiffle was speeding on to the former ; Lord Dane was coming from the latter, and they came in contact.

"Is it you, Tiffle ?" cried his lordship, gayly. "Enjoying a ramble by starlight ?"

"Oh, my lord, you are pleased to joke," simpered Tiffle. "My days for starlighted rambles is over. I leave 'em for the young now, my lord : I've had my turn. Last night I see Miss Lester walking cosy in the starlight,—the evening-star was out, at any rate, if it wasn't late enough for the others,—and I thought how romintic it was : it put me in mind of my own sentamintel days, my lord. There was a gentlemin by her side, —him that the wreck cast up.

Had it been daylight, instead of starlight, Tiffle would scarcely have presumed to fix her eyes so keenly upon Lord Dane: she believed she had thrown out a shaft that would take.

"Wrecks cast up rogues as well as gentlemen," responded his lordship, in a stern, displeased tone. "A man whom nobody knows is scarcely one to be walking by starlight with Miss Lester."

"Just the very refliction that occurred to myself, my lord," acquiesced Tiffle, complacently. "And says I to myself, 'I'll keep a sharp look-out over you, young man, for Miss Lester's sake, if you presumes to ipproach too near of her.' And so I shall, my lord."

"Quite right, Tiffle," cried his lordship, warmly. And as they parted company, a golden sovereign was left in Tiffle's hand.

This appeared to be a night prolific in adventures and encounters. Before Mr. Lydney had well removed from his hiding-place, he found himself face to face with a man—a youngish man—who was dragging himself covertly through the wood. He appeared alarmingly startled at the encounter, and leveled his gun at Mr. Lydney.

"Halloa, my man, what's that for?" cried the latter, unmoved. "Do you take me for a cut-throat?"

"If you don't say who you are, and what you are doing here, I'll shoot you," was the reply.

"I feel infinitely obliged to you. Have you any more right to be in the wood than I have? I should be glad to know."

Mr. Lydney spoke with courtesy; and the man could not fail to remark that his voice was that of a gentleman. He had feared a keeper.

"You were posted there to watch me?" he exclaimed.

"Nay," said Mr. Lydney, "I may with equal reason reverse the accusation, and say you were watching me.

I don't know who you are; I never saw you in my life that I know of; and my time is more valuable than to be wasted in looking after strangers, if yours is not. You must have escaped from a lunatic asylum."

The man let fall his gun. He had been peering at Mr. Lydney as well as the obscurity around allowed him, and at last made out that he was not a foe; at all events, not a known one.

"I ask your pardon for my haste," he said; "I thought you were somebody else. The fact is, nobody but suspicious characters are ever prowling in the wood so late as this, unless it's them dratted keepers, who are ever ready to swear an innocent man's life away."

Mr. Lydney laughed. Young-man-like, he had no objection to a spice of adventure, and he was naturally of a kindly, affable disposition; if he could do no good to a fellow-creature, he would not do him harm.

"Are you aware of the insinuation against yourself which that last speech implied? 'Nobody but suspicious characters.' I conclude you mean poachers. Poachers and keepers. Well, I am neither the one nor the other. If you choose to beat about this wood, or any other part of Danesheld, from January till December, carrying a gun in one hand and snare-nets in the other, you are welcome, for all the business it is of mine. Were they my preserves, it would be a different matter."

"You won't go and say to-morrow that you dropped upon me here with a gun?"

"I should be clever to say it, seeing I know you neither by sight nor name. But if you prefer a specific promise, you may take it. Life is short enough, my man, for the little good we can accomplish, without passing it in doing gratuitous injury to others."

The man liked the tones, and liked the words; he could not account for it, but his heart opened to the speaker, as it had not opened of late years.

"I think, sir, you are the gentleman stopping at the Sailor's Rest, whose box is missing."

"The same," replied Mr. Lydney.

"I nearly got into trouble over that box yesterday. I happened to be passing the castle on my way to my home, as the cart was unloading, and I halted for a few minutes, and looked on. Them keen police heard of it, and had me up to the station; whether they thought I had walked it off, or had seen anybody else walk it off, I don't know. I laughed at 'em. Young Shad and two or three more urchins could testify that I didn't go near enough to touch any thing on the cart."

"You must have heard the box described," rejoined Mr. Lydney. "Did you see it?"

"I did not see it, sir, to my knowledge or recollection. But if, as I hear, it was underneath the rest of the things, I was not likely to. I stopped but a few minutes, and they had just begun to unload."

"You cannot give a guess as to where it is gone, or who took it?" resumed Mr. Lydney, a thought occurring to him.

"No, that I can't. I have not thought much about it. That Shad's as ready-fingered as a magpie, but they say it was too heavy for him to lift."

"I would give a good reward if it were restored to me, untampered with," resumed Mr. Lydney.

"Would you, though?" quickly rejoined the poacher, as if the sound were music to his ears.

"Fifty guineas."

"Fifty guineas!" uttered the man, as much astonished as the inspector had been.

"Fifty guineas, and no questions asked. Provided it were restored to me before midday to-morrow. After that, a different offer may be made, *and* questions asked, pretty sharp ones."

"By jingo! that's worth looking after," exclaimed the man. "I know a fellow or two, who *have* done a little in the fingering line, sir, and I'll—I'll Be on to them. If I can hear of the box you shall have it on those terms. Honor bright, though."

"Honor bright, on the word of a gentleman. The fifty guineas shall be paid, and no inquiries made. I fancied you might perhaps hear of it among your friends."

Little cared Mr. Ben Beecher—for it was no other—for the last delicate insinuation: indeed, it may be questioned if he heard it. A golden vision had been opened to him, and in that he was absorbed.

But the two, so strangely met, were not to part without observation. Lord Dane, in walking away from his conference with Tiffle, heard the sound of voices, and began to peer about him for the purpose of ascertaining who their owners might be. His lordship's thoughts were directed to poachers.

He saw Mr. Ben Beecher, the latter passing out of the wood close to Lord Dane. But no sooner had he passed out than he passed in again, penetrating to Lydney.

"I'm afraid it's of no use saying to-morrow at midday, sir: there'll not be sufficient time for what I shall want to do, and the people I must see. Say twenty-four hours from this, and I have little doubt I can hear of it, and bring it. I would meet you here, too, by ourselves: I'd rather not go to the Sailor's Rest."

"Very well," replied Mr. Lydney, after considering, "I will give you the extra time. In this same spot," he added, after a pause; "to-morrow night at the same time."

Now the last sentence, only the last, appointing the meeting, reached the ears of Lord Dane, for Lydney raised his voice that it might catch Beecher's ear, who was again departing.

"Who can the speaker be?" thought Lord Dane: "the voice does not seem unfamiliar. I'll be down upon you, my gentlemen, to-morrow night."

Lydney! His lordship stared with all his eyes as Lydney came forth to view, and walked away.

"Then he *is* a bad character, and a poacher to boot!" muttered Lord Dane.

CHAPTER XIX.

THE WRIT.

BRIGHTLY rose the sun on the following morning; brightly, as the day went on, did it throw its rays into the little sitting-room of Wilfred Lester. On the sofa lay Edith : she did not keep her bed, but was in the habit of getting up after breakfast. Wilfred sat on the arm of the sofa making some flies for fishing.

A fair, fragile being, almost a child, looked she, as she lay there : her features attenuated, her cheeks hectic. She wore a white wrapping-gown, which possibly made her appear more of an invalid than any other dress would. She was anxious to say something to her husband, but the topic was one of dread and agitation, and she trembled to set about it.

"Wilfred," she exclaimed at length, dashing hurriedly into the subject, "where was it that you went last night?"

"Went?" he returned, bending his head over the flies. "Nowhere in particular. I was out and about, talking to one, talking to another."

"So you always say," resumed Edith, in a low tone. Why will you not tell me the truth?"

"You are not jealous, are you?" was his next remark, with an air of pleasantry.

She raised herself, and seizing his hand, drew him towards her, speaking in a nervous whisper.

"Oh, Wilfred, my husband, do not try to joke it away, but answer me. Is it true what people say? They declare that you go out with the poachers; that you are learning to do as they do."

"Stop a bit," he interrupted. "Who told you that, Edith ? Because if any man were base enough to bring to a wife such tales of her husband, I'll mark him, as sure as my name's Lester. If a woman, I'll tell her what she is."

"Is it true, Wilfred ?"

"I ask who brought you the news ?"

he reiterated. "Before I answer your question you must answer mine."

"No one brought it to me, in the sense you would imply," she rejoined. "It was—let me see—the day before yesterday. I had come down here, and Sarah did not know it; the door was ajar, and I heard some one accost her at the kitchen-window. She was ironing at the board underneath it, and I suppose had got it open. I don't know who it was, Wilfred ; I cannot detail to you what I heard ; neither did I listen purposely, but some words caught my ear. They turned me sick ; faint ; they were to the effect that you went out at night with the poachers, that you had been one of them in that late attack upon Cattley ; the words and the tone seemed to insinuate that Sarah must know it to be true. Oh, Wilfred, I have felt since that morning that I would rather die than bear the burden of the fear."

"Would it not have been as easy for you to assume the wicked tale to be false?" he inquired.

"I might have deemed it false, but for Sarah's words in answer ; I am sure I should have thought it too dreadfully improbable to be true. But she—"

"Why ! did she uphold it ?" he interrupted, with impetuosity.

"No ; she denied it," answered Edith, in a low, shuddering tone ; "but she denied it with falsehoods ; denied it too eagerly. She retorted that whoever said it, must be fools and liars ; she vowed and protested that her master—you—was never out after sunset. Now you know, Wilfred, it is after sunset—after dark in fact— that you do go out ; and some nights you have not been home till early morning. Besides, there was a tone of fear in Sarah's voice as she spoke, giving me the impression that she knew it to be true."

"And that's all ?" he asked.

"Is it not enough ?"

"No : you must not be so silly. Making me into a poacher, indeed ! a midnight attacker of keepers! You have certainly an exalted opinion of your husband, Edith. I would no more attack a keeper, than I would attack you."

"But where is it you go to when you are out at night?"

"Never you mind where, Edith. I am not attacking keepers. If I get into any troublesome escapades, it will serve my father right. I don't mean escapades that the law could touch, you foolish girl," he added hastily, seeing her terrified countenance. "Pray have you been gossiping over this to Sarah?"

Edith shook her head.

"I have not hinted to her that I heard any thing said, but I have asked her where you go to at night—I could not help it. I asked her two or three times yesterday, and she pretended to think I was afraid of your catching cold, and kept telling me not to worry myself."

"Edith," said Wilfred Lester, "a man is generally driven to good or to evil by circumstances. As they may be favorable, or the contrary, as the world uses him, so follow his own acts."

"As his conduct is, so will his circumstances be," she said, stopping what he was about to add. "Yes, Wilfred, it lies with himself to be prosperous and happy, or not; in nine cases out of ten, you will find that as a man plants, so will he reap."

"Nonsense!" returned Wilfred, "it is as he's used. Look at my case. I am used infamously by my father,—kept out of what I ought to enjoy on the one hand; on the other, I have you, whom I have made my wife, and vowed to succor and cherish, dying of want—yes, of want, Edith—before my eyes. My darling! if I went into the highway, and robbed the first man I met, none could say I was not driven to it."

"Don't think of me," she answered with eager, painful emotion, her wan, white face lifted pleadingly to his. "I shall grow stronger soon; I do not require any thing more than I

have. If you will only be patient and endure, this dark cloud will pass away. Have faith in God. But, oh, Wilfred! do not let my imaginary wants lead you to evil."

"Imaginary!" he uttered.

"Indeed, I think I shall soon be better; and you know my Aunt Margaret brings me many things. Wilfred, remember,—'we must not do evil that good may come.'"

"My wrongs make me desperate; your suffering makes me desperate," retorted Wilfred. But she interrupted him.

"It is just this, Wilfred: if you do wrong, or go wrong, you will kill me. I can bear poverty and privation; I cannot bear disgrace and ill-doing. Act so as to bring it upon us, and I shall not survive."

At this juncture, Sarah put in her head; half spoke, half beckoned to her master, and he followed her to the adjoining room, the kitchen. Edith, her fears, since the last two days, painfully alert against some obscure dread, to which she could give neither shape nor name, sprang from the sofa and unlatched the door, which they had closed.

Sarah had advanced to the ironing-board, and pointed to some beans that lay upon it.

"What's to be done for missis?" asked she. "She can't eat these, and they are every thing I have been able to get to-day. Credit's all gone, master."

"There's a partridge in the house."

"Well, master, the truth is, she can't eat partridge any longer. She never liked 'em. When at Miss Bordillion's, as I hear, if they had game for dinner, something was always got for her. There are some folks who turn against game, and she's one; and when they are sick, their fancies are all the stronger. And for this last month, pretty near, she has had nothing else. I have tried the partridges every way to tempt her; I've roasted 'em, I've boiled 'em, I've fricasseed 'em, I've fried 'em, and one day I chopped 'em up and made 'em into balls, but it didn't do; it *was* partridge, and that was enough. She makes a show of eating a bit before you; but her stomach heaves right against 'em now, and she can't pretend any longer."

Wilfred Lester stood by the board, gloomy and perplexed. He knew no way whatever of procuring any thing else for Edith: as Sarah observed, all credit was gone. If a mutton-chop would have saved her life, he must pay the butcher for it before it was sent home.

"Can't you do up some eggs for to-day?" he asked.

"I could if I had 'em. Eggs are no more to be had than any thing else, without money. And there's another thing, master, that looks blue: the coals are almost out."

Inexpressibly relieved to find the colloquy with Sarah related to no more dread topic than her comforts, Edith breathed a silent thanksgiving, and called to her husband. It was at this moment her voice was heard.

"Wilfred."

He stepped into the parlor. She was standing in it with a bright, quite a merry face.

"Do not be so anxious about my luxuries," smiled she. "I overheard your debate with Sarah. I was alarmed when she called you out,—mysteriously, as I thought,—and I opened the door. I can eat some of the beans; I can, indeed; I shall do very well. As to the partridges,—well, I confess that I am tired of them: but you must treat me as a capricious child is served; make me go without, if I cannot eat what is provided."

"And will that be the way to get up your strength? to restore you to health?" he mournfully returned. "Whilst the grass grows, Edith, the steed starves; whilst you are starving, I may lose you."

She turned away, for her eyes were filling with tears. But just then some commotion was heard in the kitchen. Sarah's voice was distinguishable, and raised in an angry tone, apparently to some one who had entered.

"Then I say he's not in, and he won't be in to-day, that's more. So be off out, please."

"I say he is in," responded a man's voice. "Not a moment ago, I see him at that there kitchen-winder. You may as well fetch him here, for I shall stop till I see him. I'm a emissary of the law, and the law can't be played with; and if folks gets into trouble against the law, they must pay for it."

Edith, her eyes full of terror, and her face ghastly, seized hold of her husband, as if her feeble arms could shield him from harm. She was connecting this unseen visitor with the wild rumors afloat of the night work; and terrific visions were dazzling her eyes of handcuffs, a prison, a public trial; perhaps death. Sarah's voice was heard again in loud remonstrance and abuse.

"Don't keep me, Edith; don't alarm yourself; I must go and see what it is," he whispered, himself agitated. "I must, my dear! we shall have the fellow penetrating to this room."

Unwinding her hands, he put her hastily in a chair, and entered the kitchen. Sarah had armed herself with the tongs, which she was presenting in a warlike manner towards the stranger, hoping to menace him away. The man laughed derisively when he saw Wilfred, put a paper in his hand, and disappeared. Sarah dashed down the tongs in a passion.

"Now why couldn't you keep away, in there?" she wrathfully demanded, more as a person in authority speaks to a subordinate, than a servant to a master. "*I* know what it is; as long as he didn't serve it, you were safe."

"He would have dropped upon me, going out. Don't make a fuss."

"No, he needn't," snapped Sarah. "You might have slied out at the back door, and over the palings when you wanted to go out, or strided out at the side-window. There's plenty of ways of dodging them gentry, if folks have a mind to it. My goodness, missis! what's the matter?"

Edith had come into the kitchen, the image of ghastly terror, and shaking like a leaf. "What is it all?" she gasped. "What's that? Show it me! oh, Wilfred, show it me!"

Her voice rose quite harsh in its agitation, and she pointed to the paper left by the man. Wilfred Lester crumpled it up in his hands to keep it from her.

"It's nothing, Edith; don't disturb yourself. Nothing but a stupid bill."

Sarah gave a snatch at the paper; Wilfred would not let go it; and the two had actually a sort of tussle for its possession, in which the paper got torn, and Sarah mastered. She opened it and laid it before her mistress.

"There, ma'am, now you can see for yourself; it is nothing but a claim on master for money. Did you not see, sir, that her fears were o' something worse; that the agony were crushing her?" added the woman, in her strong sense, as she turned again to her master.

Standing at the kitchen-door—for she had entered the house unperceived, like the unwelcome visitor had done—was Miss Bordillion, an amazed spectator of the scene.

"Have you all taken leave of your senses?" she demanded. "What does this mean?"

"It means that we have come to the end of every thing," bitterly retorted Wilfred, as he returned to the sitting-room, leaving those to follow him who would: "of food, of credit, of hope. And the next thing for me will be a prison. Lady Adelaide will hold a jubilee the night I enter it. She is at the bottom of our misfortunes. Aunt," (for so he had learned to call her) "when I go in, you must take care of Edith."

Edith stole up to her husband, her face white still; the livid white of fear, not of illness. She was unable to comprehend the paper; and certain ominous words in it.

"In the name of our Sovereign Lady, the Queen," did not tend to reassure her. "Do explain it to me," she gasped.

"It is a simple thing, easy enough of comprehension," was Wilfred's answer, his mind smarting terribly under its annoyances; "I owe—let me look at the amount—nine pounds, three shillings; that's five pounds for the debt and four for the costs; and unless I pay it by a certain day, they will take further proceedings against me. It is a writ, Edith."

"What proceedings?" she inquired.

"Oh, I hardly know. The result would be a prison; couldn't be any thing else in my case."

She still held the writ in her hand, and glanced at it dubiously.

"You are sure—sure it is only a debt, Wilfred?"

"Why, what else should it be?" he returned. "Of course it is a debt. What can your thoughts be running on, Edith?"

He took it from her, and she sighed heavily as she relinquished it. Miss Bordillion, after exchanging a few sentences with Sarah, had come in and seated herself; she was looking exceedingly perplexed and grieved.

"It does appear to me," she began, "that things cannot go on longer in this way; that they ought not so to go on, even if your creditors, Wilfred, would allow them."

"How is it to be helped?" was Wilfred's answer. "My father, who ought to help it, will not; and I cannot force him. Neither have I a claim on any one else."

"In the last few days—I may say weeks—I have reflected upon it much. I have prayed to be directed for the right," pursued Miss Bordillion, in her quiet way, "and I have at length come to the conclusion that if Squire Lester will not help you, out of favor, he must out of right."

"Who's to make him?" put in Wilfred.

"You know how very, very greatly I esteem Mr. Lester, how warm a regard I have for him," pursued Miss Bordillion, the delicate pink on her cheek increasing to brightness. "Hitherto, I have taken his part in this business; I have been unwilling to cross him, or say a word that could reflect upon him:—and you know, my dears, that you did do wrong in disobediently marrying—"

"Halt there!" interrupted Wilfred. "I do not see the disobedience. My father approved of the union in the first place; and could I be so base as to desert Edith, because Colonel Bordillion lost his fortune? No; there was the more reason for my fulfilling the engagement; and my father would never have been implacable but for Lady Adelaide."

"Well, we will not reap up the question of the marriage; it can do no good now," sighed Miss Bordillion. "The very moment I read the news of Colonel Bordillion's loss, I knew that Lady Adelaide would set her face against Edith, and induce my father to do so; and therefore I chose to act for myself. And why should she? Out of regard for me? No; but because she fears a sixpence going out of my father's pocket; if it came to me it would be that much loss to her own children. It was a black day for me and Maria when he made Lady Adelaide his wife."

Miss Bordillion thought within her that it had not been a bright day for somebody else. She resumed.

"There was a sum of money that ought to have been paid to you, Wilfred, when you came of age. You did not have it."

His cheek flushed as he listened.

"A sum of money! I had none paid to me. What sum of money?"

"Twelve hundred pounds. It was left to you like Maria's fortune was left to her: save that hers was a large sum, yours a small. Squire Lester enjoyed the interest; the principal was to be paid to you when you were of age: Maria's when she married."

"And why have I been kept out of it? why has even the knowledge of it been denied me?" fiercely responded Wilfred.

"I have spoken latterly to Squire Lester about it," sighed Miss Bordillion. "I have intimated that it ought to be given up to you; that both law and justice demand that it should be. He said, 'No, neither law nor justice;' but he would not discuss it. So then I took counsel with myself, I took counsel in my prayers, and it appeared to me that my duty lay in telling you."

Wilfred sat gazing at her, astounded at the tidings. They were too good to be received without doubt.

"Is there, indeed, no mistake?" he uttered. "Am I truly entitled, now, to twelve hundred pounds of my own?"

"It was so left," replied Miss Bordillion.

A flash of joy, not seen in his face for a long while, illuminated it to brightness. He stooped down and kissed Edith.

"You shall have something better than partridges yet, darling."

"Where are you going?" she asked, as he was leaving the room.

"To the hall. My father and I must have a settlement now."

"Edith, what did he mean about partridges?" inquired Miss Bordillion, who had caught but the one word.

"Nothing worth telling, aunt. It is only the housekeeping grievances over again."

"I know it is a hard time with you, Edith, and has been. But, Edith, has it been wholly undeserved? I know Wilfred is careless and impetuous; man-like, he does not trace cause and effect; he does not see as we do. You did act wrongly, Edith, both you and he, and I pray that your wrong-doing may be thus working itself out."

"I have thought so, long, Aunt Margaret," was the whispered answer. "I look upon it as our penance, and patiently try to bear."

"Then you do rightly, child," warmly replied Miss Bordillion. "Take up your cross bravely and humbly, and it will grow lighter with each step; let it drag behind you in discontent and rebellion, and it will weigh you down. Be comforted, Edith; God will remove it in his own good time."

A MYSTERIOUS LOSS.—*See page* 137.

10

Wilfred Lester was speeding to the hall. And who should answer his summons at the door but Tiffle! Of course it was not Tiffle's place to answer doors : she was quite above it ; but happening to cross the hall at the moment of the knock, she, in her curiosity, pulled it open. Her first impulse was a stare of unqualified surprise ; her next, to place herself in his way, and prevent his entrance.

"Who might you want, sir ?"

"Mr. Lester,—if it concerns you to know," was the reply of Wilfred, as he attempted to pass in. "I see he is in his study."

"Master's pertikelarly engaged, and can't see visitors," objected Tiffle.

Wilfred Lester's eyes flashed fire, and he raised his hand authoritatively.

"Stand aside, woman," was the imperative command. "You forget to whom you speak. This is my father's house."

Tiffle slunk out of his way, and he approached the study. It was a room on the ground-floor, whose window looked to the side of the house. Wilfred had caught a glimpse of him standing at it. He turned round when Wilfred entered, and his features assumed an angry expression.

"To what am I indebted for this visit ?" he began. "You were forbidden the house, sir."

"I do not suppose my breaking the interdict will produce permanent injury to the house's inmates," somewhat insolently retorted Wilfred, who, what with Tiffle's reception and now his father's, felt chafed almost beyond bearing. "I shall not infect it with ague or fever, nor yet with small-pox."

"What does bring you here ?" imperiously rejoined Mr. Lester.

Wilfred coolly seated himself in the chair opposite that usually occupied by its master.

"Father," he said, changing his tone, "I have come to ask assistance from you. Our position cannot be a secret: my wife is wasting away from want before my eyes ; every available article is either pledged or sold, save

Edith's wedding-ring, and that I cannot attempt to take ; I have no clothes save these I stand up in ; in short, we have eked out our resources until none are left to us. To-day I had a writ served upon me for £10, or nearly that, and my next move must be to a prison. Will you help me in my strait ?"

"You must be aware that you have brought all this upon yourselves," was the reply of Mr. Lester. "What, save destitution and embarrassment, could come of a marriage like yours ?"

Wilfred drew his chhir a little forward, and leaned towards his father.

"You make a show of punishing me for marrying her ; but, do you blame me in your heart of hearts ? Would not you have done the same, in my place ? Father, from my soul I believe that you would never have visited it upon me, but that you were incited to do so by Lady Adelaide."

"To the point," briefly spoke Mr. Lester, "State the purport of your visit, if you have any to state."

"I believe I was not far from the point. However, I am here, I repeat, to ask you for assistance."

"I cannot give it."

"I crave it as a favor."

"I will not give it, I say," tartly responded Mr. Lester.

"Then I must request it as a right. Yes, sir, and I must have it. You hold money belonging to me I believe, money that by right of law ought to be at this moment in my hands instead of yours."

"No, I do not."

Wilfred felt a little staggered ; but he rallied, convinced that Miss Bordillion had not misled him.

"Maria has her fourteen thousand pounds, to be paid to her on her marriage, you enjoying the interest until that epoch. I have in like manner twelve hundred, which passed legally into my possession when I became of age. Sir, it ought to have passed absolutely : it must do so now."

"Who has been giving you this information ?" inquired Mr. Lester.

"That, I imagine, is of no consequence."

"Not much, certainly. I conclude it was Margaret Bordillion. The money—for to set the question at rest and save trouble, I will descend to explain to my rebellious son—was left to you, twelve hundred pounds, and the intention of the donor would appear to be, to a cursory reader, that you should come into the money at twenty-one. But the deed is so obscurely worded, that upon that point a question has arisen. I have taken counsel's opinion upon it, and their advice is that you do not come into it until my death."

Wilfred paused a few moments before replying.

"And what of Maria's? That she does not come into hers until your death?"

"About Maria's there is no question. The clauses are differently worded."

"Where's the will? In Doctor's Commons?" next spoke Wilfred.

"The money was not left by will. It was a deed of gift."

"Where's the deed, then?" pursued Wilfred.

Mr. Lester pointed with his finger to a small, iron safe which had stood in his study as long as Wilfred could remember.

"It is there," he said.

"You will allow me to peruse it."

"Indeed, no," said Mr. Lester. "I think I have satisfied you pretty well, as it is. Your perusing it could answer no end: it is obscurely worded, as I now assure you, and the opinion of counsel was that you could not touch it till my death."

"Other counsel may be of an opposite opinion," persisted Wilfred. "It would be but fair to allow me to submit it, in my turn."

"And to what good?" asked Mr. Lester. "Were your counsel's opinion adverse to the one already consulted, what of that? You could only prove which was right by an action at law, and I believe you have no funds to sustain one. I tell you openly, that I shall not part with the money, until death compels me."

"Is this justice?"

"It is law."

"Once convince me that it is law, and I will urge the point no more," said Wilfred. "Suffer me to read over the deed."

"I have told you no," said Mr. Lester. "The deed is there, safe and secure," motioning once more to the iron safe, "and I will not disturb it. Our interview is over. I cannot give you any assistance; and I desire that you will not intrude here again."

Wilfred rose from his seat in agitation. "Will you drive me to a prison? Will you allow Edith to die? Look here," and he snatched the writ from his pocket, "for this paltry ten pounds, I must go into one; will you not, at least, pay that?"

Whether Mr. Lester would have relented, with the unpleasant scrap of paper placed palpably before him, it is impossible to say. Before he could speak, the door was flung open, and Lady Adelaide sailed in.

She did not look at Wilfred. She passed him with scorn, picking up her dress as she swept by, but she spoke to Mr. Lester.

"They told me your son was here, but I did not believe it. Mr. Lester, can you allow his presence?—and by so doing make light of parental disobedience in the sight of your young children?"

"He is not here by my will: he entered the house against it. I have already told you to depart," he added, looking at Wilfred.

"I wait for my answer," said the latter, still showing the writ. "Will you help me out of this?"

"Neither out of that, nor any thing else," irascibly responded Mr. Lester, whose temper did not appear improved at the implied contest between wife and son. "I tell you the interview is over."

Wilfred put the writ in his pocket; and turning on his heel, departed, bowing to Lady Adelaide,—a bow so low, so elaborate, that she might well have deemed it offered in irony.

CHAPTER XX.

THE NIGHT INTERVIEW.

As Wilfred Lester was striding home from the unsatisfactory interview, he met Miss Bordillion and Maria. Walking by their side, having just overtaken them, was Mr. Lydney. To say that Wilfred was in anger, would not be conveying half an idea of the actual rage that possessed him. He was literally foaming with passion: it was boiling over and bubbling out from every pore : the presence of Lydney—a stranger—he ignored as completely as though he had not been there ; and burst forth with all his grievances, chiefly addressing Miss Bordillion :

"I am kept out of it,—I am to be kept out of it ! The money is mine, safe enough : twelve hundred pounds, as you said : and he coolly assures me he has had counsel's opinion, and I cannot claim it till his death ! The deed is obscurely worded, he says ; and when I ask to read it over : no : he denies it, though it was in the very room. If there's justice in heaven—"

"What *are* you speaking of, Wilfred ?" interrupted Maria, who had turned crimson, but was now growing white.

"I told him Edith was dying of want ; I told him I was going to the dogs, and should soon be in prison," raved Wilfred, never so much as hearing his sister. "Look here :—dashing the writ out of his pocket :—"I positively lowered myself to show him this, and beg of him, like any mendicant, that he would help me over *this* stile ! But, no : my wife may die, and I may go to jail and rot there. It's nothing to you, Maria : nothing that you need worry yourself over," he broke off : for she was evincing painful curiosity to look at the paper : "it's only a cursed writ for ten pounds."

"Must you pay it ?" she shivered.

"Must I pay it ?" echoed he, turning ironically to Miss Bordillion. "Must I pay ten pounds, she asks, when I

have not ten pence : no : nor ten farthings. Perhaps you'll tell me how I am to pay it ?" he chafed, to Maria.

"Wilfred, when you do give way to these outbreaks of temper, you are so impetuous that there's no getting you to speak reason or to hear it," said Miss Bordillion, who had not been able until then to put in a word edgeways. "Do be calm, if you can, and tell me what it is that Mr. Lester says about the deed."

"He says the deed is obscurely worded, and that I cannot claim the money till his death. He taunted me —yes, it was nothing less—with my wings being clipped, so that I could not go to law with him. And he is right," stamped Wilfred : "they are clipped."

"I never heard the slightest doubt expressed but that you came into the money at twenty-one," spoke Miss Bordillion. "I am quite certain that such was the intention when the deed was made. Mr. Lester should have allowed you to read it for your own satisfaction."

"He had better not drive me to extremities," foamed Wilfred, "or I will break the safe open and take the deed. 'Twould be no theft."

"Wilfred ! Wilfred !" pleaded Maria, "you don't know what you are saying."

"Not know ! I should say a vast deal more, but that you are present. But it is not my father," he added, in an altered voice : "it is that false woman, who is ever at his side to set him against his first wife's children. It may come home to you yet, my Lady Adelaide."

Without further colloquy, vouchsafing no adieu, Wilfred Lester strode away. Miss Bordillion, possibly not liking him to escape in that mood, or wishing to soothe him, followed quickly in his steps, leaving Maria and Mr. Lydney alone.

"I will be back directly," Miss Bordillion hurriedly said.

They were in a retired path, near the entrance of the wood, and Maria began pacing it backwards and forwards slowly. Mr. Lydney turned with her and remained by her side. He saw that she was greatly agitated, —that even her lips were white.

'It had been more to the purpose, possibly, that I had followed your brother, than Miss Bordillion," he observed.

"I am grieved, I am annoyed that these painful family affairs should be brought under the notice of a stranger," spoke Maria, half in vexation, half in apology.

"I should be very sorry if I thought you considered me now in that light," he warmly uttered. "I was in hopes, I believed, you did not."

"In truth you are right, Mr. Lydney," she said. "When I look back and remember how very short a period it is that we have known you, and then consider the (I may say it) almost confidential terms upon which we meet, I am lost in surprise. I think," she added, with a smile, "either you or ourselves must have displayed great forwardness."

"Not so, Miss Lester. There are some people who only act upon us as repulsive elements, whom we never can like, never can unbosom to,—no, not though we were thrown into domestic contact with them for years. There are others who are mutually attracted at the first glance, who know that they have found kindred spirits, objects worthy of esteem and trust: it does not require long for intimacy to grow up between these. Let me prove myself deserving of your friendship, your confidence: hesitate not to speak unreservedly to me of your brother. From what I gather,—for it is conversed of openly in Danesheld,—he is at the present time in some straits."

He bent his handsome form towards Maria, and a flush rose to her face. It may have appeared to her that there was help, protection, in that manly figure of strength,—it had long appeared to her that there was perfect truth to be found in that earnest face. An irresistible attraction had drawn Maria to him from the first,—an attraction, not less irresistible, prompted her now to acquiesce in his last words.

"That Wilfred and his affairs are freely spoken of in Danesheld is, I believe, only too true, Mr. Lydney; and it is nothing but what must be expected. I should think no son of good family—heir, as he ought to be —was ever reduced to the plight that Wilfred is."

"He is the heir, is he not?"

Maria shook her head.

"Danesheld Hall is not entailed, and papa can, if he pleases, make one of his younger children his heir."

"Would that be just?"

"Shamefully unjust," answered Maria, her face in a glow. "Oh!" she added, with emotion, "I cannot tell you how miserable I am! I could sacrifice myself to bring comfort to poor Wilfred. When I think of his trials, his uncertain prospects, and know that they are not deserved, my heart seems as though it would break with grief and pity, for I am helpless to aid him. And when I remember his thoughtless impetuosity, coupled with his keen sense of injury, I dread, I dread—I hardly know what I dread."

"You dread that, smarting under privation and unmerited wrong, he may be drawn into some escapade, not precisely fitting for the heir of Squire Lester."

Maria glanced quickly up at him, and he bent his truthful, sympathizing eyes upon her. In that moment she became aware that he knew and was then thinking of the disgraceful rumors which were abroad to Wilfred's prejudice. An instant's struggle with her feelings, which ended in her struggling no longer, and she burst into tears.

William Lydney drew her hand within his.

"Have faith in me," he whispered. "Leave him to me: I will be his friend in every way that I possibly can; and will try, all that man can try, to keep him from harm."

"I see you know—I see you have heard," she stammered, in much distress. "My days and nights are passed in feverish dread. If any—any—disgrace fell upon Wilfred, I think I should die. I have so loved him! I have so looked up to him! Mamma died, papa was estranged from us: we had only each other to care for."

"Trust to me," he fondly reiterated, as he pressed her hand between both of his, and then released it, for Miss Bordillion was discerned returning in the distance.

Leaving Maria, giving a passing word of greeting to Miss Bordillion as he passed her, Mr. Lydney sped after Wilfred. The latter had not entered his house, but had halted near it, and was moodily leaning against a stile that led into the wood. Lydney laid his hand on his shoulder, and rallied him in a gay tone:

"Shake off dull care and send it packing. What is the matter?"

"The matter! that's good! When a fellow's out at elbows and out at heart, out of friends, and out of help, there's enough the matter. I'm hard-up in every way; and, by Jove! I don't care who knows it, for the shame's to others, not to me."

"A man never yet deserved friends and help, but he found them," returned Lydney. "No need to be out of heart."

"Tush!" was the chafed response of Wilfred Lester.

"If I am cognizant of some part of your grievances, you must thank yourself for speaking of them before me a few minutes ago: and must pardon my thus reverting to them. I—"

"I don't care who knows of them, I say," impetuously interrupted Wilfred. "I'd mount a public rostrum and proclaim them with pleasure; for the shame, I tell you, lies with others. Still, I don't see any good in your recurring to the subject."

"No good at all, unless I could help you out of them, which I dare say I can do, if you will only behave like a reasonable being. Lester," he continued, earnestly, something very like emotion checking his free utterance, "I owe my life to you; but for your brave exertions, that awful night, I should have been gone and forgotten. You saved my life at the risk of your own. It is a debt that I can never repay, but you can lessen my sense of the obligation, if you will, by allowing me to be your friend, by treating me as a brother."

"What now?" asked Wilfred, staring at him. "As to risking my life—it's not so joyous to me that I need care to prolong it."

"Suffer me to be to you what a brother would be, if you had one. You are wrongfully kept out of money. I have more than I know what to do with. Let me be your banker."

The red color flushed into the cheek of Wilfred. He hesitated some moments before he spoke. Mr. Lydney resumed:

"Borrow of me, as one chum would borrow of another,—as I dare say you and I have both borrowed before now, when out of cash. You can repay me, you know, when things come round again."

"They never may come round again," answered Wilfred; "you'd probably be done out of it forever, if you lent money to me."

"Rubbish! You'll come in for it sometime; and plenty of it. How much will you have?"

"Are you serious in this offer?" demanded Wilfred, after looking keenly at him.

"Serious!" returned Lydney, "what do you mean? Is it any thing so very great, that you should doubt, or hesitate?"

"Then you are a good fellow, Lydney, and it's more than any body else has done for me. I'll take ten pounds, to get rid of this cursed writ."

"Nonsense about ten pounds! You must take some for yourself, as well as for the writ."

"No more, no more," uttered Wilfred Lester, the crimson flush again dyeing his face. "Save me from prison, and I'll thank you; but I want none for myself."

Mr. Lydney looked him full in the face, and spoke in a low tone.

"For your wife's comforts, then."

"No," persisted Wilfred, "those who have brought us to this, upon their heads shall the consequence be. I will not accept from a stranger what it is the duty of others to perform."

That he was unmistakably in earnest, and meant to be, Lydney saw: so he urged that point no further then. And the day passed on to its close.

Brightly and clearly shone out the evening star; brightly and clearly, if less large, crept out its sister stars, shedding their refulgence over Danesheld, lighting the path of Lord Dane, as he, remembering the interview that was to take place between Lydney and the poacher, walked from the castle to take up his station in the wood and overhear it. His lordship, to give him his due, was above acting the eaves-dropper in general, but he was most anxious to find out all he could regarding Lydney, and burning to punish those troublesome poachers. That Lydney was really an impostor, a loose character, and had now joined the fraternity, he entertained little doubt. To imprison the whole lot for two years would have delighted Lord Dane.

"Good-night to your lordship."

The saluter was the inspector of police, who was passing on horseback, and Lord Dane nodded in reply to the greeting, and continued his way. The next moment, however, he wheeled around.

"Halloa, inspector! Any news of the box?"

"Not yet, my lord," was the reply, as the officer turned his horse sideways. "We shall have the bills out to-morrow, and I hope they may do something."

"Bills?" echoed Lord Dane.

"Offering a reward, my lord. They would have been posted this afternoon, but Mr. Lydney called this morning and stopped it. He had his reasons, he said, for not allowing them to appear till to-morrow. It must be a valuable box, to offer a thousand pounds reward."

"Who does offer it?" burst forth Lord Dane in astonishment.

"Mr. Lydney has given us authority. If the box is in existence still, that will bring it forth."

Lord Dane paused ere he spoke, one thought was chasing another in his brain.

"Inspector, take care you are not *done*. I know more of this Lydney and his doings than I did when I spoke with you last: he has got a thousand pounds to pay just as much as that horse of yours has."

"My lord, he said freely that the box was none of his, and that the reward would come from the pocket of the owner; not from his own. I inquired who and what he was—this Lydney—but could obtain nothing satisfactory in reply. He protested that he was of English descent, and of good family, but would give no particulars."

Lord Dane drew nearer the inspector, and resumed in a low whisper. The man's head was bowed to his saddle-bow, as he bent to catch it.

"He is in league with the poachers. I am on my way now to track their meetings in my own preserves. I was a witness to it last night, and heard the rendezvous made for this, made between Ben Beecher and Lydney. That's your gentleman of family! your thousand-pound man!"

"My lord, is it possible?" uttered the inspector.

"I told you I suspected the fellow from the first," resumed Lord Dane. "He is now showing out in his true colors. Don't you be gulled, inspector. He may have made off with the box himself, as I hinted,—stolen it! and he goes to you with this munificent thousand-pound tale, to put you off the scent."

Lord Dane turned and pursued his way as he spoke, and the inspector, after a pause, given to thought, urged his horse on his way. His lordship posted himself in his hiding-place in the wood, snug and safe.

Lydney was at the place of meeting

first—I mean before Beecher. The latter came along in a joyless, dispirited sort of way, as though he had not good news to bring.

"It has been no go, sir," was his salutation to Lydney, and Lord Dane's ears were strained to their utmost capacity, so sure was he of discovering treason. "The box has not been lifted."

"No!" uttered the gentleman, in an accent of keen disappointment, for somehow he had fed himself with the hope that it had been "lifted," and would be restored through Mr. Beecher. "Have you ascertained to a positive certainty?"

"As certain as that you and I are here, sir. I saw the right men, and I can assure you they know nothing whatever about it. Their opinion is, that it was took into the castle. Right glad they'd have been to get the fifty guineas, and we'd have shared it among us. You'd have had your box this night, sir, if they could help you to it."

Lydney paused to revolve the news."

"Would a higher reward bring it forth?" he presently asked.

"Not if you offered a bank-full—not if you offered a thousand pounds," answered Beecher, little thinking that he named the very sum to be announced on the morrow. "What they haven't got, they can't give up,—and they've not been a-nigh it at all. They think you must look for it in the castle."

"What reason have they for thinking that?"

"Well, I don't know that they have got much reason, but it's their opinion. Sharp cards they are, too, and their opinion's worth having, sir. For one thing, they say that if the box had been smuffed, they should know it."

"But Lord Dane says it is not in the castle. More than that, I hear he had the castle searched by the police, every nook and corner of it, and there was no box."

"Has Lord Dane any interest in hiding or detaining the box, sir?"

"Why?"

"Because—not that I insinuate he had, nor have I reason to think it—there's places in the castle where things may be put away, and where the eyes of the police, though they were sharpened up by a dozen magnifying telescopes, would never find 'em. I was a-talking to old father about it. Says he, 'If my Lord Dane wanted to keep that box in hiding, he could do it fast enough in the castle.' Tales go, sir, though they may not be true, that years ago, one of the Lord Danes, who was at his wits' end for cash, went snacks with some smugglers, and the booty used to be deposited in the secret places of the castle."

How did my Lord Dane's ears like being regaled with that? There's a very popular proverb which runs in this fashion :—"Listeners never hear any good of themselves."

"And if, by chance, the box should have been consigned to any one of these secret places, how,—who's to get it?" inquired Lydney.

"Why, it will never be got as long as the castle's a castle—at least as long as my Lord Dane's its master," returned the poacher. "There's not many, sir, would choose to brave Lord Dane."

"A martinet, when crossed, I suppose," carelessly remarked Mr. Lydney.

"Like all the rest of the Dane family. The old lord was a stinger, if thwarted ; and his eldest son would have been worse, had he lived to reign. Captain Dane was hot, too ; but generous."

"I have heard him, the captain, spoken of since I came to Daneshold," observed Mr. Lydney. "Did he not fall over the cliff ? or was thrown from it ?"

"It was not a simple fall, sir. He was scuffling with another man, and was no doubt pitched over. Daneshold regretted him much, and all the more when tidings came of his eldest brother's death. We should have liked the captain to reign over us. Why,

Ravensbird—the very man you are lodging with—was his servant."

"Indeed! With whom was Captain Dane scuffling?"

"It's what has never been found out, sir, from that day to this. Ravensbird was took up for it; but it wasn't him, and that was proved. And then there was a talk of a packman; but he couldn't be discovered. No, it has never been found out."

There was a pause. Mr. Lydney broke it, his voice ringing out unusually sonorous and clear in the night-air.

"The present Lord Dane—Mr. Herbert, as I hear he was called then—was he suspected?"

"My heart alive, no!" returned the poacher. "Whatever made you suspect him, sir?"

"*I* suspect him!" echoed Mr. Lydney. "My good man, don't run away with a wrong notion : I cast no suspicion towards him. Had I been in Dancsheld at the time of the occurrence, and of an age to reason, it is an idea I might have taken up. He was the one to benefit by Captain Dane's death."

"But, when the thing happened, Mr. Dane, the eldest son, was alive. Captain Dane was no more the heir to the property, at the time of his death, than I was : in fact, he never was heir at all, for he died before his brother."

"And Mr. Herbert was *not* suspected?"

"He was not suspected," answered Beecher. "Though that brings to mind that a chap which I'd rather not name, declared he saw Mr. Herbert on the heights at the time of the accident, or murder,—whichever it was. But he was three sheets in the wind, and we made him hush his tongue."

"Why make him hush it?"

"Who'd charge such a insinuation against a Dane,—though it *was* only Mr. Herbert? Besides, what should he want, attacking his cousin? No, 'twasn't likely : and we made the chap cork up his chatter."

"Who was 'the chap?'" continued Mr. Lydney.

"Well, I don't know that it matters telling; it's all over and done with. 'Twas my brother, sir."

To describe how Lord Dane in his hiding-place clenched his fists at the audacious Lydney, and would have liked to pummel him as he deserved, would be a task for a strong pen. The latter continued, totally unconscious that he had any listener, save Beecher.

"Could you give me an idea where these secret holes are in the castle?"

"No, that I couldn't, sir, and I don't know that there really are any : it may be all bosh. I'll ask father again."

"Do so. And—"

The speech was interrupted by a shot, fired not far from them. Beecher opened his ears.

"That shot's a ruse to deceive the keepers : they are not at work so low down as this. It was within an ace of being hot work last night; but the keepers got help and came out in numbers, and we made a run for it."

"What pleasure can you find in this wild, lawless life?" remonstrated Lydney. "It is full of danger."

"A spice of danger gives zest," returned the man.

"A spice may But when it comes to exchange bullets, and battered heads, and broken limbs; that is rather more than is agreeable."

"One must live, sir."

"Every man, who tries to live honestly, may live honestly : and—"

"Not when he has been at this sort of work all his life. Who'd trust him then? or help him to honest labor?"

"I would, for one," returned Mr. Lydney. "If a man who had stepped aside from the straight path, turned to it again, and set himself in a proper way to be what he ought to be, there's all the more respect due to him."

"Ah, well, sir; talking's one thing, doings another. I wish I could have found your box; that would have helped some of us on."

"Keep a look-out still : it is not impossible but you may hear of it. There's for the trouble you have already taken," he added, putting a piece of gold in his hand.

" I'll tell you what it is, sir. If we had always had such people as you to deal with us in this Dancsheld, we shouldn't, many of us, have gone wrong. Thank you, sir, and a hearty good-night to you."

The man moved quickly away; Lydney more leisurely followed him; and, last of all, emerged Lord Dane, wiping his brows like a man in a hot consternation.

"A pretty devil's plot, these fellows would like to set afoot!" quoth he; "secret places in the castle, and all the rest of it! If ever a man deserved hanging, it's that traitor Lydney. The whole set of poachers are angels, compared with him."

CHAPTER XXI.

AN ENCOUNTER WITH SHAD—TURNED FROM THE HALL.

OUTSIDE the police-station, and on every available place where bills could be stuck, appeared notices of the loss of the japanned box, with the offer of a thousand pounds reward for its restoration. The offer took Dancsheld by storm, and the crowds that were wont to collect, wherever one of these bills appeared, staring at the offer and making their comments, quite impeded the foot-traffic. The days however, nay, the weeks, and the months went on, and nothing came of it; no box turned up, and the reward was still unclaimed. The police felt inclined to adopt Lord Dane's opinion; that Lydney himself had got the box, and that the reward never would be called for.

The depredations on Lord Dane's preserves went on alarmingly, and apparently with impunity. Whole dozens of game were bagged, the poachers seemed to enjoy their full swing, and the keepers were balked, night after night. Lord Dane was losing patience, and felt inclined to offer a thousand pounds reward to catch *them*.

Heartily indeed would he have given it, could Lydney have been entrapped with them. That Lydney was occasionally seen by Lord Dane, in the wood with the poachers, at any rate with one of them, Beecher, was beyond dispute; and perhaps few in Dancsheld but would have subscribed to Lord Dane's opinion of his worthlessness, had they enjoyed the same means for judging of him.

Meanwhile, at Wilfred Lester's cottage domestic matters appeared to be going on rather more comfortably. Sarah, by some cajoling process of her own, the secret charm of which she would reveal to neither master nor mistress, had contrived to obtain a little renewed credit for meat and other necessaries. Mrs. Lester would sigh and trouble herself as to when they were to be paid for; her husband evinced that utter indifference to future consequences, which is sometimes born of despair; had Sarah pledged his credit for hundreds, it seemed the same to him. A most bitter feeling had seated itself in his heart against his father, touching the deed and the money withheld from him; at first he had been loud and noisy, vowing revenge, vowing to obtain possession of the deed by some desperate means, but of late he had buried his wrongs in silence, and spoke of them no more. In his former loud flights of temper, the only one to remonstrate against them to his face was Lydney; Edith dared not.

One frosty morning in December, Maria, in taking the wood-path to Miss Bordillions, encountered Lydney; somehow or other they often did encounter each other; but to which lay the fault, whether to him or to her, or to the two mutually, cannot be said. That a powerful attachment had sprung up between them, there was little doubt, though as yet it had been spoken of by neither. Danesheld was that morning alive with commotion, for an encounter had taken place the previous night between the keepers and poachers, in which the former were worsted, and the latter had got off scotfree. It was said that Lord Dane was foaming. Maria almost sprang to Lydney when she saw him, asking if he had heard the news. That she was trembling with an inward fear, a dread to which she dared not give a shape, her agitated manner proved.

"I heard of it hours ago," he smiled, as he took both her hands in greeting.

"Do you know—do you know"— it seemed that she could scarcely get the words out—"who were in it? what men?"

"No. Various rumors are afloat. I believe I could mention one fellow; but it's no business of mine. I saw him sneaking into the wood, under cover of the dark night, as I was going to your brother's, where I spent the evening."

Maria's countenance visibly changed, and her lips parted with suspense, as she listened.

"And what Mrs. Lester will say the next time she sees me, I cannot anticipate," he continued, not unobservant of Maria's varying cheek. "Will you believe that I was so devoid of all conscience as to stay there till one in the morning, keeping Wilfred from his bed?"

She could dissimulate no longer. Her lips turned white, her eyes became wet, and she faltered out tale-telling words in the moment's emotion.

"Oh, is it true? Are you sure you were with him?"

He pressed her hands warmly, bent low, and whispered, with a beaming smile,

"I never tell you any thing but truth; believe me, I could not do so. Maria, it is all right, there is no cause for agitation. I was with Wilfred, at his own house, till one o'clock in the morning; we got into a discussion, and the time slipped on unwarily. The encounter with the poachers took place at half-past twelve."

"How kind you are!" she exclaimed, in the sudden revulsion of feeling induced by the news.

"In what way?" he laughed. "Kind for telling you this, or for keeping Wilfred up shamefully, and running the risk of Mrs. Lester's displeasure?"

"Kind in every way, I think," she answered, her face radiant. "But for you—"

Mr. Lydney raised his hand with a warning gesture, and Maria looked round in surprise. Clearing some feet with a bound, he sprang upon young Mr. Shad, who had been twined round a tree in his usual attitude, listening with all his ears. He drew him forth by the hair of his head, Shad yelling unmercifully. Maria said farewell, and walked quietly on, leaving the capturer and captured.

"You sneaking young varmint!" uttered Lydney; "so I have caught you again at your tricks! How many times does this make? Now, what shall your punishment be? I wonder if I could get you a week or two's wholesome recreation on the treadmill?"

At the last suggestion, Shad only yelled the louder; and in the midst of the noise up came Tiffle, who was going into Danesheld, and generally chose the wood-path when she did so, though it was the longest round. She took in every point of the scene with her sly eyes, but suffered not her tongue to betray it.

"Well: if I ever heard such a noise!" quoth she; "I thought it must be some young panther let loose. And who is it? It's something like Granny Bean's Shad."

"He's agoing to kill me! he's wanting to whack me! he'd a-like to pull up my hair by the roots!" shrieked Shad. "Tell him to let me go."

"Let him go, please," said Tiffle to Lydney. "I'm sure you're too much a gentleman, sir, to ill-treat a poor little weak boy."

Tiffle essayed to pull him from Mr. Lydney, as she spoke, but Mr. Lydney put her away. He had not attempted to beat Shad: only held him tight.

"I am not going to touch him now," he said to Tiffle: "I have no cane with me; but, so sure as I catch him dodging my footsteps, or Miss Lester's, again, so sure will I inflict proper chastisement upon him. You came up opportunely, Mrs. Tiffle."

"To prevent the beating?"

"No: to hear my promise. The next time you give him orders to track me, or your young lady, remember that he shall certainly suffer for it, if he attempts to put your behests in practice. That you merit the punishment, shall not avail with me : he shall get it."

"Oh !" screamed Tiffle, with a great show of indignation, "what treasonous words is these? *I* give him orders to track people ! what have I to do with him? Am I a perlice walker?"

"You have more to do with him than people suspect, and in more ways than one," was his significant retort, as he turned round and looked full in Tiffle's face, which suddenly became the color of scarlet. "Now, my good woman, set him to watch me again !"

He quitted hold of Shad with a gentle shake, and proceeded on his way, in the opposite direction to that taken by Maria. Tiffle regained her composure, as she best might ; but the scarlet of her face turned white with rage, and she shook her fists after him, and panted forth :

"I vow I'll be revenged on him for this ?"

"I know what," cried Shad. "I saw him at the wood last night, just after the row. He'd been in it, I think."

"Where did you see him ?" eagerly cried Tiffle.

"He was a coming up the road, t'other side the wood. I see him with my two eyes. The clocks was a striking one."

"Did you see Will Lester?" returned Tiffle. "Was he out with 'em ?"

"I didna see *him*. He might ha' been there, though, and this un ha' been to take him home, for 'twas close to Will Lester's where I see him. I ha'n't seen Will Lester, this morning, nowhere : maybe, he's wounded."

"What did that divil set upon you now for ?"

"Cause I were a watching him and Miss Lester, and he twigged me," returned Shad. "I never see such a keen eyes as he's got. He had laid hold of her two hands and was a-hugging of 'em."

"Keep the sharpest look-out on him you ever kept in your life, Shad," were the concluding words of Tiffle. "Poke and peer about the woods forever, especially after dark. That Lydney's a big cut-throat in disguise, and we'll pay him off."

Vowing vengeance upon the whole world in her anger, and upon Lydney in particular, Tiffle pursued her way. She had executed her commissions in the town, and was returning, when she met Lord Dane. She had had plenty of time to cool ; but to cool down from an evil spirit was not in Tiffle's nature : she remembered the sovereign bestowed upon her by his lordship, and the words he had used ; and she stopped him now.

"Well, Tiffle, and how are you ?"— for, when Lord Dane chose, he could be affable and condescending to the lowest.

"I'm none the better, my lord, craving your pardon, for the dreadful tales of last night's blood that every shop you go into *will* tell. Is it true, my lord, that one of the keepers was cut in half ?"

"Not quite," replied Lord Dane, checking a laugh. "He is wounded in the ribs. I wish I could lay my finger on the man that fired at him."

"My lord, I think it's as likely to have been that Lydney as anybody," responded Tiffle, dropping her voice. "I have good information that he was one of them."

"Have you ?" eagerly returned Lord Dane. "Where ? how ?—how did you get it ?"

"One that's safe and sure saw him just outside the wood at one o'clock this morning. And where could he have been to, my lord, at that place and hour, but a-j'ining in the fray ? If you could get him transported; my lord, it would be a provadinshil mercy for Dancsheld and for Miss Lester."

"Ah," was the only answer of his lordship.

"She's a getting enthrilled by him, my lord; as safe as my name's Tiffle. Not a day passes but he's at our house, with master, or with my lady, and of course *she's* present. And then the private meetings out of doors!" added Tiffle, turning up her eyes. "They were in the wood together not half an hour ago, her two hands squozed in his, as if he were her lovier."

Lord Dane's face grew black as night. Tiffle did not pursue the subject: she left her shaft to tell.

"And they do say that Mr. Wilfred Lester has not been seen abroad yet, my lord. It's to be hoped he's come to no harm: though I did hear a insinivation that he was wounded."

She shot a rapid glance out of her cat's eyes at Lord Dane, then meekly dropped them, curtsied and turned away.

It is probable that Lord Dane would not so far have forgotten his courtly manners as to speak to Maria on the point of Tiffle's information touching, herself, but that he was betrayed into it in the angry heat of the moment. His road led him past Miss Bordillion's house, and seeing Maria leave it on her way home, he increased his pace and overtook her. He raised his hat, a pleasant smile on his comely face, and, joining her, walked by her side.

"Maria," he began, "when am I to be favored with my answer? Do you not think I have waited long and patiently?"

Maria's heart beat, though her spirit sank within her. Was he going to enter again upon *that* subject?

"I really beg your pardon," she stammered. "I do not understand."

"Not understand that I love you?" he rejoined, his tone one of the sweetest tenderness. "That my days are passed in one long dream—the hope to call you my wife? In truth, Maria, my patience has been sorely put to

the test; let the suspense come to an end."

"But indeed you could not have misunderstood me, Lord Dane," she replied, in agitation. "I told you months ago this could never be. I have no other answer to return. I thank you very much for your good opinion, but I cannot be your wife."

"Tell me why you would reject me," he said, after a pause.

"There is no particular reason, except—except—that I do not care for you sufficiently to become your wife," she hesitated.

"Do you deem that it would be an inexpedient alliance? Or do you fear I should not make you a good husband?"

"I never glanced at either point. Suffer the subject to drop, Lord Dane."

He looked at her with a winning smile.

"It can never drop until you are mine, Maria."

"But indeed it must," she answered, "for yours I cannot be."

"Have you seen your brother this morning?" he resumed.

"My brother? No."

"Nor have heard, possibly this rumor touching him. That he is wounded."

Had Maria been shot with one of the random shots from Dancsheld wood, it could not have had much greater effect upon her than these words. The whole of her heart's blood seemed to leave her, and she turned to him with quivering lips that refused utterance.

"It may not be correct," he continued, "but the report is certainly abroad. Maria, this is no hour for squeamishness: your brother ought to be got away from here. If he is not hurt now, it will be sure to come ere now."

"I wish he was away," she cried, betrayed out of her self-possession; "but where is he to go?"

"If you did not treat me so cavalierly, Maria, I would soon find him a post. I have one at my disposal now:

at least my interest would secure its being bestowed where I please. It is under government, and would be the very thing for Wilfred, until better times comes round for him. It is nearly a sinecure ; the pay eight hundred a-year."

Maria's brain began to whirl. Eight hundred pounds a-year on the one hand, absence from Danesheld and his grievances, home-comfort for him and Edith ! On the other, poverty, starvation, a continuance of the awful dread, companionship with his dangerous associates, perhaps disgrace, a public trial, or *killed* in some midnight encounter ! She turned her lovely face, crimson now with excitement, on Lord Dane.

" Oh, will you not interest yourself and give it him ?"

" Willingly. If you will interest yourself *with yourself* for me."

It was a cruel alternative. Maria walked on in silence, and began revolving all he had said.

" Who informed you he was wounded ?" she whispered.

" I heard it."

" I do not think it can be true. Mr. Lydney told me he was with him till one o'clock this morning ; the time flew unwarily, he said."

A strangely derisive smile curled the lips of Lord Dane. Maria knew not why, but she shrank from it.

" I do not doubt it," he significantly observed ; " I think it extremely probable that he was with him till that hour. Birds of a feather—but I should be sorry to class Wilfred Lester, with all his faults and imprudences, with a man of Lydney's stamp."

" Mr. Lydney is a gentleman," she returned, in a low voice.

" Allow me to ask what proof you have of that : whose testifying word? Maria, it is time your eyes were opened. I hear from various points Miss Lester's name coupled with Lydney's,—that they are seen abroad in company, that they appear on intimate terms of friendship. This very morning they were walking in the wood together, the young lady's hands in his : and Danesheld is ringing with it."

She turned her face in its hot scarlet upon Lord Dane, her eyes flashing, her tongue indignant.

" And what though I was in the wood conversing with Mr. Lydney ? It is a public path, open to all the world. Let Danesheld concern itself with its own business, but not with mine. My conscience is pure, Lord Dane : I met Mr. Lydney accidentally, as you might meet him, and I have done nothing unbecoming to a lady.

" I did not mean to reproach you, Maria, and I spoke but out of regard for you. I cannot bear to hear of the future Lady Dane being brought into contact with a—"

" I am not the future Lady Dane," she burst forth. " I never will be."

" Perhaps you would prefer to be the future Mrs. Lydney," he rejoined, unable to suppress his sarcasm.

Again her face grew scarlet, but she made no retort.

Lord Dane resumed.

" Maria, let us have done with this playing at cross-sticks with each other. If you will not allow me to speak to you as your future husband,—though that will come,—let me speak as your true friend. Lydney—mind, Maria, I am only asserting what I know—is here under false colors. He parades himself as a gentleman, he has obtained admission in that character to the best families, he has made himself intimate with you. Will you believe that almost from the very first I have known him to be an associate with the worst characters here, sharing in their pursuits, poaching on my preserves with them ? He tells you he was with Wilfred Lester till one o'clock this morning ; I say that it is more than likely; for it has been whispered to me that Lydney was one of those engaged in the attack last night."

She felt utterly confounded. Strange doubts and fears assailing her at all points ; but she had faith in Lydney.

" It is not possible," she gasped.

"All that you say of him cannot be possible. And it was at Wilfred's own house that he was, last night."

"Understand me, Maria. With regard to last night, I assert nothing positive; for, of his movements then, and Wilfred's, I am personally ignorant. It has been told to me that he was in the wood, it has been told to me that your brother is wounded: both may be false, for aught I know. But when I tell you that he is the associate of bad characters, and that he frequents the wood at night with them, I speak of my own positive knowledge. Is that a man to be intimate with Miss Lester?"

Maria was hard of belief, and she spoke resentfully.

"If you have known this, as you say, from the first, why have you not stopped his visits to the families of the neighborhood?"

"I have my reasons for not speaking too soon, and the police have theirs. My gentleman is being watched, and the time will come, I believe shortly, when he will be dropped upon and denounced. Private friendship would have led me to interfere, but as lord-lieutenant I have public duties to consider. The time is not yet come, I say. He made a show of offering £1000 reward for the recovery of the box—"

"He never said it was himself offered it: he was but acting for the owner," persisted Maria.

"Be it so. But whether for himself or owner, he was safe in offering it, seeing that the box is most probably in his own possession, and has been from the time it was lost."

"Who asserts that?" flashed Maria.

"It is a suspicion—not an assertion. We cannot come to any other conclusion."

At that moment Wilfred Lester came in view, walking as well as he ever walked in his life, with no sign of a wound about him. He did not stop, but passed them with a nod. Maria turned triumphantly to Lord Dane.

"You see! All the other assertions may be false as this."

"False! Thank you, Maria. I passed you my word that with regard to Lydney's pursuits and associates they were true. I did not answer for last night's doings. Can you have faith in him still?"

"It seems to me that I can never lose my faith in him," she replied in a low tone, as though she were communing with herself.

Lord Dane threw up his head with all the hauteur of a British peer, and he bit his lips with vexation. That he was very greatly prejudiced against Lydney there was no question; still he did believe him to be an unworthy character.

Danesheld Hall was in view, and Maria entered. Lord Dane also entered, and proceeded to the study of Mr. Lester. He there confided to Mr. Lester what he had never done before—his suspicions of Mr. Lydney; and strenuously urged that he should be treated as an impostor and turned from the hall.

"He appears to me to be a thorough gentleman—a gentleman in all respects," was the reply of Mr. Lester, who felt considerably astonished and staggered at the communication. "If what you say be correct, the fellow must have the impudence of—"

"It is correct," interposed Lord Dane. "Do I not tell you I have watched him myself, been a witness to his night assignations in the wood, his confederacy with the poachers? I have had my reasons for keeping this close, and the police have also theirs. Neither must it be made public now, unless we would defeat the ends of justice; but I confide the facts to you that he may have no further opportunity of working more mischief at the hall."

"He certainly shall not be admitted here again," remarked Mr. Lester. "But as to past mischief—you go too far, Lord Dane. What mischief has he brought to the hall?"

"He has tried at it, unless I am

greatly mistaken," significantly returned Lord Dane. "He has contrived to establish a pretty good understanding with Maria, out of doors and in : and young ladies often prove more susceptible to the fascinations of a stranger than to the sterling qualities of old friends."

Very indignant, indeed, felt Mr. Lester at the hint: not indignant against Lord Dane, but at the presuming intruder, Lydney. He, however, repudiated the insinuation touching Maria. Lord Dane smiled.

"These fellows, who come into a neighborhood for what they can pick up, are just the sort to draw a young lady into mischief: I mean such mischief as a secret attachment, and then a marriage. Fancy what a windfall Maria's fortune would be to this man! and you know, were she to marry without the previous arrangement regarding the money, you would be compelled to hand it over."

Mr. Lester stood as one thunderstruck. This view of the case had never struck him before, and he began to rail at himself for his blindness. Sneaking covertly after Maria, that he might grasp her fortune? Of course he was! it was all plain now. The perspiration broke out over his face like peas.

"You had better persuade her to become Lady Dane without delay," said his lordship, quietly, "and so secure her from harm. You would retain the money, and I should gain a wife, whose happiness it would be my daily study to promote."

"She shall be your wife before the month's out," foamed the disturbed Mr. Lester.

Lord Dane quitted the hall, and it happened unfortunately that Mr. Lydney almost immediately called at it before Squire Lester's indignant fears had had time to cool. He rushed out and met him as he entered ; and, with many needless words of insult, ordered him to quit the house again.

"What has occurred ? what have I done ?" demanded the amazed Lydney, while the raised tones of Mr.

Lester's voice brought forth Lady Adelaide and Maria.

"I condescend to no explanation, sir," was the retort of Mr. Lester. "Only take yourself off, and never presume to attempt crossing the threshold of my house again : you have crossed it too much."

"But you will first accord me an explanation of this treatment," persisted Mr. Lydney.

"There's the door, sir," stormed the squire, waving his hand to the open door, which the servant held. "If you do not depart instantly I shall order my domestics to put you forth."

A moment's communing with himself, and then the young man turned to obey. But he first raised his hat courteously to the Lady Adelaide, who had stood the image of consternation, and walked forth—not as one cowed by merited insult, but with a lordly step and head erect, his whole air and bearing that of a chieftain, from whom insult recoiled.

Maria shivered, crept up to her own room, and burst into a flood of passionate tears.

———————

CHAPTER XXII.

A CONFUSED PLOT—THE APPARITION IN THE RUINS.

LORD DANE was not one to do his work by halves. If he could not publicly proclaim his suspicions of Lydney's ill-doings, or if he did not choose to do so, he yet determined to damage his reputation as far as possible. The most welcome news to his lordship would be, to hear that Lydney had been driven from the place : perhaps he hoped to help on that desirable consummation. Upon quitting Squire Lester's he bent his steps to the Sailor's Rest. Ravensbird was alone in the bar, reading a newspaper : he rose up when his lordship entered.

"I want three minutes' conversation with you, Ravensbird."

The man bowed, led the way to the parlor, and handed a chair to Lord Dane, remaining himself standing of course.

"How much longer do you intend to harbor that fellow Lydney?"

"I'm sure, my lord, that's more than I can say," returned the landlord, who could take questions as coolly and literally as most folks, even from Lord Dane. "It's his business; not mine. He'll stop on at his pleasure: as long as he pays his bill, I have nothing to say against it."

"No, Ravensbird, he will not stop at his pleasure," returned Lord Dane. "I am here now to desire you to turn him out."

"Upon what plea, my lord?" asked Ravensbird.

"Give any plea you choose, to him. The one I give to you is—that it is my pleasure."

"My lord, I cannot put forth a gentleman in that fashion; one who conducts himself as a gentleman, and pays his way."

"It must be done. I insist upon it," said Lord Dane.

"I beg your pardon, my lord. Not by me."

"The fellow is an impostor, a man given to nefarious courses; he consorts with the poachers, and trespasses on my preserves at night. But, mind, Ravensbird, this is for your private ear alone, and I know you can be secret when you like. He has wormed himself into the social circles of the best families here, and may work incalculable mischief. Is that a man for you to continue to harbor?"

"What he may do out of doors, I know nothing of," persisted Ravensbird; "I see nothing wrong in him, and have heard no wrong. In-doors, he conducts himself as a quiet, well-behaved, honorable gentleman, and that's all I have got to do with."

"You are my tenant, Ravensbird, and you must do as I wish you."

"My lord, I am your tenant, but I pay you rent for your house, and am master of it. In taking the Sailor's Rest, I did not part with my respon-

sibility of action. I should be happy to oblige your lordship in many ways, but to turn a harmless gentleman (as far as I see) from it, is what I can't do."

"Say you won't, Ravensbird."

"Well, my lord, I'll say I won't, if you prefer it," answered the man, though with every token of civility and respect. "If this young Mr. Lydney behaved himself ill under my notice, it would be a different thing."

Lord Dane regarded Ravensbird with a haughty stare. The man met it equally.

"I fancy you cannot understand, Ravensbird. He has come here to engage in bad practices, therefore he must be hunted out of Danesheld. The police might do it for him, and save trouble, but he seems to take precious good care not to give tangible grounds. He's a sly one, depend upon it, and he must be got out of the place."

"All well and good, my lord, if it can be done; but I am not going to join in getting him out."

"Do you remember a certain clause in your lease, which I caused Apperly to insert, when you entered upon this house?" demanded Lord Dane. "It was to the effect that, should circumstances induce me to retake the house upon my hands, you must give up possession, and quit it at my pleasure."

"By your lordship's giving me six weeks' notice," interposed Ravensbird.

"Good. If you are to fly in the teeth of my requests in this manner, —and it is the first, I believe, that I have made to you, — you stand a chance of getting that clause acted upon, Mr. Ravensbird."

"As your lordship pleases, of course," was the sturdy answer, while Ravensbird looked full in the face of the peer. "I should be sorry to leave the house, for it suits me, and I earn a living; still, there are other tenements to be had in Danesheld. Perhaps your lordship will give it some reflection, before you compel me to quit this."

Marked independence, nay, more, marked meaning, was in his tone. Lord Dane passed from the subject to another.

"You have heard of this outrage in my woods last night."

"As all Dancsheld, has, my lord."

"What do you personally know of it?"

"Not any thing," said Ravensbird. "What should I?"

"Ravensbird," proceeded Lord Dane, bending his head forward, and speaking in an under-tone, "I could bring the officers of justice into this house now, and give you into custody on suspicion of having been concerned in it."

"Because I 'harbor' Lydney—it is your lordship's expression—and you suspect him of being connected with the poachers?" asked Ravensbird, with some freedom.

"No."

The two stood gazing at each other —for Lord Dane had risen, and now faced his tenant. It was his lordship who broke the silence.

"Last evening—it must have been near ten o'clock, not very long before the affray took place—I saw you in the wood, with one of the worst of the men, Ben Beecher. Hand in glove with him, pacing the thicket with him, your hand upon his shoulder! I saw you myself, Ravensbird."

"I was there with him," quietly replied Ravensbird.

"It is a cool assertion."

"I had a little private matter of business with Ben Beecher: and I went to the wood, hoping to find him and to transact it. I did find him, and was with him the best part of half an hour, and then I left him, and came back home. That's the simple truth, and the whole truth, my lord. Had I known there was likely to be a fight in the wood, I should not have chosen last night to go there. I take part in a poacher's conflict! You know better than that, Lord Dane."

"Yet you have been accused of a worse offence in your day," cried his lordship.

A strangely significant smile played over the lips of Ravensbird. He raised his eyes full on Lord Dane. "I may be publicly cleared of that suspicion yet, my lord, by the real offender being brought to light. I have reason to think I shall be."

"What reason?" inquired Lord Dane.

"A belief in the divine laws of retribution and of justice."

"Can you tell me the nature of your business with Ben Beecher?"

"I have said that it was private, my lord."

Lord Dane took up his hat. "It seems that I have met with little satisfaction in coming here this morning. Considering that you were once servant in my family, Ravensbird, I have an idea that it might behoove you to treat my wishes with more compliance."

A tinge of color flashed into Ravensbird's dark face. "I was servant to the Honorable Captain Dane; I was not servant to Mr. Herbert."

Lord Dane put his hat on his head and walked out, Ravensbird attending him to the door.

"By the way," cried his lordship, wheeling round, "is that other man gone? I mean the old passenger, who was likewise saved and brought here," he added, seeing that Ravensbird looked puzzled.

"He is not gone, my lord; he has not found himself well enough to go. But he is getting better now."

"Does he not go out?"

"He has never once been out of his room, let alone the house, your lordship. He is waiting for remittances, he says."

"Ah! mind you don't feed him all this while, and then not get paid. How quiet he must keep himself! I never hear it mentioned that there is such a person in the place. What does he do all day?"

"Sits and coughs, and reads the newspapers."

"What's his name?"

"When he first arrived Sophie asked it, and he answered that it was no business of hers. But I saw his medicine came in directed to 'Mr. Home.' He was so ill at first, we were obliged to call in Dr. Green."

"Home? Home?" debated his lordship: "don't know the name."

He marched up the street, and Ravensbird turned in-doors again. Certainly the man behaved more cavalierly to Lord Dane than any other of his dependents would have presumed to venture upon. The wonder was that his lordship put up with it.

It was growing dark that same evening,—that is, it may have been near upon five o'clock,—when three men met under covert of the thick wood. Later, with last night's remembrance upon them, they would not have dared to be there: a few days must elapse, ere they grew bold again. They deemed themselves alone; but, trailing flat with his belly on the ground, serpent that he was, lay young Shad, listening,—not to plans for another battue on the pheasants, but to as nefarious a scheme of housebreaking as was ever concocted. Shad had not yet been promoted to assist at great crimes; and his hair rose up on end, as he listened. What, with his personal fear (for Shad fully believed that if any untoward accident betrayed his proximity, he should be riddled through with bullets), and what with the low tone the men conversed in, Shad obtained but a partial hearing of the plot. The chief part that he made out was, that Dane Castle was to be broken into, and the plate "bagged."

Waiting till the men dispersed,—for he did not dare to move until they were gone,—Shad rose up, and tore along at the top of his speed till he gained the spot where he was in the habit of waiting for Tiffle. But no Tiffle was there. She probably had been, and was gone; for it was near eight o'clock. Shad, with all his cunning, was at fault: he scarcely dared to approach Mr. Lester's, which Tiffle had always strictly forbidden, but his tongue was burning to be delivered of its secret. He stole across the in-

tervening space, and gave a timid knock at the back-door.

"If you please, ma'am, can I speak a word to Mrs. Tiffle?" cried he, as a kitchen-maid answered it.

The girl went to the housekeeper's room, where Tiffle was.

"Mrs. Tiffle's wanted," cried she. "It's Granny Bean's Shad."

An unwelcome announcement in the presence of her fellow-servants, and Tiffle jumped up.

"Granny Bean's Shad!" uttered she, in apparent amazement. "He can't want me: it must be a mistake."

She flounced through the back-passages of the house to its outside, and there, sure enough, stood Shad. Her first impulse was to treat him to a good shaking.

"Don't you begin upon me, then, till you've heered," whined Shad. "I shouldn't a-come a-nigh, but you warn't at the place. I've been a-hearing murder, and it made my bones sweat to listen."

"Hearing murder!" ejaculated Tiffle.

"They's a going to break into the castle," resumed the boy, "murder Lord Dane, and fork the plate. I heered 'em say as there was hundreds of ounces kep' in the big chest, and they'd bag it all, while 'tother was a doing the business."

To give Tiffle her due, her badly disposed mind was more intent upon working petty ills and aggravations to her species, than great crimes. Murder, certainly, bore as much horror for her as it does for most people: and she clasped hold of young Shad in affright, and bade him speak intelligibly, and relate all he knew.

"It were them three. Drake, and Ben Beecher, and Bill Nicholson, Ben Nick's brother," said Shad, "and I've been a-lying ever since dark a-listening to 'em, with my nose in the frosty ground, and afraid to draw a breath. I couldn't make out all they said, but I made out enough: and they be a-going in for the castle plate and to murder Lord Dane."

"Did you hear them plan his murder?"

" No, but look you here," said Shad, who did not want for brains, though it was convenient to let it appear to the world in general that his head ran short of them. " They talked about the plate; and to hear of it was good to make your mouth water, spoons, and waiters, and teapots, and things; but 'tain't the plate as they's chiefly a-going in for; I made out that much. They said, while the business was a-being done, two or three of 'em could go and rifle the plate-chest, and nobody be none the wiser. And I says to myself as I listened, what *is* the business, if it's not the robbing the plate-chest? It must be to murder his lordship."

Not an improbable conclusion for Shad to arrive at. Tiffle arrived at the same.

" How many more was to be in it, besides them three?" asked she.

" I dun know. They said two or three of 'em ud fork the plate while the business was a-being done, so there'll be more in it nor them. I heard 'em speak of Lydney once, and then the rest said, Hush! and after that they called him 'L.' I'd lay that white doe rabbit of mine, what's at granny's, as he is to be in it."

Tiffle's eyes sparkled at the information, but before she could reply, one of the footmen, who had been out on some private matter of his own, came up the back-door.

" What, is it you, Mrs. Tiffle, out here! why, you'll catch cold. And young Shad, as I'm alive!"

" Come to beg a drop of my liner-ment for Granny Bean's rheumitix," responded Tiffle to the servant. " The last time I gave her some, it cured her in no time; her back's a'most double to-night, he says. Here, Shad, give me the bottle, and I'll bring it out to ye."

"A-groaning with it awful, granny was," whined Shad, quickly taking his cue; " and please, ma'am, I haven't got no bottle. I come cutting along fast, feeling for granny, and fell over a stone and broke it."

" What a careless boy you must

be!" returned Tiffle: " I suppose I must find one. Wait there."

She followed the footman in-doors; but only to return and finish her conversation with Shad. The boy dismissed, she prepared to go out herself. Lady Adelaide, with Mr. Lester, was dining abroad, so she had no leave to ask.

Her proposed visit was to Lord Dane. Apart from Tiffle's shock at the contemplated murder in itself, it put a stop (should it be carried into effect) to certain ambitious visions which Tiffle had recently, and more especially that day, been indulging a hope might grow into realities. Tiffle had cast her covetous eyes on the castle, hoping to slip in as its housekeeper, either through favor of Miss Lester, should she become Lady Dane, or through the favor of Lord Dane himself, did he remain a bachelor. Of course, were the thread of his lordship's life to be severed by any such summary process, Tiffle's visions must fade into air.

Lord Dane was seated alone in his dining-room,—the great dining-room that the reader has seen before. Miss Dane had retired, but he sat yet over his wine. The rays of the chandelier fell on the glittering table, on its beautiful service of sparkling crystal. Bruff entered.

" My lord, a person is asking to see you. It's Lady Adelaide Lester's maid."

" To see me?" returned his lordship. " What, Tiffle?"

" Yes; Tiffle, my lord. I told her your lordship was at dinner, but she wished me to bring word that she had come for something important."

" A message from Lady Adelaide, possibly," carelessly remarked Lord Dane. " Let her come in."

Tiffle appeared. Lord Dane had turned his chair to the fire then, and she advanced and stood near him. Bruff departed and shut the door.

" Oh, my lord! the most wicked plot!" she began, throwing her bonnet back in her flurry, and putting out her hands. "The castle's going to be rifled, and your lordship murdered promiskeous in your bed."

"What!" uttered Lord Dane, wondering whether Tiffle had turned crazy, and evincing a very powerful inclination to laugh. "You can sit down, Tiffle: you seem a little excited."

"My lord, it may sound like ridicul, but its gospial truth," returned Tiffle, taking the chair offered her. "Them three men have been a-plotting of it in the wood—Bill Nicholson, and Drake, and Ben Beecher; and one overheard 'em as is sure and safe, and he come and imparted of it to me. Lydney is to be with them, it's pretty apperient, for his name was mentioned once, but they said, Hush! and afterwards called him only 'L.' And they spoke of rifaling the plate-chest while the business was done,—the business object that they break in for, my lord,—and that, you may be sure, is no other than the murdering of you."

Lord Dane, uncertain still whether there might be any thing in the tale, or whether Tiffle really had lost her senses, made her go over the whole of it circumstantially. It comprised all she had heard, and some she had not heard, for Tiffle's news, like many other persons', was sure to increase in the telling; she repeated it all.

"Was it you who heard this fine plot?"

"Me, me lord! As if I should be prowling in the wood at night, a-hazarding of my repetation!"

"Oh, of course not," said Lord Dane, with a cough. "Who was it, then?"

"I couldn't impart that to your lordship."

"Then you had better not have imparted the tale. I suppose it was some — some—" his lordship was rather at a loss for a word—"beau of yours."

"Indeed, then, no!" was Tiffle's nettled rejoinder. "I've had enough of them sort of vanaties, and had rather keep 'em at arms-distance."

"Well, as it appears that something

may be in it: at any rate there's sufficient doubt to induce some sort of preparation against the possibility—"

"Some sort of preperation!" interrupted the alarmed Tiffle. "Preperation against it must be made, my lord, or you'll have the catastrify for certain."

"Just so!" said Lord Dane. "Therefore it is necessary that all points bearing upon it should be imparted to me. Tell me, in private, who this bearer was, and he shall come to no harm, nor you either. Otherwise, I must call in the aid of the police, and you must be publicly examined to-morrow before Squire Lester."

This would not have suited Tiffle at all: quite the contrary. Yet she was awake to the common-sense view of Lord Dane's argument, and to the necessity of his knowing all.

"It's not that he could come to harm, my lord, or that I have any motive to conceal it, such as you might fancy," she resumed. "But the one that heard it is useful to me; he looks about for me, unsuspected, and brings me news; and if it was once known he did so, there'd be good-by to it,— for folks would be on their guard not to speak before him. I'd tell your lordship, if you'd let it be quite private from everybody else; indeed, you might see him for yourself."

"Agreed," said Lord Dane.

"It was Granny Bean's Shad."

"Granny Bean's Shad!" he uttered, looking at her. "Why, every second word spoken by that boy is a barefaced lie."

Tiffle bent her face close to Lord Dane's: he had never seen it so earnest, so little savoring of deceit.

"That Shad will tell you the truth in this, my lord, I'll answer for it with my own life. He has less faults than folks think for, and he daredn't play the fool with me."

"I'll see him," said Lord Dane, as Tiffle rose to withdraw. "When do you say the attack is to be made?"

"Not for three nights for certain; and then none was named. They were waiting for something, though Shad could not make out for what, unless it is for the moon to go. Another thing he only half heard: those ruins were mintioned. He thought perhaps they were going to meet in them, and plot further."

"What ruins?" quickly asked Lord Dane.

"The chapel ruins opposite," replied Tiffle, extending her hand in the direction.—"They may be there now, at this very moment, for all we know."

"Tiffle," called out his lordship, as she was gliding from the room with her usual stealthy step. "Not a word of this abroad, remember. And caution that Shad."

"He's safe, my lord; and you may rely upon it, I don't eject another syllible from my lips. It's in your lordship's hands now, and out of mine."

Lord Dane remained in a reverie after her departure, and then strolled out of the castle. That an attack was being contemplated he entertained no manner of doubt, though he did not take precisely the same view of it that Mr. Shad and Tiffle had adopted. He felt surprised; for, loose in character as the three men mentioned had hitherto been regarded, taking their full delight in poaching, smuggling, and similar adventures of a venial nature, or what are looked upon by many as venial, they had never attempted great crimes, and Lord Dane felt convinced that some master head-piece was urging them on.

He stood outside the castle-gates, still thinking, taking little notice of a female form approaching from the direction of Danesheld. But the female came close up to him, and compelled his attention: he recognized the cloak and bonnet of Tiffle.

"Back again!" cried Lord Dane.

"I have abtained a little more ividence, my lord," was Tiffle's rejoinder, "and thought you'd blame me if I didn't return with it.—When I came the first time, I sent young Shad with a lantern to search the place where them smugglers had been,

thinking it not impossible but they might have left some token behind 'em; for when folks hold a meeting in the dark, and things slip from their pockets or their hands, they're difficult to be picked up again. Shad was back before I was, and he brought this."

She held out a scrap of paper to Lord Dane, and he examined it by the light of the lamp which illumined the gateway, paying Tiffle the compliment, as he took it from her, that she would have made a first-rate detective.

It proved to be part of a note, and Lord Dane read the following words:

"—— impossible to join you tonight, but to-morrow you may expect me without fail.
"W. L."

It appeared to have been written hastily on a long, narrow bit of paper, and then twisted up. The direction, if there had been any, had gone with the first part of the contents.

"Now, I can take my Bible effidavit that that writing is Lydney's," cried Tiffle, when Lord Dane had looked at it. "I have seen his handwriting at our house upon pieces of music, and I saw a note of his to Miss Lester. 'Twas only a line or two about a book, but it was that very self-same hand-writing, and I'll stand to it, my lord, with the very same autigriff at the end of it, 'W. L;' which is the short for his name, William Lydney."

"Where did Shad find this?"

"Close upon the very spot where they'd been a-plotting."

"Why did you not bring Shad up, as you dropped upon him?"

"Shad'll come to-morrow morning and ask for you, my lord, as you ordered. 'Twasn't likely I was going to bring him to the castle myself, and set your detainers a wondering and talking," was the reply of Tiffle.

She took her final departure, and Lord Dane, after consigning the paper to his pocket-book, fell into another reverie. That Lydney was an out-and-out villain he was beginning to believe, and his angry eye flashed at the thought that he had been admitted to the intimacy—perhaps gained the love—of Maria Lester. Before him stretched out the sea, broad and wide, not that he could see much of it from where he stood; on his right were the lights of Daneshold; and on his left the chapel-ruins. The moon was high in the sky, and flickered her light upon those picturesque ruins as she had done many a time before,—upon the green walls, the several apertures. Lord Dane turned his eyes towards them.

Singular to say, he had never once been inside those ruins since his return from abroad, in fact since his accession to the title: nay, it may be said, since the period of his romantic love for the Lady Adelaide. Many times had he passed them since then, walked round them, stood near them, but it happened that, either by design or accident, he had not gone inside. He bent his steps thither now, his mind full of Tiffle's surmise: the plotters might be there at that moment, for aught he knew.

Lord Dane crossed the green sward, crisp with frost, crossed it as stealthily as he had ever stolen to his appointments with Adelaide Errol; for it was not his intention to pounce upon or surprise the men, but to listen to them. He had his own reasons for suffering the plot to go on to the very hour appointed for its execution. Once inside, he halted, looked about, and kept his ears open. Nothing appeared to have changed: there were the faint remains of the altar, the traces of the graves, the ghostly-looking windows, and the moss-covered stones: all looked as it had looked in those years long gone by.

It appeared to be entirely void of human life; if any plotters were there, they remained still and silent: and, that none were there, speedily became apparent to Lord Dane, as he paced about it. His thoughts began to revert to the past, and soon, grow-ing oblivious to the present, to the lapse of years, to annoying plots, and to Maria Lester, the past was alone before him. He was dwelling on Lady Adelaide's beauty, on their mutual dream of sentimental passion, on her strangely sudden desertion: and from that topic his mind naturally reverted to the tragic accident, which had cost the life of Henry Dane, almost on the very site where he then stood.

The latter was not a pleasant subject to indulge in, with the ghostly-looking ruins around, the grave-stones beneath, and the pale white moonlight above; and Lord Dane, middle-aged man though he was getting, British peer though he was, began to find that he was not totally exempt from the sport of superstitious fancies. He turned from the altar, where he had been standing, to make the best of his way out, when at that moment a form rose up in the window aperture nearest to him, and remained silent, watching him, it seemed, in the moonlight. A half-smothered cry broke from Lord Dane's lips, his hair stood on end, and his flesh crept.

Yes they did, lowering to him as you may deem the assertion. It is true that Lord Dane had been thinking of his cousin: and imagination, especially superstitious imagination, plays curious tricks. As he stared at that figure in the aperture, its extraordinary resemblance in form to the dead man, struck upon him: he strode to the window, separated only by the wall, and stood face to face,—face to face with him who was once Harry Dane. The once-familiar features stood out pale and clear in the moonlight, far too clear for Lord Dane not to recognize them. It was then he uttered the smothered cry, and his hair bristled up from his brow.

He fell back involuntarily. He leaned against the decayed wall to recover himself. He remembered who and what he was, a man and an Englishman: shook himself, stepped to the entrance and passed out at it. That he had seen his cousin's spirit,—a ghost, as it is familiarly called,—was his undoubted conviction, little as he had hitthero believed in ghosts, given to ridicule the fancied seers of them, as he had been.

It had vanished. Nothing was to be seen outside. Lord Dane strode round the exterior of the ruins, but the ghost was gone, leaving no trace behind.

No trace, save in the physical disturbance of Lord Dane. Again the superstitious feeling came creeping over him, the dread that the dead was hovering near: and he positively started, full-pace to the castle, quickly, and perhaps as conscious of terror, as Lady Adelaide had run, shrieking, that eventful night. Bruff was standing in the gateway as his lord entered, and turned in amazement to look at him: for in the starting eyes, the panting lips, and the livid features, the man could scarcely recognize those of Lord Dane.

———◆———

CHAPTER XXIII.

THE DETECTIVE FROM SCOTLAND YARD.

A TELEGRAPHIC despatch went up to London in the course of the following day. It was sent by Lord Dane, and received by the head police-office in Scotland Yard. On the morning after, Bruff informed Lord Dane that a gentleman, a stranger, was at the castle, asking to see him.

As the reader may surmise, it was one of the chief detectives, come down in obedience to the demand of Lord Dane. He bore about him no outward signs of his profession; was in plain clothes, and a free-speaking, agreeable man,—one who had received a liberal education, and was well read. His name was Blair. Miss Dane, meeting him in the corridor, scanned him with her critical eyes,—critical when single gentlemen were in the way,—and inquired privately of her brother who he was, and whether he was mar-

ried. To the latter question, Lord Dane, at hazard, answered "Yes;" to the former, he carelessly said something about "banking firm," "private affairs," "money matters." Miss Dane, who was a great gossip, forthwith favored the household with the information that Mr. Blair was one of his lordship's town-bankers, come down on money business. And thence the news penetrated to Danesheld. He remained on a visit at the castle.

After breakfast, which Lord Dane partook of with him in the library, came the conference. Mr. Blair was put in possession of the facts already known to the reader;—of the shipwreck, of Lydney's being saved from it, of the recovery of the box, and then its loss, of Lydney's suspicious association with the poachers, his frequenting the wood, of his having been seen in it, or close to it, at the hour of the late conflict with the keepers; of his having wormed himself into the confidence of the neighboring families, especially of Squire Lester's, and his supposed covert designs on Miss Lester and her fortune; and lastly came this projected attack on the castle, to which Master Shad had been a listener, and of which Lydney was no doubt prime mover. Lord Dane threw open the whole budget.

Mr. Blair listened in silence.

"When is the supposed attack to take place?" was the first question he put.

"Better be prepared from to-night, inclusive. The boy said not quite immediately."

"And—if I gather your lordship's wishes rightly—you would prefer the attack not to be prevented; but that the light-fingered gentry should be caught in the act."

Precisely so. The neighborhood shall be rid of this pest, Lydney; therefore it shall go on to the attack. I am sorry for the other men, and would have spared them if I could, but there's no help for it, and they must share the penalty. They have been too fond of helping themselves to hares and pheasants, and of setting my keepers at defiance, also of doing a little private business in the smuggling line : but they would no more have ventured to plan such a feat as this, than I should. Lydney has drawn them into it."

"I scarcely follow your lordship yet," mused Mr. Blair. "By this lad's account—Shad, or whatever you call him—robbery appeared to be a secondary consideration : the clearing of the plate-chest is to be effected while the real object, 'the business,' is transacting, and this business a murderous assault on your lordship. How have you incurred Lydney's ill-will, that he should plan so diabolical a crime ?"

"I have given you Shad's version, —I should rather say the conclusion he jumped to," returned Lord Dane, "but I have not yet given you mine. I do not believe that any assault upon myself is contemplated. I believe they would be only too happy that I should sleep, undisturbed, through the proceedings, and wake up to find them and the plate safely off."

"But you have said the plate is not the principal object," again pursued Mr. Blair.

"Neither is it," returned Lord Dane. "I believe that Lydney's chief object is to search for this box. From the first, he has insolently and rudely accused me of detaining it in the castle ; accused me both to my face and behind my back. Now, I think it will turn out that the box is the prime motive-power, and that he has persuaded these poor fellows to join in the attack by promising them a share in the plate-booty for their pains."

"Where *is* the box ?"

"I cannot say."

"Did it enter the castle ?"

"Have I not explained that the things were all placed in my strong room and secured ; and that when they were visited—on the same day, and by Lydney himself—the box in question was not among them ? The two men who carried in the things could not remember that particular box ; my butler, who was looking on failed to

observe it ; in short, the only pair of eyes which professed to witness its actual entry, belonged to this young reptile, Shad ; and he's the deuce's own cousin for telling lies, if it suits his purpose."

"Had he a purpose ?"

"He was standing by, watching the unloading of the cart. Lydney afterwards heard of this, and offered him sixpence if he could tell where the box went to. Shad said into the castle,—having the attractions of the sixpence before his sight. The general opinion was, that the box was stolen from the cart in its progress to the castle. For my own satisfaction's sake, and in justice to my servants, I had the castle at once searched by the police ; but no box was found."

"And did Lydney know of this ?"

"He did. The inspector of police, here, informed him of it."

"Then, my lord, how can you take up the opinion that he must be breaking into the castle after the box ?"

"It is my opinion," replied Lord Dane. "Bad as he is, I do not believe personal injury to myself is his object."

"Have you cause to think he may entertain any ill-feeling against you at all ?" proceeded Mr. Blair, after some reflection.

"No. Unless—I declare, that is a point in the business that never occurred to me till this moment—unless he is cognizant that I, on Tuesday last, warned Mr. Lester against him. I found the fellow growing more intimate than was expedient with Miss Lester,—at all events trying to do so, —meeting her in her walks, and the like ; and I gave Mr. Lester my opinion of his character, with the grounds for it. I understand Mr. Lester so far acted upon it, that same day, as to turn him from the house upon his attempting to call."

"Did he know it was you who gave Mr. Lester the information ?" inquired Mr. Blair.

"Not that I am aware of. But he may have learned it."

"Quite sufficient provocation to induce ill-feeling towards your lordship, in a base mind like his," remarked the officer. "Especially if he really had cast a covetous eye on the fortune of the young lady."

"But to murder me for it!" cried Lord Dane, in a doubtful tone." That's rather strong revenge."

"Few men, let them be ever so bad, contemplate murder," answered Mr. Blair. "The crime, when committed, generally arises with circumstances. But I must lay my plans, so that this one does not succeed in it. Where is your police-station?"

"In the heart of Danesheld. I will walk with you to it."

"I understand that your lordship gives the entire charge of this business into my hands?" pursued Mr. Blair.

"Undoubtedly."

"Then you must allow me to go to work in my own way. I would prefer to visit the inspector here alone. His name is Young, I think?"

"Young. He succeeded Wilkes, who died. Your plan will be, I suppose, to place some men each night inside the castle?"

"I will inform your lordship of my plans this evening, when I shall have had time to consider of them."

Mr. Blair walked into the town, and found the police-station. Inspector Young happened to be in the first room alone, perched upon a stool. The stranger, in a summary sort of manner, began asking various questions of Danesheld and its inhabitants, of the police-station, and of other things, rousing the ire of the inspector, who was a great man in his own estimation, and considered that nobody, save a magistrate, or Lord Dane himself, might interfere in what pertained to his post.

"I should be glad to know who you are, coming in and examining into my business," cried he, resentfully.

"Should you?" was the careless reply. "I am Mr. Blair, from Scotland Yard, and I hold my private orders direct from Sir Richard Mayne."

The inspector jumped off the stool.

"I beg your pardon, sir," said he.

"Please to step into the inner room. I hope—I'm sure I hope nothing in our office here has fallen under the displeasure of Sir Richard."

"Not that I have heard," replied Mr. Blair, as he took his seat. "But now I want a great deal of information from you. Who's this Lydney that's stopping in the place?"

"Well, I don't know who he is," returned the inspector. "We can't make him out, sir. To appearance, and to speak to, he seems of the very highest degree,—you wouldn't take him for any thing less than a nobleman. But, on the other hand, he mixes himself up with poachers and disreputable people, goes into the woods with them at night, lodges at a public-house, and,—in short, we are puzzled."

"Was it his own box that was lost?"

"He says not. Very anxious he has been for its recovery, quite feverish over it. He offered a thousand pounds reward."

"When he is probably not worth a hundred pence. Had that box been produced, and the reward claimed, you might have found yourselves in a dilemma, or had to rob your own pockets to give it."

Inspector Young smiled.

"We are more cautious than that, sir, though we are countrymen. My Lord Dane dropped me a hint to the same effect; and I, in a civil way, intimated to Lydney that he was a stranger, and we could not be answerable for the reward. So he deposited the money with me."

"The thousand pounds?" uttered Mr. Blair.

"He did, sir. Of course I gave him an acknowledgment, and we hold the money still. But I had to pass my word to him that the transaction should be a strict secret: consequently it is not known."

"Not to Lord Dane?"

"Not to any one. Lord Dane's opinion is, that Lydney himself has possession of the box; but—"

"No, it is not," interrupted Mr. Blair.

" I can assure you that it is," said the inspector.

" I can assure you that it is *not*," authoritatively corrected Mr. Blair. " If his lordship has told you so, he must have had his own reasons."

The inspector did not dare to contradict again. He looked at his superior, and waited. The latter lowered his voice.

" Have you heard that Dane Castle is likely to be broken into ?"

" No !" exclaimed the inspector. " Who by ?"

" Lydney—as the chief mover. And his object, as Lord Dane thinks—one of his objects—is to search after this identical box ; the other object is the plate-chest. That is the business I am down upon."

" My goodness me !" ejaculated the inspector, after a pause. " Lydney ! well I could not have believed that of him ! I can't understand this at all, sir."

" Neither can I," returned Mr. Blair. " It was clear enough before you told me of the thousand pounds : it is not now. How can I get at a chap called Shad ? I should like a meeting with the gentleman,—accidental, you comprehend."

" That will be easily effected. He is always about the wood," was the reply of the inspector.

While they converse, let us turn for an instant to Miss Bordillion's, where Mr. Lydney was presenting himself for a morning call.

" Not at home," said the servant ; but at that very unlucky moment who should present her unconscious self at the window but Miss Bordillion. Lydney looked at her, and then at the servant, a half-smile upon his face. The girl felt angry and confused, and attempted a justification.

" It is not my fault, sir : I have only to obey orders. Though it is *not* my mistress' general custom to say she is not at home when she is."

" Miss Bordillion desired you to deny her if I called ?"

" Yes, sir, she did."

He wrote a few words on a leaf of his pocket-book, tore it out, and sent it in to Miss Bordillion.

" I pray you, as a favor, see me for a few minutes : I will not ask it again.".

" Once more can't matter," said Miss Bordillion to herself, as she read the words. " Show Mr. Lydney in, Ann."

" I thank you for admitting me," he began, as he entered. " I find, Miss Bordillion, that within the last day or two some strange rumors to my prejudice have been circulating in Danesheld. With Lord Dane, I never was in favor ; but others were friendly with me. Will you tell me candidly what these rumors are, and whence they arise. I apply to you, because I believe you are truthful and sincere, above petty prejudice, and I had learnt to believe that, of all in Danesheld, you esteemed me as a friend ?"

Miss Bordillion hesitated in perplexity. She was, as he designated it, truthful and sincere ; but she was also kind, and revolted at the thought of giving pain. Mr. Lester had favored her with his version of the reports against Lydney, asserting that they were indisputably true—as Lord Dane had asserted to him—and, Miss Bordillion felt that she could not again receive one who lay under so dark a cloud.

" You probably heard that Mr. Lester turned me from his door ?" he proceeded, finding she did not speak.

" I must acknowledge that I did."

" And you have given orders to be denied to me. Well, now, Miss Bordillion, would it not be fair to acquaint me with the grounds for that line of conduct ? A man cannot fight shadows."

" It might be fair, Mr. Lydney, but it would be a task by no means agreeable. That there are tales abroad to your prejudice, it would be folly to deny ; but I think the removing of them rests with yourself."

" In what way ? I cannot, I say, combat shadows ?"

" It appears to me that you should declare who you are. You have said that you are of good family,—a family of some note in England. I am sure I received the assertion with perfect reliance on its truth, as I make no doubt others did. But, now that these prejudices against you have arisen, it is incumbent on you to declare more particularly who your family are, and of what country. I think if you could do this, the feeling against you would, in a measure, be removed. You perceive I speak openly."

Something like amusement twinkled in his eye as he listened.

" I suppose, since the prejudice has spread, people have been searching through the peerage and baronetage, and all your other red books, to find the name of Lydney," said he.

" Something very like it, I believe," replied Miss Bordillion. " Do you not see that it is necessary you should declare yourself ?"

" Will you tell me what the rumors are, and whence they arise ?"

" Whence they arise, I do not know ; from your own conduct, I believe. People talk of you being friendly with the poachers,—of your frequenting the woods at night. For myself, I do not credit that ; I do not, indeed, Mr. Lydney ; I have better faith in you."

" Yet you have ordered your doors to be closed."

" I—I could not do otherwise," she answered, quite distressed at having to give the explanation, yet deeming it better to speak freely, now it was entered upon. " Squire Lester insisted upon it ; or else Maria's visits here must have ceased."

" I am accused, I hear, among other henious sins," he proceeded, dropping his voice to a lower key, "of entertaining covetous designs on the fortune of Miss Lester."

" Who could have told you that ?" uttered Miss Bordillion.

" It is patent to all Danesheld. You may hear it as you pass along the street. I am supposed to be doing my best to delude Miss Lester into a Gretna-Green escapade, or some such unorthodox marriage, for the sake of touching her fourteen thousand

pounds. Allow me to assure you, Miss Bordillion, that, whenever I do marry, it will be of no moment to me whether my wife shall possess fourteen thousand pounds, or not fourteen hundred pence."

" I wish you would not mention these things, Mr. Lydney, for they only pain me to hear them. For myself, I cannot but have confidence in you ; there is something about you that I have trusted from the first, and trust still. But, put yourself in my position, and reflect how impossible it is that I can act against the stream, and continue to receive you here,—especially with Miss Lester visiting me as usual. If you would be more open, as to yourself, and declare who you are, it might be different."

" The fact is," said Lydney, but in a good-natured tone, "that you do doubt me. You like me personally, you have a sort of faith in me, at least you had ; but you cannot overget the budget of inuendoes against me, now opened. I do not know that I blame you for it, Miss Bordillion ; in your position, as you observe, I might judge as you do. I will not intrude longer on you," he added, as he rose, " but I must express my hope that the time will shortly come when you will welcome me to your house again."

Miss Bordillion held out her hand in token of adieu.

" Were I you, Mr. Lydney, I would no longer remain in Danesheld ; it cannot be a pleasant spot of abode to you now."

" That proves how you share in the general prejudice," he laughed, as he released her hand. " Farewell."

" Not a word about his family—or who he is," thought Miss Bordillion, as she turned to ring the bell. " I don't know what to think."

The servant had the street-door open as he approached it, admitting Maria Lester. Mr. Lydney caught her hand and drew her into a small room or study, where in past days she and Edith used to do their lessons. He closed the door, and stood before her.

" Maria," he began, calling her in

his agitation by her Christian name, "I am going to put your friendship, your confidence in me, to the proof. Dark tales are abroad to my prejudice, insinuations that I am not what I appear to be, that I am no gentleman; nay, worse, that I am a bad character. Do you believe them?"

"No," she quietly said, lifting her trusting eyes to his.

"I will not thank you; it appears to me that if you could believe such accusations, cast on me, you would not be worth my thanks. Bold, you will say. Yes, I am bold in this moment. It is not convenient to me —you shall know why, sometime—to declare any thing more of myself than people know at present. The tales of my nefarious doings will right themselves; I do not fear them, or cast a word to them; but when you hear it said that I am no gentleman, that I am an adventurer, believe it not. Will you trust me?"

"With my whole heart and faith," she answered, the tears rising to her eyes.

"I do thank you now," and somehow he contrived to possess himself of both her hands. Holding them between his, he looked her steadfastly in the face. "It has been brought against me, that I am striving to gain the affections of Miss Lester for the sake of securing her fortune. Upon the state of Miss Lester's affections I will not enter, but I will honestly avow that she has gained mine. I say no more; I must leave it to the future; to the time when I can present myself before Mr. Lester, and ask that his daughter may be given to me for my own. In that hour Mr. Lester will find that fortune is certainly no object to me, and that he is heartily welcome to retain any she may possess. I have not offended you in saying this?" he added in a tone of the deepest tenderness.

No, he had not offended her; far from it: her heart only beat more responsively to the avowal. It was an instant of agitation; her feelings were nearly beyond control, and her

wet eyelashes rested on her crimsoned cheeks.

"It has been told to me," he whispered, "that another covets the prize for his: one whom I suspect to be my enemy. And that Mr. Lester favors his suit."

"But not I," she answered in the moment's impulse. "I never can be his, though he has made it a condition of his placing Wilfred beyond reach of want. Papa would like it: Lord Dane is rich and a man of rank."

"I will take care of Wilfred," said Mr. Lydney: "so far as any one can take care of him. And it may be in my power to offer Mr. Lester a position for his daughter, not inferior to that of Lord Dane. Only trust me, Maria," he concluded, as he lingeringly released her, and turned away.

As the maid was showing him out, a stranger passed the door, and looked keenly at him, very keenly Lydney thought. It was not, however, an offensive stare: but the eyes that gave it appeared to have a peculiar power of their own for taking in all points of any object on which they rested.

"I hope he will know me again," said Mr. Lydney, good-humoredly: "I wonder who he is."

"I know sir," said the girl. "He passed when I was in the tea-shop just now, and I heard it. It is my Lord Dane's banker, come down on a visit. Good morning, Mr. Lydney, sir."

The last sentence was uttered in a hearty tone, and with a raised voice, for Lydney had slipped half-a-crown into her hand, willing, perhaps, to prove to the girl that he cherished no resentment against her for obeying orders, and denying him. The stranger evidently caught the tones, and turned to the maid.

"Did I hear you call that gentleman Lydney?" he asked.

"Yes, sir. That's Mr. Lydney."

Mr. Blair looked after him, looked curiously, as if Lydney did not answer to the picture he had mentally painted of him.

"He does look like a gentleman,"

were the words that seemed involuntarily to escape him.

"He is a gentleman, if ever there was one," cried the girl familiarly.

"Ah!" soliloquized Mr. Blair, walking on. "Just the fellow to come into a country-place and ride the high horse. He might deceive us, if we trusted to his looks.

CHAPTER XXIV.

THE ATTACK.

It was Sunday evening, and several days subsequent to the arrival of Mr. Blair. In the large dining-room at Dane Castle he sat, Lord Dane with him. Both gentlemen had finished their wine, but the decanters and dessert remained on the table. They were in earnest conversation, when suddenly one of the windows was shaken, and Lord Dane rose hastily, pulled aside the white blind, the curtains not being closed, and found himself face to face with Mr. Shad, the glass only between them. He had mounted the iron railings outside, and was standing on the spikes, leaning forward, and holding on by the frame of the window.

"You young imp!" uttered Lord Dane, as he drew back the window, which opened in the middle, after the manner of the French, "what the deuce brings you here?"

"They're a-coming on this very night, my lard,—I know they is," cried Shad, his face working with excitement. "They're in the wood now, and a-tying black crape to their hats; I see 'em a-tying of 'em on, and I thought I'd come and tell ye."

Mr. Blair was by the side of Lord Dane, and he seized the boy and deposited him inside the room.

"I see the 'lumination in this here parlor," proceeded Shad, "and made bold to get up and look if it was your lardship in it, but the blind hindered me. I was afeared to go to the big gates, for the servants would on'y ha' druv me back again."

"How many did you see?" asked Mr. Blair.

"I see four. Two tall, and two short," answered Shad. "There was the three what I heered a-planning of the thing days back, and the 'tother, the tallest of all, was like—; I didn't see his face, though,"—he broke off. "He was a-sitting down all the time, and the black hung afore his nose."

"How can you tell that he was tall, if he were sitting down?" demanded Mr. Blair.

"'Cause he was," was Shad's reply. "I twigged his long legs."

"Who were you going to say he was like?"

"Well, I never heered him speak, and I never see him get up—but he was like Will Lester."

"Nonsense!" angerly interposed Lord Dane. "What should Wilfred Lester want, breaking into my house? The boy's a fool, Blair, and has always been deemed one. Do you think it was Lydney?" he sharply added, turning to Shad.

Now the boy was not a fool; he had a vast deal too much cunning to be a fool, and that cunning he was incessantly calling into requisition. It did not in the least matter to Shad whether the silent gentleman in the disguising crape might be Mr. Lydney or Mr. Wilfred Lester; his opinion was that it was the latter; but as the suggestion appeared to give offence to Lord Dane, who would evidently be better pleased to hear that it was Lydney, Shad's cunning prompted him to veer round.

"Well, I dunno," said he, with admirable simplicity. "Lydney's tall, too, he is; and I think the man was broad, here," touching his chest, "like Lydney's is. Yes, I does think he looked more like Lydney. 'Twas the leggins made me think o' Will Lester; but I see Lydney with a pair on, one day."

"Safe to be Lydney," murmured Lord Dane in the ear of Mr. Blair. And the latter nodded.

" What did you hear ?" he asked of Shad.

" I didn't hear nothing, sir. They warn't a talking, above a odd word 'bout the veils; and I cut off, and left 'em, to tell his lardship."

Mr. Blair spoke for a moment in an undertone with Lord Dane, and then gingerly lifted Shad out at the window again, on to the spikes, telling him to jump down. Lord Dane addressed the boy:

"You go home at once, to bed, Shad. You are not wanted, and there might be a danger, you know, of your getting shot, in mistake for one of the thieves, if you lingered near the castle. If these men get dropped upon through your information, you shall have such a reward as you have never seen in your life. Make the best of your way home."

Away tore Shad, as if in a hurry of obedience. But the moment he was beyond view of the castle, he stopped dead, threw up his arms, capered with his feet; performed, in short, all sorts of antics, and spoke out with his tongue:

"Go home to bed, my lard says! Not I; I hain't agoing to bed; I'd like to see the fun. And as if I didn't know Will Lester, though he have got the black crape over his face! He—"

Shad found himself pinioned. Strolling about and smoking a cigar, was Mr. Lydney, close to whom Shad had unconsciously been dancing, and who had heard his words.

"What is that about Will Lester and black crape, Shad ?"

Shad began to howl. He was a-going home to his granny's to bed, he was.

" You little hypocrite !" exclaimed Mr. Lydney, "do I want to hurt you, do you suppose ? Look here, Shad, you cannot play the simpleton with me, so just put off that idiotic folly. I ask you what you meant, when you alluded to Wilfred Lester's having black crape over his face, and I ask to know. If you don't choose to tell me, I will take you off now to the police-station, and you shall tell them.

What fun is going on to-night ? I heard all you said, and that Lord Dane had ordered you home to bed. Did you ever see a sovereign, Shad ?"

" I have seed 'em," returned Shad, with a stress on the "seed."

" Would you like to possess one ?"

" Oh !" aspirated Shad, in trembling delight, his mouth beginning to water.

"I said I would give you sixpence if you told me the truth about that box; I believe you did tell me the truth, and I gave it you. Tell me now the truth of what is agate, touching Mr. Wilfred Lester, and I will give you a golden sovereign."

For that tempting bate Shad would have sold Danesheld and everybody in it, himself included. But Shad was somewhat puzzled. If this was the night of the grand expedition, and Mr. Lydney was strolling about enjoying idleness and a cigar, he could not be in it, as had been surmised. Shad's cunning came to the rapid conclusion that he was *not* in it, and that they had been under a mistake in supposing so.

"I daredn't tell," said he, "I'm afeared as you'd tell on me again, and they'd kill me dead, some of 'em."

" You may trust my word, Shad, better than I can trust yours; I will not tell upon you. See how bright it looks."

Mr. Lydney struck a fusee, took a sovereign from his pocket, and held the light close to it. The attraction was irresistible, and Shad speedily made a clean breast of it, and put Mr. Lydney into possession of as much as he knew himself.

" The castle was a-going to be broke into that night, and the plate chest stolen," was its substance.

" It is not possible that Wilfred Lester would join in an expedition of that sort !" debated Mr. Lydney in incredulity. " It's not possible, I say, Shad."

"I see 'em; they be a-tying the black crape over their faces at this very time," was Shad's eager rejoinder. "There's Drake, and Nicholson, and Ben Beecher; and Will Lester was

LYDNEY AND THE POACHER.—*See page 154.*

a-sitting down, ready. My lard broke out upon me sharp, a-saying it warn't him; he said it was you."

"Lord Dane said it was I !" repeated Mr. Lydney.

"Leastways," cried Shad, retracting, lest he might be getting himself into hot water, "he said, 'Was it Mr. Lydney or was it Will Lester?' 'cause both was tall. So I said as I couldn't speak to neither of 'em for certain, when I see it angered him. As if I didn't know Will Lester!"

After some further colloquy, Shad was dismissed, and Mr. Lydney remained in a state of the utmost perplexity and discomposure. That Wilfred Lester had joined in certain night expeditions of the poachers, touching game, he had made himself only too sure ; but that he would rush madly into crime, was incomprehensible. One of two things was certain ; he must have lost his senses, or become utterly reckless.

How could he, Lydney, prevent its taking place ? at any rate prevent Lester's joining in it ? It was indispensable he should be prevented, not only for his own sake, but for his family's ; and a deep flush rose to Mr. Lydney's brow, as he thought of the terrible disgrace it would reflect on Maria, should her brother be taken and tried for housebreaking. As he thus mused, he became conscious that several policemen were passing him, not together, but singly, and at different times, as if not to attract observation ; the connection of their errand flashed into his mind—they were going up to guard the castle ? All that he could do was to follow them, place himself in a position that would command the approach to the castle, watch for the appearance of the robbers, and intercept Wilfred Lester.

The only retainer of Lord Dane's who had been made privy to the expected attack, was Bruff. The rest had been suffered to retire quietly to rest, night after night, unconscious that any armed force was at watch in the castle. Suffer it to be known to

them, and it would no longer be a secret in Danesheld, was the argument of Mr. Blair ; in which case the attack would not take place. On this Sunday night, the police were admitted privately as usual ; the household went to bed ; but Lord Dane, Mr. Blair and Bruff remained up. Mr. Blair told the officers that the attack was expected.

They waited and waited ; the men at their appointed posts, Mr. Blair anywhere and everywhere, Lord Dane and Bruff in excitement ; they waited, and waited on. The clock struck one. "It is very strange they don't come !" muttered Mr. Blair.

Suddenly, shots were heard in the wood at a distance, and the men came stealthily out of their hiding-places ; Lord Dane and Bruff also rushed into the hall.

"Back, every one of you !" was the stern order of Mr. Blair. "It is coming on now."

"They have met with some obstacle, and are fighting it out in the wood," exclaimed Lord Dane. "Hark at the shots."

"Back, I say, all of you !" was the reiterated order of the detective. "Those shots are a *ruse* to draw the attention of the keepers from the castle should any be near it. I expected something of the sort. They'll be here directly, now. Back ; and silence ; and whatever you may hear or see, let none stir forth till I give the signal."

Back they cowered, and the castle returned to silence. And still they waited and waited on.

Lydney also waited in his place of ambush. Like those within, he wondered what was keeping the villains. He heard the town-clock strike one ; and, not long after, he heard the shots in the wood. It did not occur to him to take the view of them that the detective had done, and they disturbed him much : but he could not quit his present post. It was a muggy, disagreeable, damp night ; the early part of it had been clear, but the weather was changing,—any thing but a pleasant night to remain on the watch in the open air.

Suddenly, a noise stole on his ear: not, however, a sound of the covert footsteps of more than one, as he was expecting, but of one pair of boy's feet scampering over the ground with all possible haste and noise. Mr. Lydney looked out and encountered Shad.

"So you are here! instead of having gone home to bed!"

"Don't hold on me then, please, sir," panted Shad, who was out of breath. "I'm a-going to the castle to tell Lord Dane. I know he's up, a-waiting."

"To tell him what?"

"'Taint the castle they be on to. It's the hall"

"What?" screamed Lydney.

"They've a-broke into it: they be in it now. I've been a-dodging on to 'em all the night, and they be gone right into the hall, 'stead o' coming here. They took a pane out at one o' the winders."

All that had been dark grew clear to Lydney. Wilfred Lester was after the DEED,—the deed relating to his property, which his father withheld from him. He had persuaded these men into the expedition, and they, no doubt, were after doing a little private business on their own account, touching the plate-chest. And this was correct. When Shad had heard, or partially heard, the planning, he had mistakenly concluded that the castle was the object, never giving a thought to the hall. The castle, however, had never been threatened. And Wilfred Lester (but this need scarcely be observed) was not cognizant of the men's intentions to steal. He purposed and believed that the abstraction would be confined to the deed. He looked upon that as his own, and deemed he was committing no sin to take it, under the circumstances of its being so unjustly and unlawfully denied him.

With a half cry of dismay, Lydney sped towards the hall; but, ere he had gone a yard, he stopped and grasped Shad.

"You must not go to the castle,

Shad: there's no need to acquaint Lord Dane with this. I will not have you go there."

Shad lifted his cunning and covetous eyes.

"They be on the watch, they be; and if I goes and tells his lardship as that lot hain't a coming, maybe he'll give me a half-a-crown."

"And a pretty thing you'd do!" returned Mr. Lydney, meeting cunning with cunning. "You would put them off their guard at the castle; and how do you know 'that lot,' as you call them, may not take a turn up there, after they have done with the hall? Would Lord Dane reward you for that?"

Shad opened his eyes. The notion had not struck him.

"You be quiet, Shad, that is all you have to do. Be entirely silent as to the doings of this night, and especially as to Wilfred Lester: if I find that you are, I will do something better for you even than the sovereign."

He flew towards the hall, as he concluded, and Shad followed more slowly after him.

Lydney seemed to gain the hall in no time. He passed through the gates, and stood there to reconnoitre, before approaching close. The house seemed silent as the grave; nothing could be seen, nothing heard; the blinds appeared drawn before the windows, and the inmates were no doubt sleeping peacefully. Lydney began to question whether that iniquitous Shad had deceived him, when he was startled by the loud report of a pistol inside, and at the same moment some object seemed to come forth from the hall-door, and disappear among the shrubs; but who or what he could not decide. He darted forward to the house and entered it, his head full of Wilfred Lester, his ill-conduct, and his danger.

Shad had not used deceit. The men were in. Drake had entered by means of the window, had then opened the back-door and admitted the rest. They waited and listened when they were fairly in; but not a mouse seemed stirring—nothing but the beating of their own hearts.

Silently went Wilfred Lester to his father's study, the others with him; and silently he applied himself to open the safe, where his father had told him the deed was deposited. He had come armed with a key to unlock it harmlessly, so that no discovery should be made of its having been opened by unfair means. Drake kept the room-door against surprise, Ben Beecher held the light, and Nicholson did nothing. It may be wondered that Wilfred Lester should enlist three men in the expedition, when plunder was not the object, and there would be no booty to carry off; but the men had obstinately refused to go with him singly: all would risk it and stand by each other if surprised, or none. Young Lester yielded in his recklessness.

Strange objects they looked there, on that dark, midnight expedition, the black crape disguising their faces. The safe was soon opened; but there appeared a mass of papers within, and Wilfred could not get at the deed without search. Other deeds were there: other papers: some tied with red tape, some sealed, some unfastened. They were disposed of in order, and there was no difficulty in looking them over,—only it took time. He came to one: "Will of George Lester, Esquire;" and the temptation to tear it open and read it was great: he felt sure he was disinherited: that he, the heir by right of birth, had been discarded for Lady Adelaide's children; but he resisted the impulse, and threw it aside with an angry and hasty word. Presently he came to the one he wanted: his own name on the back guided him to the right parchment, and he clutched it with a suppressed shout of joy.

"All right, boys! I have it at last."

There was a murmur of congratulation given under their breath; and Wilfred began putting in order again the papers he had disturbed. While doing this, Robertson and Drake attempted to steal out of the room. Wilfred turned to them.

"Where are you going? Stop where you are!"

"Why, you'd never go to begrudge us a snack of bread-and-cheese, and a draught of beer?" returned Drake. "We shall find it in the pantry, and 'twont be missed."

"You know the bargain," said Wilfred Lester, in suppressed anger. "Nothing must be touched in the house; no: not a crust of bread; they shall not have it to say that we came in like thieves, for common plunder."

"I'll take a stroll through it, at any rate," answered Drake, hardily. "And as to not touching a bit and a sup, if I see it—"

"I will shoot the first man who lays his finger upon any thing in my father's house, no matter what it may be," was the stern interruption of young Lester, as he drew his pistol. "Drake! Nicholson! you know the agreement, I say. I have promised you a reward for helping me; and having secured the deed, I shall be able to pay it you; but the house and its contents must remain intact."

They were callous, bold men, and not to be balked in that way. Having entered on the expedition with their own views of self-benefit, it was little likely they would be turned from them. A low whisper of conversation went on between Drake and Nicholson; something to the effect that they must accomplish their purpose by stratagem, rather than come to an open broil with Wilfred Lester *there* and *then*; and they debated how best to work it. Wilfred, meanwhile, continued to arrange the papers in the safe; it was soon done, and he closed the door again, and locked it.

"Now then," said he, "to get out as cleverly as we came in."

That was easier said than done, for more reasons than one. Wilfred Lester quitted the study, with his companions, and locked the door, leaving the key in the lock as he had found it.

"We'll go out at the hall-door," he whispered, pointing to it; "it is more handy, and I know the fastenings."

Stealing over the oil-cloth, he gained it, undid the bolts, drew it cautiously open about an inch, and looked round. The men stood as he had left them; not one following him; and Beecher was putting the candle on a bracket that rested against the wall.

"I tell you what it is, Master Lester," whispered Drake, who appeared to be more ready with his tongue than the others, "we have helped you on to your ends, and you must help us on to ours; or if you won't help, you must wink at 'em. We come into this house with a resolve to pay ourselves, or we shouldn't have come in at all, and you may as well hear the truth, and make no bones over it. If we takes away but a spoon a-piece, we will take it, for we don't go empty handed."

Wilfred Lester's reply was to raise his pistol and cock it,—not to fire upon them, but to coerce them to withdraw under fear that he would. Ben Beecher, believing life was in danger, stepped close and threw up Lester's arm. The pistol went off; the bullet shattering the glass of a door at the back of the hall.

"Fools!" bitterly exclaimed Wilfred Lester; "save yourselves, and be quick over it. Fools! fools!"

He sped through the hall-door, leaving it open for them to follow, and darted amidst the shrubs, on his right-hand, whence he could readily gain the road by scaling the iron rails. Nicholson and Beecher would have escaped with him, but Drake seized hold of both.

"Don't show yourselves what he called ye—fools," cried he, in a hoarse whisper. "We may get the forks yet; if they be sleeping sound, that shot mayn't have roused 'em. Wait and see: plenty of time to get off then."

But an interruption took place at that moment that they did not bargain for. The hall-door was pushed wider, and in rushed a tall man. But that there was no crape on his face, they might have thought it young Lester

come back again. He came close up to them, and they saw it was Lydney.

"You misguided, miserable men!" he uttered in agitation. "Where's Wilfred Lester?"

Before they could frame an answer —whether it would have been one of civility, repulsion, or attack—Nicholson's eye caught sight of something white on the staircase, and a human face staring at them through the balustrades. It was in a crouching position, and might have been there some time. The sound of the pistol had also done its work: doors were being opened and shut in consternation.

"It's all over!" stamped Drake. "A race for it now, boys."

"Wilfred Lester?" panted Lydney in emotion. "Is he in the house, or not?"

"Not. I swear it. I won't deceive you, Mr. Lydney; he escaped as you came in." It was Beecher who answered.

Now, all this, since young Lester's egress, though it may seem to take time in telling, had really been the work of but a few instants; but the noise was already great, for the figure on the stairs—a female, by her voice—began screaming and shrieking fearfully. The men rushed through the door; and Lydney rushed after them, in his pursuit of Wilfred Lester.

"What in the name of confusion is the matter?" was heard above the hubbub in the voice of Squire Lester, as he descended in pantaloons and slippers, while a crowd of timid ones aroused out of their sleep—ladies, domestics, children—cowered in the rear. And the female on the stairs, who was no other than Tiffle, sobbed out in answer:

"It's a crowd of villyans with blackened faces, broke in to murder us."

With all possible speed, Squire Lester and his men-servants made search. But the "villyans" were gone.

Exceedingly surprised, not to say discomfited, was the great London detective, Mr. Blair, to find that while he had snugly made all preparations for the defence of the castle, that edifice had been left to repose in security, and the hall had suffered the attack. Lord Dane was far more confounded to hear of it : for it sent all his calculations out to sea. What could Lydney want at the hall ? he could not expect to find his box there ; and it was hardly to be supposed he broke in to steal Miss Lester. Nothing had been missed, nothing displaced in the house ; Squire Lester testified that he did not believe a thing had been touched ; therefore robbery had scarcely been the object. But of course the outrage must be investigated.

It is the custom in some parts of England for country magistrates to hold examinations of prisoners, when in a preliminary stage, at their own houses. Whether it be in strict accordance with law is another matter. Country justices, especially in remote districts, pay more attention to convenience than law.

About eleven o'clock on Monday morning, there was a gathering at Squire Lester's to inquire into the night's outrage. Lord Dane, Mr. Blair, a neighboring magistrate or two, and the squire himself, were present ; Lady Adelaide and Maria, the latter with a face of emotion, now crimson, now white; Inspector Young and a policeman ; Mr. Apperly, who had been sent for ; and—having obeyed the mandate to attend, half-request, half-command, borne from Mr. Lester by Inspector Young— William Lydney. That it was not a strictly official inquiry, only an irregular one, the reader will understand, by the ladies being present. There was no appearance of a court ; they came in as morning guests might do, and took their seats anywhere ; some stood. Maria held some embroidery in her hand and made a show of working at it ; Lady Adelaide did nothing, save hold a screen between the fire and her delicate face. Mr. Blair appeared merely as a friend of Lord Dane's. He took no part in the

proceedings, and his real character was unsuspected. The last to enter was Lydney, accompanied by Inspector Young : he looked exceedingly grave, not to say troubled, as he approached Mr. Lester, though as little like a housebreaker as it was possible to conceive. His elegant form, in its plain, gentlemanly morning-costume, was drawn to its full height : it would seem that he might suspect the accusation to be made against him, and would not abate one jot of his dignity : very attractive did his high, pale features look that morning.

"I have been favored by a message from you, Mr. Lester, desiring my attendance here," he began, after saluting Lady Adelaide and Maria, and the rest of the company generally. "May I request to know for what purpose ?"

"Yes, sir," dryly replied Mr. Lester. "You may be aware that my house was broken into early this morning. I am about—in conjunction with my Lord Dane, and some of my brother-magistrates—to make some inquiry into it ; and, from circumstances which have transpired, we deem it right that you should be present at the sitting. Are you ready to be so, of your own free-will ?"

"Perfectly ready," replied Mr. Lydney.

"Good !" said the squire. "Otherwise we must have compelled your attendance."

Now, it must be remembered that none save those in the secret knew of the suspected attack on Dane Castle. Mr. Lester and his brother-magistrates were in ignorance of it : the police, receiving their orders from Mr. Blair, did not mention it,—Mr. Blair forbidding it at the earnest request of Lord Dane. Certainly the preparations for defence, and the posting the police inside could have had nothing to do with the attack on the hall. Lord Dane strongly urged on Mr. Blair that the three men, spoken of by Shad, should not be told upon, and he spoke with all the high authority vested in the county's lord-lieutenant: to such authority the officer could do little else but how. In the first place, urged Lord Dane, nobody was sure that they were the men, they had only the word of that little liar, Shad, for it. In the second place, even if they were the men, they had, beyond doubt, been beguiled by that traitor, Lydney,—whom it would be much more in accordance with justice to punish for the whole. Thus, it occurred that nothing was likely to transpire beyond the fact of the actual entrance into the hall. Shad was not alluded to in the business, and the only person who appeared likely to give evidence was Tiffle.

Tiffle was introduced to the drawing-room, curtseying, ambling and shuffling. Squire Lester desired her to speak out what she knew to Lord Dane and the magistrates.

"I retired to rist last night, my lord," began Tiffle, choosing to address his lordship particularly, "and what the reason was, I am inable to say; but the more I tried to get to sleep, the more pertineshously I lay awake. Well, my lord, it was getting on, I'm sure, for two o'clock, when I started up in bed, a-thinking I heard something down-stairs. The flurry it put me in is undescriptable, and I went out of my room to listen. If ever I heered voices in the hall, I heered 'em then: I thought some of the household had got down-stairs at their pranks,—for a tight hand I'm obligated to keep over the servants in this house,—and I crept to the last flight and peeped through the bannisters. I never could have done it if I had known, but I no more thought of bulgarious robbers being in the hall than—"

"What did you see or hear!" interposed Lord Dane.

"My lord, I saw this. I saw three horrid maranders with their faces blackened, and I saw another which I couldn't distinguish nothing of but his coat-tails a-whisking out at the hall-door. Then, or whether it was just before it I can't be sure, a dread-

ful pistol went off, and I nearly fainted. I wouldn't faint, however; I come-to; knowing the family's lives were at stake, and I looked down again, and there I saw the man whisk into the hall again, and I'm sorry to say "—Tiffle coughed and dropped her voice—"that it was Mr. Lydney."

There was a dead pause.

"What next?" said Lord Dane.

"My lord, nothing. Except that they all four, him, and the black bulgarians, talked together for a minute, and then they blew out the candle which had been flaring, level with their heads, and tore away, one trying to get off faster than another."

Mr. Lydney glanced round at Maria. She sat there with a white face, her hands clasped. He smiled at her; it did not look like the smile of a guilty man.

"You hear?" exclaimed Squire Lester.

"I do hear," replied Mr. Lydney.

"Can you offer any explanation?"

"I swear it was him," broke forth Tiffle. "If he denies it he will commit perjury. I saw him as plain as I see him now. I didn't know the others, because their faces were deguised in black, but his was not."

"I did enter your house last night, Mr. Lester, but only once," he calmly said. "If a person went out of it, before I came in, as your servant testifies, it was not myself."

Every soul present appeared struck with consternation at the boldness of the avowal. When the sensation had subsided, Lord Dane inquired haughtily if he could plead any thing in justification.

"If you will allow me five-minutes' conversation with you in private, Mr. Lester," said Lydney, turning to that gentleman, "I will enter upon my justification. Probably you may deem it a satisfactory one."

Mr. Lester repulsed the request indignantly. He was not accustomed to grant private interviews to midnight burglars. Had Lydney any thing to say, he must speak out.

"Then I have no resource but to be

silent," observed Mr. Lydney, after a pause of thought. " Nevertheless I am innocent of any offence."

" You have called yourself a gentleman," cynically remarked Lord Dane. And Lydney took a step forward and threw his head back with dignity.

" I am at least as much of a gentleman as your lordship—in all points," was the firm answer. " Possibly, did we come to examine and compare rank and rights, I should take precedence of you."

The whole room (save one) resented the speech, and were ready to cudgel Lydney for the insult to my Lord Dane.

" Let it pass," said his lordship, good-naturedly. " I can afford it. Will you make out the warrant for his committal, Mr. Apperly ?"

" For my committal !" interrupted Lydney, half angry, half inclined to laugh. " Committal where ? and for what ?"

" To the police-station, for the present, while we look after your companions, and for the crime of breaking into Danesheld Hall," sharply spoke Squire Lester.

" This is beyond a joke," cried Lydney. " You cannot possibly suppose. I broke into it, or was one of those who did ?"

" Silence, sir !" said Lord Dane. " The opportunity of explanation was offered you, and you declined to make use of it."

Lydney remained silent: not in obedience to his lordship, but for self-communing. The warrant for his committal was made out, and Inspector Young laid his hand upon him.

" You are my prisoner, William Lydney."

Then Mr. Lydney roused himself, and appeared as though he would have entered upon his justification ; but, as he was turning to Mr. Lester, his eyes rested on Maria, and it seemed to change his intention. He hesitated, and finally remained silent.

" You need not touch me," he quietly said to Inspector Young, " I will

yield to your authority. But do not treat me as if I were guilty."

The audience was broken up, and the room rose. In the confusion, William Lydney found himself near Miss Lester. There was a whole world of sincerity, of truth, in his smile of tenderness.

" Appearances are dark just now, Maria," he whispered. " Can you trust me still ?"

" I trust you more than ever, William. I will trust you through all," she answered fervently.

" It shall be well repaid, my darling." And Inspector Young called him, and marshalled him forth, an ignominious prisoner.

CHAPTER XXV.

THE DEAD IN LIFE.

IN the invalid's room—for so they called that at the Sailor's Rest, tenanted by the stranger, Mr. Home—there was great bustle. Ravensbird was in attendance, his wife also, and Dr. Green was there ; all gathered round Mr. Home, who lay on the sofa, very, very ill. Ailing from the first, he had now been taken alarmingly worse, and the physician gave little hopes that he would recover.

" Tell me how long you think I shall last," said Mr. Home to him. " I do not fear death ; but if I am near it, I must settle many things."

" Of immediate death, hourly death, there is no danger," was the reply, " and I think you will rally yet. But I do fear your life will not be much prolonged."

" That is, I may rally so as to last a few days ? Speak out."

" Yes," said the physician, reluctantly.

" Then the sooner Apperly is brought to me, the better," was the invalid's answer. " Do you hear, Ravensbird ?"

Dr. Green shook hands with his patient, and went out. Mr. Home spoke again, anxiety in his tone. His voice was as energetic as it had ever been: his intellect as keen.

"Ravensbird, there's no time to be lost. Send for Apperly."

"Immediately, my lord," was the man's answer.

But, it so happened, that as Dr. Green left the Sailor's Rest, he was overtaken by the group who had emerged from Danesheld Hall. Apperly was among them; and Inspector Young walked by the side of Lydney. Dr. Green informed Apperly that he was wanted at the Sailor's Rest in his professional capacity, and the latter went in at once, and proceeded to the door of the sick-chamber.

"I am told the old gentleman wants me, who is lying here," quoth he to Sophie, who came out to him.

"Yes, he is very ill," answered Sophie. "But you need not call him old, Mr. Apperly: he is not as old as you are. You can go in."

She held the door open for him, quitting the room herself. Mr. Apperly advanced to the couch, near which stood Ravensbird.

"I am sorry to hear you are seriously ill, sir," he began. "Mr. Home, I believe."

The invalid turned his head towards him. His high features, somewhat attenuated now by suffering, his keen eyes, and his white hair. A handsome man still. Mr. Apperly gazed at him, and then backed a few paces, astonishment, mingled with terror, on his countenance.

"Good heavens!" he uttered, as he wiped his brow. "It—it—can it be? It *is* Captain Dane! come to life again."

"No, sir," rejoined the invalid, very sharply for one so ill, "it is not Captain Dane. I am Lord Dane. And so I have been, ever since my father's death."

The lawyer looked bewildered. He turned from the sick man to Ravensbird, from Ravensbird to the sick man.

"Is it not a dream?" he gasped.

"It is not a dream," said Ravens-bird. "It is my old master, sure enough; my lord now. I have been proud to know it ever since the day after the shipwreck."

"Why you—you—are supposed to be lying in the Danesheld vaults, sir—my lord. Goodness help me!" broke off Apperly in his former hot fashion; "if you are in truth Lord Dane, who is he,—the other Lord Dane at the castle?"

"If I am in truth Lord Dane!" retorted the invalid. "What do you mean, Apperly? I am my father's son."

"Yes, yes, of course; but these sudden changes confuse me, my lord. Who is he at the castle, I say? I can't collect my senses."

"I should think you can't," was the reply of the true Lord Dane. "He is an usurper; not an intentional one; we must give him that due. He is plain Mr Herbert Dane, and never has been any thing else, though he has reveled in all the rights of a peer for these ten years."

"It will take me—it will take me a week to get over this; a week before I can comprehend it," ejaculated Apperly. "Were you really not killed, my lord?"

"If I was killed I came to life again," said Lord Dane, intending the words as a joke. "The fall over the cliff took away my senses for a time, and otherwise injured me; but I recovered. A moment yet, Apperly: there will be some work for the lawyers between me and the false Lord Dane; which side do you enlist upon?"

"Yours, my lord, certainly; yours by all means."

"Then I retain you as my adviser, and I will tell you my tale. But I should wish somebody else to be present. Ravensbird, where's Mr. William?"

"He has not been in, my lord, since he went this morning to Danesheld Hall."

"Did he go to Danesheld Hall?" asked Lord Dane.

"Yes," was Ravensbird's answer "Squire Lester sent for him."

"And a pretty kettle of fish he has got himself into, if you mean the young man lodging here, William Lydney," put in the lawyer. "He is taken into custody on remand. Young has just walked him off to the station-house."

"Walked Mr. Lydney off to the station-house!" uttered Ravensbird, while Lord Dane stared, in unqualified astonishment.

"A shocking scapegrace, I'm afraid, gentlemanly as he looks," explained Mr. Apperly. "Reports have been abroad, connecting him with the poachers, for some time; but he has got himself into real trouble now. He and three more, with blackened faces, broke into the hall last night, for robbery no doubt, but that they were disturbed. Lydney is the only one of the lot taken as yet."

"How dare you so traduce him, and in my presence?" cried Lord Dane, his eyes flashing wrath. "You don't know what you are saying, Apperly. Are you aware who he is?"

"Not I, my lord. I know nothing of him, except that his name's Lydney; or he says it is. Danesheld looks upon him as an adventurer."

"He will be Danesheld's chieftain, sir; I can tell you that," returned his lordship, with emotion. "Ay, you may stare, but he will. He is my own lawful son, and will be my Lord Dane before many days are over, for I shan't last longer."

"Why, it is mystery upon mystery!" exclaimed Mr. Apperly, who certainly did stare, in no measured degree. "He goes by the name of Lydney."

"He is my own son, I tell you, the Honorable Geoffry William Lydney Dane. Geoffry is his first name, but we have always called him William: my wife, a lady of French extraction, used to say her lips would not pronounce the Geoffry. And you assert that he is in custody?"

"He is in custody beyond dispute, for I made out myself the warrant for his committal," was the answer of Mr. Apperly. And he forthwith proceeded to give Lord Dane a summary of the circumstances, so far as he knew them: dwelling on the fact that Mr. Lydney did not deny having been in the house, as testified to by Tiffle.

"One thing is certain," said Lord Dane, "that William is incapable of a mean or dishonorable action. If he was in Lester's house, he was there for some good and legitimate purpose, and so it will turn out; not for a bad one. Pshaw, sir! speak of housebreaking in connection with William Dane, a future peer of England! I will stake the rest of my poor life that Herbert Dane—my lord, as you all call him—is at the bottom of these rumors against him. I do not suppose he suspects who William is; but I think it likely that he fears I am alive, and goes upon thorns, lest I should turn up."

"My lord, may I ask you why you did not assume your rank and your rights when you first returned?" said Apperly. "Why you have lain on here in obscurity, suffering Lord Dane— Mr. Herbert, I should say—to continue in his honors?"

"All in good time," replied Lord Dane. "I have had my reasons. You know that box that so much has been said about?"

"Well, my lord?"

"I must get that into my possession, if I can, before I alarm Mr. Herbert Dane. I would almost barter my boy's future title to have it safely by my side now. Apperly," continued Lord Dane, after a pause, given to reflection, "it has been in my mind some time to have a detective officer down. Keen men are those London detectives; they ferret out every thing; and perhaps by those means I may arrive at the box. I was only waiting for my health to get better; but it has got worse instead. You shall telegraph for one this day."

"A London detective is at present in Danesheld, at the castle," replied Mr. Apperly. "His name is Blair, and he passes as Lord Dane's banker; business brought me in contact with him some time ago, and of course I recognized him, but he gave me a hint that he was here incog. He might suit your lordship's purpose as well as another."

"Not if he be a friend of Lord Dane's, as you persist in calling him."

"I beg the true Lord Dane's pardon," smiled Mr. Apperly; "but we have called Mr. Herbert Lord Dane so long, that we must call him so, I fear, by many another slip of the tongue. I could ascertain by two words to Blair himself, whether he is at liberty to give his energies to your cause."

"Then go and do so at once," was the command. "Let him understand that he will have to act *against* the present Lord Dane of the castle, but do not mention me otherwise than as Mr. Home. When Dr. Green was called in to me,—I could not send for Wild, because he would have known me,—he asked my name. I replied, 'Mr. Home,' for I was thinking of my own home at the moment, and the word did as well as any other. If this Blair will assist, bring him back with you, for it is high time to act, and the plot is thickening. The Heir of Dane in custody for felony! Do you hear it, Ravensbird?"

As Mr. Apperly walked towards the castle, not knowing where else to look for the detective, it occurred to him that he was not bent upon altogether an honorable errand. To seek Mr. Blair in his host's residence, purposely to ask him to act against that host, was certainly not altogether clear steering; but lawyers are thick-skinned, most of them, and so was Mr. Apperly. It happened, however, that he had not to seek Mr. Blair at the castle, for he met the latter walking from it.

"I was going in search of you," began Mr. Apperly. "A gentleman down here has need of the services of a detective officer. Could you act for him?"

"Yes; for the business that brought me down is so far over that I am no longer needed, and have now quitted the castle. What is it?"

"I must premise that you will have to act against Lord Dane, though in what manner I do not precisely understand myself. Will your private feelings allow you to do so?"

"An officer must have no private feelings," was Mr. Blair's reply. "Lord Dane demanded a detective from town, and I was sent down. My business with him is concluded; and if I am required by another party, I have neither plea nor wish for refusing, whether my services may be put in requisition against Lord Dane, or against any other lord. Does it relate to this business of breaking into the hall? which I confess I cannot fathom,—at least Lydney's share in it."

"In a manner it does; and I can fathom it as little as you."

"I fancied so. I thought Squire Lester might be calling upon me for aid."

"I am not the agent of Squire Lester," replied the lawyer, as he took Mr. Blair to the Sailor's Rest.

Lord Dane was then off the sofa, pacing the room by the help of Ravensbird's arm. The complaint that he labored under was an inward one, telling little upon his general appearance and his apparent health.

"This is Mr. Blair, my lord," said Lawyer Apperly.

"Sir," said the peer, stopping in his walk, and facing him, "I have need of advice and assistance. I have been wronged by Herbert Dane, — Lord Dane, as he is called,—whom I hear you have been visiting. Can you aid me?"

"I have no doubt I can," was Mr. Blair's reply; "at least I can inform you whether any thing can be done, if you will put me in possession of the circumstances."

"Very good. But before I enter upon my tale, which is a long one, allow me to inform you that I am Lord Dane."

The detective gave a sort of cough, impressed with the sudden belief that the gentleman before him was laboring under a mania, and wanted a keeper, rather than a police-officer. His eye glanced at Mr. Apperly.

"His lordship says right," observed the latter. "He is the true Lord Dane."

"The true, veritable William Henry, Lord Dane, only surviving son of the old Lord Dane, of whom you may have heard," continued the peer. "You look astonished, Mr. Blair: I thought police-officers were surprised at nothing."

"The present lord has enjoyed the honors so long," remarked Mr. Blair, recovering himself. "He is not like one who succeeded yesterday. Sir Richard Mayne himself would be surprised at this."

"I dare say he will be, when he hears of it," returned Lord Dane. "And now for my story,—when you will learn how it happens that he has enjoyed them."

Lord Dane seated himself on the sofa, Ravensbird disposing the pillows for his support, and then taking his stand by his side, while the lawyer and the detective occupied chairs opposite,—and Lord Dane began:

"You may probably have heard, Mr. Detective, that Captain the Honorable William Henry Dane, as I was then, went over the cliff, one moonlight night, by accident or by treachery, and lost his life; that his body was turned up by the sea some weeks afterwards, and buried in the family vault."

"I have heard this," replied Mr. Blair. "Bruff, the butler at the castle, a sociable spirit if encouraged, has been fond of visiting my room since my sojourn here, and entertaining me with various items of the family's history. All in good faith: he is proud to tell laudatory tales of the Danes."

"I had been staying at home for some time," proceeded Lord Dane, "and was engaged to my mother's niece and ward, Lady Adelaide Errol. I don't mind telling you, Mr. Blair,—for you may have lost your head for a woman yourself,—that I was madly and blindly in love with her, fascinated by her beauty. I say blindly,—had

I not been blind, I might have seen that her love was given to another. This was the man to enlighten me," —touching Ravensbird's arm. "He came to me in my chamber one morning, in his true regard for my welfare and honor, and warned me that Lady Adelaide was deceiving me; that she loved my cousin, Mr. Herbert Dane, and that he returned her love. When he went on to say that they met almost nightly in the ruins of the chapel, —you know them: on the edge of the cliff,—met for their lovers' endearments, their confidential converse, their ridicule and deceit of me,—then my passion broke forth, and I kicked him, Ravensbird, my faithful friend and servant, down the stairs, discharging him on the spot. In my blind infatuation for Lady Adelaide, I thought he was but traducing her, and I visited it upon him. What made me more angry than any thing, was the accusation that she stole out at night to visit the ruins and meet her lover—my childlike, gentle Adelaide!"

"Danesheld never could come at the cause of quarrel between you and Ravensbird," put in Mr. Apperly, but Lord Dane went on.

"A friend of mine, Colonel Moncton, had his yacht in the harbor. I had dined with him on board the previous evening, and on this morning he came up to call at the castle. I walked out with him afterwards, and was showing him the locality. We went into the ruins, and there I picked up a small bow of pink ribbon, whose centre was a pearl, which I knew Lady Adelaide had worn on the front of her dress the previous evening, for I had seen her dressed for dinner before I went down to the yacht. All in an instant it flashed upon me that Ravensbird had told me truth—for, unless she had visited the ruins the previous night, the bow could not have come there. My blood was boiling over, and I determined that not a day should pass, before I had it out. I met Herbert Dane, and told him I should step into his house to smoke a cigar that evening; intending in my own mind to tax him with the treachery."

"He said he was expecting you," again interrupted Mr. Apperly. "And we found him at home, waiting for you, after your fall from the cliff."

"Not *waiting* for me," significantly returned Lord Dane. "Evening came. I had promised Moncton to dine on board and say farewell, for the yacht was to sail with the tide. I did not go. I had brooded over my wrongs all the afternoon, and felt in no fit state even for Moncton's society, and I dined at home, with Lord and Lady Dane, and Adelaide; we had no guests that evening. After dinner I took my way to the ruins, resolved to watch the meeting between them, should there be one. I felt half mad to think that I had been so gulled; to know that Adelaide had but tampered with me; to feel that her love was another's. Inside the ruins I waited, and presently I saw Herbert Dane come stealing over the grass, keeping as much in the shade as he could, for I think the moon was never brighter. Cautiously he came up, came inside, and all but touched me, as I stood close to one of the apertures. Whether he heard my breathing, whether I made any movement, I don't know, but he evidently became aware that some one was there. He took it to be her for whom he waited; 'Adelaide, my dearest, is it you?' he whispered—and the words unnerved me. In my passionate rage I seized hold of him and shook him; I reproached him with his base treachery; I told him he should fight me on the next day. He retorted—and quarrelling vehemently, we made our way outside the ruins, close to the edge of the cliff. There it came to a struggle, and there I saw Lady Adelaide, who must have come up meanwhile, quickly step out of the ruins, and gaze at us. In the same moment, we got on the edge, and I lost my footing and fell—"

"Then it was Herbert Dane who flung you over?" eagerly inquired Mr.

Apperly, in his eagerness. "We have never known whom to suspect,"

"It was Herbert Dane. I do not think it was purposely done. He was trying to fling me to the ground, but not over the cliff; I was trying to fling him, and I lost my footing I say, and fell. In the instant of the fall my ear caught Lady Adelaide's shrill scream."

"She ran screaming back to the castle half dead with terror," exclaimed Mr. Apperly, whose mercurial temperament could not be still. "But she did not recognize either you or Herbert Dane."

"She recognized us both," returned Lord Dane; "it is absurd to suppose otherwise. It was light as day,· I say. I know that she denied it; I have talked it all over with Ravensbird, over and over again since I lay here, and I say that Lady Adelaide must have recognized us. Love for Herbert Dane may have kept her silent; or fear lest her own name should be brought in did she betray that it was with him I struggled. I hear that, after this, she refused to continue her friendship with Herbert Dane. I am glad she had so much grace."

"She may have looked upon him as a murderer in intention as well as in actuality. Most persons thought the murderer was a packman."

"Oh, that packman was nothing," said Lord Dane. "As I was crossing the heights to the ruins some fellow accosted me, opened a small box or tray of wares, and importuned me to buy. I refused, harshly enough, I dare say, for I was in no mood of suavity, and the fellow grew loud and insulting. I promised him if he did not be off I would call forth the servants from my father's castle to convey him and his pack to the lockup, and away he hurried."

"And how were you rescued after the fall?" again began Mr. Apperly, while the detective sat perfectly silent, as he had done from the first.

"By one of those interpositions of

Providence that no doubt come direct from Heaven," solemnly repeated Lord Dane. "Moncton, disappointed of seeing me on board, anxious to bid me farewell, caused his yacht to heave-to, when she was abreast of the castle, put off in the boat, with a hand, and came to the very spot where I was lying, intending to seek me at the castle. Now, mark you, he was not well acquainted with the coast, and he mistook this small spot of beach for the larger one above, where steps wind up the cliff; what do you call that but Providence? He found me lying there insensible; he thought dead; and he found that there was no road to the heights from that place. He put me in the boat with the help of the sailor, and they pulled back to the yacht. I revived. I was very much bruised and hurt, but no bones were broken. They had a surgeon on board, a young man who had come with them from the States for what he called a spree. Moncton was for putting the yacht back to port, but I—smarting under the infamous deceit of Lady Adelaide—preferred to go on with him on the voyage. I did not care if England never saw me again, and the farther I was away from it the better. The yacht touched here and touched there, reaching the States at last, long before I was well; in fact this complaint that I am dying from was no doubt induced by that fall. I ought to have written to them at home, at least to tell them that I was in the land of the living, but I put it off and put it off, and the next thing that overtook me was a fever; a long, nervous fever, rendering me incapable in mind and in body. When I was sufficiently well to hear the news, Moncton informed me of the death of my mother; he had seen it in the papers many weeks back; had kept them, now put them into my hand. 'I must write to my father now,' I said to him, but that very same day fresh newspapers came in, bringing accounts of the death of Lord Dane."

"Ah! they were not long apart," said Mr. Apperly. "My lord went off quite sudden at the last, and never signed his will. Mr. Herbert succeeded then."

"Yes, Herbert succeeded," replied Lord Dane, with emotion, "but I never suspected that he did. I saw mentioned occasionally in the English journals, 'Geoffry, Lord Dane,' and it never occurred to me that it was other than my brother Geoffry, the direct heir. Had I known it was Herbert, and that I myself was the true Lord Dane, the first and fastest steamer would have brought me over. I had not been friendly with my brother Geoffry; he was overbearing and tyrannical, and I did not care to return, neither did I care to write. England had lost her attractions for me, and I had ceased relations with her. I knew that I should inherit nothing under my father's will—my fortune had been paid to me when I came of age. Therefore, I stayed on, giving no token home of my existence, my residence being chiefly in America, though I travelled pretty well over the globe, Europe excepted. When I found my health failing, failing probably to a fatal termination, then I turned my thoughts to home, and lost no time in returning hither. We took our passage in the 'Wind,' eleven hundred tons register, New York. She brought us safely to this, my own native spot, and wrecked us on it. That was strange," he musingly added, but after a moment's pause went on. "But for my son's interest I do not suppose I should have troubled the old country again—"

"Your son?" said Mr. Blair, interrupting for the first time.

"Yes, sir, my son," returned the narrator, his agitation rising. "The gentleman whom you and Squire Lester and Herbert Dane have, between you, ordered into custody to-day on a charge of midnight plundering, he is my son."

"He! William Lydney!" continued the inspector, astonished for once in his life.

"He, and no other, sir. He is the

honorable William Dane, one of your future peers. Do you think *he* broke into George Lester's house?"

"By Jove!" exclaimed Mr. Blair, surprised out of his equanimity.

"I had never lighted upon any account of the marriage of Lord Dane, (always supposing it to be my brother Geoffry), and, failing in children of his own, of course William was his heir, after me; for that reason, and to establish his rights, I came home. We were wrecked—and saved; all that we had with us went down, save a few papers and letters in William's pockets, who was dressed when the catastrophe occurred, sufficient to establish our identity with the agents in London of our American bankers; otherwise we might have been at a temporary strait for money here—"

"Never, my lord," put in Ravensbird, "so far as my narrow means could prevent it."

"Knowing me for Lord Dane, perhaps not, Ravensbird," smiled his master. "But you might not have been so ready to help two distressed unknown shipwrecked travellers."

"My lord," spoke Mr. Apperly, who was dying to have his curiosity gratified, "how *does* that young gentleman come to be your son? You must have made an early marriage."

"I did make an early marriage," replied Lord Dane. "I was not much more than of age. I married the daughter of a French merchant and banker, who had settled in the States, and I married her in secret. Her father had a bitter prejudice against the English, arising from a grievous wrong done to his family by an English officer in her time of the Napoleon war. I was an English officer, and he told her plainly he would rather see her in her grave than my wife. On my own side, I knew that my family, always a haughty one, would never sanction my alliance with a merchant's daughter, and the result was that we married in secret, and contrived to keep it a secret. My wife lived on, unsuspected, at her father's home, making plausible absences from

it occasionally. During one of these William was born, and was christened Geoffry William Lydney. As the boy grew he was introduced by my wife to her father's house as the child of a friend, and from that time there was no difficulty in her having him there much, for the old gentleman grew to like him, and to ask for him. Still, we did not dare tell our secret, and the years passed on. We waited patiently for the time that death, in the course of nature, would take him, and release us from our bondage. Alas, death came, as it often does come, where it is not expected. The old gentleman died; that *was* expected, leaving his accumulated riches to his daughter; but ere we had well declared our position, and inherited, she also died; died from a neglected cold. After the lapse of a few months, I came on a visit to England, and to my father's at Dane Castle, and there my senses became enthralled by the charms of Lady Adelaide. I did not tell Lord and Lady Dane of my marriage, or of my boy; I had no particular motive for the reticence, save that I felt a constant unwillingness to enter upon it. You must remember that I was not the heir, my brother Geoffry's was a good life, and I never cast a thought to the probability of inheriting. Had I done so I should have been the first to declare that I had a son. I did tell Adelaide. In one of our confidential interviews I told her I had made an early and secret marriage, and that my wife was dead. I bound her in honor to secresy, and so far as I know, she has observed it. I did not mention William; a feeling prompted me not to; but I meant to have told her of him before we married. William's very large fortune in his own right, inherited from his mother, would prevent any jealous unpleasantness on pecuniary scores. Now you perceive how it is that William Lydney—as he has called himself here—is my son."

"It's like the winding up of a comedy," cried Mr. Apperly.

"The comedy's not wound up yet,"

retorted Lord Dane. "And now, Mr. Detective," he added, turning to that gentleman, "I come to the part that more particularly concerns you. There was cast up from the wreck a box, which was claimed by William, —a japanned box, with the initials 'V. V. V.' upon it, surmounted by a Maltese cross. While he came here to get assistance to remove it, my Lord Dane goes on the beech, sees the box, and orders it up to the castle. Why did he do this?"

Lord Dane stopped, but his question was not answered.

"Because he recognized it; recognized it as my mother's box,—one that she had given me when I first went abroad. There is not the slightest doubt that he must have known it again, for he had seen it many and many a score of times at the castle in earlier days; and Mitchel, whom Ravensbird questioned, says that he appeared struck with its appearance. The initials stood for her maiden name, Verena Vincent Verner, General Vincent having been her uncle : and the Maltese cross had been added to them, in a freak, by her brother, young Verner. He had borrowed the box of her, and when it came back it was embellished with the cross. This box she gave to me when I was going out with my regiment, and the very day I was putting my papers and best treasures in it, Herbert Dane stood by and helped me. Yes, he recognized the box, and that's why he laid his hasty hands upon it and sent it to the castle."

Mr. Blair drew his chair a few inches nearer Lord Dane. His part was indeed beginning now, and the plot was getting interesting.

"What he may have feared, what he may have thought, I do not pretend to say, when he saw it on the beach. He may have arrived at a doubt whether I was not yet alive ; or he may have feared that some one was bringing my effects to England, and was preparing to denounce him as my destroyer. I say I cannot fathom his precise thoughts and mo-

tives, but that he holds that box securely housed in the castle—unless he has destroyed it and its contents with it—is my unshakable conviction."

"Permit me," said Mr. Blair, interposing. "Will your lordship inform me what its contents were?"

"They were varied, sir. Papers and documents relating to my property in America, for my money is invested there, and to that of my son. My will was also in it. All these can be replaced : but what I fear can never be replaced, are the testamentary papers relating to my marriage and to my son's birth. The clergyman who united us is dead, the witnesses are dead : altogether, if these are lost, I might never be able to prove, to the satisfaction of British law, that William is my veritable, legitimate son. See you not how valuable to the suppression of them would be to Herbert Dane? I cannot last long, and failing the proof of William's title, he would be the next baron by right of law."

The detective nodded his head ; he saw it all now clearly.

"That box has been the cause of my remaining on in this house in secresy and seclusion," continued Lord Dane. "I never intended, you may be sure, to return home otherwise than openly, than as my own proper self : but the moment the life-boat had saved us—for which we may thank young Lester—came the knowledge that the box was lost, and all else we had had with us. I told William that night it would be better to remain incog, for a time, till we could see what must be done. I did not choose, you see, to bring him home and introduce him as my son and heir, without being able to prove the fact, were I challenged to do it. Then burst upon me the knowledge that my own brother had long been dead, and that he who reigned as the Baron was Herbert Dane. All the more cause for my going to work cautiously. The box at present may be intact ; at any rate, not destroyed ; but were I to make a

13

stir, and it came to his knowledge that I am here, and that William is my son, he might burn the contents whole-sale."

"I understood that the castle had been thoroughly searched, and that no such box was there," observed Mr. Blair.

"So did I," said Lord Dane. "William brought me home the news from the police-inspector, and it has troubled me much. But for that, I might have gone about matters in a bolder manner. The fact is, I have been ill all along, in daily hopes of getting better, and I put it off until I should be so. It appears now that I never shall be."

"The chances are that he has removed it from the castle," mused Mr. Blair. Young told me the search was as efficient as he could make it. But again, it was, by all accounts, very heavy, and he must have had help to do this : would he risk that, under the noise that has been made ? I suppose," he continued, stroking his chin, and speaking half in a soliloquy, half as a question, to Lord Dane, "that there are no secret hiding-places in the castle ?"

"I cannot say ; if there are, I do not know of them," was the emphatic answer of Lord Dane. "I never heard the supposition mentioned till the other day. William came in contact with Ben Beecher—a loose, devil-may-care set those Beechers always were—and, by something that accidentally transpired, William thought Beecher or his companions had been concerned in the abstraction of the box, and that through Beecher he might get it again. It came to nothing, but he has met Beecher occasionally since—the box, mind you, being the object—and the man persists in it to him that there are secret places in the castle, old Beecher vouching for it."

"I know of one," observed Mr. Apperly, while they all turned to him with interest.—"In the strong-room—"

"Which do you call the strong-room ?" interrupted Lord Dane.

"The death-room, as it was in your

time, my lord ; but the present owner of the castle chose to change the name, not liking, possibly, the associations the word death gave, as connected with your supposed fate. In the trestle-closet in that room there is a hidden spring ; press it, and the side of the closet slowly opens like a door : plenty of space there to conceal any thing. It came to my knowledge by accident. I went to the death-room once in search of the old Lord Dane, and he, not expecting me or any one else, had the place open. He commanded my secrecy : tradition went that the castle had once, it was in his grandfather's time, been a refuge for the booty of smugglers, and his lordship, honorable and haughty, liked not that coloring should be added to the tale. I informed the present lord of that place—I mean Mr. Herbert."

"You !"

"I did, my lord. It was just after he came into the title. We were speaking of the castle and its rooms, and I told him of that hiding-spot, and showed it to him. He was the only and legitimate lord, as I believed, and had more right to the secret than I."

"Then, by heaven, that's where my box is !" uttered Lord Dane, rising from his seat in excitement. "And now what's to be done ?" he feverishly asked of the detective.

"Plenty of clue to work upon now."

"Your lordship must give me a few hours for deliberation. As you have observed, we must act cautiously, lest he become alarmed and destroy it. We might get a search-warrant for the castle, but he is the lord-lieu-tenant still, and might cancel it. None in the county possess his authority. There is no immediate hurry for to-day, and I must mature my plans. It may be necessary for me to apply to Sir Richard Mayne."

"And my son ?" imperiously spoke Lord Dane. "Will you suffer him to remain in custody ?"

"That he cannot be guilty, is perfectly clear to my mind," returned

Mr. Blair, "and I will release him on my own responsibility, provided he shall satisfactorily account to me for his presence at Mr. Lester's with those men last night. Can your lordship explain it?"

"No, I cannot," replied Lord Dane. "I will drop a few pencilled words to him, and tell him to confide in you. He *may* do it."

"In all security. He may tell me as a friend, not as a detective."

The words were written, and Mr. Blair departed with them to the police-station, leaving his lordship, the lawyer, and Ravensbird setting their wits to work over the box and the hiding-place.

CHAPTER XXVI.

THE HEIR OF DANE.

WILLIAM LYDNEY sat quietly enough in the strong-room of the station, expecting a visitor. He had requested to be allowed an interview with his landlord. Ravensbird, and Inspector Young, had appeared to acquiesce, and to send a messenger for him. In point of fact, the messenger was despatched to the castle to inquire Lord Dane's pleasure on the subject. The door opened, and William Lydney rose in expectation, but he saw only the stranger who had been at Lord Dane's side that morning at the examination,—the London banker.

"I bring you a line from Lord Dane," began Mr. Blair, putting the folded paper in his hand.

William looked at it, and then at his visitor.

"From whom did you say?"

"From the true Lord Dane," was the whispered answer. "And I believe I have now the honor of speaking to the future lord. Your father, in that note, bids you confide in me,—he has done so. Perhaps it may be in my power to order your release."

"But what can you possibly have to do with it?" exclaimed young Lyd-

ney. "You are a friend of—of him at the castle; his town banker."

"You have been flourishing in Danesheld under false colors, Mr. Dane; so have I. I am not Lord Dane's (the title will slip out) banker, and how the report got wind is more than I can say. I am one of the chief detective-officers of the police force. Your father has called in my aid to assist him, and I am ready to assist you. First of all, what did bring you to Mr. Lester's with those companions last night?"

"I cannot explain; I cannot tell you any thing about it," was the quick response.

Mr. Blair looked at him, doubts arising.

"You could not have broken in with those men for a nefarious purpose, surely!" he slowly debated, feeling very unpleasantly perplexed in his own mind.

"I!" returned William Dane, as haughtily as any Dane had ever spoken. "You intimated but now your cognizance of my rank; I do not forget it, I assure you, or yet disgrace it."

"Will you give me your reasons for not confiding in me?"

"I do not know that I need object to that," said William, after deliberating. "I could not prove my own innocence without compromising another."

"I told your father you might confide in me, as a friend, not as a detective officer. Do so, that I may be enabled to assist you; and I declare to you, upon my sacred word, that what you may tell me of any other party shall remain locked up in my own breast,—it shall never be used against them."

"Never be spoken of? never betrayed?"

"Never, so long as I breathe, unless by your permission. I am not retained to work out this business at Mr. Lester's; it is nothing more to me than to any idle spectator, therefore I can safely give you the promise. Let me know the whole, from beginning to end. A curious suspicion has occurred to me more than once, having its rise from some words dropped last night, by that respectable member of society, Shad. Is it possible that Mr. Lester's son has been the actor in this, and not you ; that the woman-servant —Tiffle, or whatever her name is— mistook you for him in the confusion ; and that you have been bearing the stigma to screen him ?"

William Dane saw that it would be the best plan to confide the whole truth to Mr. Blair ; and he did so. That Wilfred Lester was indeed the culprit, and that he had rushed in after him, having waited for him in vain near the castle, through Shad's tale, rushed in, hoping to bring him to his senses, and rescue him from his alarming danger. He gave the history of the deed as the motive of the in-break, not plunder ; he told that the object had been accomplished, and the deed was then in Wilfred's possession, unsuspected by Mr. Lester. It was William Dane, who, finding Lester amidst the shrubs, had torn the crape from his face, and seen him into his home.

"You see," he concluded, "I cannot declare these facts, without awfully compromising Wilfred Lester, and it is not my intention to do that."

"The facts must be confided to Squire Lester, and he must stop proceedings."

"I don't know. He is very bitter against his son. If he knew me for the true heir to Dane, I might have some influence with him," continued William, smiling, "and it should certainly be exerted for Wilfred. It may be better to wait and see what will turn up, so long as Wilfred is not suspected."

"You seem wonderfully easy under your own incarceration," observed Mr. Blair, gazing on his handsome face.

"A man with his conscience at peace, is generally easy under most circumstances. And as to the accusation—pshaw ! I need only point my finger, and say there is the true Lord Dane at Ravensbird's, come home to assume his rights, and you may know me for his son ; Danesheld would soon scatter the accusation to the winds."

"I think I can do that," said Mr. Blair. "Come with me."

He led the way into the general office, where sat Inspector Young on his usual stool, writing. At the same moment, the messenger, who had been despatched to Dane Castle, entered.

"Did you see his lordship ?" inquired the inspector of the latter.

"Yes. And he says no person whatever, especially Ravensbird, is to be admitted to the prisoner."

"The interdict will not be necessary," coolly observed Mr. Blair, as he turned to the inspector. "Young, I am about to relieve you of your charge. This gentleman must be set at liberty."

The inspector stood in mute consternation.

"Where's the warrant for it ?" he presently ejaculated.

"Your warrant is, that you are bound to obey my orders," said Mr. Blair. "Let that be your answer to any one who has authority to question you."

Mr. Blair opened the door, and bowed slightly, with every mark of respect, as Lydney passed him. Had the inspector possessed ten eyes, they could not have stared away his astonishment ; it was not lessened when Lydney, laughing and looking back, spoke :

"I will not cherish resentment against you, inspector, for holding me your prisoner. But the day may come when you will thank your stars for not having made an enemy of me. Better, for your self-interest, that you made one of my Lord Dane."

As Mr. Blair and the ex-prisoner left the town behind them, and were nearing the Sailor's Rest, who should come full upon them, in a not-very-frequented part of the road, but Lord Dane. He was swinging down from the castle to the station, to enforce his prohibition personally against any one's being admitted to the prisoner. To describe his amazement when he saw Lydney, free and at large, would be difficult; he gazed, and rubbed his eyes, and gazed again, believing his vision must be deceiving him.

"What is the meaning of this? what brings that man here? at liberty?" demanded he fiercely of Mr. Blair. The latter signed to his lordship that he would speak to him privately, and Lydney, slightly raising his hat, which motion Lord Dane might take as one meant in courtesy or mockery, just whichever he pleased, strolled gently on.

"Circumstances have come to my knowledge since the examination this morning, my lord, which render it inexpedient that Mr. Lydney should be kept in custody. I have deemed it my duty to release him."

"What on earth do you mean?" ejaculated Lord Dane. "'Circumstances!'"

"They have, indeed. Mr. Lydney is no more guilty than you or I. I *know* it, my lord."

"I think you must be mad," returned Lord Dane, in his anger. "It was proved beyond doubt that he was guilty; Tiffle proved it; Shad proved it; the piece of letter Shad found the first night—"

"The letter is explained," interrupted the detective. "It was not written to any poacher; it was written to a gentleman in the neighborhood, Mr. Wilfred Lester, who must have dropped it out of his pocket in the woods, using part of it probably for wadding for his gun."

"Do you remember that, in thus releasing him, that you have set my warrant, my authority at defiance?" resumed Lord Dane. "Have you forgotten who I am?"

"No, certainly, I have not forgotten. But my duty was plain before me, and I could but act upon it. I am only responsible, my lord, to one person, and that is my chief, Sir Richard Mayne. I am prepared to lay my motives before Sir Richard, and I am certain that he will approve them, and say I did right to release Mr. Lydney."

Lord Dane felt staggered. He knew how high in the force Mr. Blair was, and that he was a clever, prudent man.

"What are the circumstances you speak of—that could induce you thus to act?" he asked, in a less haughty tone.

"I am not at liberty to relate them, save to Sir Richard only, but I can assure your lordship they are such as to justify me. Certain private facts have been disclosed to me in my official capacity, and I have acted upon them."

"How dared Young connive at the escape of the prisoner, while he held my warrant for detaining him?" foamed Lord Dane. "He shall suffer for it."

"Young had no choice, my lord. When I issue orders, he has not the power to disobey."

"I shall go this instant, and order him to take that thief, Lydney, into custody again," cried Lord Dane.

"I must submit—with all due respect to your lordship—that it will be waste of time for you to do so. So long as I am here, I am chief of the police force, and Young is as my servant."

Lord Dane felt beaten on all sides. Never, since he became Lord Dane, had he been so bearded. Hastily determining to pour out the full grievance before Squire Lester, whom he looked upon as more injured than himself in the proceeding, and quite as much insulted, he turned on his heel to retrace his steps, vouchsafing no further word to Mr. Blair,—and then his eyes lighted on a sight which did not tend to restore his temper to equanimity. Bending down till his face was nearly on a level with hers, and her hand retained in his, stood Lydney, talking to Maria Lester.

Away strode Lord Dane in his fury. Scarcely knowing what he did, he would have pulled Maria from her companion, with words of cutting insult to Lydney, and of reproach to Maria for "degrading herself."

"I beg your pardon, Lord Dane," William said, calmly putting him aside and shielding Maria. "Allow me, Miss Lester: I am quite capable of taking care of you."

"What would your father say?—to see you thus lower yourself to *his* level, Maria?" asked Lord Dane, controlling his voice to her. "An associate of dark villains, a midnight housebreaker! It is indeed fitting society for Miss Lester!"

Maria was exceedingly agitated, but she looked up at Lord Dane, and spoke words of denial.

"He is not that: you do not know what you are saying."

"I heard he was cajoling Miss Lester to some purpose," retorted Lord Dane, in his anger; "that he had nearly prevailed on her to forget social ties and decency, and unite her fate to his! I shall begin to believe it."

"As your lordship has entered upon the topic, I may as well avow that the first hope of my life is, that Miss Lester shall some time unite her fate to mine," he coolly said, while Maria fell into pitiable embarrassment. "Should she entrust her life's future to me, she shall find happiness, so far as I can make it. I may be able to effect that better than your lordship would. Maria," he added, turning to her and clasping her hands in his emotion, "I cannot yet explain; but you will trust me still."

"Yes," she answered, in the impulse of her heart's affection, "I repeat that I will trust you still, and forever. Let the whole world forsake you and speak ill of you, I will not. Lord Dane, you have provoked me to say this: you do not know what you are doing when you accuse *him* of housebreaking."

"Do you know, young lady," began Lord Dane, his lips turning rather livid, "that this style of conversation, of heroic avowal, is very like a taint on the future Lady Dane? Do not fancy I shall give up my bride to a criminal adventurer, although she may have been duped into a passing fancy for him."

"She shall be no bride of yours, Lord Dane," said William, a radiant expression lighting his countenance. "Not at least if I can prevent it, and I think I shall have her voice on my side. Be firm, my darling," he whispered, bending lower : "put your trust in me, and believe that I will make good all the words I have ever said to you. Though indeed," he called out, as he walked away with Mr. Blair, who had come up, "should things turn out as—as—they may, there does, I fear, stand a chance that you may be Lady Dane."

Maria could neither understand the words nor the expression of his face, save that it spoke of deep, earnest love for her. She turned towards her home, and Lord Dane, all fire, strode by her side.

"No, no; I never will mistrust him," Maria was repeating over to her own heart. "The instinct that attracted me to him at first, whispering me that I might confide in him as I would in myself, that he was true as steel, stands by me still. Let the whole world turn against him, I will not. Was it unmaidenly to say what I did? Lord Dane should not have provoked me ; and this dreadful fear, which I dare not mention, as to the real truth of last night's work, is terrifying me beyond control. Lord Dane is rich, powerful, and he is William Lydney's enemy ; but God's mercy is over all."

At the outer gate of Danesheld Hall they met Squire Lester, who appeared somewhat perturbed.

"Dane, have you heard this extraordinary news?" he began, when he was still some yards from them. "One of my servants declares that Lydney is at liberty, and walking about unmolested : he ran home hastily to tell me."

"He is at liberty," said Lord Dane, arresting his steps. Maria stopped also. "I was coming to inform you. The police have set him at liberty on their own responsibility."

Squire Lester looked as though he could not understand. The police set at liberty a prisoner who had broken into his house, and been committed by

Lord Dane ? What could the world be coming to ?

"And the first use he made of his liberty was to dare to stop Maria in the street, take her hand, and converse with her in private," resumed Lord Dane. "Mr. Lester, I beg you to *a'low* for my thus speaking to you. You have sanctioned my addresses to your daughter, and that must be my excuse : surely this intimacy with a banned man is neither seemly for her, as Miss Lester, or as my future wife. Had she permitted me to remonstrate against it, I should not have called upon you to do so."

"How could you, for shame, suffer him to speak to you ?" demanded Mr. Lester, turning his angry face on Maria.

"Papa," she answered, in a low tone, "he is not guilty : he is not what you think him."

"Your warrant for saying so, young lady ?" Mr. Lester contemptuously rejoined.

"I have none that I can give : I have only the conviction of my own heart," she answered, much distressed.

"The conviction of your own folly," retorted Mr. Lester. "Am I to have two disobedient children ? Go to your room, Miss Lester, and spell over the word 'disgrace.' Do not come from it until you can tell me you will eschew it. I am proceeding to the police-station, and you had better accompany me," he added to Lord Dane. "If the police dare to beard me, I will convey this man to the county-prison myself. Last night's work *shall* be investigated."

"Oh, papa, don't, don't !" uttered Maria, clinging to him as if to hold him back, as she burst into tears. "You don't know what you may do, —what dreadful secrets it might bring to light. Has it never struck you that some one else may have been concerned in this instead of Mr. Lydney ?"

"Why, what do you mean ?" exclaimed Mr. Lester in consternation. "Are you going mad ?"

"I dare not say what I mean,—I dare not say it. But, papa, if you have any regard for your own honor and happiness, you will not press for an investigation into last night's work."

She retreated towards the house as she spoke, sobbing grievously. Mr. Lester looked after her in angry perplexity.

"What does she mean ? Is she really mad ? or can she have become so enthralled by that cursed adventurer as to fear his being brought to public punishment ?" soliloquized Mr. Lester, while Lord Dane tossed his haughty head, and curled his lip with withering scorn.

CHAPTER XXVII.

THE TRESTLE-CLOSET—MARIA LESTER.

IT was evening, and Lawyer Apperly was walking at a strapping pace towards Dane Castle. Not to call upon its master,—or Lord Dane and Mr. Lester, and several more *dons* of the vicinity were assembled in Danesheld, at a county-dinner, and the fact was well-known. Airing himself at the castle-gate in the cold—a pastime he rather favored—was Mr. Bruff. He gave the good-evening to the lawyer as the latter came up.

"Good-evening, Bruff," was the response. "I want you to put on your top-coat and take a walk with me."

Mr. Bruff was surprised. "A walk, sir ?"

"At the request of Lord Dane. He is waiting for you."

"Waiting for me !" uttered Bruff. "Why, what can he want with me ? He is not taken ill, is he ?" he added more quickly,—the idea occurring to him.

"He is very ill," gravely responded Mr. Apperly. "I am not sure that he is not ill unto death."

"For heaven's sake, what's the matter with him ?" demanded Bruff. "Where's he lying ? who is with him ? Never mind my coat. When he stepped into his carriage here, an hour ago, he was perfectly well."

"Now, don't put yourself in a flurry, Bruff," returned the lawyer; "ill though he is, that will do him no good. He has need of your services, and has sent for you."

"But to be ill unto death!" cried Bruff, closing the castle-gate, and turning towards Danesheld, side by side with Mr. Apperly. "Mercy prevent any thing happening to him! He's the last of the race, and the title would become extinct."

"A sad calamity, that," remarked Mr. Apperly, taking a pinch of snuff. "You are attached to the Danes, Bruff."

"It's only natural that I should be, Mr. Apperly, serving them so long. I wonder who would have the castle then? The crown? or Miss Dane?"

"Neither has got it yet," was the lawyer's rejoinder, in a tone of significance. "But—"

"This news reminds me of the other night," broke in Bruff. "I was standing at the gate, sir, like you found me to-night, only that I was talking to a friend, and my lord came up the very image of a corpse, his face and hands a livid blue. I did not like to accost him, he seemed so scared and strange; he looked for all the world like a man who—"

"Had seen a ghost," interrupted the lawyer.

"A ghost!" uttered Bruff, disdainfully. "Like a man who has not many hours off his death-bed, I was going to say. Some sudden pain or inward illness must have attacked him: perhaps it's the same thing now. Pray goodness he gets over it!"

"I did not fancy you owned any ultra fondness for his lordship."

"Not as I did for the past family," spoke Bruff, with emotion; "especially for the old lord, and for Mr. Harry. I never did greatly like Mr. Herbert. But the rest are dead and gone, and he is Lord Dane. He is a good master."

"Could the old family—any one of them—rise from their graves to life, should you deem yourself bound to serve them or the present lord?"

"Why, the present lord would not be Lord Dane in that case," debated Bruff, after a minute given to consideration.

"Of course he would not."

"I should naturally serve the old family, whichever of them it might be," returned Bruff. "But where's the use of reaping up impossible speculations, sir?"

"Very true. Better put forth our best steps to the Sailor's Rest."

"The Sailor's Rest!" echoed Bruff, in astonishment. "Have they taken my lord there? What, in the name of stupidity, did they do that for? If they moved him at all, they should have brought him home."

Mr. Apperly said little more. Arrived at the Sailor's Rest, he marshalled Bruff up-stairs and introduced him to the chamber. Bruff cast an impatient glance around; he saw Ravensbird, young Mr. Lydney, and some one seated on the sofa, whom he took but a passing glance at.

"Where is my lord?" he cried.

"There," said Mr. Apperly.

Lord Dane rose from the sofa, took a few steps alone, and stood before Bruff with a smile. Bruff's face grew long as he gazed, and he backed against the wall.

"Don't you know me, Bruff? I am real flesh and blood."

"It—it's the living image of what Mr. Harry once was, save the hair!" ejaculated Bruff, staring from one to another in hopeless perplexity. "But it can't be!"

"Yes it can, Bruff. Mr. Harry was not killed by his fall over the cliff, and Mr. Harry is alive still. I thought you would have known me better."

The water rushed into Bruff's eyes, and his very hands trembled with emotion, as he knelt down before Lord Dane.

"My lord! my true and veritable lord! I do know you now!" he uttered, the tears streaming down his cheeks. "Old Bruff has lived long enough, now that he will see one of the real family reigning at the castle !"

Lord Dane extended his hand, and bade him rise.

" I shall never reign there, and you will not serve me, Bruff; for, to the best of my belief, a few days will see me where I am supposed to be—in the castle-crypt. But," added Lord Dane, motioning his son towards him, and resting his hand upon his shoulder, " I hope you will serve another, as truly and loyally as you would serve me. This will be the castle's future lord."

" He is— ?"

" Another Geoffry, Bruff: the Honorable Geoffry William Lydney Dane; he is my only son. Be faithful to him, for his father and grandfather's sake."

" I said he was a chieftain !" declared Bruff, his delighted eyes glistening ; " the first time he ever came to the castle, I saw he was born to be a chieftain. Miss Dane declared he was like my lady ; she did indeed !"

" Like my mother? Yes, the resemblance has struck me ; but he has the high Dane features too. I am dying, Bruff ; and I require a service at your hands first. Will you execute it ?"

" Ay, my lord ; any thing for you and yours. Though it should be to the laying down of my life."

" But, understand, Bruff, it will involve treachery to him at the castle. We must meet treachery with treachery. He has been treacherous to me, and now comes my turn. You don't ask who it was sent me over the cliff."

Bruff did not ask, even now. A dark suspicion was stealing over him. " It was Herbert Dane. But not in treachery. The treachery touching that, lies in his having duped everybody afterwards by passing himself off for innocent and unconscious. It is done and over ; but something else remains. Where's that box, Bruff ?"

" The missing box ?" said Bruff, shaking his head. " My lord, I don't know ; I have never known."

" It was my box, Bruff, and my mother's before me. You have seen it many a time. There is not the least doubt that Herbert Dane recognized it on the beach, and has got it in the castle. Now, that box I *must* obtain. I have a detective at work, but it has struck us that you may serve the cause more effectually than he ; though he seems a keen man, does Blair."

" Blair ! Blair a detective ! What does your lordship say ?"

" Your friend Mr. Blair's a detective, Bruff, unsuspicious of the fact as you may have been. You must get this box for us out of the castle tonight."

Bruff was wandering out to sea again. He did not believe the box was, or could be, in the castle. Mr. Apperly explained, at a sign from Lord Dane.

" In the death-room there's the trestle-closet, Bruff, and in the trestle-closet there's a secret hiding-place. The box, we think, is in it. If found to be there, will you get it here by stratagem ?"

" Yes, I will," replied Bruff. " If the box is my lord's, he has a right to it ; and I look upon myself as his retainer now, not Mr. Herbert's."

A little conversation, and their plans were put in execution.

Bruff and Apperly proceeded at once to the castle,—a man waiting outside it with a truck. Bruff held the keys of the death-room, and he admitted Mr. Apperly to it through the outer passage, where they were not likely to be met by any of the servants : and Lord Dane was safe at the dinner. The lawyer pressed the spring in the closet, and the side slowly opened.

They found themselves in a room seven yards square, a room where an immense booty could have been stowed away, had smugglers ever so willed it. It was empty now, save for one small object in the middle,— the missing box.

The missing box, open. Lord Dane had contrived to wrench back its lid. He had found, however, what he had not bargained for—an hermetically-sealed case inside, which he had *not* yet succeeded in opening. Probably he had wanted tools and opportunity; possibly, having it safely in his possession, he did not haste to penetrate its contents.

"I'll tell you what," said Bruff. "He must have lugged this in here himself at the moment of its arrival, while I was seeing the miller's men out. Though how he could have had the strength to move it, is more than I can conceive."

"A desperate man finds strength for any thing," returned the lawyer. "When he recognized that box as Captain Dane's, the very uncertainty of what was turning up, and what should bring it back in England, would make him desperate. We shall have a pull, to carry it from here to the cart."

"I say, Mr. Apperly," cried Bruff, in a whisper, "only to think of its having been Mr. Herbert who threw the captain over the cliff! Didn't he dissimulate!"

"He could do a paltry trick or two, could Herbert Dane. He served me one: it was about the lease of the Sailor's Rest. I accepted Mitchel for tenant, under the old lord's approbation, and the deposit was paid: my lord turns it all topsy-turvy as soon as he comes into power, gives it to Ravensbird, and I had my trouble and some cost for my pains. Steady, Bruff; get firm hold of the end. The case is of lead, you see; it is that which causes it to be so heavy."

Just about the time that they were moving the box, or a little earlier, Maria Lester was quitting her own house for a hasty visit to her brother's. She had not seen her father since the afternoon when he ordered her to her room. Whether his mandate implied that she was to keep it exclusively until restored to favor, she did not know: had it been so, she was too miserable to obey. That WILFRED had been the real criminal of the preceding night, she had little doubt, and the fears, the distress that haunted her, nearly drove her what Mr. Les-

ter had called her,—mad. She did not dare to hint at her suspicions to her father; she believed he might be capable of prosecuting Wilfred: but, ever and anon, in the midst of her sick suspense, there would rush over her a vision of hope, of brightness,—that, after all, she was judging him wrongly; that he was not, and could not be guilty of so base a deed.

Have you ever felt the rack of suspense, reader? How far more terrible it is to endure than the actual reality? Then you can understand why Maria Lester stole out of her own house, almost like a criminal, hoping to gain some tidings, some little word of certainty, whether it might be of good or of evil, did she go for five minutes to her brother's.

It was dark night, but she took no attendant: was she not about to visit her proscribed brother? was she not disobeying commands in going out at all? She drew her veil over her face, and walked swiftly along.

Edith was alone when she entered, sitting in her low chair by the fire. She was beginning to gain strength and look better; for Sarah contrived in her unaccountable manner to procure all sorts of renovating dainties, not excepting wine.

"Where is Wilfred?" asked Edith, glancing nervously round the room.

"He has just stepped out to take a walk,—expecting, I fancy, to meet Mr. Lydney," replied Edith. "I do not think he is very well."

"Who? Wilfred?"

"I mean Wilfred. He has been in quite a nervous state all day; actually nervous, Maria. So extraordinary for Wilfred, who is naturally careless and calm."

"Nervous in what manner?" asked Maria, her heart beating.

"Disturbed; restless. When people have come to the door, he has started to the kitchen window to peep out and see who it might be: once, there was a loud knock; he happened to be in the passage, and he came rushing in here and held the door to. I asked what he feared? what was the matter?

he would not speak, but he was certainly agitated. He has seemed all day to be frightened at his own shadow."

Terrible confirmation! Maria sat on, feeling frightened at her own. Mrs. Lester resumed.

"Maria, what can be the true meaning,—the facts of that business last night at the hall? Wilfred will not say a word. Any one would suppose that he might have gone out to-day, and learned the details, but he did not. I can never believe that Mr. Lydney is guilty: and he has been released from custody!"

"Yes, he is released," murmured Maria.

"Upon what grounds? That his innocence has been indisputably proved?"

"I do not know."

"Sarah, too, has been in rather a queer way all day," pursued Edith. "When she heard that Mr. Lydney was arrested, it put her out unaccountably, for she has taken a wonderful fancy to him. And she has seemed as fidgetty as Wilfred over the knocks at the door, reconnoitering from the window before she would open it to any one."

"Was Wilfred out last night?" inquired Maria, in a low tone.

"Well, now, that's what I'm unable to tell you. I went to bed very early, and fell into one of those sound sleeps from which you do not wake easily: I suppose it is my weakness sleeping itself off. Wilfred was in bed when I woke this morning. I asked him what time he came up, and he said he thought the clock had gone eleven. But, Maria, there was a tone in his voice which did not sound a true one, and I fancied he might be deceiving me; so I asked Sarah, and she answered in that cross way she has, when put out, 'What should have taken him out?' Between the two I can get at nothing satisfactory."

Maria rose. In her desperate fear she would have put the question plainly to Wilfred, could she have seen him, and implored him to tell

her the best and the worst; but it was uncertain what time he might come in, and she did not like to remain out long, not caring that Lady Adelaide should miss her. She wished Edith good-night: and Sarah, hearing her departure, went to the front-door and opened it.

"It's quite dark, Miss Lester. Shall I put on my bonnet and run with you?"

"Oh, no, it will not do to leave your mistress alone, and I shall be home in a trice. You don't happen to know which way my brother is walking, I suppose, Sarah? I would meet him if I could, for I wish to speak to him."

"No, miss, I don't know. I wish I did," she added, in a marked manner.

"Why?" distinctly asked Maria.

"Because I should be apt to go after him and pull him home: he is safer at home than out," was the woman's emphatic reply.

"Was he out last night?" inquired Maria, speaking in the strong impulse of the moment: and she knew that Sarah was faithful; she knew also that she was not blind to the doings of Wilfred.

"He was out," answered Sarah, sinking her voice. "And if he cannot be stopped at his game, Miss Lester, he'll come to—to—something bad."

"Sarah! I am sure you know all!" she wailed. "Where was he?"

"I know pretty well. Folks must be sharp to deceive me where my suspicions are wakened. But it's not for your ears, Miss Lester."

"My suspicions are awake, too, Sarah,—awake to dread, to agony," she whispered. "Tell me what you know. It will be more kind to me than the letting me remain in suspense."

"He went out last evening as soon as missis had gone up to bed, and he never came in again till two o'clock, or past, and it was Mr. Lydney who brought him to the door," said Sarah, without further circumlocution. "I saw his hat this morning, Miss Maria."

"His hat! What do you mean?"

"There had been black crape pinned on the inside of it," she proceeded. It had been torn out, but the pins and the edge was left."

Maria raised her trembling hand to her damp brow. The avowal was nothing more than her fears had suggested, but it turned her sick and faint. Visions of a felon's bar and he standing at it, rose before her eyes, and she felt that she would willingly sacrifice herself for Wilfred.

"I took the pins out, and I burnt the nasty edge of crape," added Sarah. "And I'm sure every knock that has come to the door to-day has brought my heart in my mouth, thinking it might be the officers of justice. If this comes out to Miss Edith—bother! I'm always forgetting and calling her that!—it will just kill her."

Maria walked away with her shivering dread. In every tree she feared an enemy; in every turn of the road an ambush,—the officers of justice, as Sarah called them, watching for her brother. She was in view of her own home, and was passing the corner of the wood where Tiffle was wont to favor young Shad with her presence, when she came upon a tall, still figure, gathered under the shade of the trees. At the first movement she thought it was Wilfred, and threw up her veil.

"Is it you? out here alone?"

The speaker was William Lydney. He took Maria's hand in his, and told her he was looking for her brother, who had promised to meet him somewhere about there that evening, but who did not appear to be in a hurry to remember his appointment.

"I have been to his house," she answered, "and, going there, did not desire any of the servants to attend me. I—I—"

"You are ill—or agitated?" he rejoined, perceiving that she could scarcely speak. "Which is it, Maria?"

"Both, both!" she uttered, giving vent to the feelings that so terribly oppressed her. "Oh, William, tell me the truth about last night! The suspense is killing me."

"The truth! You do not doubt me, Maria?"

"Doubt you!" she echoed, clasping his hand between hers in her heart's trust, in her deep agitation. "I know that you are the firmest friend man can possess,—that you have suffered this guilt to rest upon yourself to shield Wilfred. It was he who was the housebreaker last night. He was one of those men with the crape on their faces! he had crape on his! it has been told to me beyond dispute. I suspect that you followed him in to draw him out of the crime."

He did not answer.

"Will you not let there be confidence so far between us, Mr. Lydney? It will not betray to me more of my brother than I already know."

"Call me William! Call me William!" he hastily exclaimed. "The name sounds sweeter to me from your lips than it ever did before. You are right. Wilfred did so far forget himself as to join those men,—or rather get them to join him. The knowledge that they had entered the hall came to me in a singular manner, and I made speed to enter it also, with the view of getting Wilfred out of it. But I arrived when the deed was done. Wilfred was already gone. I found him, tore the crape from his hat, and saw him safely home. That's the whole truth, Maria."

"And his object? That deed?"

William nodded.

"As I supposed. Did he get it?"

"He did."

"Papa has not discovered its loss, then?"

"No. I gathered that this morning. Had he done so, it might have helped him to guess at the real offender."

"And you have generously borne the odium to shield him! you are bearing it still. While Daneshold is calling you thief, adventurer,—turning you from its doors! If they did but know what they are doing! and I may not declare it. You can never be repaid."

"I am amply repaid now," he whispered, as he threw his arm round Maria's waist, and drew her beside him. "Let them say of me what they will, so long as you will be my heart's confidant, and take my part, their words fall on me as the idle wind."

"But I cannot take it openly."

"That will come yet, Maria. A little time, my dearest, a very little time, and I may ask Mr. Lester to give you to me."

"Oh, William, do not speak of it," she interrupted; "it may never come. All this day, since this new and dreadful fear has been upon me, touching Wilfred, now it is a certainty, I have asked myself whether I ought not to sacrifice myself for him."

"Sacrifice yourself in what manner?"

"By marrying Lord Dane," she whispered, throwing her two hands before her face, as one does in mortal pain. "My father hinted to me that it should be the means of making his peace with Wilfred; he said that on my wedding-day, he would restore Wilfred to favor, and allow him an income."

For a single minute, William Dane held a battle with himself,—whether he should not confide to Maria who he really was. But he remembered the word passed to his father not to breathe a word of his rank until he could assume it, and he resisted the temptation.

"Maria," he gravely said, "you have trusted me before, trust me still. Mr. Lester's wish that you should become Lord Dane's wife, does not arise from any particular love for him, but for his rank, his wealth, his social position. I believe that, as my wife, your position will not be inferior to what it would be as his, and that Mr. Lester will acknowledge the fact. Promise me that until the relative merits of myself and Lord Dane can be publicly compared, you will hold yourself free."

She lifted her eyes to his in the starlight. "I do not know what there is about you, but you seem to possess the power of persuading me against my judgment. I do promise."

"I must have another boon from you yet, Maria,—the permission to speak to Mr. Lester, as soon as I shall find myself in a position to do so. Give it me now, and set my heart at rest."

"But that will imply—it will be giving you—" Maria stopped: she could not get on.

"It will imply that I am dearer to you than any one on earth: it will be giving me the hope of proving my love and gratitude to you throughout my whole life," he softly whispered, as he, for the first time, pressed his lips to hers. "My darling, give it me."

"Yes, yes," she answered, her heart wildly beating.

They stood a moment in silence. Maria broke it.

"I do not know why I trust you. We were, until recently, strangers. I know nothing of who you really are; and yet I do revere and confide in you above all, under God. But you may say I am lightly won."

"When I do say it, then reproach me," he answered, with emotion. "With God above us, and those bright stars, his witnesses, hear me vow to you, that truly and fervently as I shall undertake to cherish and love you at the altar, so *will* I do it all the more fervently as the years go on. You may register the vow, Maria, for it shall be sacredly kept."

"Why did you tell me this morning that I might yet become Lady Dane?"

"Ah! thereby hangs a joke," he laughed. "Perhaps you may have no choice yet."

"Choice of what?"

"Choice between becoming my wife and Lady Dane."

"William, I cannot understand you."

"Not yet, my darling. But you have promised to trust me: don't forget that. I will see you to the gate," he added, for she was about to move away.

Maria hesitated, deliberating whether it were better, should they be met, that she were seen abroad after dark, with William Lydney, or by herself. However, the distance was so short that she made no objection. He drew her arm within his, and they walked on, slowly enough, it must be confessed.

We are apt to assure children that they never do a wrong thing but they are dropped upon. Just so it happened with William Lydney and Maria; though whether they were doing any thing very wrong the reader must decide for himself. They had all but reached the gate, when two persons came hastily out of it, and faced them, —Mr. Apperly and the Lady Adelaide Lester.

CHAPTER XXVIII.

LADY ADELAIDE'S INTERVIEW.

The box had arrived in triumph at the Sailor's Rest. Covered over with a cloth, that it might not attract attention going in, and so set gossips' tongues to work before their legitimate time, it was lifted from the truck and up the stairs. Lord Dane's mouth worked convulsively as he saw it, saw that the leaden case was intact, for now any doubts that might have arisen reflecting on his much-loved son were dispelled forever. He silently leaned back on the sofa, covered his face, and gave thanksgiving to God.

But, just previously to this, William had gone out, on the fruitless errand of meeting Wilfred Lester, who never came to his appointment. He met Maria instead: which was, perhaps, to him quite as satisfactory. Anxious enough, though, was he to see Wilfred, to get a promise from him, if possible, that he would henceforth forswear these disgraceful and dangerous escapades,—for that was his hope and purpose. The previous night, or rather early morning, when

he had found Wilfred in the shrubs, escaping from his father's house, and had hurried him to his home, he asked him to appoint an interview, for that was no moment for speaking, and Wilfred had done so for the following night after dark. "Somewhere in the road skirting the wood near the hall," he named: he probably feared that a chance word might reach the ears of Edith, did he fix it at his own home. It thus happened that when the box came in, William was absent.

"Put it there for security," said Lord Dane, indicating a closet at the foot of his bed, "and give the key into my possession. That may prove a safer stronghold than the secret closet at the castle: it is certainly a more legitimate one. And now, Apperly, do me a favor: go and get Lady Adelaide here."

"Lady Adelaide Lester! To-night, my lord?"

"I have a fancy for seeing her. I shall see everybody by degrees, now the box is found. What's the hour?"

"It's between eight and nine. What shall I say to Lady Adelaide to induce her to come? And she may not be at home!"

"Any thing you please, save telling her who it is that wants her. It is the evening of all others that she is likely to be at home, and the evening when she could best come. This county party takes the husbands, and the wives are solitary."

Mr. Apperly proceeded to the hall, and was shown into Lady Adelaide's presence, who was alone. He had been concocting his tale as he went along. What her ladyship should think of him afterwards, he little heeded: all his business was to obey Lord Dane.

"An old friend of mine come to Danesheld, and lying ill at the Sailor's Rest? and wants to see me instantly?" cried Lady Adelaide. "I never heard of such a thing!"

"I may go further than an old friend, my lady, and say a relation," pursued Mr. Apperly. "I beg your ladyship not to delay ; I will attend you thither."

"But I never heard of such a thing," she repeated.

However, Mr. Apperly contrived to gain his point, and she went out with him. It was at this juncture that they met William Lydney and Maria.

"Ah, ha, Mr. William, so we have caught you, have we," cried the lawyer, while Lady Adelaide stood in speechless astonishment. "Beauing about the young ladies, sir. I shall acquaint Lord Dane."

Now, of course, the words "acquaint Lord Dane" bore very different sounds for their several hearers. William only laughed ; Maria's pulses beat with confusion ; Lady Adelaide, in her pride, resented the indecorous familiarity.

"Do I see *you* here, Miss Lester?" she haughtily asked. "And with that man !"

Maria would have withdrawn her arm from Mr. Lydney's. He would not suffer it : he held her under his protection, and stood with her, frank and upright, before Lady Adelaide.

"Mamma, I have been to Wilfred's ; I had an urgent reason for going," she said, her voice trembling. "It was but at the corner, here, in returning, that I met Mr. Lydney."

"Degenerate girl ! you had better take up your abode with Wilfred ; two choice scions of one stock !" retorted Lady Adelaide. "My house shall not much longer hold you, or my children be disgraced by your companionship."

"Your ladyship will at least allow her an asylum a short while yet," spoke William, and his words and tone were harsh with mockery. "Until—"

"Until what, may it please you, ✿ ?" asked Lady Adelaide, in the same bitter tone, for he had paused in hesitation.

"I was about to say until Lord Dane shall remove her from it," he replied, bending forward till his face nearly touched Lady Adelaide's, as if he would speak for her ear alone.

Maria felt utterly confounded at the words, while Mr. Apperly enjoyed the scene amazingly, and understood the allusion to "Lord Dane." He saw how matters stood between the heir and Maria Lester.

"How dare you presume to speak thus familiarly of Lord Dane ?" cried Lady Adelaide, in her wrath. "Unhand that young lady, sir. Quit his arm, Miss Lester. Do you hear ?"

"In obedience to you, her stepmother, she shall do it," quietly returned William.

He released Maria, but continued to walk by her side the few steps that intervened between them and the gate. Lady Adelaide sailed majestically past them, and rang a violent peal on the bell.

"Show Miss Lester in-doors," she authoritatively cried, as one of the men-servants came flying to answer it. "And now, sir," she added, to William, "have the goodness to remove yourself from before the hall, or you may be breaking into it again, as you did last night "

"You will think better of me sometime, Lady Adelaide," he answered, without the slightest resentment in his tone, as he raised his hat and turned away to pursue his path homewards, though not without having first shaken hands with Maria.

"How is it possible, in the name of common-sense, that you lawyers and magistrates and people can permit that man, Lydney, to be at large ?" asked her ladyship, as they also walked on.

"I fancied he was rather a favorite of yours, my lady."

"A favorite ! Well, so he was, before all these dreadful suspicions and things came out against him. But, now that he is proved to be a black sheep, we can only take shame to ourselves for having suffered his companionship."

"Except Miss Lester," put in the lawyer, who appeared somewhat given to aggravation that night. "She sees no shame in his companionship, if one may judge by signs."

"Were Miss Lester my own daughter, I should ask by what right you dare thus to speak of her to me," stiffly rejoined Lady Adelaide. "As it is, I wash my hands of her and her doings: if she chooses to go unmitigatedly to the bad, as her brother has done, by allying herself to this evil character, she must do it."

"She might go further and fare worse, my lady."

"She might—what?" ejaculated Lady Adelaide.

"She might go further and fare worse than in allying herself to William Lydney; that is what I said, my lady," was the composed answer of Mr. Apperly.

"Of course she might. She might ally herself to Jack Ketch, the hangman: rather worse, of the two, than one who probably will come to be hung," was the vexed retort of my lady.

"Very true, so it would," quoth Mr. Apperly.

"I expect my madcap brother has arrived in Danesheld, and is playing me this trick," resumed her ladyship, loftily quitting the previous topic. "It would be just like him; to send me word he was dying, and then laugh at me when he gets me there."

"No, I do assure you you are mistaken, my lady. I had the honor of seeing the Earl of Kirkdale when he visited Danesheld; this gentleman does not resemble him in the least; is an older man, in fact."

Lady Adelaide vouchsafed no reply. She had little doubt that it would prove to be the Earl of Kirkdale, and she observed silence until she entered the Sailor's Rest. Mrs. Ravensbird came forward, full of obeisance to her former lady.

"Sophie," began Lady Adelaide, walking unceremoniously into Sophie's parlor, "is it Lord Kirkdale who is here?"

Sophie was overwhelmed with astonishment. First at the Lady Adelaide's coming there at all; secondly, at her question, touching the earl.

"Lord Kirkdale, my lady!" she repeated. "His lordship has not been here: I don't know any thing of him."

"No! Who is it then that wants me?"

"My lady, I am unaware that any one does. I don't understand. We have no strangers staying at the Sailor's Rest."

"Don't come to hasty conclusions, Mrs. Ravensbird," said the lawyer. "The invalid up-stairs has asked to see her ladyship."

"Oh!" uttered Mrs. Ravensbird: and the accent expressed so much consternation, not to say alarm, that Lady Adelaide gazed alternately at her and at Mr. Apperly. The latter quitted the room.

"Sophie, what is this mystery? Who is it that can want me?"

"Oh, my lady, I cannot tell; I dare not. I never thought he would be sending for you."

"Will you walk up, Lady Adelaide," said Mr. Apperly, re-entering. "He is waiting for you."

"Well, now, that's a cruel thing," debated Sophie to herself. "They ought not to take her without warning. She'll be terrified out of her senses." Acting on the impulse of the moment, she ran forward and touched Lady Adelaide. "My lady," she whispered, "be prepared for alarm, —you are going to see the dead back in life."

Between it all, Lady Adelaide began to wonder whether she had lost her senses, or whether they had. She only stared at Sophie in reply, and followed Mr. Apperly.

The first object on which Lady Adelaide's eyes rested as Mr. Apperly threw open the door, was William Lydney. She leaped to the conclusion that a hoax was really being played upon her, and that he was its perpetrator. He advanced as if to receive her, and slightly bowed,—indignation flashed forth from her eye and lip.

"Is this your doing? Did you dare insolently to concoct a tale that should bring me from my home?'

SERVING THE WRIT.—*See page 158.*

14

"It was I who sent for you, Adelaide," interrupted a voice behind him.

She started at the sound : she looked to whence it came. There stood, holding out his hands, Harry Dane,—if ever she had seen him in her life,—Harry Dane, who was lying in the family-vaults, sent thither by her treachery and Herbert's violence. She shrieked, shivered, and would probably have fallen, but that William was ready with his help. Lord Dane advanced, feeble as he was, and held out his arm to lead her to the sofa.

"You need not be alarmed, Adelaide. It is I, myself, and not my ghost. Take my hand and feel it: you have not had the opportunity to do so for ten years."

She sank on the sofa, sobbing. Lord Dane made a sign, and they were left alone. He then applied himself to reassure her.

"Harry! Harry!" she uttered.

"Did he then not kill you ?"

"Who ?"

"Herbert."

"You did know it, then ? A heavy secret to bear, Adelaide, throughout these ten years."

"A secret that has made the curse of my existence," she wailed. "In the day's bustle, in the midnight's dark solitude, I have had one awful scene ever before me,—the struggle between you and Herbert on the heights, and your fall over. In the social daily intercourse, in conversation with my friends, when the thought has flashed over me, I have stopped to shudder ; in the dark night I have seen it over again, and woke up shrieking from the terrific dream. They say in the house that I am subject to the nightmare. As a heavy burden weighs down the body, so has that awful burden weighed down my spirit,—and I have not dared to tell it."

"Herbert bound you to secrecy ?"

"Not so. He does not know to this hour that I recognized either him or you. He may suspect: I cannot tell : but he can be at no certainty. The subject has been a barred one between us. He has not lived here : he has chiefly stayed abroad."

"Altogether, then, my disappearance—death, as it has been looked upon—did not bring you happiness ?"

"Happiness !" she reiterated. "It has made my days a living misery. From that hour, I have never had a minute's real peace. I would have given my own life willingly to recall yours."

"But for your own conduct, Adelaide," he resumed, leaning towards her, "that night's work never would have had place."

"I know it, I know it," she answered, putting up her hands, as if she could shut out remembrance. "And it is that knowledge which has brought my share of the cost."

"Why did you deceive me ?" he abruptly asked.

She clasped her hands on her knees, and made no answer.

"You suffered my love to grow almost into idolatry. Why did you do so ? why did you not stop it at the outset ? When I first came home you must have loved Herbert."

"Passionately," she whispered.

"And your motive for allowing me to beguile myself into the same passionate love ? What was it ?"

"I acted heedlessly,—some might say wickedly. I thought the attentions of another would draw observation from me and Herbert ; and Lady Dane was already partially awake to it."

"Every action of yours at that time was one of deceit to me. Should you have married me ? or broken your promise, and openly jilted me when the time came ?"

"It is past and over," said Lady Adelaide.

"Yes, it is past and over. Romance has yielded its place to the realities of life. I am older than my years and *dying;*—you are a married woman, and the mother of many children. Therefore we may well converse upon the past, as freely as though we had not been the actors in it."

"Who says that you are dying?" she quickly uttered.

"I say so; the medical men say so; my wearing frame says so. I do not imply, Adelaide, that I am going to die this night: but an incurable disease is upon me, and is doing its work. That fall from the cliff injured me internally: and though I have appeared well, have gone about like others, have traveled, have enjoyed myself, I have never been the same man since. In the last year it has shown its progress rapidly, and there is no mistake that the end is drawing near. Very near I thought it was this morning; but I have rallied again, and may yet enjoy a few days' deceitful health and strength,—deceitful as you were, Adelaide. I ask you whether you would have married me?"

"I do not know," she sighed. "I did not know then whether I would, though the question did sometimes cross me. I believe—if this is to be a confessional of truth—that I buoyed myself up with the hope that Herbert might get some good appointment, which would enable him to speak out. And another faint hope was cherished by both of us,—one less justifiable."

"Tell it out, Adelaide."

"We hoped—I will not say that Lord Dane would die, but that *when* he died, it would be found he had remembered Herbert. Had it been but equivalent to a thousand a-year, we should have married, and risked it."

"Throwing me over to the dogs, or anywhere else that I might go!"

"I loved him before you came near us," she said, in a half-pleading tone.

"And you might have told me so at once. Why did you not marry him when impediments were removed? When I was gone, and he Lord Dane?"

Lady Adelaide turned half round to the questioner, something like horror in her eyes.

"Marry him then! When I thought him a murderer?—by accident, if not by deliberation. I should have looked for your spirit to appear to us when we completed the contract. Many a time I have asked myself was he guilty in intention."

"No, Adelaide. I believe him to be innocent, so far. We were scuffling in angry passion, each for the mastery; but murder, or any serious injury, was no doubt thought of as little by him as by me. He cannot have impressed you, by words, with the belief that he was guilty?"

"By words! Do I not tell you that it has been an interdicted subject? Herbert Dane has never spoken to me of that night. When I ran away from the ruins, I could not control my shrieks. They broke from me in my nervous trepidation, but I had sense left not to betray cognizance of what had taken place. That I was a witness to some sort of scuffle, they forced from me afterwards, for they put me to the oath; but," she added, in a lower tone, "even the oath could not wring from me who were the actors in it."

"Did you witness it all?"

"I suppose not. When I reached the ruins, I heard sounds, as of dispute, and I ran through the chapel, and saw two men engaged in contest. I heard my own name. I heard sufficient to gather that I was the cause of enmity, and a dreadful sickness came over me when I recognized you and Herbert. In that same moment you fell over; I thought he had hurled you; and I had no peace afterwards, for I felt—I felt that I was almost as guilty as he. Herbert questioned me subsequently. What had I seen? he asked. What had terrified me? I would not satisfy him. I interdicted all mention of the subject; and interdicted it remained. He would have returned to our former confidential intimacy. He spoke seriously of our marriage,— you were gone, Geoffry soon went, and he was the heir to Dane. No, no I and Herbert Dane have remained strangers ever since; and I never gave him my reason for it."

"Did your love for him cease with that night?" resumed Lord Dane.

"Can love cease as rapidly as it

comes on?" she returned, her accent one of sharp pain. "Though I refused Herbert Dane, though I took him for a murderer, I yet loved him. I believed that what he had done, he had done in the heat of passion, in his jealous love for me, and the feeling may have softened my judgment and my heart. All I know is, that it was years before I overgot my tenderness for him. I do not think it had quite left me when he returned recently from abroad."

"Yet, in the very midst of this love, you married George Lester!"

"I had the choice of two alternatives: to return to Scotland—hated Scotland—or to marry George Lester, and I chose the latter. He has been an indulgent husband to me."

"Very much so, as I hear," remarked Lord Dane, "more so than to Katherine Bordillion's children"

Lady Adelaide's cheeks flushed at the allusion. She did not pursue it. She began to question Lord Dane of his escape from death, of his sojourn abroad, and he gave her a brief summary of its history.

"How could you think of not letting us know you were alive?"

"Let who know? My father and mother were dead, and you the wife of George Lester: there were none left in the old country who cared to hear from me."

"But to go off in that strange way in Colonel Moncton's yacht. And the castle close at hand for you to have been brought to!"

"That night was the turning-point in my life, as well as in yours," was Lord Dane's pointed answer. "It opened my eyes to the fact that Adelaide Errol, my promised bride, was but playing a game with me,—that while her shafts of ridicule, of dislike, were thrown into me, she kept her heart's love for Herbert. Smarting under the blow, was there any wonder that I should become an alien, Lady Adelaide?"

Again she bent her face down,—her face still so lovely,—and the bright color rose upon it, almost as fresh as it had used to do in its damask purity.

"Have you married since then?" was her next question.

"No."

"Lord Dane—I mean my uncle—wrote to the States to make inquiries as to your fortune, after your supposed death. You had never told him what it was invested in, he said."

"I am aware I had not. It was all safe, though, and at good interest."

"He wrote, I say, but he could learn nothing satisfactory. And before he could pursue further his inquiries, he died."

"And Herbert did not, when he succeeded. That is easily understood. A man who had sent, or thought he had sent, another out of the world, would scarcely care to grasp his fortune. I expect my remembrance has not been one of sweet odor to Herbert Dane."

"That it has not! Others wondered why he went abroad, on coming into possession, and stayed away for years. I could have told them: that the sight of the old spot was unbearable to him."

"Yes," responded Lord Dane. "And he may have felt himself safer when beyond the pale of British law. The fear of detection, of the discovery that he was the actor in the night scene, Harry Dane's assailant, must have caused him many a night-sweat: the coroner's verdict was 'wilful murder.'"

There was a pause in the conversation: each was occupied with the past. Lady Adelaide was the first to interrupt it.

"When did you arrive at Danesheld?" she asked, as the thought occurred to her. "To-day?"

"Last September, when the turbulent sea cast me ashore. But for your step-son's exertions with the life-boat, I had never again seen Danesheld."

"Last September!" she repeated, quite shrieking in her astonishment. "Was it you who were saved,—who have been lying since at the Sailor's Rest? Why have you done so?"

"I tell you, as I told Apperly, when he put to me the same question —for reasons. Perhaps from the delicate motive of not wishing suddenly to deprive my Lord Dane. of his title and rent-roll."

There was a grim smile on the speaker's face, and Lady Adelaide slightly started as the full import of the words struck upon her.

"Why, yes; as you are here, Herbert cannot be the rightful possessor," she slowly said. "You—must—be—Lord Dane!"

"I am Lord Dane. Herbert is not, and never has been."

"Then why in the world did you not return when your father died?"

"We will let that subject rest, Adelaide. I never supposed it was Herbert who was reigning. I thought it was my brother Geoffry. I have heard a rumor that Herbert Dane seeks a wife in Maria Lester. A pretty child she was ten years ago."

"I have not interfered,—I would not interfere in Herbert Dane's *marriage*. I expect she would have been his wife by now, had not her fancy become enthralled by another, one William Lydney. I saw him in your room as I came in; you would shun him, did you know his character. Why, Harry, he is a dreadful man; an adventurer and a robber. He broke into our house last night. He is pursuing Maria for her fortune,—that fourteen thousand pounds she is entitled to."

"Indeed!" composedly returned he. "Grave accusations to bring against a Dane."

"Against a Dane! of course they would be; but I am not speaking of a Dane."

"I am. William Lydney is a Dane, and was born one."

Lady Adelaide sat with her mouth open, half stupefied. Lord Dane touched her arm.

"You may remember that I informed you of my early marriage. I did not tell you that I had a son born of it, but I intended to acquaint you, Adelaide, before I made you my wife. It is he whom you Dancsheld

people have been converting into an adventurer, a house-breaker, a poacher,—I know not what. He is my own son,—Geoffry William Lydney Dane."

"Why then he—he—will be—surely—Lord Dane!" uttered she, when her consternation allowed her to speak.

"The very moment the breath goes out of my body, he is Dancsheld's lord. A better *parti* for Maria Lester than Herbert Dane."

"My goodness me!" gasped Lady Adelaide. "And I have called him —I don't know what I have not called him. Every thing but a gentleman."

"Adelaide," said Lord Dane, awaking from a fit of musing into which he fell; "take it for all in all, life has not been to you all flowers and sunshine."

"Taking one thing with another, it has been to me a wretched life," she answered, bursting into tears. "The world speaks of 'The gay Lady Adelaide;' it has more cause to speak of the repentent one. My own deceit has come home to me,—as Herbert's must have come home to him."

"As we sow, so must we reap," concluded Lord Dane. "Deceit is a crime that, sooner or later, entails its sure punishment."

And take you note of the words, reader, for they are full of truth.

CHAPTER XXIX.

TAKING DANE CASTLE BY STORM.

LORD DANE (we call him so a little while longer) and Miss Dane were seated at breakfast, in the castle, or to speak more correctly, after breakfast, for the meal was over, though the things were not removed. Miss Dane was airily attired, as if in opposition to the winter weather; gay colors predominated in her dress, and her ringlets were no less flowing than usual. They were holding an argument about William Lydney.

"It's of no use trying to convince me, Geoffry," said she, persisting in her own view of things. "I know that he is no more what you call him, than I am. He is the best looking, the most polite, the most gentlemanly man in Danesheld; and he does pay the sweetest compliments. A midnight house-breaker! just as much as Tiffle is. She must have dreamt it."

"Pshaw!" returned Lord Dane, with apathy.

"Had those police creatures kept him in custody, I should have gone in the carriage and made a morning call upon him at the station. I should. Just to testify my regard for him, and to show Danesheld how very much I resent the opinion they have taken up respecting him. I asked him one day, whether he was rich,—rich enough to keep a wife; he laughed and answered, Yes, and a gilt coach-and-six for her. A man with those means is entitled to every respect," concluded the lady, with a great stress upon the "every."

"Possibly you would like to offer him a wife in your own person, as well as a morning call, and enjoy the benefit of the gilt coach," drawled Lord Dane.

"Oh, dear!" simpered Miss Dane, "oh, dear! I'm sure you have no cause to say that. If he does admire me, which is evident from his looks, and if he has paid me a little attention, he has not said any thing—yet. But he is a most fascinating man; it can't be denied; and I expect him here every minute."

"Expect whom here? Not that fellow, Lydney!" cried Lord Dane, aroused out of his apathy.

"Indeed, yes, he and no other," she smiled. "I despatched a note to him yesterday evening, after I heard of his release from the fangs of Young and those harpies, requesting him to be here this evening at ten o'clock, on important business. I want to offer him my congratulations, and to assure him of the fact that the more Danesheld abuses him, the higher he stands with me."

"You always were a weak fool, Cecilia, and you show it more every day," was the complimentary retort of Lord Dane. "With regard to that impostor, I shall stand no further nonsense: he goes out of Danesheld, or I do. I wrote to Sir Richard Mayne, last night; these police underlings shall find out what it is to beard a lord-lieutenant. And you may as well understand me, now and for the future. Should your friend Lydney attempt to darken my doors, the servants shall kick him out."

"How remarkably impolite you are, Geoffry, and you do take such unaccountable prejudices!" was Miss Dane's rejoinder, who, whatever may have been her other deficiencies, possessed one of the meekest of tempers. "It is my home as well as yours, and I shall receive my own friends in it, of course."

"Any friend you please; but not Lydney. If Miss Dane cannot keep herself from degrading associates, I must beg leave to do it for her."

"Ah, but you can't," she returned, gently clapping her hands in triumph, as she looked from the window, "for he is already come."

Out of the room strode Lord Dane, and down to the hall. Lydney was in the middle of it, being shown in, and Bruff was crossing to meet him, bowing low.

"What do you do here, sir?" he foamed.

"I am here in obedience to a request of Miss Dane," was the answer, delivered courteously. "My visit is not to your lordship."

"I am the master of this castle," foamed Lord Dane, "and there's the door. Go out of it."

He laid his hand on Lydney's shoulder, possibly to enforce compliance in no very gentle manner, but Bruff positively forced himself between them.

"Oh, my lord, don't, don't!" he pleaded in excitement. "You may be sorry for it afterwards. This gentleman may have as much right as your lordship to—to—enter castles."

Whether Lord Dane would have flung Bruff out, for his interference, and Lydney after him, cannot be told; for at that moment advanced Mr. Blair, who had followed Lydney in.

"Sir," he said to Lord Dane, "will you grant me an interview before dealing further with this gentleman?"

"Sir? Sir!" repeated Lord Dane, astonished at the style of address. For ten good long years he had left the "sir" beneath him.

"I speak advisedly," was the whispered answer. "I have strange tidings to communicate to you."

Lord Dane glanced around him, and was seized with an inward panic. The detective stood calm and stern; Lydney self-possessed and dignified, yet with somewhat of pity in his countenance; Bruff was troubled and fearful, but testifying to Lydney the utmost respect. Lord Dane noted it all, and his courage failed him, almost his self-possession; yet he had no suspicion of the nature of the calamity to come.

"Pass in here," he said to Mr. Blair, motioning to Bruff to open the door of the dining-room; and, as the old butler hastened to obey, he saw the same livid look on his master's face which it had worn the night he passed him in the gateway. They were shut in, and Lord Dane motioned to the officer to take a chair.

"I have come here to prepare you for a most unpleasant surprise," began Mr. Blair, somewhat at a loss for words to break the unwelcome tidings; "and I have but a minute or two to do it in, for one is following me close at hand who—who—must cause a startling effect upon you; and it will be well for you that I speak first. But you are ill!"

"No," replied Lord Dane, as unconcernedly as his quivering lips, which he was biting in his agitation, allowed him to speak. "Proceed."

"You were surprised at my addressing you as 'sir,' and naturally so. I am sorry that it should have fallen to my task to inform you of the change hanging over your head; but I must do my duty, however unpleasant. When I released William Lydney from custody, you questioned my motives, my right,—I believe my good feeling. I would have explained matters to you then, had I been at liberty to do so; but they were not sufficiently ripe. I must do it now, and I can only ask you to *bear* it as a man."

Lord Dane made no reply. He stood with his arms folded, and his pale face turned on the speaker. That he only controlled himself to calmness by a very great effort was evident.

"Ten years and some months ago," proceeded Mr. Blair, "a catastrophe occurred in the Dane family. Captain the Honorable Harry Dane met his death, as was supposed, in falling from the heights, struggling with an assailant. Until a day or two back, it was neither known nor suspected who the other was; but it is at length discovered to have been you. He—"

Mr. Blair paused, alarmed at the appearance of Lord Dane, whose agitation was fearful to behold.

Well it might be. All that he had dreaded for years was come. Lady Adelaide had spoken of her burden, but what was hers compared to the one he had carried? One perpetual nightmare had lain upon his soul. In his ghastly visions by day and by night, one perpetual terror had ever been upon him,—the day of DISCOVERY, when he should be dragged from his high pinnacle to answer for the murder of his cousin Harry; perhaps to suffer for it a felon's punishment, death upon the scaffold. That the officer now before him was about to arrest him, and was thus preparing him, in his humanity, he entertained no manner of doubt. The perspiration broke out on his brow in large drops of anguish, and he threw up his hands to Mr. Blair in an attitude of entreaty.

"It was not wilful murder," he gasped, in a tone of the sharpest pain. "If you arrest me for it, you will do me a foul wrong, for I am innocent. We were quarreling, and it came to blows; he struck the first, as

I have a soul to be saved! he attacked me! We got too near the edge of the cliff, in our strife, and he went over, but I did not push him : I swear I did not. I was as guiltless of intentionally causing his death as I am of causing yours. Could Harry Dane speak to you from the next world he would say so."

"Nay, but there is no cause for this violent agitation," interposed Mr. Blair. "Had you heard me to an end—"

"I have thought for some days that it might be a warning that this was coming upon me," continued Lord Dane, in a dreamy tone, as he leaned against a side-board, never so much as hearing the interruption. "Harry Dane appeared to me."

"What?" uttered Mr. Blair. "Appeared where?"

"Ay, ridicule it. I am a strong man, sir, a man of enlightened education, of intellect; and, as all such must do, I have ever cast the most contemptuous disbelief, the veriest mockery on supernatural tales. Ghosts, visions! appearances!—they might be fit marvels for children, but not for men. Nevertheless, I tell you now, in the broad light of day, I, Goeffry, Baron Dane, in full possession of my mind and senses, I tell you that some evenings ago I saw the apparition of my cousin Harry. Never, since the fatal night of his death, had I entered the ruins, but the story told by Shad, that the plotting might be there, sent me to them. It was the night preceding the day when I telegraphed for you. I stood in the ruins, my thoughts naturally cast long back to the unlucky night and its events, when I was last there. I raised my eyes, and there, at one of the apertures, gazing in upon me, was the form of Harry Dane. I saw it as plainly as ever I saw it during his lifetime."

Lord Dane's voice faltered, for sounds—he deemed them ominous ones—seemed to arise from the next apartment, the hall. Mr. Blair's ears were opened to the same, but before he could say another word to Lord Dane, or impede his movements, the latter had drawn the door gently open, so as to allow of peeping out. You may forgive the tremor that shook his frame : he believed that the officers of justice had arrived for him.

Not much like officers of justice, however, did the group look that met his view. Standing in the hall, his left hand affectionately laid on the shoulder of William Lydney, was a tall, upright figure, his high features bearing an unmistakable likeness to the Dane family. In spite of his pallor and his white hair, none could mistake him for any other than Harry Dane. "In the body or the spirit?" may have thought one who was gazing. The old servants of the castle were gathered round,—some standing, some positively kneeling, all with tears in their eyes. Bruff's eyes were overflowing ; and in the background stood Ravensbird and Lawyer Apperly.

"I said you would know me again," he smiled, his own eyes full, and his right hand grasping those of his father's old retainers. "I did not think I should live to return to assume my proper position amongst you ; but God has been merciful to me, and I am here."

A low murmur of congratulation, intermixed with sobs, was heard in answer.

"Not for long, my dear old friends, not, I fear, for many days. You will only regain me to lose me again ; but I shall leave one—"

The hall was rent with a shout.

"Long live Lord Dane! Thank God for restoring the dead to life! Long live and bless the true Lord Dane!"

"No, no, it will not be for long," he answered ; "for the old grim enemy who must take us all at last, is coming swiftly on for me. I was about to introduce you to one who will fulfill my place to you in all ways when I shall be gone. Look at this young man by my side, and tell me who he is like."

They looked attentively. Seeing the two side by side, they compared their height, their features; and some voices were heard to answer, somewhat timidly:

" He is like a Dane."

" Yes, he is like a Dane. You may have known him only as plain William Lydney; you may have heard him traduced as an adventurer, a suspected criminal. My friends, Danesheld little guessed who it was accusing. He is my only son, your future lord, the Honorable Geoffry Dane."

Geoffry Dane held out his hand, all pressed round to clasp it. There was another shout, while poor old Bruff sobbed outright. One, who was not overwhelmed with brains, was heard to ask how he could be Geoffry Dane *and* William Lydney.

" Must I give you his name in full ?" smiled Lord Dane. " He was christened Geoffry William Lydney; so, you see, though he was known in Danesheld as William Lydney only, he did not sport false colors. My dear friends," he added, with emotion, " there is nothing false about him. He is a genuine Dane, honorable, upright, open. He never gave me a minute's uneasiness in his life, and that is what can be said of few sons. Serve him truthfully in all good faith ; as he will be faithful to, and protect you. He will not belie his race."

But what, of all this, had heard Herbert Dane ? — henceforth Lord Dane no more. Nothing, save the shout, " Long live Lord Dane ;" for they were at one extremity of the great hall: he at the other. But he had *seen*. He turned his perplexed face upon Mr. Blair, its expression asking for the information that his lips did not.

" Yes, it is your cousin, Harry Dane, and if you saw him, as you state, the other evening, though I had not heard of it, you *saw* him in the flesh, not in the spirit. He did not die when he fell from the cliff: he was preserved, and has now returned to claim his own. You are not about to be arraigned as a murderer, the conclusion you jumped to," continued Mr. Blair, with a smile, " but you

must put up with the loss of your title and fortune. *That* is Lord Dane."

" And he ?" pursued Herbert, pointing with his finger to Lydney, the conviction flashing over his mind in the same moment that he had been all along laboring under some extraordinary delusion as to the young man's doings and character.

" His son: the Honorable Geoffry William."

Herbert Dane wiped the drops from his face, and went forth. The crowd opened, and they stood face to face gazing at each other.

" Herbert !"

" Harry !"

In a moment their hands were locked ; and alone, save for William, they retired to the dining-room, Lord Dane leaning upon Herbert.

" First of all, Herbert, let me say that I forgive you—"

" It was not purposely done," interrupted Herbert Dane, in agitation, while William retired to the window out of hearing. " I never pushed you ; I never knew we were so near the edge until you went over. Harry, I swear it."

" Not for the encounter : I have as much need of your forgiveness for that, as you have of mine, for I believe I was the aggressor. But you might have come to see after me, or sent assistance to me when I was down."

" I never supposed but that it must have killed you, and in my cowardice I dreaded detection and punishment. As for assistance, I saw that one of the preventive men was underneath."

" What I would forgive you for is the *provocation*,—the deceit practised towards me by you and Adelaide. Do you realize what it must have been to me ? I forgive you, as I have forgiven her. I am hastening on to my long journey, and I could not enter upon it without first squaring up my accounts : so I sent for her last night and gave it her."

" She was worth neither you nor

me, Harry. She jilted me afterwards, like she had been ready to jilt you. Many a thousand times have I wished that I had let you win her: it would have been better for all of us."

"Ay. But we will drop the subject. You played me a sneaking trick, Herbert, about that box. What induced you to steal it—and conceal it?"

"The box frightened me. I have feared detection in every leaf and sound for this last ten years, and when the box, that box, stared me in the face on the beach, I cannot tell you my sensations. Remember, I never cast a thought to the idea that you might be living, and if rights came to be measured, I, the only Dane left, might surely claim the box. I concealed it, and would have opened it to see what it contained, but the inner case baffled me. I will give it up to you; it is in the castle."

"I don't fancy it is," said Lord Dane. But he resumed. "And now comes the last question touching your misdoings. Why is it that you have so persecuted my son?"

"He terrified me as being the owner of the box. I no more supposed him to be your son, than I supposed him to be mine; but I did fear he might be coming over to denounce me as having helped you to your death. And I really have had a bad opinion of him, from his consorting with the poachers."

"'Consorting' with them!" returned Lord Dane, some scorn in his tone. "He was after the box—that's what took him into the poachers' company; and looking after Wilfred Lester, who was going to the bad as headlong as he could go. Who but Wilfred Lester, do you suppose, broke into his father's house? William went there to get him out of it."

Herbert Dane made no answer, in his surprise. The past was becoming clear to him.

"Herbert," said Lord Dane, bending towards him, "did such a thing ever cross your mind as RETRIBUTION? Have you remarked how surely our own doings bring forth their natural fruit? We plant an acorn, and it springs up an oak-tree; we sow an ear of wheat, and it ripens into corn; we set an noxious weed, and it comes up tares. Just so is it with the moral world: according as we plant, so must we gather.' You and Adelaide Errol did me a bitter wrong: it was not the injury of a moment,—that which may be committed in a whirl of passion, without premeditation; but it was a concerted, long-continued wrong,—a deception that you carried on through months of time—one day planning how you should best blind and deceive me on the next. But now, what has that conduct borne for you in the end? Adelaide looking upon you as a murderer, would not have you, jilted you, as you term it, and married George Lester, entailing a life's misery upon herself,—for she loved but you. Her ill-treatment of, and ill-feeling towards George Lester's son drove him, the young man, nearly desperate; his life was worth nothing to him, and in his recklessness to preserve it, he put off in the life-boat the night of the shipwreck, saving me and William. None but a man whose life was valueless to him would have manned, and by his example induced others to man, the boat on that desperate night. Thus Adelaide is the remote but certain cause of our safety; the cause of your being put down from your high pinnacle, the cause of your losing your wished-for bride,—for that Maria Lester will be William's there can be no manner of doubt. See you not how it has all worked under Providence? —that the original deceit is recoiling on yourselves?"

Herbert Dane did see it. Who would not? and a recollection flashed into his mind of William Lydney's triumphant look, when he had said Maria might yet be Lady Dane.

"I have come to remain, Herbert," continued Lord Dane. "The castle from to-day must own me for its lord, and you must be my guest. Do not think I will turn you abruptly out of it: we will discuss plans for your future amicably, and I will take care that you are better off than you were when you were last Herbert Dane. Some persons might come upon you for the back rents of the past ten years," he added, laughing, "but you need not fear that I shall. How is Cecelia?"

"More flighty and absurd now than ever. The present crotchet in her head is, that William Lydney is in love with her."

"Oh, indeed. Well, she and Maria Lester must settle that between them. Poor, harmless Cecelia!"

"May I come in?" cried a voice at the door, which proved to be from Cecelia herself. "I don't think I shall ever have my understanding clear again; it is being turned upside down. They tell me that Harry is come back as Lord Dane, and that William Lydney—Harry! is it indeed you?"

"That William Lydney is not himself but somebody else," laughed William, turning from the window, after the meeting between her and his father was over. "I must introduce myself as your cousin, Miss Dane."

"Oh, dear! cousin!" echoed Miss Dane, a blank look arising to her face. "Why, to be sure you are, being Harry's son; and not a first cousin either." And away flew she up-stairs to consult her prayer-book as to the forbidden ties of consanguinity; opening it at that part which begins, "A man may not marry his grandmother."

CHAPTER XXX.

SQUIRE LESTER was seated in his study, in a very cross and disturbed mood. Various things were giving him trouble. In the first place, the discharge of Lydney from custody, and the positive refusal of Inspector Young to retake him, was an offence that worked up his blood to bubbling heat; in the second, an interview he had just held with his daughter, increased it to boiling-point; and in the third, the uneasiness and vexation he endured on the score of his son, sent it flowing over. He *could not* deaden all natural feeling for Wilfred, though he had striven to do so lately; he began to fear that something must be wrong on his side; and to doubt whether Lady Adelaide's constant incentives to the persecution of Wilfred were altogether the precise line of conduct he ought to have fallen in with.

Of his wife's expedition to the Sailor's Rest the previous evening, under the convoy of Mr. Apperly, he knew nothing; Lord Dane having demanded a promise from her that she should for the present be silent as to his return. His anger against Marie arose from this: he had sent for her to his study that morning, and told her to hold herself in readiness to espouse Lord Dane; and Maria, calling up her whole stock of courage, had told him that she could not.

"You would prefer to marry that villain, Lydney!" spoke Mr. Lester, in his wrath.

Maria bent her head, crimsoning painfully. All that she reiterated was, that she could not marry Lord Dane.

Mr. Lester was obliged to wait for his rage to subside sufficiently to speak.

"Look you here, Maria. I will give you the day to consider of it. If you do not tell me to-night that you are ready to accept Lord Dane, you must leave my house. You can take up your abode with Wilfred: I will not suffer you under my roof any more than I did him. Had I followed the advice of Lady Adelaide, you would have gone to them months ago. Disobedient, disgraceful children!"

"Oh, papa!" she said, the tears streaming from her eyes, "have a little compassion for us both! Give some aid to Wilfred, save him from utter ruin, and do not force me upon Lord Dane!"

"Your answer to-night, Miss Lester," was all the rejoinder he vouchsafed to give.

Maria escaped : Mr. Lester sat on, fuming and fretting, when he was interrupted by the appearance of Mr. Blair, that gentleman having made his way to the hall immediately after his interview with Herbert Dane.

"Good-morning, Mr. Lester. I am disturbing you early, but business must be my excuse. I have had a telegraphic dispatch this morning from town, from Scotland Yard. The lord-lieutenant wrote to Sir Richard Mayne, last afternoon, regarding this house-breaking affair of yours, and Sir Richard has communicated the fact to me. A fine invention, this electric telegraph! I look upon it as one of the greatest connected with science! He would receive Lord Dane's letter at eight, and I got his message at half-past."

"May I inquire what was the object or the nature of Sir Richard Mayne's communication to you?" inquired Mr. Lester, who felt most considerably astonished.

"None whatever: except to inform me of the appeal having been made to him by the lord-lieutenant. You appear surprised, Mr. Lester: you have, I believe, looked upon me as my Lord Dane's banker, but I must assure you I am nothing half so important in a commercial point of view. I am a detective officer; one of the chief."

"Bless my soul!" ejaculated Mr. Lester.

"I came down here to watch the doings in Danesheld. A communication reached me that an attempt was to be made to break into Dane Castle, and I laid my plans accordingly. Would you believe, Mr. Lester, that on Sunday night the castle was protected by policemen, waiting for the robbers?"

"No!"

"But we were on the wrong scent I, with all my penetration and experience, was misled. While we were cunningly guarding the castle, the hall was entered : and that, not the castle, was the object from the first. Now, by stating particulars to you so far, you will readily give me credit for being in possession of the whole, and I must inform you that it was upon my authority William Lydney was discharged from custody,—which induced the lord-lieutenant's haughty appeal to Sir Richard Mayne."

"But what could possess you to discharge him?" sharply asked Mr. Lester. "The man is as great a villain as ever walked. Have you done it to screen him from the consequences of his guilt?"

"Hardly," responded Mr. Blair : "my office is to bring to punishment, *not* to screen. I discharged him because he was *not* guilty. Listen, Mr. Lester. In the attack made on your house, there was a ringleader, one who planned it, and on whom, in my opinion, nearly the whole guilt rests. The fellows he induced by promises to aid him, some of your loose poacher chaps, have neither the brains nor the courage to enter upon a house-breaking expedition on their own account."

"It is precisely my opinion," eagerly acquiesced Squire Lester; "it is also Lord Dane's. Those poachers are not worth punishing, and therefore we have not moved heaven and earth to take them. The ringleader is the guilty man, and that ringleader was Lydney."

"Mr. Lester, give me credit for being assured of my facts before I speak. William Lydney was *not* the ringleader."

The officer had dropped his voice to a low, earnest key, and his look had changed to one of solemn meaning. Mr. Lester, he could not tell why, did not like it.

"I am here to tell you who the ringleader was; but I warn you beforehand, Mr. Lester, that it will not be pleasant to your ears."

"It must have been Lydney," was the faltering answer, all Mr. Lester's assurance gone.

"It was Wilfred Lester."

Up started Mr. Lester, overturning the inkstand before him, his face red, and his tongue loud.

"How dare you traduce my son?" he cried, as he paced the room. "Do you forget who he is; that he is a gentleman? He is under the cloud of my displeasure just now, and it drives him to be wild, random: to associate with loose company. But a midnight house-breaker! You shall eat your words, Mr. Blair."

"I am not sorry to hear one admission from your lips," equably returned the officer, who had sat with professional coolness until the burst was over: "that it is the being under the cloud of your displeasure which *drives* him to be wild and to join bad company. You speak truth, Mr. Lester. Whatever ill your son may be guilty of, you have driven him on to it. He *was* the house-breaker into the hall last night,—that is, the mover in the step,—the ringleader."

"Perhaps you will say I drove him on to that!" chafed Mr. Lester, whose feelings were taming down from indignation into pain.

"Yes, I should, if you ask my opinion. Mr. Lester, allow me—it is of no use to contend against facts, or to resent what it is my painful duty to tell you. Knowing, as you now do, who I am, you may be sure I should not come to you with a half-substantiated story. It was your son who planned and carried out the attack on his father's house, the poachers being persuaded and bribed by him to help in it."

"But what for? what was his motive?" gasped Mr. Lester. "There was nothing taken; did he want to cut our throats?"

"There was no robbery, in the ordinary sense of the word, and the pistol you heard discharged was raised by him at one of the men, who had hinted that it might be pleasant to effect a little business of that sort on his own cheek. There was something taken, however."

Mr. Lester looked round, as if to make sure that the chairs and tables were all in their places.

"What was taken?" he inquired, his accent savoring of incredulity.

"Have you examined your iron safe?"

"No." But Mr. Lester turned short round and examined it then; that is, gave a stare at the outside.

"I fancy his object was to get into his possession a certain deed, relating to some money he believes he is entitled to, but which you withhold. And I fancy he succeeded."

After a pause of astonishment, Mr. Lester hastily drew some keys from his pocket, and unlocked the safe. He knew precisely where to lay his hand upon the parchment, and essayed to do so.

"The deed is gone!" he uttered, turning round in perturbation. And Mr. Blair nodded.

"You now perceive your son's motive. I don't defend him: mind that. I don't defend him; but some may deem that he had provocation. Whether the money ought by law to have come to him when he was of age, I cannot offer an opinion upon. He expected that it should, and the least you could have done, was to allow him to peruse the deed. When you shall deliberate the past over with less prejudice than you have probably been in the habit of doing, you may arrive at the same conclusion as myself,—that had Wilfred Lester been treated differently by his father, he might never have forfeited his good name."

"Are you going to arrest him?" was the rejoinder of Mr. Lester, who was cutting rather a sorry figure: as most men do when a conviction of their own bad conduct is brought home to their shame.

"To arrest him is not in my department. If you choose to give him into custody, you can hand your warrant and instructions to Inspector Young. Your son might get the punishment, but I know who would get the odium. When the whole facts were disclosed, the miserable course of his past treatment, there's not a judge upon the bench but would recoil from sentencing him,—thinking of their own children."

Squire Lester gave his brow a rub, which was apparently growing hot. "I am not going to give him into custody," he sharply said. "You need not preach."

"But that I felt convinced Mr. Lester was a good man at heart, and had been led away (he best knows by what influence) to act harshly, I should not have disclosed to him the true culprit," observed the officer, looking him steadily in the face. "I knew he would shrink from bringing public punishment on one who is his son, and ought to be his heir, thereby furnishing further food for scandal in Danesheld."

"Further food!" retorted Mr. Lester. "I have furnished none yet."

"My good sir!" returned the officer. "If you only knew the hard words bestowed upon you from one end of the place to the other, you would not think that. Wilfred, with all his ill-doings, is popular and respected, compared with you."

"You are bold," chafed Mr. Lester.

"It is the fault of my trade," was the answer, given with a knowing smile. "It is a good thing, and you may thank your stars for it that some one else has been more compassionate to your son and his wife than you have been: or else I am not sure that they —she, at any rate—would be alive now. I speak of a gentleman who has lately been regarded as a wolf, come to Danesheld to devour lambs,—William Lydney."

"Ah! William Lydney!" was the fierce response, as if Squire Lester wished to indemnify his anger for momentarily forgetting him. "However you may excuse my son for being here last night, you cannot palliate *his* guilt. He had no deed to get."

"I will let you into a secret, Mr. Lester. It came to William Lydney's knowledge that your son was in the wood on Sunday night with the rest of the ruffians,—the convoy engaged

in the respectable employment of tacking black crape to their hats. That may have been about nine o'clock. He waited out in the cold damp air till morning, watching for Wilfred Lester, resolved to snatch him from the crime he was contemplating. Unfortunately Mr. Lydney, like the rest of us, believed it was the castle that was threatened,—he did not give a thought to your house,—and when the truth reached him, they were already in the hall, and he was too late. He came here just in time to find the deed accomplished, and the jail-birds flying; but he found Wilfred, and got him safely home. William Lydney saved your son from prison; William Lydney has helped him in other ways, which I am not going to speak of. I went ferreting about last night amidst the odds and ends of Danesheld population, picking up what information I could about William Lydney and Wilfred Lester, and I picked up a good deal. Lydney's character has been pretty nearly taken from him for frequenting the haunts of the poachers; but he was looking after your son, to keep him from the evil. They had grown friendly."

"Wilfred always had a hankering after low company," said Squire Lester.

"If he never gets into lower company than young Lydney's, he won't hurt," returned Mr. Blair, bursting into a laugh.

Something in its tone upset Mr. Lester's equanimity.

"Why, who is Lydney?"

"Oh, as to that, you can ask him when you next see him. I should treat him with civility, were I you, squire, if only in return for his taking your son's guilt upon himself. It is not every man who would quietly be given into custody for another."

"What possessed him? He must have been possessed by some powerful motive."

"Or motives. True. Wilfred Lester saved his life, and he may have been actuated by gratitude. A feeling is abroad also that he would do a great deal to save from disgrace one who is so nearly related to Miss Lester."

"He is a ruffian and a villain! and I will maintain that he is, so far as his behavior goes in this house," fired Mr. Lester, disturbed by the allusion. "Who but a villain would set himself out to rival Lord Dane, and gain my daughter's affections?—ay, and I can't answer for it that he has not succeeded. Can you defend him in that, sir?"

"I think I had better leave him to defend himself."

"Were I Lord Dane, I would shoot him?"

"Were you Lord Dane, I do not fancy you would," laughed Mr. Blair.

The conference came to an end, and Mr. Blair felt assured that no more appeals would go up to Sir Richard Mayne. He left the house, and Mr. Lester paced his study in a most uncomfortable state of perplexity. Would it be best to take Wilfred into favor, or to go on disowning him? And how was he to get back the deed? And what would my lady say?

Meantime there came a summons to the hall-door. The servant admitted three gentlemen, who had descended from a carriage. One, a commanding-looking man of attenuated features, a stranger to the domestic; Mr. Apperly, and—very dubiously looked the servant, not knowing whether to deny him admittance or not—William Lydney.

"I wish to see Mr. Lester," said the stranger.

The man bowed, and led the way to the study. He laid his hand on handle of the door, and turned.

"What name, sir?"

"Lord Dane."

"I—I beg your pardon, sir," stammered the man, in his surprise. "I asked what name?"

"Lord Dane," was the distinct repetition; and the servant wondered what old madman had got in, as he announced it. He looked round for the other two, but found they had not advanced, so he closed the door on the one who had.

"Show me to Miss Lester," said Mr. Lydney.

"I'm sure I don't know," said the man, familiarly. "She's at home, and my lady's not down yet. But, about admitting of you in—"

"I bid you show me to Miss Lester," interrupted Lydney, in a quiet tone of command,—and the man felt that it might not be disobeyed.

Maria was in the drawing-room alone, the traces of tears still upon her cheeks. She brushed them away hastily, and advanced to receive the guests.

"My visit is not to you, Miss Lester," began Mr. Apperly, in a joking manner, "but I have taken the liberty of following this young gentleman to your presence, thinking it may be as well to introduce him,—Mr. Dane; Lord Dane *to be*."

William Lydney smiled; Maria looked from one to the other. She scarcely noted the words, strange as they were; all her thoughts were directed to the imprudence of his appearing at the hall.

"Does papa know you are here?" she timidly asked.

"Not yet; but I have scarcely transgressed his prohibition. He forbid William Lydney to enter; he did not forbid Geoffry Dane."

"I expect you can settle it yourselves now, without me," cried Mr. Apperly, as he quitted the room.

"Maria, answer me truly. Does not Mr. Lester wish to force you on Lord Dane?"

"Yes," she answered, bursting into tears. "If I will not give the required promise before to-day is over, I am to be turned from my home."

"Give it, my darling," he whispered, as he caught her to his heart and held her there. "*I* ask you. Promise that you will marry no other than Lord Dane."

"What do you mean?" she uttered, in agitation.

"Promise me to be Lord Dane's wife," was all he reiterated.

"William!" and she strove to draw away from him.

"OH, MY LORD! THE MOST WICKED PLOT!"—*See page 181.*

"Will you promise, then, to be mine?" he fondly whispered.

"Oh, that I might promise it!" she said, in her distress. "Gain my father's consent, and you have mine."

"I think his will be gained before the day is over," he replied, gazing in her face with his triumphant air of tenderness. "My dearest, you trusted the unknown William Lydney. He was obscure, under a cloud, and he could not declare himself. I told you that the trust should not be misplaced. I am Geoffry Dane."

"What *do* you mean?" she exclaimed.

"To be Lord Dane, I fear—I fear—ere much time shall have elapsed. I puzzled you, Maria, when I said you might come to be my Lady Dane yet, if things worked well. But you cannot suppose I alluded to him whom you knew as Lord Dane. He is no longer Lord Dane, and, in point of fact, never has been."

"Then—who—is—Lord Dane?" returned Maria, bringing out the words slowly in her excessive astonishment.

"My father—who is at the present moment with Mr. Lester. The Captain Harry Dane who fell over the cliff when you were a child, Maria. He did not die."

"Can this be true?"

"It is undoubtedly true," he returned, with a smile. "As true as that I shall hold you to your promise to be mine—my darling, my darling wife!"

She started from his embrace, for Lady Adelaide entered. If anything could have added to Maria's wonder of astonishment, it was to see her shake hands heartily with William, and call him "Geoffry."

But we have not quite finished with Mr. Lester, whom we left pacing the study in excitement. He was interrupted by the announcement of Lord Dane, and turned to receive him. Instead of Lord Dane, there entered, walking slowly, as if from feebleness, but not stooping, a fine, upright man. with white hair. Mr. Lester supposed

some mistake had been made, or that Lord Dane was following; but as he scanned the features of the visitor, he felt strangely startled, and drew back.

"I—I—thought he said Lord Dane," broke from him, in his embarrassment.

"So he did," was the stranger's answer, as he held out his hand. "Don't you know me, George? Who else, but myself, should be Lord Dane?

Mr. Lester staggered to a chair and sat down, utterly petrified.

"Harry Dane did not die, George: and he has come back at the eleventh hour to claim his own. I should have been home ten years ago, had I dreamt that it was *Herbert* who was representing the Dane peerage; I never supposed but it was my brother Geoffry."

Mr. Lester clasped his hands and welcomed him, and at this juncture, Lawyer Apperly entered, and the events of the past were cursorily explained to Mr. Lester's almost disbelieving ears.

"What a dreadful blow for Herbert Dane?" was his first comment.

"Dreadful in one sense, inasmuch as that it deprives him of his rank," assented Lord Dane; "in another sense, it is a boon: a relief."

"Relief from what?" asked Mr. Lester, but Lord Dane evaded the question.

"Danesheld says—it has lost none of its gossiping talents—that he wished to marry your daughter."

"Why—yes," was Mr. Lester's slow answer, as he ran over probabilities and improbabilities in his own mind; "but—I don't know now. Of course this change will involve loss of income as well as loss of title."

"Undoubtedly. And he may think himself well off that I do not call upon him to make good the revenues of the estate, which he has enjoyed for the last ten years," Lord Dane added, laughing.

"I do not see that he can now think

further of Maria," Mr. Lester observed, shaking his head. "And she does not like him."

" Were she quite free, I would have made her an offer on the part of my son," resumed Lord Dane.

" Your son !" echoed Mr. Lester.

" Oh, to be sure, you have just said you have one by an early marriage. Is he in this country ?"

" He is in this house ; he came with me ; but I sent him to wait in the drawing-room, until my first appearance to you should be over. By accepting him, your daughter's anticipated position will not be changed ; she will still be Lady Dane. In point of wealth she will be better off, for Geoffry has an immense fortune from his mother's side."

"A most flattering, munificent offer," cried the gratified Mr. Lester, " and if Maria can only be brought to hear reason and to entertain it—"

" Oh, don't fancy we would force Miss Lester's inclination," interposed Lord Dane ; "she must be allowed to decide for herself. You had better let my son be introduced to you. Apperly, suppose you go and bring him in."

" I shall be most delighted, most proud to make his acquaintance," spoke Mr. Lester, in the exuberance of his spirits. "I wonder what Apperly can be chuckling at," he thought, looking after him ; " but I don't fancy he ever did cordially like Herbert Dane."

Mr. Apperly went away chuckling, and Mr. Apperly came back chuckling. Lydney was with him ; and Lady Adelaide, and Maria followed them. Mr. Lester flew in a rage.

" You here ! You audacious man ! How dare you presume to intrude into my house ! I beg your pardon, Lord Dane, but this man Lydney—"

Mr. Lester stopped, for Lord Dane had linked his arm within the " audacious man's," and was leading him up.

" An instant, George Lester," he said ; " you shall tell me about Lyd-

ney when I have made the introduction. My son, Geoffry Dane."

The consternation of Mr. Lester was pitiable.

" He !—he your son ?" he gasped, when he could speak.

" My own and only son,—Geoffry William Lydney Dane, styled the Honorable. Ah, Lester ! you and Danesheld have been abusing him,— have been laying all sorts of outrageous sins to his charge, deceived into it by the calumniations of Herbert Dane ; but Maria was more clear-sighted than any of you. She saw that his nature was what it is, all honor and goodness, and she trusted him. I think you should give her to him in recompense."

Lady Adelaide advanced, her cheek flushed with emotion, as she addressed her husband.

" George, I never urged you to give her to Lord Dane—to Herbert ; I do urge you to give her to Geoffry."

" I can but ask you to hold to your promise, sir," interrupted William, looking at Mr. Lester with a sunny smile. " You have vowed she shall only marry to be Lady Dane, and the sole chance of her becoming so—since my father is not a candidate for her hand—is by accepting me. Give her to me," he yearningly pleaded. " I will love and cherish her forever."

" I'll draw up the marriage settlements for nothing, if you will say yes," cried out Lawyer Apperly, in the fullness of his satisfaction. " I could walk a mile on my head, to-day."

" What in the world is the matter with you all ?" exclaimed Mr. Lester, above the confusion and in his own emotion. " You are beseeching me as if for some great boon, hard to grant ; I think the boon will be bestowed on me. Take her," he added as he grasped William's hand ; " take her, and keep her, and forgive me the past."

" And, now that that is all right, I must be going," said Lord Dane."

" Where ?" asked Mr. Lester.

" Where ! why to show myself in

Danesheld with my son, and to make a few more calls on friends, as I have made here, previously to holding my levee at the castle. I shall go about it rather charily, Lester, lest timid people may fancy it is a ghost coming in. Herbert thought me one the other night in the chapel-ruins. It was the only time I ventured out, while I was at Ravensbird's. The night was fine, I felt unusually strong, and I managed to walk as far as the ruins. Herbert Dane it seems had walked to the same spot, and we met. I know he took me for my own apparition, for he scuttered off like a man scared by one, while I stepped to the next window, and got inside. Are you ready, William? We go first to Wilfred Lester's."

"To Wilfred Lester's!" involuntarily uttered Wilfred's father.

"Yes, sir, to Wilfred Lester's." replied Lord Dane, somewhat sternly. "His own flesh and blood have forsaken him, have abandoned him to the charity of a cold world, so it is time the world took him up. I intend to carry him and his wife to the castle, to-day—pretty little Edith as she used to be, more ready with her kisses for Captain Harry Dane than Maria was—and there they shall stop, my guests and William's, until somebody can see about a home for them. In a measure I look upon this as my duty. Various tales have come to my ears—Danesheld gossip again!—that my cousin Adelaide has set the father against the son. If so, I feel sure that Adelaide has had some base and crafty adviser,—possibly she may find it to have been a member of her household. At any rate Wilfred stays with us until you and she come to your senses. Do you hear, Adelaide?"

Lady Adelaide did hear, and looked terribly conscious and confused. But, what was more to the purpose, she looked repentant.

They left the ball, and were about to step into the carriage, when they encountered Miss Bordillion, who was calling at it. Like some others had done, and like many others were destined to do before the day closed, she started back at the sight of Lord Dane. The facts were hastily explained to her.

"I told you that the time would soon come for you to welcome me again," smiled William, as he held out his hand. "Your door will be open, I hope, to Geoffry Dane, though it was not to William Lydney."

"And Maria?" she uttered, unable to take in at once all the wonders.

"Oh! I had serious thoughts of running away with Maria," laughed he, "but Mr. Lester has obviated the necessity. He tells me I may take her without."

Miss Bordillion gazed after the carriage, as it swept round the gravel-drive, and at William's face, which still smiled upon her from the window.

"I never will be persuaded out of my senses again," emphatically uttered she. "My judgment trusted him, my heart spoke for him : but because others turned against him, I must needs do the same : and now I am just paid out."

Lady Adelaide had gone up to her chamber with their departure, and there sat Tiffle on a stool of thorny impatience. She was big with news.

"Not but what I'm grieved to have it to disclose, my lady, for its awful inaquitty," quoth she "Knowing your ladyship was not down, and hearing voices in the drawing-room, I made bold to put my eye to the key-hole, and there I saw—but it's too barefaced to tell your ladyship, and makes me red all over, down to the extrimities of my toes."

"Tell it on," said Lady Adelaide.

"My lady, there was that advinterer there, that Lydney, and he had got Miss Lester all held close to him, her face upon—if you'll ixcuse my mintioning the word—his breast, my lady, and was a-kissing of her like any thing."

"You and I may have been kissed in our days, Tiffle," was the cool response of Lady Adelaide. "I expect she will soon be his wife."

"His wife!" shrieked Tiffle, in her amazement. "Lydney's? What, and go out with him a Botamy-Bay convict?"

"Tiffle!" reprimanded her ladyship, in a sharp, haughty tone. "Have the goodness to recollect yourself: you are speaking of Miss Lester."

She pointed to the door as she spoke, and Tiffle retired, cowed and thunderstruck. One of the under-servants met her, and said that Shad was outside the back-entrance, asking for her.

"Shad! come here asking for me!" responded Tiffle, in a great amount of wrath. "I'll teach him to come after me, ondacious little reptile! That Granny Bean is forever wanting fresh stuff for her rheumitix."

"Granny said I was to cut and tell ye, and not to mind calling at the house for once," began Shad, in an undertone, when Tiffle reached him. "Lord Dane's come back."

"Come back from where?" cried Tiffle. "Where has he been?"

"Not him at the castle: he ain't Lord Dane no more. T'other's come, him what they says fell over the cliff, but he come to life again. He have took up his footing at the castle, and t'other'll have to turn out. Granny said I was to tell ye as Lydney—"

"Well!" said Tiffle, impatiently, staring with all her eyes. "Get on quicker."

"As Lydney have been here in disguise, a-looking after what folks did wrong, but not a-helping of 'em, as was thought. He's t'other's son, and his name's Geoffry Dane, and he'll be Lord Dane after him."

Tiffle gathered in the words, gathered in her own politics of the past, and fell back in a real fainting-fit.

CHAPTER XXXI.

LORD DANE'S LEVEE—THE FLAG HALF-MAST HIGH.

NEVER sure was such a levee seen or heard of. It had no parallel in history, ancient or modern. Her majesty sometimes has a crowded court, her subjects pressing in to do her honor; but her crowds are all of that class who bask on the sunny side of life: no Lazarus must mix with them. The levee at Dane Castle was of a different nature.

It appeared that Lord Dane, with his induction to the home of his ancestors, had taken a new lease of life, so well did he appear. His malady was of a nature to cause him at times excruciating agony, varied with interludes, lasting perhaps a week or fortnight, even more, of freedom from pain. His last attack at the Sailor's Rest, when he sent for Mr. Apperly, had been so violent as to induce a belief in himself and Dr. Green that the end was fast approaching, but he appeared now to have completely rallied from it. Excitement is of benefit in some cases; perhaps it had been so to him.

The castle was thrown open at ten o'clock on the morning of the levee,—a brilliant morning in winter, with a blue sky and a bright sun. It was known to be Lord Dane's pleasure that all should attend it, of whatever degree, high or low,—of whatever character, bad or good. Not confined to the Dives of life was it,—the aristocratic few of Lord Dane's own rank, who might claim the right of entree; not confined was it to the still more scanty few of the good and great; the poor fisherman was as welcome as the exclusive gentleman; and the poachers and smugglers were expressly told to be there. The lower end of the large hall was lined with the Dane retainers, in their handsome livery of purple, their white coats laced with silver. Bruff and Ravensbird stood behind Lord Dane: uncommonly proud was Bruff that day.

How fast the visitors flocked in, none could tell, save those who witnessed it, all pushing eagerly to welcome and do honor to Lord Dane. Had he been made of hands, there would scarcely have been sufficient to satisfy the ardent crowd. He stood with them both outstretched; he had a kind look, a low, heart-felt word for all. His son stood at his right hand, and he presented him individually to all. Wilfred Lester was also very near him, treated by him with marked affection and distinction: Lord Dane was determined to do what *he* could towards bringing Wilfred back to his proper standing in society,—towards reinstating him in the respect of the world. Men saw with surprise that day that Squire Lester also paid consideration to his son: it must be remembered that the last and worst escapade, the breaking into the hall, was not known or suspected to be his work.

"Ah, my lord," cried Mr. Wild, the surgeon, as he, too, offered his greetings to Lord Dane, "but it was not well of you to be attended by a stranger at the Sailor's Rest. Doctor Green has been but two years in the place, and I grew up in it; your father thought me skillful enough for him."

Lord Dane laid his hand on the doctor's shoulder.

"Wild," he laughed, "I appoint you surgeon in ordinary to me from henceforth; not that I shall live to employ you long; you must get my son to fall ill after I am gone, and exercise your skill on him. Why, man, don't you see the reason of my calling in a stranger instead of you. You would have known me for Harry Dane at the first glance, and would have gone crowing with the secret all over Danesheld: that would not have suited my plans just then."

Mr. Wild shook his head.

"It has taken me down a notch, though, to think that you should have called in a stranger."

When the hall was full, and people had done coming in, so far as could be judged, William Dane—no longer William Lydney—left his father's side and mixed with the crowd. Nearly the first his eye lighted particularly on, was Inspector Young.

"I hope, sir, you won't remember past times with resentment," began he, "and visit your displeasure upon me when you come into power as chief of Danesheld."

"What an idea!" laughed William. "I gave you credit for better sense, Young; or at any rate believed that you would give me credit for better. You did your simple duty, and none of us can do more. We shall be famous friends," he added, holding out his hand, and the gratified man took it graspingly. His night's rest had been spoiled by the thought that he had taken into custody and treated as a common prisoner, the Honorable Geoffry William Dane.

Who should William come upon next, skulking near the door behind the servants, and not daring to advance, but Ben Beecher. It was the first time they had met since the midnight encounter in Squire Lester's hall: Beecher and his two companions had been keeping themselves close and quiet since, but they had ventured to the castle this day, arguing that their absence might tell against them worse than their presence; so they had assumed what bold faces they might, and followed in the wake of the stream. Their share in the exploit was known to two or three; it was perhaps suspected by Squire Lester; but there was no fear that further notice would be taken: for since the disclosure relative to his son, Squire Lester had become as anxious to hush up the affair, as he had previously been to investigate it. William Dane knew this.

"Is it you Ben Beecher, come to pay me a visit in my own house?" he cheerily began. "More space to welcome you here, than I had at the Sailor's Rest. Why don't you come forward to my lord? your father has already had his confab out with him."

"Sir, how could you go on deceiving us and blinding us in that way?" returned Ben Beecher, in a tone of timid deprecation. "If we had dreamt that you were the Lord Dane—or as good as the lord—should we ever have let you know our secrets? Why, there's not a thing about us but what you know, even the very worst."

"I am glad I do," replied William.

"It has just stopped our fun forever!" uttered Beecher.

"I hope it has," he laughed. "That is the very best calamity that could happen to you."

"Yes, sir; but may just have us all took up to-morrow, and transported upon your sole evidence."

"No, Beecher, I shall not do that," he gravely answered. "I would much rather keep you here, in the hope that you will be loyal dependents of mine when I do become your lord. I wish that time might be very far off, Beecher; but I fear it is all too close. You say I had knowedge of the worst: I certainly did know of your ventures in the poaching line, and I did hold to the hope that there your sins ended: I never could have believed that you would rush upon the crime of midnight housebreaking. I should have been the first to give you into custody, had I known it. What could have possessed you to engage—"

"Hush-sh-sh!" interrupted Beecher, glancing round him with a pale face. But the room was too full of humming commotion to afford a chance of its overhearing. "The whole fault was Wilfred Lester's; he beguiled us into it; I swear he did. Sir, he never put it to us in the light of a crime; he harped upon his own wrongs, his father's cruelty, and said would we help him to get out his own deed. I'm sure what he said might have talked a regiment of saints into helping him."

"It was a crime and a disgraceful one," repeated William Dane; "all the accessories were bad. The disguising crape alone would have stamped you villains. It is all very well to lay the blame on Wilfred Lester,—I do not deny he bears the chief share of it,—to say the abstraction of the deed was the object; unless I am mistaken, your object was the plate chest."

"When men of our sort get put right in the way of temptation, you, being what you are, sir, can't understand how well-nigh impossible it is for 'em to go aside from it," was Beecher's answer.

"Yes, I can, I can understand it all," interrupted William. "Once inside the house, took into it, too, by the squire's own son, and the plate chest handy, it was hardly in the nature of man not to help themselves," pleaded Beecher. "We should never have put our necks in the noose of our own accord, but Will Lester, he took us into it; and that's how it was. If it was the last word I had to speak, we never did such a thing afore, and the fright has been such a lesson to us, that we shall never do it again. Passing on shore a bit of tobacco, or taking off a hare, or a stray goose, or a chicken, have been in our line, but not them graver things. There is a set who dodge about Danesheld and other neighboring places, as their work or the police let them, and go into worse things, and we know 'em, and are friendly with 'em; but we have never joined 'em, and we wouldn't do it, and that I declare's the truth. It was them I thought might have helped themselves to the box when it was missing, Mr. Lydney."

"Mr. Dane," corrected William, with a smile.

"Dash my memory! I wish it never had been Dane, though. Is Squire Lester going to issue a warrant against us—does he suspect it was us?" continued the man, again glancing round him.

"Whether Squire Lester suspects or not, I cannot inform you; he does not know. Do you know what my opinion is, Beecher?"

"What, sir?"

"That the better mode of proceeding for all parties, will be to do nothing; but to let the affair die out in silence. Were I Lord Dane, I should recommend that to Squire Lester with all my influence."

"Ah, if he would!" uttered Beecher, his eyes sparkling.

"Allow me to recommend you,—all of you who were engaged in it,—to be entirely silent. Never speak of it even among yourselves; never let the name of Wilfred Lester, as connected with it, escape your lips. It is the only safe plan. Were he brought to book for it, you must inevitably be brought also; my own evidence, which I should be called upon then to give, would convict you. Remember, I saw and recognized you three in the house, but I did not see him in it."

"True, true," whispered Beecher. "Oh, sir! if you would but be merciful to us, and keep our counsel! We'd promise faithfully never to go upon your lands in return for it. I'm sure if we had known, that night, that it was the young Lord of Danesheld who pounced upon us in the hall, and not Mr. Lydney, I for one should have been fit to go and hang myself. As to splitting upon Wilfred Lester, we should never do that for our own sakes."

"Beecher, will you make a bargain with me? If I undertake that—through my influence, or my father's, with Squire Lester—you shall never be proceeded against for this midnight crime, even should your participation in it come to Squire Lester's ears, will you promise, on your parts, to drop the disreputable lives you have hitherto been leading, eschew expeditions against game and game-keepers, and let the Dane lands alone?"

"Yes, we will," answered Beecher, eagerly.

"In our first encounter in the wood, which you may not have forgotten, I told you that it was no business of mine did you prowl about the Dane preserves all day, a gun in one hand and snares in the other, seeing they were not mine. Virtually they were mine, at least my father's, but actually they were in possession of him who was then called Lord Dane. I told you also, that if they were mine, the affair would be very different. You must see that it is, Beecher. It is my duty now to protect the lands, and I shall do it."

"I can't gainsay it, my lord," returned Beecher, who seemed lost in thought.

"What slips of the tongue you do make!" merrily cried William. "I am no more 'my lord' than I am 'Mr. Lydney;' you were dreaming of the future, I expect. The ex-lord, 'Mr. Herbert, had a reverence for game, people say; I have more reverence for one man's well doing than I have for all the game in England; nevertheless, I respect and shall uphold the game-laws. Cannot you and I contrive to remain friends, Beecher, in spite of them?"

"Friends!" echoed the man, with deep feeling.

"I said friends. It will be your fault if we are not. You cannot suppose I shall take advantage of the past in any way; of the knowledge which circumstances brought to me touching your pursuits. You once said, Beecher, that had you been dealt with in a kinder spirit, you might have been different men. Suppose you begin to be so from this day, and I will help you. Wrong doings will not fit you for the next world, or speak for you when you get there."

Beecher made no answer; his face was working.

"You shall have constant work on the estate, and be well paid for it in fair wages; a more safe and certain living, that, than what you obtain from your night expeditions. The estate has been well kept up, but its laborers have been neglected; I shall hope to go upon a different plan, to make it a model one."

"The estate or the men?" cried Beecher, with little regard to the laws of grammar.

"Both," smiled William Dane. "The men must be true to me, and I shall be true to them. They must give me their best service, not eye-service, and I will ever consider their true interests in a kind and watchful spirit; in short, I intend that we should be friends in the best sense of the word, they and I, identifying our interest one with the other. Will you be one, Beecher?"

The man half stole his hand out before he answered.

"Ay, I will, sir; I'll do as you wish me; for I'm pretty near tired of the life I have led."

"A bargain! and we will neither of us go from it," whispered William as he shook it.

But there was another colloquy, one perhaps more interesting to the reader, taking place in a further corner of the apartment! and those holding it were Herbert, ex-Lord Dane, and Richard Ravensbird.

"Concealment for us all is over with it's necessity, Ravensbird," Herbert Dane was observing. "Your conduct of the past puzzled me: let me hear its explanation."

Ravensbird looked at him steadily.

"Are you speaking of the time of the accident, sir? when my master fell from the heights?"

"I am. I thought your manners then were remarkably strange. To begin with, you protested to me that you could lay your finger upon the man who had caused it. What induced you to say that? and to whom did you allude?"

"Shall I speak out freely, sir? I must, if I speak at all."

"I wish you to speak out, otherwise I should not have desired you."

"Then, sir, I entertained no manner of doubt that my master had been deliberately pushed over; murdered. And I believed it was you who had done it."

"The doubt was upon me at the time that you suspected me. But why should you have done so?"

"Because I knew that both you and he were after my Lady Adelaide. I was his servant, firm to his interests, and it was I who told him she favored you and not him. I had been the previous evening in the ruins, and I saw your meeting with her. Sir, why frown upon me in that haughty man-

ner? I am speaking out at your request, but I can be silent if you will. I told my master that you and she were in the habit of meeting there, and I got kicked out for it. When, that same night, a struggle took place on the heights close to the ruins, ending in my master's destruction, I naturally looked abroad for motives that might have induced it. Danesheld gave me the credit for it. *I* knew that I was innocent,—that I had not been near the place; and my own suspicions naturally flew to you. I, felt as certain, Mr. Herbert, that you had done the deed, as that I had not done it; and if I could have entertained doubt at all, you yourself, sir, drove it away."

"In what manner?"

"You told me that you could hang me,—that the threats against Captain Dane which I had uttered in your presence in the morning would be sufficient to hang me, if you chose to disclose them. I said to you, then, why did you not hang me? and you replied that you would not go out of your way to do it, for you had no ill-will against me, and that if you got me hung on the nearest tree, it would not recall the past, or bring the dead back to life. I had my common-sense about me, and I knew that if you were innocent, you would be the first to tell of those threats. I was but an obscure servant,—you were one of the Danes, and *his* cousin. Just for a little moment that story of the packman staggered me; but I soon threw it away as worthless. Sir, you and I were playing a crafty game with each other then. You saw I suspected you; I felt sure that you saw it; you urged me that it would be better if I quitted Danesheld; I answered that I should stay in it, and I boldly demanded of you the preference, when you were granting the lease of the Sailor's Rest. Mr. Herbert, I felt that you would not dare to refuse me."

"What could have been your attraction to Danesheld?" inquired Herbert Dane. "One would have thought you would be glad to quit it, after having been arrested for the murder."

"That is just the reason I remained in it, sir. I felt as certain that the time would come when I should be cleared, as certain as that the cloud had fallen. It occurred to me at the time to declare my suspicions to Lord Dane; but in the first place I had no proof that it was you, and in the second, my lord was so bitter against me, believing I was the transgressor, that he would probably have refused all credit to any thing I might have said Thank a good Providence that it is at last cleared !" fervently continued Ravensbird, "and in a brighter manner than any of us expected."

"Ay," echoed Herbert Dane, in a tone of unmistakable relief. "If I lose my wealth and honors, Ravensbird, I gain peace. There is one thing never accounted for: your absence from the Sailor's Rest for an hour and a-half that same night, and your refusal to state where you were."

"I was in no mischief," answered Ravensbird, a comical look on his grim countenance. "I was doing a bit of courting, and I did not choose to proclaim my private affairs for the benefit of Danesheld. I had spoken a hasty word to Sophie when I left the castle, in the morning, and whispered her to meet me in the evening, when my Lady Adelaide should be dressed for dinner. Sophie came, and we were pacing about in the field-path behind the castle all the while. It was bright moonlight."

"Pray did you honor me by imparting your suspicions of me to Sophie—after the catastrophe occurred ?"

"Not I, sir," returned Ravensbird, shaking his head. "Sophie's no better than other women, where the tongue is concerned, and it would pretty soon have been all over Danesheld. I never disclosed them, Mr. Herbert, to a living soul; if I suspected you myself, I did not do you the injury of trying to put you wrong with others. Many and many a time,

though, have I wondered that Sophie did not suspect, because she knew about you and Lady Adelaide, and also that I imparted it to Captain Dane before he kicked me out; but she never seemed to glance at that phase of the question, and I was glad she did not."

"You must have been thunder-struck when the life-boat brought *him* ashore."

"Thunderstruck !" echoed Ravensbird, "that's not a strong enough word, sir; there's no part of speech in the English language that is; and I thought what a jackass I had been, to mistake that body, cast up, for his. I did not know him till—let me see, I think it was the next night: he had kept himself covered over with the bedclothes, and hid his face with that purple shade, so that I had not had any look at him, to speak of. The next night he began talking about Danesheld, saying he had once been near the place; and what with his astonishment at hearing of its changes, and what with finding that I was as true and attached to him as ever I had been in my life, why he pushed the shade up and let me see his features. The surprise pretty well knocked me down. We were obliged to tell Sophie, because she would have recognized him as readily as I, and he could not always keep his face hid; and his eyes got well directly, affording no excuse for the shade.— How Sophie succeeded in keeping the secret, and mortifying her tongue as long as she did, will always be a joke against her; but my lord threatened her with unheard-of penalties if she disclosed it."

"You must have known that Captain Dane, when he fell, had a son living in America ?"

"Of course I knew it, sir; but I did not consider I was bound to disclose it. I like to let other people's business alone. I argued that the young gentleman, who was then fourteen, would be safe to come over and see after his father, and it would be time enough then for me to bear testimony here that he was truly his son. When the years went on, and Master William never came, I used to fear he was dead, and wondered who had inherited all the money. But that I did not care to leave the inn and Sophie to take care of themselves, I might have gone over to the States to see how it was, for the lad was always a favorite of mine; worth his weight in gold: and thankful I am that he has turned up all right at last."

The levee came to an end, and the castle resumed its quietness. Herbert Dane remained for the present the guest of Lord Dane, as did Wilfred Lester and his wife; and the strange sensation caused by the return was beginning to subside in Danesheld.

A family dinner-party was about to be held in the castle, no guests invited save the Lesters and Miss Bordillion. Miss Dane, who still officiated as the castle's mistress, made her appearance in the drawing-room on the appointed evening, a perfect marvel of gauze, ringlets, flowers, and pretty colors. Edith was with her, quiet and sad; and soon arrived Lady Adelaide, her husband, and Maria; next, Miss Bordillion In short, all had assembled except Lord Dane.

"Dinner is served, my lord," announced Bruff, throwing wide the door for them to pass out; but William spoke hastily:

"His lordship is not here yet, Bruff."

"Oh,—I beg your pardon, sir. I understood James to say that dinner was being waited for."

"Bruff, you had better apprise my lord," cried out Miss Dane.

He went across the corridor to Lord Dane's room, and knocked at it. There was no reply. Bruff knocked again. Still there came no answer, and the man then tried the door. It was fastened. He went back to the drawing-room, and beckoned out William.

"Sir, I can't get into my lord's room, and I cannot make him hear. I fear he must be ill."

"Dead," was on Bruff's tongue, remembering the precarious state of Lord Dane, but he did not utter it. William hastened to the door. The rest, who had caught sight of Bruff's alarmed countenance, followed him. William put up his finger for silence, and his ear to the door, but not a sound was heard.

"My dear father, are you ready? We are waiting for you," he said, in a clear, distinct voice.

No response.

"Do, pray, speak just one word, Lord Dane, if only to assure us you are not in a fit," cried Miss Dane, in coaxing and trembling accents, for she was easily alarmed. "Harry, then! won't you speak?"

"I shall break open the door," said William, hurriedly. "Had you not better"—he looked at the ladies—"go back to the drawing-room?"

The door was forced, and there lay Lord Dane on the bed. He was not dead, but he appeared to have fainted; feeling ill, he had probably thrown himself on the bed for a few minutes' rest.

"Mr. Wild and Dr. Green, instantly," whispered William to Bruff. Lord Dane revived to speech and consciousness before they arrived, but death was upon him.

"The night will close it, William," he said, "but I have waited for it long. Maria," taking her hand, "you will be William's wife?"

"Yes," she answered, through her tears.

"Don't wait for months and months to elapse first, because I have but just gone," he continued to them both. "Remember, it is my wish that you marry shortly: and I leave my blessing upon it. William will be here alone. Where is Adelaide?" he resumed, looking round, after a pause.

She had remained in the drawing-room with Miss Dane. One of them went for her.

"Come close to me, Adelaide," he said, when she came in: "stand by your husband; between your husband and Wilfred. Old grim Death has come for me, child : but I must say a few words to you before he penetrates quite in. Did it ever occur to you that you must sometime lie where I am lying ?—on you death-bed ?"

Very pale and troubled looked Lady Adelaide, but she did not answer.

"There is but one thing will serve you when you come to it,—a clear conscience. I look back now on my past life, and vainly gasp forth the yearning wish that I had in many cases acted differently : though, of wilful injustice, I cannot charge my memory. It is not, however, to tell of my faded life, my sins and my atonements, that I speak : they lie between me and my merciful Father, to whom I am hastening. Adelaide, when you come to this hour, what will your conscience say to you for the manner in which you have treated Wilfred Lester ?"

She burst into tears; the last sentence was uttered imperatively.

"My dear, you have been guilty of terrible injustice : and I think that your eyes must have had perverting scales thrown before them," pursued Lord Dane. "Wilfred is your husband's eldest son; he has an equal right to partake of his substance with your own children; but you have driven him upon the world without means or resource, that they might enjoy the more. Do you imagine that injustice such as this, can be acceptable to God ? or that it will be permitted to prosper ?"

A deep silence, broken only by the sobs of Lady Adelaide.

"You must change this course of conduct, and repair the injury, if you would obtain peace at last. I speak to you, more than to Lester, because you have been the chief actor and mover. What could possibly have so set you against Wilfred Lester ?"

"It was Tiffle," broke out Lady Adelaide, in her emotion. "She is always exciting me against him."

"Show Tiffle the door," returned Lord Dane, with a touch of his old fire. "I must leave you reconciled."

He took Wilfred's hand in his open palm, and looked at hers. She immediately put hers into it. Mr. Lester did the same.

"And now yours, Edith," said Lord Dane.

The four hands were clasped together,—token of the reconciliation, the good feeling, that from that hour was to dawn upon them.

"Love and unity," murmured Lord Dane. "Strew your path with them, and they will stand by to serve you ever; scatter it with thorns, and they will turn and prick you at the last. Adelaide, they are my dying words to you !"

———

All too quickly there was another levee at the castle; but this time the world came in with saddened faces and subdued tread, pressing on to the death-room. The flag floated half-mast high over the gate, and the trestles stood on the flag-floor, bearing their bier,—William Henry, seventeenth Baron Dane, lay on it.

Never were there half the followers at any funeral of the Danes, as at this. The interment took place on a cold, bright day,—the blue sky overhead, and the white snow covering the ground and the landscape. A marked contrast did that long, sable train present—all walking—to the glitter of the snow, as they wound round from the castle-gates to the private chapel at a short distance,—not the chapel of the ruins. The officiating clergyman advanced first in his surplice and hood ; the coffin was borne next, attended by its pall-bearers ; after it, bareheaded and alone, walked Geoffry William, now Lord Dane ; behind him came Herbert Dane and Squire Lester ; next, the Earl of Kirkdale and Wilfred Lester ; others followed ; and last, the servants, Bruff and Ravensbird heading them. And thus the true William Henry Dane was at length consigned to the vault of his ancestors, side by side with that unknown stranger who had been buried for him.

Mr. Apperly produced the will on their return to the castle. It was dated but very recently,—after the late lord had taken up his abode at it. A handsome sum was bequeathed absolutely to Herbert Dane, equivalent to twelve hundred a-year: Miss Dane gained an annuity of three hundred. A remembrance was left to Lady Adelaide, and five thousand pounds to Wilfred Lester, as "a thank-offering for having saved my life, and that of one far more precious to me: my dear son, Geoffry William." A thousand pounds was left to Bruff, and two thousand pounds to "my faithful friend and servant, Richard Ravensbird;" a like sum—two thousand pounds—was directed to be equally divided between the castle-servants; and the rest of his large fortune was bequeathed to his son,—not counting the revenues of Dane, which came to him by law.

"What a wealthy man he has died?" quoth the gossips.

So he had. But he had spent nothing like the whole of his income abroad. William Lydney had been fully justified in asserting that Squire Lester was entirely welcome to Maria's fourteen thousand pounds.

CHAPTER XXXII.

A WEDDING-BREAKFAST—THE LAST SCENE ON THE HEIGHTS.

ONCE more there was a large gathering of the people at Danesheld. But this time it was not of a sad nature, neither did it take place at the castle, but at the residence of Squire Lester. Following the injunction of his father, William had not long deferred his marriage, and on as balmy a day as May ever brought forth, he was united to Maria.

They had returned from church, and were now seated at the breakfast, a goodly company. Lord and Lady Dane in the middle of the table; opposite to them, Mr. Lester and Lady Adelaide; Wilfred sat by his sister's side, and Edith by Lord Dane. Many friends were present Bruff, in at-

tendance on his lord, paraded his portly form by the side-board, to the admiration of Squire Lester's less exalted staff of servants, and Ravensbird had invited himself, to wait upon anybody.' As to Sophie, she had quitted the Sailor's Rest for the hall at six o'clock that morning, protesting in all her national vanity that nobody but herself could turn out Miss Lester fit to be seen.

Miss Dane was present, in the most ravishing of costumes,—so coquettish and airy that it was difficult to believe anybody but Sophie, with her French taste, had had a hand in it. Herbert Dane was not there. He had left, to take up his residence in Paris, and there he would probably remain for a permanency. He had always favored the gay city, and England was no longer a sunny land to him. Miss Dane lived in his house covered with the ivy:—the reader visited it one evening when he was Herbert Dane. Very vexed was she to leave the castle, but where was the help for it? Soon after Lord Dane's death, when future plans were being talked over, and Wilfred and Edith had returned to their own cottage, her brother told her she might occupy his old house, as he did not intend to do so.

"Oh, thank you all the same, Herbert," was Miss Dane's hasty reply, "but I would prefer to stop at the castle."

"At the castle! How can you? You will not be wanted here. Ask William if you will."

Miss Dane, rather offended, went off on the spur of the moment to find William. In a pretty little speech, all airs and graces, and Lydia-Languish looks, she proposed to remain with him as housekeeper.

"But I shall soon be bringing a housekeeper home, Cecilia," was his reply, in a laughing tone of remonstrance.

"Oh, dear! then it *is* true! I never did put the question direct to you or to Miss Lester, and could not think of paying attention to the insinuations of others. I should manage the household better than she will, being accustomed to it; I wish I could stay, William—only as a cousin, of course," simpered she, casting down her eyes and her blushing cheeks.

William thought it about as direct an offer as a gentleman could well receive. He suppressed the merriment in his eye, and replied in a grave tone.

" I fear you have spoken without counting the cost. I am young; you are—young too ; what would scandal-loving Danesheld say ?"

" Oh, dear !" shrieked Miss Dane, with a start, " would it, do you suppose? I never did think of that. Then I may as well accept Herbert's offer of his house."

She hastened from the room, her silk apron held before her eyes, and William burst into a violent fit of laughter ; so prolonged and irrepressible that the sober Bruff, who just then came in, thought his young lord had suddenly gone crazy.

Miss Dane, therefore, took up her abode in the offered house, with a cordial intimation that the castle would be delighted to welcome her at any and every opportunity ; and here she was at the wedding. Perhaps the next best thing to being the bride, was to be one of the bridesmaids, for in that capacity did Miss Dane officiate this morning.

The breakfast had proceeded to the toast-giving. The health of Lord and Lady Dane had been drunk, and William was standing, a flush on his handsome face, to return thanks, when the door slowly opened, and a tall, spare stranger, with a military air, and his sallow features bronzed, stood at it, leisurely surveying the company. The company, in their turn, surveyed him, and William paused. He seemed to strike upon their senses somewhat after the fashion of Banquo's ghost. A dead silence supervened, and not a few of the visitors began to wonder whether this could be a second Lord Dane sprung from the dead.

" Which is Edith ?"

Curious words to come from him, and the sea of faces stared in blank consternation, Edith's not less blank than theirs. Suddenly, there was a faint, yearning cry, and Miss Bordillion sprang towards him.

" My brother ! I am sure it is my brother !"

" Yes, it was Colonel Bordillion. He had just landed from India, having come home without apprizing any one.

Oh, there was congratulation ! Mr. Lester pressed forward, Lady Adelaide, others who had known him many, many years ago,—all with their eager welcome. Edith could not remember him ; he had parted from her, a little child of six, when she was sent over from India ; and she stood confused, scarcely understanding who it really was. He looked around, perhaps naturally, for the youngest and the fairest, and drew close to her and Maria, surveying each alternately.

" You are Edith," he said, laying his hand on Maria.

" Oh, papa, papa, no,—it is I !" said Edith, then, as she fully realized that it *was* her father, and flung herself into his arms with a burst of hysterical tears. *I* am Edith."

" And you ?" said Colonel Bordillion, smiling upon Maria, after he had given a few moments to Edith.

" I am Maria Lester," returned she, totally oblivious at the moment of her new name.

" And you must be Wilfred ?" continued Colonel Bordillion, surveying the tall, handsome form that rose between Maria and Edith.

" Not so, papa. This is Lord Dane. Wilfred is standing at your elbow."

Colonel Bordillion greeted his son-in-law, and then turned to Lord Dane, his eyes ranging over his noble features and manly bearing.

" It is the face and form of a Dane," he said. " But I knew not that there was a young heir to inherit. And what is the cause of this festive assemblage ?"

" Nothing but a wedding-breakfast," laughed Lord Dane. " I have been making this young lady my wife."

" Why, you have just told me your name was Maria Lester," cried Colonel

Bordillion, smiling down upon her blushing face."

"Forgetting that she has laid it aside forever," put in Wilfred. "She should have said Maria Dane."

Colonel Bordillion sat down with them. He was an exceedingly guileless, open-speaking man, and he entered without ceremony upon his own affairs before everybody.

"I have done with service," he observed, "and have come home to rest during the remainder of my days. You and I can live together, Margaret."

"Oh, yes, yes," she answered; but there was a little catching sob of the breath as she remembered how very poor a house it was to welcome him to."

"A sad affair that bank going," exclaimed one of the guests. "Quite ruined you, did it not, colonel?"

"I thought so at first. It was believed there would not be a shilling for anybody, but it has turned out quite differently. We have got back more than fifty per cent. of our losses. Over thirty thousand pounds they have refunded to me."

Over thirty thousand pounds! The poor Colonel Bordillion! Squire Lester sat and stared at him. Margaret stole a glance at Edith, and laid a hand upon her own beating heart.

"Why, you must have been a sixty-thousand-pound man, colonel!" exclaimed peppery little Lawyer Apperly. "What an immense fortune!"

"What do you wear out your lives in India for, but to make fortunes?" laughed the colonel. "I assure you, the very instant I could draw my dividend—"

"Thirty thousand, you say?"

"Rather more. The instant I drew it, I made arrangements for returning home to relieve my honored friend and connection, Squire Lester. It has fallen to him to supply his son and daughter-in-law with an income hitherto, and I thought it high time I took my turn at the cost.

If ever a flush of shame darkened a man's countenance, it dyed at that moment George Lester's. How had he supplied them? Left them to starve: nearly allowed Edith to drop into her grave from sheer famine: suffered Wilfred to go to ruin as fast as he pleased! Lady Adelaide, too! she glanced at Edith,—a pleading glance from her burning eyelids; it seemed to say, "Do not, in pity, expose me!" So Edith understood it, and a sweet look of loving assurance went back to Lady Adelaide. The least concerned of all, was Miss Dane, shaking out her ringlets, and taking shy peeps at Colonel Bordillion;—she was speculating upon whether the colonel was or was not too old for her, and whether it might be worth while to set her cap at him.

Later, when Lord and Lady Dane had left, and the guests, saving the immediate family, had dispersed, Squire Lester retired to his study, and desired that Sarah should come to him, she being at the hall that day, partaking of the festivities of the servants. It had been troubling the mind of Mr. Lester, what he could do towards repairing the past.

"Sarah, take a seat," began he, for Sarah had once been the valued nurse in the Lester family, during his first wife's lifetime. "I want to know whether there are not some standing debts, owing from your house. They were not all paid up."

"Yes, they were, sir. After Mr. Wilfred came into the money left him by Lord Dane."

"Some, I know, were paid. But what was it that was said about your obtaining so many things on credit, even wine? Wilfred told me he could get no explanation from you about them, and that they were not settled. I should like to pay those debts myself."

"There never were any to pay," returned Sarah, a smile stealing over her hard features. "Why, sir, you can't think I should have been able to get the credit renewed that had been stopped so long. I thought at the time how soft folks must be to fancy so. Every bit and drop that came in I went for with the money in my hand." " Where did you get the money from ?" asked Mr. Lester, in astonishment.

" From one that Danesheld was pulling to pieces as a thief and a ragabond," was Sarah's answer. " I have wished when I heard 'em, I could tie the whole place together, and bump 'em for it. He made friends with me, and told me I must join him in a little bit of deceit, for he could not see my master and mistress's state without relieving it, and I did. He found the money, and I laid it out : and it is thanks to him, William Lydney, that Miss Edith is alive to see her father this day. If ever a young lady has gained a prize, it's your daughter, sir, in marrying him."

" I think she has," said Mr. Lester, with emotion.

" I know she has," was the retort of Sarah. " He was just going to the dogs as fast as he could go, was Mr. Wilfred ; yes, sir, you are his father, but I'm not going to eat my words ; racing to 'em he was, and William Lydney saved him, bearing all sorts of suspicion and scorn for Wilfred Lester's sake. People talk of the noble Danes ; but I'll be whipped if ever there was one of the race half as noble as the present lord."

The next morning, while the Lesters were at breakfast, a violent noise, as of fighting, was heard in the hall. Lady Adelaide's thoughts flew to her children, and she sprang to the room-door and opened it. There stood Shad and Tiffle, engaged in a pitched battle, scratching, biting, tearing, and shrieking at each other.

The cause was this : Shad had presented himself at the back-door, apparently in a state of much excitement and fear, and demanded to see Tiffle. The girl, who answered it, ungraciously told him to " Go and hunt for her :" for the fact was, Tiffle, who had got up in a most vile temper, had been making several of the servants suffer, and this girl more particularly. Away

16

went Shad up the passages, looking here, peeping there, until he came to the hall where he caught sight of Tiffle, who was standing with her ear to the keyhole of a door, which happened to be that of the breakfast-room. Shad stole stealthily up behind, and laid hold of her. Tiffle, in her terror, for she thought she was caught, began, when she saw who it was, to pay him off by sundry tingling slaps on the cheeks and pullings of the hair. Shad, in his terror, not to say pain, retaliated, and the result was the battle.

" What is the meaning of this ?" demanded Squire Lester, advancing " Tiffle !"

Tiffle softened down to meekness : only by the flashing of her sly eyes could one have told how false the meekness was. Shad only howled.

" I'm sure I beg parding, sir, and my lady," returned she. " This wicked raggamuffyan of Granny Bean's come a-starting of me to throw me over, just as I was going into the breakfast-room to ask a question of my lady about little Miss Ada—".

" You wasn't a-going in," raved Shad in his anger : " you was a-stopping at the door a-listening."

" The ready lies that these young creatures invent !" apostrophized Tiffle, turning up her eyes. " I would not have cared for his startling of me, but it vexed me, sir, to see one like him a-pushing of himself into a gentleman's house. Be quiet, you vagabone, and come along with me. I'll soon put him out, my lady."

" Stop," said Mr. Lester. " How did you get in, Shad ?"

" I come to the door and I asked for Mrs. Tiffle," sobbed Shad ; " and the young woman she told me to come and find her—"

" Asked for me—me !" put in Tiffle, in a glow of indignation. " The impidince of that !"

" What be I to do ?" howled Shad. " Granny's dead, she is, and I be afraid to stop there. Who be I to tell ?"

" Granny Bean dead !" returned Mr. Lester.

" I'm sure on't," sniffed Shad. " She's

a-sitting back in her chair, with her face blue, and her mouth open, and her eyes a-staring. I wondered as she didn't screech at me to get up; so I lay abed, and when I went to her her face was like that. And, because I comes and tells, I'm kicked at and my har tored out."

"Please, sir, hadn't I better go back with him, and see what it really is?" asked Tiffle, as mild now as milk.

"I think you had," replied Mr. Lester; "but step in here an instant first. Shad, you sit down there," added he, pointing to a chair in the hall. Tiffle went in, and closed the door.

"Lady Adelaide and myself have come to the resolution of parting with you, Tiffle. We have not been satisfied with you for some time, but suffered you to remain until Miss Lester's marriage was over. You will quit the hall this day month."

Tiffle turned her face, growing livid with surprise and anger, from her master's to Lady Adelaide's: both looked calmly resolute.

"To pa-pa-part with me!" gasped Tiffle. "What have I done?"

"What have you not done in the way of mischief?" returned Mr. Lester. "Ask your own conscience. But for your underhand plots and wicked doings, I should never have been opposed to my son in the manner I have. A servant, who peers into private places, and listens behind doors and hedges, will no longer suit Danesheld Hall."

"I!—I listen behind hedges!" shrieked Tiffle: "when do I go out to listen? It's a lie!"

"Tiffle! how dare you speak so before your lady? If you have not listened behind hedges yourself, you have taken care that your respectable friend, Mr. Shad, should do it. What is the nature of the connection or relationship between you and Shad?" abruptly concluded Mr. Lester.

The question seemed to drive Tiffle wild. A connection between her and Granny Bean's brat, Shad, she raved who dared to insinuate it?

"It is of no consequence," replied Mr. Lester. "Remember that you are out of the house this day month. And let me recommend you to drop your favorite employments—looking and listening—before you try for a situation in another family."

Then out broke Tiffle: her rage mastered her, and she was as a very fiend let loose. She abused her master; she insulted Lady Adelaide. The servants came flocking in astonishment, and Mr. Lester put her out of the house there and then, paying her on the spot the balance of her wages due. She bestowed some benedictions, more loud than holy, upon the hall, as she flounced out of it, pulling Shad with her.

Sure enough Granny Bean was dead. Tiffle took up her residence in the hut, announcing that she should remain in it for the future, and boasting that she had well feathered her nest, and could live in comfort. What was to become of Shad? people asked. But, alas! that young gentleman turned out to be the offspring of the immaculate Tiffle. It came to light through some recent revelations of Granny Bean's. Tiffle at first denied it with glowing indignation, but when she found her denial was only laughed at, then she turned upon them and brazened it out.

"Well, he was; and she was proud of him, there!" Well she might be, for he was the very image of herself.

The sun was sinking beyond the sea on one of the evenings in June, its last rays illumining a busy scene. What could be going on at Danesheld? It seemed as though all its population had dressed themselves in gala clothes, and had turned out to crowd the heights. Anxiously were their eyes directed to the farther extremity of the road; and as a carriage wound round the corner into view, symptoms of excitement arose. It was a chariot and four, its panels bearing the Dane arms and coronet. Inside it sat Lord Dane and his wife. They were returning from their bridal-tour. Simultaneously with the sight of the chariot to the crowd, came the sight of the crowd to the inmates of the chariot.

"What can this mean?" exclaimed Lord Dane, in the surprise of the moment. "Look, Maria!"

No need to ask how long what it was, or why they had assembled there, for the low murmured tones of greeting grew into deep and heartfelt shouts—"Welcome home to Lord and Lady Dane!" The carriage advanced at a foot-pace; it could not get on quicker, unless it had crushed the people; and Lord Dane bowed on all sides, the frank smiles on his handsome face pleasing the shouters as much as the bows.

"William, I do believe that everybody is here!" exclaimed Maria, as rich and poor, high and low, were caught sight of in turn. "There's your friend, Ben Beecher."

Lord Dane looked out till he caught his eye, and gave him an especial smile and bow all to himself. Ben reddened with pride.

"And there's Sophie, William! Do look! she is shaking her handkerchief! And there's Mr. Apperly, shouting himself hoarse. How kind they all are!"

Maria stopped, for at that moment a lovely bouquet was dashed into the carriage, nearly catching her on the cheek. She took it up, laughed, and leaned forward.

"Thank you, thank you, Sophie!" for it had come from Mrs. Ravensbird.

A few paces more, and Lord Dane, taking his wife's hand, pointed to a certain spot where stood two people, somewhat apart from each other. A woman in a gay, new, scarlet shawl, and gay yellow bonnet, with pink bows inside, and a young gentleman in a suit of corduroy, ornamented with fancy metal buttons.

"See there, Maria."

"Shad and Tiffle! Maria uttered. "I wonder she should have that boy with her. And how strangely she is dressed! What will mamma say?"

"As to her having Shad with her, I have a strong suspicion that Shad has more right to be with her than

with anybody else," said Lord Dane.

"What do you mean, William?"

Lord Dane only laughed, and there was no time to pursue the theme, for the crowd grew denser.

The gates of the castle were thrown open, and the entrance was lined with the Dane retainers. Gathered before them stood welcoming friends: Mr. and Lady Adelaide Lester and their children, Wilfred and Edith, Colonel and Miss Bordillion, Miss Dane and others. It was the last appearance of Wilfred Lester and his wife. In a day or two they were to depart for town, an excellent appointment under Government having been obtained for him, through the Dane interest.

The carriage drew up, and as Lord Dane stepped from it, there was a flourish of trumpets, and a new and stately flag shot up from the centre turret, to wave majestically over the castle. The beams of the departing sun shone upon it, and acclamations rent the air.

A few hasty greetings to relatives, and then William turned to give his final bows of thanks to the crowd. He was interrupted by a yellow bonnet, which had pushed through the ranks and planted itself before him.

"Here's wishing of your lordship every happiness in life, and the same to your lordship's lady," curtsied the false and brassy Tiffle. "Though I have been shamefully used and abused, and turned out of my place since your lordship's departure, I'm not one to bear malice, and says I to Shad, 'We'll go up with the rest, and offer our kingretilations this onspicious day to Lord and Lady Dane.'"

"Lord and Lady Dane beg to thank you," was William's response, somewhat coldly spoken.

"And I've taken up my risidince in the cottage which was Granny Bean's, having accumulated enough for a small indepindince," answered Tiffle. "And if I can serve your lord or ladyship in any way, I shall be gratified to do it."

"Have you taken to Shad, as well as to the cottage?" pursued William.

"Yes, my lord, I have. Not being ashamed to acknowledge in the faces of inemies that he's mine," was the assured response.

"The best thing that could be done with Shad would be to send him to a reformatory; the next best place for him would be a school," returned Lord Dane. "I promised the boy I would do something for him: and he must be rescued from his present vagabond life, if he is to escape utter ruin. I am ready to place him at an industrial school, where he will be taught to earn his living, and where what good may be in him will be brought out."

"And it's with thanks for your lordship's intintions, but I don't intind to do myself the pleasure of excapting of them," spoke Tiffle, in a tone of resentment. "Shad's no more a vagabone than other folks, and he'll stop and have his abode with me, and no power shall tear us apart."

Shad melted into tears and whined out a chorus, one eye turned up to Lord Dane, the other down at Tiffle. He'd do a'most anything his lordship wanted of him, but he couldn't leave his dear mother, Mrs. Tiffle.

"Very well," said Lord Dane to Tiffle. "I am ready and willing to rescue him from the temptation to evil; if you refuse, and then allow Shad to run into the evil to break the law, I shall surely punish him. And, mark you, I shall have him watched. I shall suffer no more loose doings in Danesheld. You had better think it over, Tiffle; and remember that the boy has a soul to be saved."

William turned, and faced the crowd, standing bareheaded, his wife upon his arm. They were cheering themselves deaf. He bowed his acknowledgements, he smiled his thanks; to those immediately around, he spoke them. It was a scene worth depicting. The stately old castle and its waving flag; the hundreds gathered before it in their homage and affection; and the fine young chieftain standing there, free and noble, his face lighted by the slanting beams of the sun. As they gazed on his earnest, thoughtful eyes, and his brow of intellect; on his serene features, and the unmistakeable expression stamped on them, —goodness,—they felt that thenceforth Danesheld, in its lord, would possess a *friend.* Maria leaned on him, her cheeks blushing, and her eyes wet. Perhaps there was scarcely a dry eye in the crowd, as the last cheers went up—"Long life, peace, and blessings on Lord and Lady Dane!"

THE END.